Trapped. She ~~truly trapped.~~
truly trapped.

Panting with exertion, Cat stared up at the face a scant inch from hers. 'Twas too dark to see, but she could feel their hearts beating in wild counterpoint to each other...and something more alarming. His manhood swelling against her thigh. "Nay," she cried, renewing her struggles.

"Be still." He let her take more of his weight, making her aware of the power he leashed. "Be still or you'll goad me into doing that which you fear."

Cat ceased fighting, but didn't relax, couldn't. "So...'tis not just my father's ruin you want," she managed to say.

"I'd be a fool and a liar if I denied you stir me. I've been long without a woman and you're uncommon fair. But your honor...such as it is...is safe with me. I'd sooner bed a pox-ridden whore as Ruarke Sommerville's get!"

Dear Reader,

With the first three books in her series featuring the Sommerville brothers, Suzanne Barclay earned a nomination for Best Medieval Historical Romance from *Romantic Times*, a Bookrack award for Series Romance, a 5★ rating from *Affaire de Coeur* and a 5★ rating from *Heartland Critiques*. This month, we are very pleased to be able to bring you the next book in the series, *Knight's Ransom*, the story of a French knight who captures the daughter of his enemy to avenge the murder of his family. Don't miss this exciting return to the ongoing drama of the Sommervilles and the de Laurens.

In *The Wedding Bargain*, Emily French tells the emotional tale of a widow, Charity Frey, who defies her Puritan community and marries Rafe Trehearne, a bondsman who has been wrongly accused of treason.

Also this month, RITA Award finalist Laurel Ames is back with *Tempted*, her new novel that *Affaire de Coeur* calls an "exciting, unusual, and delightfully quirky Regency." And Ana Seymour's sixth title for Harlequin Historicals, *Gabriel's Lady*, is the first of two connected books set in the wilds of the Dakota Territory.

We hope you'll keep a lookout for all four titles wherever Harlequin Historicals are sold.

Sincerely,

Tracy Farrell
Senior Editor

Please address questions and book requests to:
Harlequin Reader Service
U.S.: 3010 Walden Ave., P.O. Box 1325, Buffalo, NY 14269
Canadian: P.O. Box 609, Fort Erie, Ont. L2A 5X3

SUZANNE BARCLAY

Knight's Ransom

Harlequin Books

TORONTO • NEW YORK • LONDON
AMSTERDAM • PARIS • SYDNEY • HAMBURG
STOCKHOLM • ATHENS • TOKYO • MILAN
MADRID • WARSAW • BUDAPEST • AUCKLAND

ISBN 0-373-28935-9

KNIGHT'S RANSOM

Copyright © 1996 by Carol Suzanne Backus

This edition published by arrangement with Harlequin Books S.A.

Printed in U.S.A.

Books by Suzanne Barclay

Harlequin Historicals

*Knight Dreams #141
*Knight's Lady #162
*Knight's Honor #184
†*Lion's Heart* #252
†*Lion of the North* #272
†*Lion's Legacy* #304
*Knight's Ransom #335

*The Sommerville Brothers
†The Lion Trilogy

SUZANNE BARCLAY

has been an avid reader since she was very young; her mother claims Suzanne could read and recite "The Night Before Christmas" on her first birthday! Not surprisingly, history was her favorite subject in school and historical novels are her number-one reading choice. The house she shares with her husband and their two dogs is set on fifty-five acres of New York State's wine-growing region. When she's not writing, the author makes fine furniture and carpets in miniature.

If you would like to receive a more detailed Sommerville Family Tree, please send a large SASE to: Suzanne Barclay, P.O. Box 92054, Rochester, NY 14692

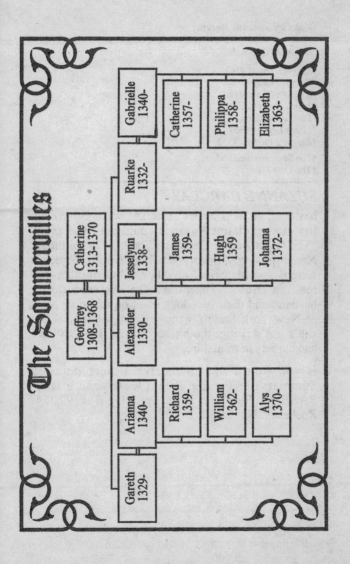

The Sommervilles

Geoffrey 1308-1368 = **Catherine** 1313-1370

- **Gareth** 1329-
- **Arianna** 1340- = **Alexander** 1330-
  - **Richard** 1359-
  - **William** 1362-
  - **Alys** 1370-
- **Jesselynn** 1338- = **Ruarke** 1332-
  - **James** 1359-
  - **Hugh** 1359-
  - **Johanna** 1372-
- **Ruarke** 1332- = **Gabrielle** 1340-
  - **Catherine** 1357-
  - **Philippa** 1358-
  - **Elizabeth** 1363-

Prologue

*Bordeaux, France
August 10, 1375*

"Which ones are we going to steal?" asked Maslin.

Bernard de Lauren glared at his henchman. "None if you keep shouting our intent for all and sundry to hear."

"You couldn't hear a catapult being launched over the din of so many beasts galloping about," Maslin grumbled, but he stooped from his great height to whisper the words in Bernard's ear.

Though he hated to be corrected, especially by a hireling, Bernard silently conceded the point. Between the thunder of so many steel-shod hooves and the whoops of the knights putting them through their paces, it was hard to hear. Still... He glanced surreptitiously at the other spectators.

Seasoned knights, veterans of the English campaigns in France, stood alongside youths eager to win a rich purse in the tourney being held two weeks hence to celebrate the peace treaty between France and England. The men's attention was firmly fixed on the mock battle being staged so they might judge the merits of the stock Ruarke Sommerville had offered for sale.

Bernard had been judging, too, but he hadn't come to buy.

"Sommerville charges a fortune for these grays, but from what I've seen, they're worth every livre," Maslin said.

"If a man intended to buy. Which I don't. I'd not enrich these cursed English by one sou." Bernard spat the last word.

Maslin winced but resisted warning his volatile master against such open displays of hatred whilst they were in English territory. Bernard was not rational when it came to the English. Despite the peace treaty just concluded, the English would doubtless leap at the chance to hang the infamous Bernard de Lauren did they realize he was here. For the thousandth time since embarking on this scheme, Maslin wished it hadn't been necessary to leave the rest of their men leagues away in Toulouse. However, Bernard could hardly have upheld his image as an honorable knight come to attend the tourney if he'd appeared with his band of cutthroats at his back.

" 'Twill be pleasant to even the score by stealing from a knight who played such a major role in conquering our country," Maslin said. "Despite this peace treaty, King Charles may even restore your sire's titles when he hears how you bested Ruarke."

"What care I for Charles's favor or an empty title? I want money and revenge against these English bastards. Had they not killed my father and put it about I was a traitor, I'd not have been forced to change my name and hide inside Crenley Keep."

Actually, Maslin knew Frenchmen had killed Odell de Lauren after he had attacked them. And as to the rest, reputedly Odell had been ruthless beyond belief, and Bernard had taken up where the old man had left off. 'Twas the main reason Maslin and his brothers worked for Bernard, or Jean Cluny as he was known to his extensive band of outlaws. Though Bernard scoffed at what they'd gained, few brigands lived as well as they did. "This peace with the English will cut mightily into our livelihood. 'Twill be difficult now to raid the farms of the Languedoc or waylay rich merchants on the roads and blame the attacks on the English."

"Aye." Bernard spat onto the grassy plain. "A pox on them and their peace. We'll starve do we not find another source of revenue. With the profit from these horses, I'll buy lands of my own and tenants to farm them."

"First we must get the horses. And it won't be easy."

"I know. We've spent the past three days watching them."

Actually Maslin had sat in the rain and thus knew how closely guarded was this valuable horseflesh. The grazing pastures were ringed by Sommerville's tents, and at night the patrols guarding the horses were doubled. Nor would they be easily overpowered. Ruarke had retired from soldiering some years before, but he had put his considerable expertise to use. His men trained daily on these very grounds, honing their skills under the exacting eye of the man King Edward had declared the greatest knight in his realm. "It won't be easy at all. Mayhap we should wait until after the tourney, then follow some of the victors and relieve them of their prizes."

Bernard scratched at the whiskers on his pointed chin. He was still a handsome man, but forty years of hard living had marked him. His skin was pasty, his eyes red-rimmed. "The idea has merit, but I want Ruarke Sommerville's horses."

"What did he do to make you hate him above his countrymen?"

"'Tis not who he is, but what." Bernard transferred his scowl from Sommerville's silken tents to the young men fighting their mock battle. Equipped with the finest armaments, their mail so highly polished it gleamed in the autumn sun, they fought with wooden swords and brightly painted shields. "All this was bought and paid for with booty wrested from France."

Maslin nodded, familiar with the story. Ruarke had left England an impoverished third son and returned a hero laden with plunder. Though he'd refused the grand titles his grateful king would have granted, 'twas rumored Ruarke was the wealthiest man in England. "We also turned a tidy profit from the war."

"Tidy profit?" Bernard snarled. "All the rich prizes were snapped up by the English. I mean to make my fortune ere peace settles over the land and stifles it. And Sommerville's horses will make a fine start. Why, I may even keep one. Mayhap that huge stallion he rides."

A roar from the onlookers drew Bernard's attention back to the field. The battle had ceased, and the warhorses were lined up for closer inspection.

"Have you seen one that interests you?" asked a deep voice, and Bernard found himself facing the very man he'd come to rob.

Clad in a black wool tunic finer than Bernard's feast-day best, Ruarke Sommerville sat tall in the saddle, staring down his haughty nose at Bernard. Despite his, what, three and forty years, Ruarke had the bearing of a man half that age. His broad shoulders and thick chest tapered down to a lean belly. The tiny lines fanning out from sharp brown eyes and a hint of silver in his sandy hair were the only signs of aging.

"They are fine specimens," Bernard said, his hatred increasing.

Ruarke's expression grew distant and wary. "You come from the South of France."

"How can you tell?" Bernard asked, masking his apprehension.

"My wife is from there, so I recognized your accent."

"Ah. I was born in Narbonne," Bernard lied. "But I've lived outside Paris for many years. My name is Jean Cl-Clarmont," he stammered. Jesu, he was so rattled he'd nearly forgotten there might be men here who'd recognize his false name as readily as his birth name. "And this is my groom, Maslin Sauveur."

Ruarke inclined his head, but his eyes lingered overlong on Maslin's scarred face and serviceable sword, and Bernard could read the disbelief in them.

"The cessation of hostilities have forced many of us to find new occupations," Bernard said smoothly. "Yourself, as well. Who would think to find the hero of Poitiers turned horse breeder?"

The flattery didn't take the chill from Ruarke's rough-hewn face. "My older brother and I have worked hard to build up the finest fighting stock in all Christendom."

"Well, they are certainly that, and 'twas clever of you to come so early to Bordeaux. With the tourney drawing fighters like bees to honey, you are sure to sell the lot."

"Has one of them caught your eye?"

"Ah, several." Bernard blew a lock of lank brown hair from his face and looked away lest that piercing gaze read his intent. He seized upon the first horse he spotted. "That large stallion looks promising. The one ridden by the lad in blue."

"Lad in blue?" Ruarke turned his head. "Ah." The corners of his hard mouth softened in unmistakable affection.

Bernard blinked. Lord Ruarke favored boys? Interesting, and mayhap a weakness upon which he could capitalize. Not that he shared such a fetish. Girls were his preference...the younger the better. His blood warmed as he recalled the pair awaiting him at home. Thirteen-year-old twin sisters acquired when he'd attacked their merchant father. The sooner this business was done, the sooner he could get back to teaching them his preferences.

"Philippe," Ruarke roared, stopping conversation on the whole field and making Bernard cringe.

A knight clad in Sommerville's crimson and black materialized at his elbow. "My lord?"

"Sir Jean would take a closer look at Thor. Have the lad bring him hither."

"Lad?" Philippe followed the sweep of his lordship's arm. "But Thor is being ridden by—"

"I know who rides the stallion," Ruarke said softly. "But Sir Jean has not yet met the lad."

"Ah." Philippe shot Bernard a grin and departed.

"Did you watch the lad during the exercises?" Ruarke asked.

"Aye. He rode well."

"That he did," Ruarke boomed proudly.

"You, er, taught him yourself?"

"Aye. Though we had to sneak about for fear his mother would discover what we were about."

"I see," Bernard murmured. "It has been my experience that if you pay them enough, the parents don't object."

Ruarke's rugged features tensed. "What the hell are you talking about?" he demanded, his voice like the crack of a whip.

Bernard recoiled but was spared a reply by Philippe's arrival. "Here is the lad, milord," the knight announced.

"Shall I put Thor through his paces for you, sir?" inquired a low, melodious voice.

"Er, I suppose." Bernard glanced up. The slender build and smooth cheeks were expected, the thick lashes framing the dark eyes were not. It took him a moment to realize the rider was a female...another to realize the eyes laughing down at him weren't blue but a startling shade of purple.

Purple! He'd only beheld their like once before. On his sister Gabrielle. He'd last seen her nineteen years ago on the road to Chinon. She'd been surrounded by the soldiers who'd just chopped off their father's head. Bernard had left her there and saved himself. Served her right. Prissy little bitch. He'd always hated Gabrielle... and thus hated this unknown woman on sight.

Still, Bernard had been forced to play many roles in his life and knew well how to hide his feelings. Schooling his features into a mask of chagrined surprise, he exclaimed, "By the rod, Lord Ruarke, you've tricked me well. What is such a comely wench doing fighting in the melee?"

Ruarke grinned. "This is my daughter, Lady Catherine."

"Daughter!" Bernard cried, while Maslin choked on what sounded like laughter. Bernard felt like biting something...preferably a Sommerville. "My apologies." He gritted his teeth instead and forced himself to

bow, his hatred of these haughty, rich English so strong
it nearly choked him.

"Accepted," the chit said cheerily. "Papa is ever the
trickster," she warbled, smiling fondly at her parent. The
look that passed between them was ripe with love and
understanding.

Bernard flashed back to his own youth and the night
Odell had gifted him with his first woman. A girl, no
older than Bernard's thirteen years. They'd beaten her,
then shared her. Too bad the old man was dead. Odell
would have liked the twins.

"Papa, I think you've discomforted Sir Jean."

"Nay." Bernard pasted on a smile. "I was but thinking that a melee, even a mock one, can be dangerous. 'Tis
surprising you would agree to allow so tender a maid—"

"Allow?" Ruarke threw back his head and laughed.
"I gave up on trying to manage Cat when she was still in
the cradle."

"Are you hinting I'm spoiled?" She shoved back her
hood to reveal a coronet of honey-colored braids. She
was older than Bernard had supposed, mayhap seven-
teen or eighteen, but lovely. The aura of fragility was ruined only by her determined chin.

Willful, Bernard thought. No doubt her doting papa
had indulged her shamelessly. It occurred to him that al-
though she was only a female, her father seemed to value
her greatly. An interesting fact, that. One he might be
able to use, though just how he did not yet know. Anxious to be away and make plans, he said, "It takes spirit
to control such a large animal. You are indeed a fine
horsewoman, and I will definitely consider putting in a
bid on your Thor."

Bernard took his leave, but he and Maslin had gone
only a few paces when a troop of thirty men-at-arms

trotted onto the field, led by a pair of knights. Between them rode a woman dressed in blue velvet. Gold chain glinted at her neck and waist; a fortune in pearls banded the hem of her skirts.

"Mama!" Catherine Sommerville cried.

Bernard stopped and looked back just as the lady drew rein before Ruarke and their daughter. "This is a pleasant surprise, my love." Ruarke's powerful baritone had dropped to an intimate purr. His austere features glowed with the joy usually seen on small children at feasts.

"You received a message from the king," the wife said.

"What does Edward want?"

She cocked her head. "What makes you think I read it?"

"Because I know you." He leaned forward in the saddle and gave his wife a surprisingly passionate kiss . . . considering they had likely been wed for many years.

Bernard watched with interest this confirmation of his earlier theory that the fierce warrior had an uncommon fondness for his daughter and wife. 'Twas the sort of weakness he had learned to identify and then turn to his advantage.

"I did read it," the wife admitted when Ruarke released her. "We are called home to England."

"What?" Ruarke shouted. "But we've only just gotten here."

The lady's sigh was audible over the shifting of onlookers anxious for a bit of court gossip. "The Black Prince's health has taken a turn for the worse and he would speak with you. Princess Joan needs me to come and bolster her spirits."

Ruarke scowled as he looked around the field at the horses. "I'll go, of course, but . . ."

"I would be honored to stay and see to your business here," said Sir Philippe.

"My thanks. We had a devil of a time getting this lot here, and I'd just as soon not ship them back home."

"What of me?" Catherine edged her mount closer to the center of the discussion. "Must I leave before the tourney?"

"Absolutely," her father said. "I'd not leave you here unguarded." His voice dropped off to a whisper, but Bernard was adept at reading lips. "Not after what happened with Henry."

The girl flinched, and her chin came up. "That was two years ago. I'm older...and wiser. What say you, Mama?"

"I hate to cheat you of the spectacle." She turned to smile at her daughter, and Bernard got his first good look at Ruarke Sommerville's wife.

The shock of recognition punched the air from his lungs. "Mon Dieu . . ." he gasped.

"What ails you?" Maslin growled in his ear. "You look as though you've seen a ghost."

His henchman's words broke the spell, awakened Bernard to the danger. "Aye. I have." Trembling with disbelief, he spun around and tucked his chin into the neck of his cloak. A shiver worked its way down his spine as he pulled the cowl over his head for good measure. "I thought she was dead. She should be dead." He quaked again. "How comes she to be here, wed to Sommerville?"

"Who?"

"My sister."

"Your sister? Where?" Maslin looked around.

Bernard grabbed his arm and shoved him in the direction of their horses. "Come. We must get out of here. Gabrielle might recognize me, though it's been years, and

I've . . . aged. She hasn't, though. She's still as beautiful as ever. The bitch.''

By the time they reached their mounts, Bernard had pulled himself together. "We will ride back to the inn," he said. "Slowly, as though naught had happened."

"What will we do then?" Maslin asked, fascinated by the change in his usually fearless master.

"We will pray Gabrielle didn't recognize me. Tomorrow we will return to Toulouse and gather my men."

"Without Sommerville's horses?"

"They'll do me no good if Gabrielle recognizes me. It's been nineteen years since I tried to kill the Black Prince, but the English still have a price on my head."

"What will we do for coin, then, rob a merchant or sack a nunnery?" Maslin asked, knowing neither would yield much.

"We could kidnap Sommerville's daughter and hold her to ransom," Bernard said softly.

Maslin stopped mid-stride. "What?"

"We'll take the daughter. You've seen how Ruarke values her and his wife. Much as I'd enjoy having Gabrielle as a hostage, she's leaving for England. But Catherine . . . Did you hear if the spoiled brat had cajoled permission to stay behind?"

"Aye. At least I think so." Maslin risked another look. "His men will guard her even more diligently than the horses."

"True, but once the tourney starts, they'll be busy."

"We're returning for the tourney? I thought you said there were people coming who might recognize you."

"So there are. But none will know my nephew."

"Gervase? How will you get him here? He has done naught this past year but slave to rebuild that stupid keep of his."

" 'Tis for exactly that reason Gervase will come. He hates the English even more fervently than I do. With good reason. They destroyed everything he held dear." Bernard grinned. "He'll get the girl and bring her to me."

Chapter One

Bordeaux, France
August 20, 1375

'Twas four nights before the tourney, and the great hall of the castle was packed to capacity. Knights drawn from as far away as Italy by the promise of blood sport and rich prizes mingled with men too old to fight and ladies who had come in search of a more intimate sort of adventure. The light of a thousand flambeaux shimmered on their silken garments, winked off the golden chains hung around their necks and the precious gems banding their gowns and surcoats. Two stories above the glittering crowd, the banners of French cities captured by the English fluttered in silent testimony to the long, costly struggle waged between the two countries. Ended now by the peace treaty just concluded.

Peace! Gervase St. Juste spat onto the ground beneath the open window where he'd paused to take stock before entering his enemy's stronghold and presenting himself to John, Duke of Lancaster. He'd not know peace while his people still suffered.

"Can you pick her out in this press?" Perrin asked, straining to peer over Gervase's shoulder.

"Not yet, cousin." Gervase buried the hatred he'd nurtured for so long and swept the crowd with narrowed eyes, searching for the woman his uncle had described to him. Bernard had only seen her once, and since the noble ladies all had their hair covered by those ridiculous headdresses 'twas difficult to tell which were blond.

"There are two men in the Sommerville red-and-black livery." Perrin pointed to a pair of hulking brutes who stood a few feet away, their backs to the window, facing a small circle of smiling, laughing nobles. "How odd. They look more like men-at-arms than knights. How do you suppose they came to be invited to the duke's grand fete?"

"Because their lord is a personal friend of both the duke and his brother, the king." Ruarke Sommerville, English hero of Poitiers, scourge of all France. "Pity he was called back to England ere the tourney began," Gervase said tightly. He'd have enjoyed crossing blades with Lord Ruarke and to hell with the scheme that had brought him hither.

"Look, there's a woman with them." Indeed, one of the Sommerville retainers had moved aside to reveal a lady. 'Twas she, not the men-at-arms, who was the focal point of the posturing lords and knights. "It could be Ruarke Sommerville's daughter," Perrin added in a whisper.

Gervase nodded, noting the wisps of blond hair peeping out at her nape where it was caught in a jeweled caul. "'Tis likely." His first impression was of a slender woman in formfitting blue velvet. How fragile she looked, he thought, and his determination to see this through faltered. Then he caught sight of the gems in the trim banding her surcoat and his jaw clenched tighter. Such wealth would have kept his people in food for a month.

"She must be as lovely as your uncle Bernard claimed, for these men gaze at her like fatuous fools."

"With a dowry as large as hers, she could be an ugly cow and prospective suitors would still sing odes to her beauty."

A short, dumpy girl edged her way into the circle of admirers. Catherine turned to greet the newcomer, baring her profile to the torchlight—delicate bones, a slim nose, smiling lips and a surprisingly firm jaw. Willful, Gervase thought. Willful, spoiled and so certain of her allure she dismissed her courtiers with a wave of her pale, beringed hand. Linking her arm with the homely girl's, Catherine started toward the window.

Gervase stiffened and backed away, but for an instant, his gaze locked on Catherine's. The incredible eyes his uncle had likened to violets widened with shock, mirroring the awareness that arrowed down Gervase's spine. It exploded in his belly with the impact of a mailed fist. Shuddering against the wash of desire, he turned and melted into the shadows.

He'd been watching her.

Catherine stopped and blinked. When she reopened her eyes, the man was gone, but she knew he'd been there, standing in the courtyard just outside the window. Watching her.

"Cat? What is it?" Margery tugged on her arm.

"Naught, I..." Cat shook her head to clear it, then walked the few steps and sank down onto the bench beneath the window.

"'Tis likely the heat," Margery said, plopping down beside her. "Or the excitement."

Cat Sommerville swept the crowd with a jaundiced eye. Despite the anticipation spicing the heavy air, there was an undercurrent of animosity. The English and French walked about stiff-legged as rival dogs spoiling for a fight. Her own nerves jangled with rising irritation and something she'd come here in hopes of curing... boredom. She might as well have returned to England with her parents ten days ago. At least at Wilton she enjoyed a small measure of freedom, and she wouldn't have had to put up with the cattiness of the shallow women who'd come here.

"You look lovely this evening," said her friend.

Cat forced a smile. "As do you, Margery."

The girl laughed, a pudgy hand plucking at the skirt of her silken cotehardie. "I look like a short, puce cow in this," she said merrily. "But Mama insisted I wear it instead of the black, which at least doesn't cling to these horrid hips of mine."

"The color is most becoming on you," Cat replied, unable to truthfully say the close-cut style of the gown complemented Margery's full figure.

"What a diplomat you are, Cat." Margery laughed again, transforming her plain-as-pudding features to something approaching pretty. "May I say your gown fits you to perfection and the blue deepens the violet of your eyes. Or has Sir Archie already said so?"

Cat rolled the eyes in question. "Thus far I've not seen him this eve. 'Tis probably too much to expect he's drunken himself into a stupor and won't attend."

"How you speak about the most ardent of your many admirers," Margery teased without the slightest hint of jealousy or envy. "And you know Sir Archie doesn't overimbibe." Planting a hand on her ample bosom, she crossed her eyes in fair imitation of the love-struck knight and intoned, "Moderation in all things, that's my by-word...except in my adoration of you, my fair Catherine."

Cat laughed and shook her head. "You've a wicked sense of humor, Margery."

"No more so than your own. 'Tis why we've become such fast friends, you and I."

"Aye. Your friendship is all that's made Bordeaux bearable."

"Never say you're lonely. Why, you've a string of men trailing after you that's made you the envy of every woman here." Every woman save Margery. Which was but one of the reasons she was Cat's friend, her only friend. "Especially Lady Clarice. When I went looking for you, I had only to follow that woman's malevolent stare to find you," Margery added.

"I don't understand why she hates me so."

"She's jealous of your beauty and wealth."

"But she has both in abundance, and I've made it plain to everyone here that I do not desire any of the men at court."

"The men, contrary creatures as they are, desire you all the more for your aloofness. And who wouldn't choose you over her? True, she is pretty and she inherited a rich estate from her poor dead husband, but she's shallow and vicious, without a care for anyone save herself. While you are good and kind and patient."

"Patient." Cat laughed. "I wish my family could hear you say that last. Even I admit I'm impetuous and headstrong. Because you are my friend, you see only my good points." As she turned to smile at Margery, she spied Clarice.

The woman wrinkled her nose as though she'd scented something bad, then leaned to whisper in the ear of one of the silly women who trailed after her. What were they saying about her? Apprehension trickled down Cat's spine, making her shiver.

"Don't give them a thought." Margery seized Cat's hand and squeezed. "There is naught bad they can say about you."

If you only knew. Cat repressed another shiver. Each time a new person arrived from England she braced herself, wondering if they'd be the one to reveal her ugly secret. Though two years had passed since the sordid incident, 'twas the sort of thing that lingered on people's minds and leaked out their lips. So deep was her shame she hadn't even mentioned Henry to Margery, to whom she'd bared all her other foibles and dreams. And if Lady Ela, Margery's proper mother, learned of the aborted elopement, she'd forbid her daughter to speak with someone as tainted as Cat.

"They're just jealous because all the men are wild for you."

Cat grimaced. "I'd settle for one man who was more interested in me than in Papa's money. Someone who accepted me as I am . . . warts and all."

"You do say the oddest things, and I doubt you'll find such a paragon here. 'Tis a greedy group that's come to Bordeaux." Margery glanced about, frowning. "The old ones have come to relive their glory days, the youths for fame and fortune. Those who can't earn it in combat, seek to marry wealth . . . or steal it."

"True." Cat sighed, heartily sick of being pursued by men with gold lust, not love in their eyes. Before leaving, her mother had warned Cat to be on her guard. "Philippe will watch you as zealously as he would his own daughters, but you must do your part. Take care you are never alone with any of these men. Most are even less honorable than that disgusting Henry Norville was, and God knows we don't want a repeat of that disaster,'' Gaby Sommerville had added, never one to mince words.

As if Cat would *ever* leave herself vulnerable to a man again. She drew in a breath of hot, stagnant air and released it noisily. "How I long to leave this stifling court behind and ride out for a day," she said wistfully.

"'Tis too dangerous." Margery's eyes widened. "Never say you are going to sneak out and ride alone as you used to do at home."

"Nay. I may be bored nearly to death, but I'm not stupid." She gestured toward the two hulking men-at-arms, who stood with their backs to the tiny alcove, giving the illusion of privacy. "Gamel and Garret guard me so zealously I cannot even visit the garderobes without them. I wish..."

"Mon Dieu. I've never seen *him* before. Who do you suppose that is?" Margery murmured.

Cat followed Margery's gaze to the man who'd just entered the hall. Tall and wide shouldered, dressed all in black, he stuck out like a raven in a room full of peacocks. Looking neither right nor left at the gawking nobles, he walked toward the dais and their host, John, Duke of Lancaster. The sight of the crowd instinctively parting to permit him passage reminded Cat of her father. Though the stranger was more leanly built, he had the same proud carriage, determined stride and stern expression that made men stand aside for Ruarke Sommerville.

Power. It radiated from this man the way heat did from sunbaked rocks. Here was a presence to be reckoned with, Cat thought, going up on her toes to get a better look. Torchlight flickered over his rugged profile, high forehead, a straight nose and solid jaw. Inky hair fell past his nape, accentuating his deeply tanned skin. She gasped softly, recognizing him as the man who'd stared at her through the window. Who was he?

"Whoever he is, he's causing a stir," Margery whispered. "Lady Clarice looks like a child ready to pounce on a sweetmeat."

Cat realized her own jaw had dropped open, snapped it shut and forced her gaze from the magnetic stranger. "He's likely some impoverished knight. Why, he isn't wearing a bit of gold chain."

"He's impressive enough without."

Aye, he was. And that rankled. Cat fought against the insidious pull of something she'd sworn she'd never feel again. Desire. Only Henry had never affected her this strongly.

The stranger stopped before the dais and inclined his head. "Gervase St. Juste begs Your Grace's leave to enter the tourney." His low baritone raised Cat's heart rate another notch. Though his form was correct, uttered by hundreds of men anxious to participate in the tourney, his voice had an edge the others had lacked. Pride, she thought. And mayhap anger, as well.

"I bet he never begged for a thing in his life," Margery said, and Cat was disposed to agree.

Lord John leaned forward, the disinterest of the past two weeks absent from his leathery face. "From whence do you hail?"

"I've a small holding called Alleuze in the Languedoc."

"Hmm. Have you fought before? We want no inexperienced lads injuring themselves in their quest for glory."

The strikingly beautiful Clarice sidled up. Her red lips and the black kohl lining her eyes contrasted vividly with her white skin. "Oh, I doubt Sir Gervase is *inexperienced.*"

"If he is, you'll soon cure that," someone shouted. A round of laughter and catcalls greeted this.

Cat waited for Sir Gervase to acknowledge Clarice's unspoken invitation. A muscle twitched in his cheek, but his gaze remained locked on the duke's. "I think you will find me an adequate foe."

"Foe? Have you forgotten we are here to celebrate the peace between our two countries?" Lord John asked sharply.

"I forget naught," Sir Gervase replied in kind.

"He's certainly a prickly fellow," Margery said.

Cat nodded, taken with the way he'd ignored Clarice, yet wary of his animosity. "He doesn't seem to welcome this peace."

Apparently the duke agreed, for his gaze narrowed as it swept the bold knight from head to toe. "I crave peace. These continued hostilities have taken a toll on both our peoples."

Sir Gervase's raven head bowed a fraction, and his shoulders sagged as though some terrible weight had dropped on them. Then he straightened. "On that we are agreed. Peace is necessary."

"So you have come to fight in the tourney. Do you seek to bash a few English heads under the guise of sport? Or is it ransom you are after?"

The knight started. "What?"

"Ransom. The taking of prisoners in the melee in order to get rich by ransoming them back to themselves or their families."

"I am familiar with the process," Sir Gervase growled. "But I want naught I do not deserve. I come to celebrate the peace."

Now why did she think that wasn't strictly true? Cat was intrigued by this big, mysterious stranger. He wasn't for her. Even had she been in the market for a husband, which she wasn't, her father would never approve her marrying an impoverished French knight. Still there was something about him that caused a purely feminine flutter deep inside her.

"Cat!" Margery's padded elbow landed in her ribs. "His Grace is calling for you."

Frowning, Cat lifted her skirts and worked her way through the crowd to the edge of the dais. "You wanted me, Your Grace?"

A knowing grin split the old war-horse's face. "Caught you daydreaming, eh, m'dear? I said Sir Gervase has a harsh opinion of us and I thought meeting some of our lovely ladies might soften him toward us. This is Lady Catherine Sommerville, daughter to Lord Ruarke and goddaughter to my brother, the king."

Excitement shivered across Cat's skin. He was totally unsuitable, yet he fascinated her. "Sir Gervase," she murmured. Relieved by the steadiness of her voice, she glanced up at the knight. Her heart slammed against her ribs as her curious gaze met his. Gray. His eyes were an unusual shade of gray, she thought. Cool and mysterious as fog on water, fringed by long black lashes. The expression in his eyes changed to something totally unexpected. Contempt. Shock held her immobile.

"A pleasure, Lady Catherine." His smooth words at odds with his expression, he took the hand she'd instinctively held out. The brush of his mouth on the back of her hand sent a frisson of heat up her arm.

Alarmed, she snatched her hand back.

He straightened, brows winging up over eyes as blank as polished silver. "Have I somehow offended?"

"Nay...of course not."

"I am glad." A slow, intimate smile lifted the corner of his mouth, making her think she'd imagined his disdain. He had no reason to dislike her. "I'd hate to see His Grace's plan fail."

Intrigued, she smiled. "As would I. Have you supped?"

He nodded, taking her arm and steering her away from the dais. "I ate with my men after we'd set up camp, but the ride in was dusty. A cup of wine or ale wouldn't be amiss."

She signaled a passing page, who returned with two cups of wine just as they reached the window seat she'd recently vacated. "You're out near the tourney fields, then?" She sank down onto the bench, feeling unaccountably nervous and...and vulnerable with this stranger, though the hall was still packed with people and her bodyguards lurked nearby. "Why not here in the city?"

"All the inns were full." He leaned one shoulder against the wall of the tiny alcove, looking big and solid as the stone behind him. His body blocked the light from the hall, creating an intimate bower for the two of them.

Recalling another time and another man bent on seduction, Cat was half tempted to flee. Pride wouldn't let her. Eventually she must wed to have the children she wanted. Which meant she'd have to learn to deal with men on an intimate level. Gervase St. Juste could never be her husband, but he was enticing, dangerous. Tempting her to boldness.

"Fortunate you are to be outside the city," she said, low and husky, keenly aware of the muscles bulging beneath his velvet tunic as he crossed his arms over his chest and the way his knitted hose hugged his long legs and sturdy thighs. Very dangerous. Very tempting. "The noise and smells of so many people living so close together makes sleep difficult."

"Do they?" He stood so near she could smell the soap mingling with the faint muskiness of his skin and see an odd light flare in his eyes. "Have you had trouble sleeping?"

"Nay," she said, startled by his intensity. "Well, I am a bit bored, is all, so..." So she gazed out the chamber window and wished she were riding across the hills distantly glimpsed.

"Mayhap I can help allay your...boredom," he said silkily.

Cat stiffened, wary yet intrigued. "How?"

"Mayhap a walk in the gardens...for a start. We'll see where that leads us."

Into danger. "I am not that sort of lady."

"What sort is that?"

"The sort who goes walking with a stranger." The walk she'd taken, the one that had cost her so much, had been with a man she thought she knew. A man she'd thought loved her.

Gervase's smile was ripe with masculine challenge. Her stomach fluttered in response and her palms grew damp. "You'd go if you knew me, then?" he taunted.

Aye. Cat knew then that she was in way over her head. "Possibly." She stood, shaking out her skirts to hide the trembling in her hands...her limbs.

"Afraid of me?" His smile deepened, another challenge.

Aye, but more so of herself. She angled her chin up to meet the arrogant tilt of his. It was a mistake. In the blink of an eye, he leaned forward, his mouth closing over hers in a fiery kiss. Only their lips touched, but she felt the impact shudder through her body, sapping it of will and breath.

A groan filled her throat, of protest or surrender, she wasn't certain. Beneath her feet, the ground shifted. Dizzy and disoriented, she brought her hands up, clenched them in the front of his tunic. The growl of satisfaction that rumbled through his chest broke the spell. She tore free of him, cheeks burning, heart thundering. "How could you do that to me?" she asked.

"Quite easily, it seems," he drawled.

Cat drew back and slapped him as hard as she could... or she would have had the blow landed. Instead he caught her wrist a scant inch from his cheek.

"Don't ever attempt to strike me."

"I wouldn't have had to if you hadn't molested me." She shook off his hand.

"Quarreling already?" Lady Clarice asked, gliding in to wrap a slender arm through the knight's muscular one.

Cat smiled, displaying the teeth she longed to sink into Sir Gervase. "Nay. But we have run out of things to discuss."

"Ah. It seems I came just in time. My repertoire is more... extensive," Lady Clarice murmured. Smug as a cat making off with the cream, she led her trophy away. Just before the crowd swallowed them up, Sir Gervase glanced back over his shoulder and gave Cat a long, simmering look that promised this wasn't over.

Margery charged into the alcove. "How dare Clarice take—"

" 'Tis all right, Margery," Cat said hastily. "Sir Gervase and I, er, found we have very little in common."

"Why are you so angry? What did he say?"

"Naught, he..."

Oscar, the third member of Cat's guard, a man of medium build, unswerving loyalty and sharp wits, appeared behind Margery. "Fat lot of nerve the knight's got, running off with that woman. Do ye want we should go after the lout and drag him back?" Flanking him were Gamel and Garret. The twin giants flexed their thick arms and clenched fists the size of hams.

Cat smiled. "Tempting as the offer is, the duke has strictly forbidden fighting off the tourney field, and I'd not see you three land in trouble over a petty slight."

Gamel swung his shaggy head toward the far end of the hall where Lady Clarice and her friends plied the knight with wine and charm. " 'Tis no small thing to us, m'lady," he snarled.

"Actually, I found Sir Gervase's company tedious. Clarice is welcome to him." Cat glared at the knight, who stood taller than any present save Gamel and Garret, and seriously contemplated squashing his black head with something damaging... a pike, mayhap.

As though sensing her regard, Gervase turned suddenly and their gazes locked. Triumph kindled in those wintry eyes of his, so quickly gone it might have been a trick of the torchlight.

Now what do you suppose he's about? she wondered.

Lady Clarice was as difficult to shake as a Mediterranean squid and seemed to have more arms. Gervase finally escaped by claiming he needed to visit the jakes, then ducking into the shadow-draped gardens behind the castle. Scarcely had he closed the gate behind him when someone grabbed his arm.

Gervase yelped and yanked his arm free.

"Easy, 'tis just me." Perrin's voice came out of the gloom.

"Thanks be to heaven." Gervase sagged against the trunk of a birch tree. "I thought it was her."

"Lady Catherine?"

"Clarice. The stink of her perfume still pollutes my nostrils and I swear there are marks on my chest from her nails."

"The perils of court intrigue. What of Lady Catherine? I expected you'd have gotten her out here by now so we could be on our way."

"She proved . . . difficult." Gervase pushed away from the tree and dragged a hand through his hair as he paced the path.

"Losing your touch with the ladies?"

"Small wonder. This past year I've been too busy keeping the brigands from our door and tilling the fields like a common peasant to woo a woman." Gervase sighed in exasperation. "But I could think of no other way to get close to her except to swallow my hatred for her family and pretend to court her. Who would think 'twould be so difficult to get her alone?"

"Aye. She is surrounded by admirers, and two of those Sommerville men-at-arms go everywhere she does. How will you get her away before the tourney starts?"

"I'm not certain I can. We may have to stay and participate in a few of the events in hopes that during the confusion we will find an opportunity to take her."

"Oh? And what will you do for a suitable mount? Or will you ride old Jock in the jousting lists and the melee?"

"I have yet to figure that out...but I will. After all, we've lived on our wits these past six years."

An hour later, Cat finally slipped away from the hall to walk in the gardens. The cool night air eased the heat from her cheeks and cleared the stench of smoke and unwashed bodies from her nostrils, but for once the familiar scent of roses and herbs failed to lift her spirits.

Sir Gervase's attempted seduction had shaken her, and when Philippe had arrived a short while later, she'd asked to leave the castle and stay in her father's tent.

"A tent is no place for a lady," Philippe had replied.

"I've stayed in them since I was little." Nor could he deny that. "The castle is crowded beyond belief with so many nobles come for the tourney. True, Margery and I are more fortunate than most, since there are only two of us in our bed, but six other ladies spread their pallets on the floor each night. I can scarce arise at night to use the pot but what I step on someone."

"You are more comfortable here," he insisted.

"I have never been more uncomfortable in my life, and well you know it. 'Tis a nest of greedy vipers and back-biting she-cats. Margery is the only one with whom I feel at home."

"If anyone bothers you, you have only to tell me and I will bring the matter to His Grace, the duke." Philippe's expression sharpened. "Are you certain this Gervase St. Juste didn't insult you? Oscar seemed to think—"

"We merely...argued. The man is arrogant and surly. I can look out for myself. However well-meaning, Lord John's interference would only make things worse, for there are some who think our family's connection with the king's has given me airs."

"You? Never." His brown eyes danced. "I know you'd rather be mucking out a stall than dancing with...what was it you called them...ah, yes, those lead-footed nobles."

"Then you see why I'd rather stay in the tents than—"

"Out of the question. Your sire was most specific in his instructions. You are to stay within the castle except whilst attending the tourney events. Gamel and Garret are to be with you at all times, and one is to sleep across the doorway of your chamber at night." Nor could she shake Philippe's determination. Having served her father for some nineteen years, first as squire, then as a knight, he was not only loyal, he knew the folly of disobeying Ruarke Sommerville.

Sighing, Cat turned her back on the castle and walked along the gravel path.

"Are you certain Gervase St. Juste didn't insult you?" Garret grumbled as he and his brother fell into step behind her. "I've not seen you so angry in years."

Too true. Clearly her initial impression of him had been in error. He might have her papa's size and commanding presence, but Ruarke Sommerville would never have stooped to insult a woman. Obviously Sir Gervase was an arrogant lecher. He and Clarice deserved each other. Yet the few times Cat had surreptitiously glanced their way, she'd been stunned by the pang she felt at the sight of his tanned face bent close to Clarice's pale one.

"Mayhap, Sir Gervase will be wounded in the tourney and thus God will punish him for his meanness," Cat said with forced cheer. Determined not to let the knight ruin what was already an unpleasant visit, she continued along the path. On either side grew the flowers and herbs

Princess Joan had planted here when she and the Black Prince first came to Bordeaux.

"Gamel, do you know what that one is?" she asked.

The giant swung his sword scabbard out of the way as he hunkered down beside the plant in question. His thick, scarred fingers stroked the leaf with surprising gentleness. "Horehound by the smell and these white flowers."

"Very good." Cat beamed at her pupil. The brothers had learned much in the two years since Henry's treachery had made them her guardians. She'd been confined to Wilton's grounds, then, under the guise of improving the gardens. Talking about herbs had eased the tension of having someone following her at all times. "There are few things here even I recognize. I wonder if the local herb woman—"

"Lady Catherine. Ho, Lady Catherine," called a horribly familiar voice. Before she could bolt behind a bush, Sir Archie was upon them. He grabbed her hand in one of his slender ones and pressed his wet lips to her fingertips.

Cat repressed a shiver of revulsion. Archibald de Percy meant well, he was just so...soft. With his curly hair and big, vapid eyes he reminded her of a brown sheep. A wealthy, handsome sheep, 'twas true, but a sheep nonetheless.

"My dearest Catherine. I cannot tell you how sorry I am that preparations for the tourney kept me on the training grounds and thus I am so late in arriving." He pulled a linen square from inside his tunic and dabbed at the perspiration on his clean-shaven face. His short crimson tunic was the height of fashion, as were his shoes, the toes of which were so long they flopped when he walked. "I chased all over the castle looking for you.

What say we sit over there?" He pointed to the arbor at the end of the garden.

Cat groaned. This must be her night for seductive males. The out-of-the way corner and its concealing trellis overgrown with grapevines was a favorite for lovers who wished to dally without being seen. "I don't think—"

"We cannot let her out of our sight," Garret growled, and for once Cat was glad of her father's precautions.

Archie drew himself up to his full height of some five feet ten inches. It brought his aristocratic nose level with Garret's breastbone; still he managed to look down on the man as he snapped, "I assure you, my intentions are most honorable."

"That may be." Garret stared at Archie the way a bird might a worm. "But we've got our orders. And unless Sir Philippe says differently, the king himself is not getting our lady off alone."

"Of all the ridiculous, disrespectful..." Archie grumbled and complained but had to content himself with sitting in the arbor with Cat while the brothers stood at attention a few yards away, in full view of the shadow-draped interior. "I don't see why you put up with them." He dusted off the seat with his damp handkerchief, then swept her a low bow. "Lovely lady..."

Cat bit the inside of her cheek to keep from giggling. "They mean well... and they do have their orders."

"How can Lord Ruarke expect a man to court you with those two staring over his shoulder?"

"Court?" Cat swallowed a groan. "Sir Archie, I—"

"I told you my intentions were above reproach. I wouldn't dream of doing anything untoward till after we're wed."

"Wed," she said weakly. "But we've only known each other for a few short weeks." It seemed like months.

"Some couples don't meet until their wedding day," he reminded her. "Naturally I'd prefer to speak with your father before saying anything to you, but he was unable to see me before he left for London. And with so many eligible men prowling about for a wife, I'm afraid you'll be snapped up before I can."

"I'm really not in the market for a husband at the—"

"All women want to marry." He took her hand and gazed earnestly into her eyes. "But I know a lady of your, er, prospects must guard against unscrupulous men."

Cat braced, half expecting him to mention Henry's name.

"I assure you 'tis you I want, Lady Catherine," he added. "My estate is smaller than your dear sire's, but I would cherish you and love you all your days."

His declaration was a balm to an old wound. Too bad she hadn't the slightest interest in being Sir Archie's wife. "Sir Archie, I...I am flattered by your regard, but I don't know what to say." *How to get rid of you without hurting your feelings.*

"You need only agree and tell me how to contact your father. I will do the rest." The dozen or so rings he wore on his fingers winked in the faint light from the torches set around in the garden. Such an ostentatious display of wealth offended Cat and reminded her of how simply Gervase had been dressed. "Come. What say you?" Archie tilted his head, and Cat noticed his eyes glittered as avidly as his rings. He might say he wanted her for herself alone, but he lusted after her fortune, as well.

Still Cat couldn't bring herself to denounce Archie. 'Twas the way of the world. Men sought heiresses to wed.

'Twas her misfortune to be one. "My father won't approve the match."

"Why? I love you," he cried. "I will do everything in my power to make you happy. I swear it," he said wildly.

Alarmed by his fervor, recalling where Henry's passion had led, Cat cast a desperate glance at Gamel and Garret. They were nearby, but they'd turned away to give her a measure of privacy. Beyond them she saw other couples strolling through the gardens. If she called out, her guards would come running and pummel Archie into the ground. She didn't want him hurt, nor, to be perfectly honest, did she want to be the center of yet another scene. Better to dent the fool's ego than his brain.

"Sir," she said through her teeth. "My papa would never let me marry a man who was not an earl and richer than we are."

He flinched, his face flushing. "I had not realized you were so cruel. You led me to believe you cared for me. You let me court you when all the while you knew there was no hope." He stood and flung down the handkerchief like a gauntlet. "Did it amuse you to have me trail after you?"

Though she knew she'd done none of these things, had in fact done her best to discourage him, Cat accepted the role in which he'd cast her. "'Tis the way of the court, is it not?" She mimicked the brittle tone and cutting words she'd heard Clarice use to dismiss an unwanted admirer.

"I loved you," Archie wailed.

Belatedly Cat realized he meant it . . . or thought he did . . . and wished she'd found a gentler way to do this. "Archie, I—"

"Nay!" His eyes filled with tears. "I will not stay and let you continue to flay my bleeding heart." With a dramatic toss of his head, he stalked away.

Gamel and Garret started as Archie went past them, then turned to look at her. "About time, too," Gamel said cheerfully. He'd never liked Archie, or any other man who'd tried to get close to her. "Will you come within now?"

Cat sighed and shook her head. "I need a moment." Spirits drooping, she leaned back against the wooden trellis and closed her eyes.

"Resting up for the next victim?" inquired a deep voice.

Cat jerked, eyes flying open. Someone watched her from the other side of the trellis. The dim light cast a crisscross pattern of gray and black on his face, but she knew him instantly. "S-Sir Gervase, what...?"

"I was eavesdropping," he admitted without remorse. "I wanted to see if I was right about you."

"Right?" she asked, still dazed to find him here.

"I was. You are a spoiled little vixen."

Cat bolted upright, generations of Sommerville pride driving out confusion and shock. "I am not. You don't know me."

"I see that the reason you wouldn't walk out with me is that I'm neither wealthy nor titled."

"You arrogant, rude..." Cat's voice trailed off as she realized she was speaking to thin air. Gervase St. Juste had left as stealthily as he'd come. But his insults lingered on the air, tainting the sweet scent of the summer night.

Why was he spying on her? What did he want?

Chapter Two

"**Y**ou have to admit she is very beautiful."

Gervase didn't need to ask which *she* Perrin meant. The besotted fool had done naught but speak of Catherine Sommerville since leaving the castle last eve. In no mood to discuss the woman whose face had haunted his dreams, he stared between his horse's ears at the rutted road leading from the castle to the tiltyards. In order to keep up the pretext of participating in the tourney, he had to secure a mount. He had little money, and most of the horses were likely gone by now.

"Her eyes are like violets drenched in dew."

"Next you'll be writing verse," Gervase snapped.

"'Twould better serve our purpose than your approach. I do not understand why you twice insulted her instead of charming..."

"I am not charming."

Perrin's brows rose. "Not at the moment, mayhap." Nor for many years, but Gervase could be charming and amusing. Well Perrin remembered the companion of his early youth, ever the prankster, full of mischief. All that had changed when Gervase was two and ten and the English killed his sire, Sir Denis, leaving the boy to be raised by his cold, strict grandparents. A hard blow, but not as brutal as the crime committed by Ruarke a year ago. That heinous deed had ripped Gervase's heart to shreds and turned him into a hard, embittered man. Still . . .

" 'Tis hard to believe she's the daughter of a vicious man like Ruarke Sommerville," Perrin said thoughtfully.

"Of course she is not a murdering savage like her father. Women, even one born of his evil seed, are weak creatures, but last eve I had ample proof she is cold and heartless."

"Just because she refused to wed Sir Archie? Be reasonable, if she accepted every man who trails after her, she'd be a bigamist twenty times over."

" 'Twas the way she did it, wounding both his heart and his pride when a simple nay would have sufficed. She may not be a murderer of women and babes like her sire, but she's shallow and cruel." He'd had doubts about this plan when his uncle had proposed it. No matter what Ruarke had done, to kidnap an innocent lady went against the principles Gervase's grandparents had literally beaten into him. But after meeting Lady Catherine, his conscience was clear. And his course of action. "That so vicious a soul is wrapped in a pretty package makes it all the worse."

Perrin grinned. "I should think 'twould make your task all the more pleasant. After all, she'll be your prisoner, locked up in Alleuze with none to say you nay did you decide to—"

"I may be many things, Perrin, but I would not stoop to despoil a woman in my care." The words came out more sharply than Gervase had intended.

"Nay, you are too honorable for that." Too honorable for your own good sometimes, Perrin thought. He'd

seen how the horrors of war, the bloodshed and senseless violence had eaten away at Gervase's soul. But he'd
also seen the way his friend looked at the vivacious Lady
Cat. There'd been a heat in his gaze that had been absent when he'd looked at his poor dead wife. "I was surprised you agreed to this scheme of your uncle's."

"What choice do I have?" Gervase growled. "My
people are starving. Alleuze is a charred ruin without
even a roof to keep out the rain, and I have no coin for
seed or building materials."

"Aye. And my heart also bleeds for all we lost, but
such things happen in war."

"War. I know all about war...we've done little save
fight for the past ten years. What Sommerville did to Alleuze went beyond war. 'Twas barbarism of the worst
sort." Gervase's gaze clouded over, and Perrin knew he
remembered the gruesome sight that had awaited them
when they'd returned home. Knew, too, that Gervase
blamed himself for having been off fighting for King
Charles when his family needed him. "Uncle Bernard is
right," Gervase said. "Ruarke should be made to answer for his crimes."

"True. But Bernard's motive in all this puzzles me, for
I've never known the man to do aught that didn't benefit him."

"You are as bad as my grandparents, trying to turn me
against Bernard. He came to our aid years ago when my
father was killed, and lent Grandfather the troops to re-
gain Alleuze."

"And left straightaway when old Lord Jacques
wouldn't give him half of the estate as payment for his
help."

"So Grandfather said, but he ever hated Bernard for
being a de Lauren and never let me forget I shared that

blood,'' Gervase said stiffly. "If you find this business abhorrent and wish to leave my service, I will understand."

"I'd never leave you," Perrin exclaimed. "You are more than my overlord and cousin. We've been friends since birth." He cursed the upbringing that made Gervase hold everything inside. "You are right, our situation is perilous. We must do whatever is necessary. I—I just hate to see Lady Cat hurt by—"

"Hurt! I have no intention of harming a hair on her vain, foolish little head. The worst that will happen is she'll spend a few uncomfortable weeks at Alleuze deprived of the luxuries to which she's addicted. Why, she'll likely return home more appreciative of her considerable wealth."

"Aye, she is a great heiress. If you wed her, her dowry would buy food and stone enough to keep us—"

"Wed her! Perrin, have you lost your wits? If I planned to marry again, which I don't, I could not overlook the fact she's the daughter of the man who murdered my Marie and little Eva."

"I know, but—"

"I'd speak of it no more," Gervase snapped. Bad enough his sleep had been ruined by thoughts of Lady Catherine, he'd not have his daylight hours consumed by her, as well. Ahead he spotted the tents of the nobles and merchants arranged around the field where the tourney would be held four days hence. "I need a horse to ride in the joust, and I'd have your advice on the matter."

"A destrier?" At Gervase's nod, Perrin lifted his visor. He and Gervase both had the St. Juste swarthy complexions and black hair, but Perrin's eyes were brown, clouded now with concern. "How will you pay for such an expensive beast?"

"I'll trade my father's sword for it, with the understanding I'll buy it back with the prize money I win in the tourney."

Perrin grinned. "Certain of yourself, aren't you?"

"Aye. Desperation can lead a man to greatness." But they both knew 'twas no idle boast. Gervase was unequaled with a sword and lance. Had he not been needed to protect his lands, he might have made his way as a mercenary or fighting in tourneys.

"If you earn enough, you'll not need to kidnap Lady Cat."

"Perrin," Gervase warned. "'Twould be difficult to win what Bernard says we can get for her."

"The prospect of bashing a few English heads tempts you."

Gervase grinned with a hint of his former humor. "Ah, you've caught me out. That and the fact that we'll need coin to feed our people till the Sommerville ransom is realized."

"But if you should win more than you expect, will you still go through with this mad scheme?" Perrin asked.

"Mad? Aye, I suppose I must be, but the chance to punish Lord Ruarke is too good to pass up. Now that Uncle Bernard has put that notion in my head, I cannot shake it."

"Hmm," Perrin said. What he couldn't shake was the notion this was wrong, but he owed Gervase his life and his loyalty. "As to the horses, I understand the best beasts were those bred by Lord Ruarke and most of them have been sold."

"I'd not buy from him if he had the last horse available."

As it turned out, that is exactly what he did have. After visiting every horse trader, Gervase ended up at Sommerville's.

"Aye, we've a stallion for sale," said the groom. That his tunic, emblazoned with the Sommerville crest, was newer and finer than those Gervase and Perrin wore did not escape the fellow's notice. "But ye'll not be able to afford him."

Gervase had had a bellyful of Sommerville arrogance. "I'll be the judge of that. Who is in charge here?" he demanded, one hand on the hilt of the sword at his hip.

The groom scowled, then turned to the youth lurking in his shadow. "Run fetch Sir Philippe, lad."

The boy ran off between the tents, great silken tents finer than the hovels where Gervase's people were forced to live, returning moments later accompanied by a mailed knight. Obviously the man had been training, for his helmet was tucked under his left arm and sweat slicked the hair to his head. He looked young to be in charge of Sommerville's men. Likely he was some flunky sent to see what these impoverished interlopers wanted, Gervase thought, and his temper soared.

"George?" Sir Philippe inquired, one brow cocked.

"They've come to buy a war-horse," the groom growled.

"Ah." The knight looked at Gervase, brown eyes cool and neutral. "We've only one left. Thor is his name, and he's a big brute, but you've the size to handle him."

"If not the skills?" Gervase added softly.

Sir Philippe smiled. "You would know that better than I, sir knight. You hail from the south."

It was a statement, not a question. Gervase cursed silently. "I speak both Norman French and that of the south."

"As do I. I'm originally from these parts," Sir Philippe said lightly, "so I hear nuances in speech others miss. Have I the honor of addressing Gervase St. Juste, the man who quarreled with my lord's daughter?"

"How did you know?"

"I came late to the festivities at the castle yestereve, but soon heard what had transpired between you and Lady Cat."

"I'm certain the *lady* was quick to complain about me."

Sir Philippe frowned and shook his head. "She'd be the last one to do so. 'Twas Oscar, leader of her bodyguards, who said the two of you had argued."

Bodyguards? Damn. Those two great brutes he'd seen last night *were* her bodyguards. Another impediment to surmount. "With so many brigands about, you are wise to see your lady well watched," Gervase replied with feigned casualness. Beside him, he felt Perrin shift and knew the news would elicit another round of complaints the moment they were private.

"Lord Ruarke is determined to see no harm befalls his eldest daughter." Philippe scowled. "What did you say to offend her?"

So the lady had not told her guardians of his clumsy attempt at seduction. Interesting. "She is English, I am French. Our countries have been warring for years." Gervase shrugged as though that said it all. "If you'd rather not sell one of your war-horses to the enemy…"

"It makes no difference," Philippe said quickly. "We are at peace now, and many French knights have bought milord's horses."

Gervase nodded. "I'm in need of a destrier. My own was injured en route here and had to be put down." A stretch of the truth. The battle had been years ago, but the pain of having to slit Damien's throat was fresher. He'd raised the stallion from a colt and had hopes of siring a string of bay war-horses.

"Come look at Thor, and we'll see if you two are suited." Sir Philippe motioned for Gervase to follow him. The knight was either a courtier or had time to burn, for he'd not mentioned the horse's price or asked if Gervase could pay it.

A log fence enclosed the grazing horses, each of which was chained to a huge boulder. The paddock itself was more closely guarded than the town of Bordeaux, ringed by no less than twenty pikeman. Tents flying the Sommerville banner formed a second outer ring. The area bustled with activity, squires cleaning armor and weapons, men-at-arms training with sword and ax.

Sir Philippe stopped at the rail of the fence and called to a man inside. "Fetch Thor for me, Sim." He spoke firmly but not harshly, still the man raced off to do his bidding.

"This knight seems a goodly sort," Perrin murmured. "Not at all what I'd expected from one who serves a monster."

"His lord is not here," Gervase growled. "And with so many important people come for the tourney, they are doubtless on their best behavior."

"This is Thor," Sir Philippe said.

Gervase looked around and fell instantly in love. The stallion was magnificent...sixteen hands high, heavy muscles rippling beneath sleek gray hide. He held his head up, alert but not tugging on the stout lead rope. The instantaneous attraction to Sommerville's horse angered Gervase even more than had the dangerous lure of his too-beautiful daughter. "He seems docile to be effective in battle," Gervase sneered.

"You think so?" Philippe grinned and nodded to the groom, who led Thor nearer to the rail. "Touch him if you can, Sir Gervase," the knight taunted.

Gervase extended his hand. The stallion's nostrils flared as he scented a stranger. In the blink of an eye, he was transformed from a thing of beauty into a wild beast. Screaming a challenge, the stallion lashed out with both front feet. A steel-shod hoof crashed into the fence, splintering the wood. Thick yellow teeth snapped at Gervase's hand.

"Bloody hell," Perrin exclaimed, tugging Gervase to safety. "That thing's a menace. He should be put down."

"He requires a strong hand on the reins, I'll grant," Sir Philippe said, still grinning as the groom and six helpers worked to calm the irate horse. "But you'll find no better mount in battle. He's bred to it, you see. He'll carry you till he drops, stand over you and chase off all comers if you fall."

"Saddle him," Gervase said, his gaze pinned to the stallion, who now stood still. Thor's rolling eyes and heaving sides were the only indication of the earlier outburst.

Philippe laid a cautionary hand on Gervase's arm. "There is one proviso, sir. No whips. If you cannot control him without, I cannot sell him to you."

"I've never beaten a horse, nor would I own one I couldn't manage," Gervase said tautly.

Philippe nodded. "Let us see how you manage, then."

Gervase had a moment of trepidation when he swung up into the saddle and felt the horse tense to repel him. "Nay, you do not." He tightened his knees. Thor screamed and ducked his head, ready to buck. Gervase shouted a curse of his own and drew back sharply on the reins. The battle was joined. Thor pranced and jumped and twice tried to scrape the unfamiliar presence from his back. With the skill of long experience, Gervase countered every move with one of his own till finally the horse admitted defeat and stood still in the center of the ring.

Hot and exhausted but triumphant, Gervase gingerly walked Thor over to the string of onlookers lining the fence. "He's magnificent," Gervase said. "I will take him."

Philippe grinned and named a price twice what Gervase had expected to pay.

"I . . . I do not have the coin."

"Ah, too bad. I am afraid I cannot sell you the horse for a promised share of your booty in the coming tourney."

"Nor would I expect you to." Even the strongest knight with a string of victories to his credit could be unseated or killed in the fierce fighting. "I would offer something more certain. Perrin, would you take the sword from my pack?"

From his vantage point on Thor's back, he watched his friend uncover the sword. Sunlight flowed like fire along the tempered-steel blade, struck sparks off the jewels embedded in the hilt. A gasp of wonderment swept through the Sommerville retainers.

Philippe whistled through his teeth. " 'Tis a beauty." He lifted the sword in both hands, testing its balance before looking up at Gervase. "How come you by such a sword?"

"You mean a tattered knight like me?" Gervase asked stiffly. "I didn't steal it, if that is your meaning. It's been in my family for generations, brought back from the Crusades."

"I wonder you can bear to part with it."

"I don't mean to be for long," Gervase replied. "I want your guarantee I may buy it back with what I win in the tourney."

"Agreed," Philippe said at once. "I will summon the clerk to draw up the papers. Lord Ruarke has a fondness for old weapons and would be pleased to add this sword to his collection if your plans don't succeed. If they do, rest assured you may have it back for the price of the stallion."

"That seems most fair," Gervase said grudgingly. So this Philippe was honorable. That didn't make his master so.

Just then a party of riders cantered across the field, halting a few yards away. Recognizing the woman who rode in their midst, Gervase gritted his teeth.

"What is going on here, Philippe?" Lady Cat demanded.

The knight walked over to where she sat, glaring down from her sleek brown mare. "I've nearly concluded selling Thor to—"

"Nay. You cannot sell Thor to him," she cried.

Philippe frowned. "I already have, milady."

"Well . . . well, unsell him."

"Fortunately you have no say in this," Gervase taunted.

The fire vanished from her eyes, replaced by a searing cold. "Papa said the man who bought Thor must ride him without a whip."

"Aye," Philippe replied, trying to gauge the undercurrents flowing between the proud knight and the volatile Cat. "Explosive as black powder," Oscar had said of their confrontation the night before. True. But having been with the family since her birth, Philippe knew Cat better than did her bodyguard. Better, mayhap than she did herself. He'd never seen her look at a man thus, head thrown back, nostrils flared like a mare confronted by an unfamiliar stallion. Just so had her mother looked at Ruarke when she'd met and married him... all in the same day. "He controlled Thor as ably as your sire does," he assured the fuming Cat.

She lifted her chin another notch and glared at Gervase's worn garments. "I doubt the man has the coin to pay."

"Better than coin." Philippe gestured to the sword.

Cat's eyes widened. "Where did he get it?"

Witch, Gervase thought. Spoiled, arrogant little witch. When he got her to Alleuze he'd see she worked for her food alongside his people. Aye, a fortnight of scrubbing floors should bring her down a peg. "He got it from his father," Gervase said icily.

"Lord Ruarke would welcome such a fine piece, my lady," Philippe said in the chilly silence that followed. "As his agent I've agreed to exchange Thor for the sword and hold it till after the tourney when Sir Gervase will redeem it with his winnings."

The color rose in her cheeks and her mobile mouth thinned in frustration, but surprisingly she didn't rail against the inevitable. "I hope he falls on his ass ere the melee starts," she snarled. Tugging on the reins of her horse, she spun and galloped away. Her escort scrambled after her.

Despite his pique, Gervase noted they numbered some thirty or so heavily armed men, led by the pair he'd seen with her the night before. Thirty against the twenty men he'd brought with him. Clearly he must find a way to improve the odds, or get her by herself in order for his plans to succeed. And the way things stood between them, he had as much chance of getting her alone as he had of being crowned king of France.

Mayhap 'twas time to mask his rage and see if he still remembered how to be charming to a woman.

Chapter Three

"He's still watching you," Margery whispered.

"Oh?" It took Cat a moment to locate him, lounging against the fireless hearth, one shoulder propped against the marble mantel. He had on the same unadorned black tunic he'd worn the first night. Its simplicity made the brightly garbed nobles look silly and frivolous by comparison. His dark head was bent in conversation with his friend, Perrin, but Gervase's gaze was full on her. Cat shivered as the impact of those pale, glittering eyes worked its way down her spine and lodged in her belly.

Why him, of all men? she thought angrily. Tossing her head, she turned away and fixed her eyes firmly on the pair of tumblers cavorting in the center of the hall. Part of her was excited by this game of cat and mouse he seemed to be playing with her; part of her was afraid.

Three days had passed since the disputed purchase of Thor. Gervase had spent them on the training field, coming late each night to the castle for the feasting and the entertainment Lord John had arranged. In all that time, he had not spoken to her or tried to approach her. But he'd watched her.

Sweet Mary, how he watched her. Openly, relentlessly. His visual pursuit left him time for little else. He drank sparingly, flirted and danced not at all. Even with Clarice, who had smiled, teased, pouted and finally flounced off after easier game.

Gamel and Garret had been all for waylaying him in the dark and teaching him respect for his betters. Oscar, who had a bit of a romantic streak, had forbidden it. "There's no harm in a knight being smitten by a lady. Courtly love, the minstrels call it." Cat scoffed at that. There was nothing courtly in the way Gervase St. Juste's hot glance followed her about. The only place she was safe was in her chamber, and she refused to hide there like some miscreant. She'd done that for weeks after her father rescued her from Henry. Never again.

"I think he's trying to impress you," Margery murmured.

"By making me uncomfortable?"

"Why would Sir Gervase's regard make you uneasy? Half the men in the hall stare at you."

"I . . . I do not know." Liar. Gervase unnerved her because there was something about him that made her want to stare back.

"Mayhap he is trying to work up the courage to ask if he may wear your favor in the tourney."

"He has a strange way of doing so."

"Oh, I do not know. You've yet to give a token to any of the many men who have asked." Margery grinned mischievously. "Mayhap you are waiting for Sir Gervase to approach you."

"Margery!" Even as she scrambled to deny it, Cat's eyes strayed where she'd bidden them not to—across the circle of people cheering the entertainers. He was gone.

"Were you looking for me, my lady?" a deep voice asked.

Cat started and turned her head. Her gaze fastened on the mouth that had haunted her dreams, then moved up. The eyes that had made her waking hours as tortured as her nights sparkled with suppressed laughter. 'Twas the last straw. Her temper—never an easy thing to control—broke its leash. "I would speak with you in private," she snapped.

"I am at your disposal, Lady Catherine. May I suggest the garden, in five minutes? Without your two guards."

"The garden it is," she hissed back, conscious of the curious stares they were drawing. "But I could not leave without Gamel and Garret, even did I wish to... which I do not."

Disappointment flared briefly. "Afraid to be alone with me?"

His low voice sent her pulse racing with possibilities. She angled her chin higher to counter them. "I'd not sully my family's good name by comporting myself in an unseemly manner."

"Ah, your family. Of course. They must come first."

"Always," she replied, not certain what had doused the fire in his eyes and hardened his jaw.

"We will *all* meet in the garden in five minutes." Gervase took grim satisfaction from her grudging nod, then worked his way to the side door where Perrin waited for him.

"I have learned your uncle was right. There was a scandal involving Lady Cat and a man named Henry," his cousin whispered.

"What kind of scandal?" Gervase's jaw tightened as he watched the lady in question take the arm of a stout man in shocking green velvet with pear appliqués and join the dancing.

"Sim was a little sketchy on details. Either because he didn't know them or because the ale I'd plied him with had finally dulled his brain," Perrin added. "Apparently she ran off with a man . . . Henry Norville, a young groom."

Gervase stiffened. So she not only played the whore, she was one in fact. "Did she wed him?"

"Nay. Sim says his lordship was too quick on their trail. I gather the family doesn't speak of it and the man in question is no longer alive to do so."

Gervase looked away from the dancers. "Ruarke killed him?"

"That is one of the details I didn't get. Only that Lord Ruarke was mightily upset and hired those two hulking brutes." He inclined his head toward the twin towers of bone and muscle hovering at the edge of the dancing. "The smaller, scar-faced man we've seen her with is Oscar. The others are Gamel and Garret . . . experts with the dirk and cudgel respectively."

"Not to mention their fists. They look more like bears than men." Gervase sighed and closed his eyes briefly, tired of the intrigues of court, sick of worrying about how he'd get Cat Sommerville off by herself and away from here.

"And then there are the forty men," Perrin said. "The ones who will be guarding the lady during the tourney."

"Forty," Gervase said faintly. "Damn. I stayed in hopes we'd be able to steal her away during the excitement and confusion."

"I'd forget that, if I were you. Nor does the lady seem overly interested in a dalliance with you."

She was interested. His practiced eye had caught the flare of desire in hers. "I'm not rich enough. She won't sully her precious family name by associating with the likes of me."

Perrin grunted. "What will you do, then?"

"I'm not certain. I've managed to rouse her ire, at least. I'm to meet her in the gardens in a few moments, along with her guards," Gervase added. "I wonder if she plans to set them on me?" His gaze narrowed as he picked Catherine out from the swirl of dancers. Her eyes outshone the amethysts shimmering in her elaborate headdress. She was the very image of everything he detested—pampered, polished, spoiled, English. Her gowns and jewels bought with the blood of his conquered countrymen.

Her lips curved provocatively as she laughed into the adoring face of the man who partnered her. Feral heat bloomed in Gervase's chest. He hated that unknown man for the possessive hold he kept on Catherine's slender waist. And he hated her, too, for so thoroughly besotting every man who crossed her path. Himself included. No matter who or what she was, if he wasn't careful he could easily slip under her spell.

"I thank you for learning about that young fool she ran off with," Gervase said, clasping Perrin on the shoulder. "I may have need of the information to force her into doing what I want."

Lady Clarice's lips pursed thoughtfully as she spied Sir Gervase and Sir Perrin with their heads bent together in whispered conversation. Their faces fairly shouted guilty secrets. As she watched, Gervase left his friend and slipped out the door leading to the gardens. Should she pursue him and see if he'd changed his mind about dallying with her?

A scant moment later Catherine Sommerville abruptly left the dancing and quit the hall for the gardens with only her guards for company. Interesting. Especially given the way the two had been eyeing each other. Clarice had undertaken enough clandestine meetings in her time to recognize the signs in others. Seeing an opportunity to cause trouble for the pair who'd slighted her, Clarice excused herself to her next dancing partner on the pretext of visiting the garderobes.

Once out the side door, she hiked up her velvet skirts and made for the back gate into the gardens. Careful to keep clear of the faint circles of torchlight, she scurried along the wall and ducked in behind the trellis. From within the shadowy alcove came the sounds of two voices rasping and gasping in the throes of passion. But when Clarice peered in through the lacy grapevines, she realized this was not the pair she sought and moved on. Nor was the couple trysting in the maze Gervase and Catherine.

Clarice had nearly decided her instincts had failed her when a familiar voice sailed out from the clump of birch at the far end of the garden.

"Why have you been watching me?" Cat Sommerville demanded.

Gervase replied, "You know the answer to that."

Fascinated, Clarice bent down and crept along the path till she'd reached the hedge of hazelnut. Parting the branches slightly, she saw her quarry facing each other. Cat's two guards stood a distance away, their backs to the confrontation.

"I have told you I am not interested in any... any alliance with you," Cat said stiffly.

"So your lips say. But your eyes... they tell a different tale. You've been watching me as I do you."

"Nay." Catherine's hand came up to her throat. She backed up a step. "You...you are mistaken."

He stalked closer, but he didn't touch her. "I think not. If I were not a penniless French knight, you'd gladly spend time with me. You, Lady Catherine, are a snob."

"I am not." She clenched her fists and glowered at him.

"Your protests are as false as your pose of innocence."

"Wh-what do you mean?"

"I know all about your elopement with Henry Norville."

"Sweet Mary." Catherine sagged against the tree behind her, her face ashen in the filtered torchlight.

Shock nearly caused Clarice to fall through the bushes. Oh, this was too good to be true. Imagine...

"You are afraid I will talk of what happened two years ago and ruin your reputation. But that is not my aim. All I want is to be treated as you would a man of wealth and position. A few dances...a few walks in the garden... alone. Mayhap your favor to wear in the jousts."

"'Tis...'tis blackmail," Catherine replied.

"It seems the only way I can persuade you to spend time in my company," Gervase replied just as harshly.

"You...you wretch." She looked toward the solid backs of her guards. "I've a mind to call Gamel and Garret and let them pound some manners into you."

"'Tis no more than I'd expected of so shallow and spoiled a lady," Gervase said scathingly.

"I am not." Catherine stamped her foot for emphasis, two red splotches coloring her pale cheeks.

"Prove it, then, and give me a chance to prove myself in turn. I vow I have no desire to ruin your reputation, only teach you not to look down your nose at a man for lack of wealth."

"I ... I do not know...."

"Think on it. I will seek you out tomorrow for your answer."

Catherine nodded, turned and fled.

Oh, this was too good to be true, Clarice thought. Imagine, sweet Lady Catherine was really a harlot. As she slunk off into the night, Clarice's mind seethed with ways in which she might use this new knowledge. One thing was clear, once the information became public, no man would want Cat as a wife, which would leave the field clear for Clarice. What a lovely notion.

Winded and perspiring from the last set of dances, Cat declined an invitation to join another set and wandered toward an open window. Three men trailed after her with offers of food and drink. She agreed in order to get rid of them. 'Twas hell staying here, keeping up a carefree facade when she longed for privacy to try and sort out her problem. If not for the questions it would have caused, she'd not have returned to the hall after her meeting with Gervase. Blackmail. The nerve of the man.

At least he had not followed her into the hall. Trying to keep up a pretext of gaiety under his intent gaze would have been impossible. What was she going to do? Though he'd not asked for much—only a bit of her time—the notion of bowing to blackmail went against everything she believed in.

Feeling wretched, Cat scanned the room and spied Margery standing off by herself, eyes wide, tears trickling down her full cheeks. Had some man slighted her? Had one of the catty women said something to wound poor, defenseless Margery? Lifting her skirts, Cat stalked off to the rescue.

"Margery." Cat grasped both Margery's icy hands in hers and gave them a squeeze. "Only tell me what has happened."

"Oh, Cat." Margery cried harder. "'Tis terrible. I...I cannot think of a way to tell you," she stammered between sobs.

"Hush, dearling." Cat wrapped an arm around the girl's heaving shoulders. "Come, let us find a quiet corner."

"Margery! Come here this instant." Lady Ela snapped her fingers imperiously and motioned for her daughter to join her by the hearth where she stood with a group of staring women.

"I...I have to go." Margery darted away.

Cat started after her, but Oscar blocked her path.

"'Tis late and ye should be abed. I like not the mood of the crowd," he added in a low voice.

Indeed, the dancing had ceased and the nobles hung about in small groups. They chattered like a flock of crows, eyes darting about the hall, faces animated with what looked like malicious glee. Had Gervase told them about Henry? Nay. It profited him not to betray her before he had her answer. Still Cat suddenly felt alone and vulnerable. "See what you can find out."

"Likely everyone has had too much to drink. Come, milady, we'll escort you to your room." With Oscar in front and the brothers following, they swept from the hall and up the stairs to her chamber. Cat was deposited inside and her maid given strict orders to see her mistress stayed within.

"See here. I will not be ordered about." Cat jerked the door open and ran into the solid wall of Garret's back.

Nor would he let her leave. "What of Margery and the other ladies? Where will they sleep if you bar the way?"

"I've orders to let them pass when they come up," Garret said. "But Gamel and I are to remain here the night, and you're not to leave till Oscar or Sir Philippe says 'tis all right."

Cat sighed and closed the door.

"Whatever's going on, milady?" The maid's narrow face was pinched with concern, her hands knotted in her apron.

"I don't know, Etta. 'Tis likely naught, but I'll find out as soon as Margery and the others retire." Stiff with dread and frustration, Cat moved through the undressing process by rote, absently lifting her arms as first the sideless velvet surcoat, then the silken undertunic were removed.

"You'll feel better when this is off." Etta released Cat's hair from the braids coiled over her ears.

Cat didn't feel better. Clad at last in her night shift, she sat on the stool before the fire while Etta tended her hair, but the rhythmic stroking of the ivory comb failed to soothe her frazzled nerves. Nor did any of the ladies appear who shared her room. The watch called midnight, the castle settled down to sleep, except for the occasional muted sounds of a few male voices drifting up from the hall.

Frightened, Cat crept to the door and cracked it open on the darkened corridor. "Garret?" she whispered.

"Aye. We're here."

"What news from below?"

A long pause, then, "I dunno. Oscar says he'll come by and tell ye in the morning," Gamel replied.

"Then there is something. Does…does it involve me?"

"Oscar didn't tell us," Gamel replied. "Only said ye were to stay here till he'd gotten to the bottom of things."

Things like her sordid past?

That question had Cat tossing and turning all night. She rose early, splashed cool water on her face, hastily braided her hair in a single plait and dressed in a simple woolen gown. Leaving Etta asleep on her pallet by the door, Cat eased the oaken portal open.

Gamel's face materialized in the still gloomy hallway. "You're supposed to wait within."

"I'm starving. What harm can there be in going down to the hall for a bit of food?" And information. "'Twill likely be deserted, for the men have all gone to the tilt-yard to practice for tomorrow's tourney," she added, having heard them clatter out of the courtyard when it was still dark.

"Etta could bring something up," Gamel said.

Cat shook her head. "I need to stretch my legs. If I have to stay cooped up here another moment, I'll go mad."

Gamel and Garret exchanged frowns, then Gamel sighed. "I'll take ye down to break yer fast whilst Garret gets Oscar."

Cat jumped at the opportunity, though eating ranked below finding Margery. During the long, sleepless night she'd decided Lady Ela must have become angry because the men pursued Cat and ignored her daughter. Doubtless the lady had told Margery to stay away from Cat so as to not suffer by comparison. 'Twould be easily set to rights. Cat would promise to dance no more dances, talk to no more men. 'Twas a small price to pay, for Margery's friendship was more important than the attentions of any man.

Especially Gervase St. Juste. Cat's hands clenched into
fists and her steps slowed on the narrow stairway. Any
man who would stoop to blackmail deserved to be denounced to the world. Sweet Mary, he was worse than
Henry Norville, who had at least been honest enough, in
the end, to admit 'twas her father's money he'd wanted.
If she hadn't feared exposing her sordid past, she would
have shouted Gervase's crime from the rooftops.

Cat paused at the entrance to the hall. Most of the men
had indeed left to polish their skills for the morrow, but
many women and older nobles sat at the trestle tables
partaking of ale, bread and lively conversation. Her
mood lightened as she scanned their familiar faces. These
were her peers, her friends. With the exception of Clarice and a few of her cronies, these people liked Cat,
wished her well. Fatigue and irritation with Gervase must
have caused her to imagine the chill in the air last night.

Cat spied Lady Ela seated at the far end of the room,
with her usual crowd of older matrons and Margery with
them. With Gamel at her heels, she swept into the hall.

The noble diners fell silent suddenly as though they'd
all been struck mute at once. Heads swung in Cat's direction, smiles turned upside down, glances narrowed as
they looked down their noses at her. Their contempt
stopped Cat in her tracks.

Contempt? What had she done to...?

Nay! It couldn't be, yet she knew with dread certainty
that it was. Gervase had spread the word of her ill-fated
liaison with Henry. Shame fired her cheeks and clogged
her throat; she prayed for the floor to open and swallow
her. When it didn't, instinct urged her to bolt from the
room. Pride kept her rooted to the spot. Damn. Damn.
What was she to do?

Hot tears stung the backs of her lids, blurring the sea of disdainful faces. Drowning in misery, Cat sought out the only one whose opinion truly mattered. *Margery, how can you think ill of me?* she silently asked.

To her credit, Margery stood and started forward, her own eyes brimming with tears. Her lady mother grabbed her arm, jerked her down onto the bench and held her there.

"Come, let us leave." Gamel plucked at Cat's sleeve.

Aye. Cat twitched with the urge to flee the hall and keep running till she was back in England, safe in the protective bosom of the loving family who had stuck by her despite her mistake. But her parents had imbued her with their steadfastness. A Sommerville did not run; she stood and faced trouble head-on.

Raising her chin a notch, Cat cast about for an empty table. The only one sat on the dais. Lord John was not here, but by right of her family's connection with the Angevines, she had often been asked to sup there with His Grace. "I will break my fast before riding out to the tourney field," Cat said to Gamel. Spine as stiff as her resolve, she marched down the center aisle of the hall, mounted the single step to the raised platform and took the low-backed chair to the left of the duke's lofty one.

A sullen maid, pressured to serve her by Gamel's furious glare, set the food down so abruptly ale sloshed over the rim of the cup. Cat watched the liquid pool on the polished oak and felt her throat fill with tears. Though she doubted she could swallow past the fullness, she tore off a bit of bread, popped it into her mouth and chewed. It took two gulps of ale to get the first bit of bread down, but she kept eating.

Gradually the others went back to their own food, and the hum of voices rose to replace the awkward silence.

That they discussed her was a certainty. Unable to meet their eyes, Cat stared at the crossed axes decorating the far wall and contemplated burying one in Gervase's treacherous skull. Thank God, her parents weren't here to relive the horror of two years ago, the veiled slurs on her honor and on theirs.

Somehow she got through the meal, though the bread sat in a lump in her belly and her throat was tight with unshed tears. As she stood, an expectant hush once again fell over the assembly. This time she forced herself to look around at those she'd thought were her friends. The women regarded her with disdain. The men, even the old ones, were openly speculative, wondering no doubt if she'd be amenable to a tumble. Only Margery looked back with any measure of empathy and fondness.

What shallow, petty fools, Cat thought, so quickly swayed by a vicious rumor. Though she longed to crawl away and lick her wounds, she'd come to Bordeaux to cheer the Sommerville forces to victory in the tourney, and she'd not be driven away by such as these. "Come, my friend." She looked to the hovering Gamel. "I'd take a turn in the garden to clear my nostrils of this place."

Her comment made several of the ladies gasp in outrage, but Cat was beyond caring. Her misery had given way to rage. She was staying for the tourney and attending every function. And she'd find a way to repay Gervase for dragging her name through the mud.

Chapter Four

"She's here," Perrin muttered. He didn't need to explain further, for Lady Catherine Sommerville's name rushed through the crowded hall like an ill wind.

Gervase stiffened, but he didn't turn to watch her progress through the throng of knights, nobles and ladies assembled for the tourney banquet. "I'm surprised she dared show her face."

"They are snubbing her... just as we'd heard they did this morn," Perrin added unhappily. "She is ignoring them all. Damn, but she's a brave one, her head high, her eyes fierce."

"Do you think I wanted this?" He'd hoped to blackmail her into keeping company with him, the better to steal her away. Now she'd think he had spread the rumor and would shun him totally.

"I suppose not, still I don't like hurting an innocent."

"Innocent?" Gervase snorted. "We know she is not that. And I swear she won't be harmed, only held till her sire renders up—"

"She's already been harmed," Perrin muttered. "Thanks to us, her reputation here is ruined. The only men who'll be pursuing her now are those looking for an easy tumble."

"I did not spread that rumor." A quick investigation pointed to Lady Clarice as the source. Still Gervase's hand tightened on his cup, the crest of the English kings biting into his flesh. A reminder of why he was here. Catherine Sommerville was a means to that end. He couldn't afford to feel anything toward her, not pity and certainly not this inconvenient desire. "Who's to say she was not bedding them all on the sly," he growled.

Jealous, my friend? Perrin wondered. Though Gervase was adept at hiding his feelings, Perrin had not missed the flash of hunger in his lord's eyes when he looked at the lady. Poor Marie had never kindled that kind of fire in her husband. Nor had any other woman, come to think of it. Pity Lady Cat was not only English but the daughter of one Gervase hated above all others.

"Thor shows great promise," Gervase said suddenly.

Perrin sighed and accepted the change of subject. "He's magnificent, but I wish you had longer to work with him ere the tourney. He's strong willed and not yet used to your ways. Which could be a liability, especially in the melee."

"With another horse, that might be true. But Thor is disciplined and responsive to my commands."

"Aye, and the other Sommerville horses we observed on the tiltyard were likewise fine specimens. 'Tis a puzzle, is it not, that a man as vicious in war as Lord Ruarke would have the patience and sensitivity to raise such fine beasts?"

Gervase's smile fled. "I doubt he had a hand in it, but even so I am trying to forget I bought Thor from that bastard."

"Speaking of bastards, Sir Malkin approaches Lady Cat."

Gervase whirled, his hand reaching reflexively for his sword and coming up empty. By order of the duke, all weapons were forbidden at the banquet, lest an excess of drink and strong emotions lead to trouble. Sure enough, the worst lecher in all Bordeaux, the man whose tastes were so depraved 'twas said the whores charged him twice the going rate, was bowing over Cat's hand. The din in the hall covered Malkin of York's words, but they leached the color from her face.

"Bloody hell," Gervase muttered, teeth clenched as tight as his gut. He shouldn't care, didn't want to, but the instinctive urge to protect prodded him forward. He'd only gone a step when her two bodyguards moved in front of her and chased Malkin off.

Embarrassed by his reaction, Gervase changed direction and headed for one of the long trestle tables where the servants were just setting out the meal. Swinging a leg over the bench, he sat and reached for the wine pitcher. Though 'twould take more wine than there was in Bordeaux to wash the guilt from his mouth.

"She shouldn't be here," Perrin said, sitting beside him.

"Agreed." Gervase drained his cup and set it down with enough force to jar the nearby platter of roasted hare. "Why did she come? Surely she must have realized what 'twould be like."

"Pride." Perrin grabbed a joint of meat and set it on his manchet bread trencher. "Fragile as she looks, the lady has courage and pride in abundance."

"Gall, more like. She doubtless enjoys being the center of attention, even if 'tis the attention of one such as Malkin."

"She didn't appear to welcome his advances, and she doesn't look one bit happy now."

Against his will, Gervase followed Perrin's gaze to the dais where Lady Catherine occupied the end seat. Beautiful, he thought, her crimson surcoat the perfect foil for skin pale as the pearls banding the neck. Unnaturally pale. And were those shadows beneath her eyes a trick of the light or lack of sleep? He forced the notion away and remembered instead the destruction that had greeted him when he'd returned to Alleuze, the charred walls, the pitiful graves of his wife and daughter. The mementos left behind to mark Lord Ruarke's passing through the valley. Lady Catherine's discomfort was naught to what his people had suffered at her father's hands.

"If she doesn't like it, she can leave," Gervase said gruffly, and turned his attention to the food. It tasted like ashes, but he forced himself to eat, knowing he needed to build up his strength for the tourney events.

"The cook has outdone himself," Perrin said. "I swear we've put on a stone since coming here. Weight we both needed."

"A year of eating only what little our ravaged land would yield made us skinny," Gervase replied bitterly. "Would that we could take some of this bounty back to our people when we leave."

"We'll soon be able to buy whatever we need . . . seed to plant, meat, flour, beans and such to tide us over till the crops are ready to harvest. And stone to rebuild." Perrin grinned. "Aye, we'll be warm, dry and well fed this winter."

"Hush," Gervase warned as three people took their places on the other side of the table. An older knight, his lady wife and their daughter, a plump young woman he recalled seeing much in Catherine Sommerville's company.

"May I at least speak with her?" the girl asked.

"Nay, Margery," her mother snapped. "You'll stand no chance of attracting a husband if you're seen in such loose company."

"Cat's not like that, Mama. She isn't. I...I know it's a terrible mistake. If only you'd talk with her—"

"Me?" The woman's jowls trembled with agitation. "And have these good people think I condone such behavior?"

"Good people." Margery's eyes narrowed. "I think they are terrible to treat her so for an unfounded rumor."

"'Tis not unfounded," the mother replied. "I had it from a woman whose maid knows the duke's squire that Lady Catherine did indeed run off with a man...a horse trainer," she added in a horrified whisper. "Some nobody named Henry Norville. Her parents hushed up the disgraceful business as best they could. The duke knew of it, apparently, and swore his people to secrecy, but since all was revealed last night..."

"I still think 'tis mean to condemn her for one mistake."

"A costly error, that," her father interjected. "With her bloodlines and dowry, Lord Ruarke could have made an excellent match for her. But now...no honorable man will want her." He cleared his throat and scowled. "Wed a woman who'll spread her thighs for anyone and no telling who'll sire your children."

"Too true," his wife said.

Gervase slammed down his cup and quit the table before he did something stupid, like defend a woman he didn't even like. 'Twas the principle of the thing, he told himself as he threaded his way through the tables. But then the English were known to be petty and narrowminded. Sickened by the stench of so many English bodies, offended by the way their tongues twisted the Norman French, he made for the garden.

"Well, you wanted her isolated," Perrin said, the moment they stepped outside. "Now she's even deprived of Margery's comfort."

"Don't you have anything to do besides hound me?"

"Not at present."

"Then ride out to camp and check on Thor," Gervase growled. "So handsome a piece of horseflesh may attract thieves. And take with you some meat and wine for Vallis and the others. They are as needful of a good meal as we."

"Why not come with me?"

Gervase shook his head. "I have promised to speak with Lord Etienne de Vigne after supper, and then I must decide which of the French parties we will align ourselves with for the melee."

"I thought you had settled on Henri Gaston. He's the strongest and, if we fight in his group, we will be able to concentrate on capturing the richest prizes."

"True." Gervase glanced about. Dark had fallen and the torches cast golden circles over the beds of flowers, but beyond their reach the shadows were thick, concealing. He lowered his voice. "Lord Henri's methods are not to my liking. Any man who orders his troops to hamstring fallen knights to prevent their escape or cut the horses from beneath them ..."

"English knights and English mounts," Perrin said.

"If we were speaking of war, such deplorable actions might be necessary, but this is a game, a means to fortune and glory, not a matter of life and death. Lord Etienne's forces may be smaller, but he is a man of honor." He sighed and scrubbed a hand through his hair, weary of plotting and calculating. "Go and make certain all is well at camp. I've heard tell there are those about who would like to improve their own chances in the tourney by disabling their opponents' mounts and men beforehand.''

"All the more reason not to have you riding back to camp late at night and alone."

"Since the feasting is like to stretch far into the night, and I don't know when I will be able to speak with Etienne, I will remain here tonight. Expect me early on the morrow." There would be last-minute preparations for the tourney to oversee.

"Where will you sleep?"

"In the stables if there is room. If not, under some convenient bush as we did when we were campaigning."

Perrin grinned. "Lady Clarice would doubtless be happy to help you find . . . accommodations."

"I'd have to be blind drunk to bed an English-woman," Gervase snarled. "Think of all the English have cost me."

"I know, I know." Perrin clasped Gervase's shoulder and squeezed. "But you have endured and will yet triumph. Shall I leave Armand with you?"

"Nay, take him." The castle was no place for his young, impressionable squire. "That way I'll have only myself to see to." For a time after Perrin left him, Gervase wandered aimlessly in the garden. The sweet scent of rosemary took him back to his mother's garden and home. Set high on the side of a lush valley, Alleuze had not the grandeur of larger keeps, but its sun-washed rooms had been filled with love and laughter. Now it was a hollow shell, a place of blackened walls and shattered dreams. With his family dead, had he the will to restore it? And for whom?

The crunch of footfalls and the murmur of voices warned his privacy was about to be breached. Having no wish for company, he ducked behind a towering yew and watched to see who came.

"We think you should return home," said an unfamiliar male voice. "Come morn, I'll assemble thirty men and escort—"

"Nay, I'd not cheat them of their chance to ride in a tourney they've been preparing for these two months," replied one he had no trouble recognizing. Lady Catherine Sommerville.

Gervase withdrew farther into the shadows as they came abreast of him and stopped.

"But... but this is intolerable." The speaker was Oscar. Behind him, their broad faces echoing the smaller man's concern, hovered Gamel and Garret. "At least let me send for milord."

Catherine's back was to Gervase, but he saw her shoulders move, heard her sigh. "Nay. What could Papa do save fret? And he has enough on his mind with the prince so gravely ill."

"He could run the lot of them through," Gamel growled.

Her laugh was low, tinged with sadness. "No doubt he'd want to... Papa has ever tried to vanquish whatever foes beset me, but I fear his sword would not restore my tarnished honor."

"Do not speak so," Garret cried. "Ye are the most virtuous of ladies. 'Tis these... these bastards who have no honor. To shun ye and besmirch yer name so with their whispers and lies."

"But we know they are not lies." Her voice was so soft Gervase barely heard the words over the rustle of wind through the trees, yet he felt her pain.

" 'Tis not right ye should still continue to suffer for a single mistake in judgment," Oscar said gruffly.

"Aye, Henry was surely that, but I fear my error will haunt me all my life." She turned and lifted her face to the breeze, exposing the pure lines of her profile to the torchlight, high cheekbones, straight nose and a pointed chin that wobbled a bit before she firmed it. "The air smells good after the stuffiness of the hall. What I wouldn't give for a good gallop."

"Don't even suggest it," Oscar muttered. "I'd give ye anything else ye ask for, milady, but Lord Ruarke was most specific about not allowing ye to tear around the countryside."

"Even with an escort." She smiled sadly. "I know. And he is right, the woods are full of brigands, still . . ."

Gervase felt her sigh all the way to his soul, and damned himself for it. Why her? Of all the women he'd met—including his poor dead wife—why did this one woman stir him so?

"Ah, there you are, Lady Catherine. I saw you leave the hall and thought you might like some company," Sir Archie drawled as he slid into the light. Like the snake he was, Gervase thought, his hackles rising as the man kissed Catherine's hand.

"Sir Archie," Catherine said coolly.

The knight smiled, then flicked a dismissive glance at her escort. "Kindly remain here. I'd walk a pace with your mistress."

Oscar bristled. "She goes nowhere without us."

"A wise precaution, but I mean her no harm. I but thought she might like to sit a few moments on yon bench, away from the prying eyes of friends and foes alike."

A kindly offer, given all Catherine had been through these past two days, yet it struck Gervase wrong. So while her three guards remained on the path, he crept through the brush and came around behind the trellis shielding the bench from view. A strong sense of déjà vu struck him as he knelt in the grass. 'Twas here he'd listened while Archie had proposed and was rejected.

"I am sorry to see you so vilely treated," Archie began as soon as they were seated.

"Thank you," she said stiffly. "But if you are truly my friend, you'll understand why I'd rather speak of other things."

"Of course I'm your friend." His voice dropped to a purr. "But I'd like to be more."

"What? Oh, I'm sorry, Archie, but I meant what I said a few days ago. I cannot wed with you."

"Wed?" Archie's laugh was harsh, grating. "Nay, I had a more satisfying but less permanent arrangement in mind."

Through the trellis, Gervase saw her head jerk around in surprise. "What . . . what do you mean?"

"Why, to make you my mistress, of course."

Shock held Cat immobile while Archie filled in the lurid details of the relationship he had in mind. *How could I have considered kissing that mouth?* she wondered as the filth spewed forth. *How could I have thought him gentle and kind?* she added as he trampled her character and honor into the mud with his assumptions and insinuations.

She wanted to scream for Oscar, but feared she'd be sick if she opened her mouth. She wanted to run, but her body was weighted down by the crushing burden of all she'd endured these past few days, the humiliation, the rejection, the . . .

"Well, what say you?" Archie demanded.

"Nay," Cat whispered. "Nay, I..." She swayed, dizzy and very much afraid she'd either faint or vomit.

"How dare you malign the lady with your filth?" growled a deep, horribly familiar voice. A dark figure detached itself from the shadows to the right of the trellis and walked into the light cast by a nearby torch.

"St. Juste!" Archie leapt up. "This is a private conversation. I must ask you to leave."

"Begone before I run you through." Gervase took her hand, drew her to her feet and tucked her arm through his with a proprietary gesture. "It grows late, Lady Catherine, and we have yet to discuss what colors we will wear for the processional."

"Colors? Processional?" Cat said weakly. The only thing keeping her upright was his hold on her arm.

An indulgent smile lifted the corners of his mouth; his eyes fastened on hers, hooded, intimate. "'Tis customary for a knight and his fair lady to be garbed in matching colors when she leads him into the tourney ring."

"His lady!" Archie roared. "Never say you've allied yourself with this... this French nobody," he shrieked.

Of course she hadn't. But at the moment she'd have thrown in with the devil to put Archie in his place. Raising one brow in fair imitation of the queen at her scathing best, she said, "To me, he is *not* a nobody." To Gervase she gave her most dazzling smile. "I'd say black would best suit your coloring and my reputation, sir knight."

"Harlot!" Archie swore, and strode off into the night.

The moment he was gone, Cat tugged her hand from Gervase's arm. "Now leave me alone."

"What, no thanks for getting rid of him?"

"You made him think I am your mistress."

"I am sorry for that, but at least it will put a stop to the pursuit by wretches like him and Malkin."

Cat's fingers curved into claws she longed to sink into his handsome face. "You have made good your threat to ruin me."

"Nay, I did not tell anyone." Torchlight flickered over his features, stripping them bare of pretext. "I traced the origin of the rumor to Clarice. She must have followed us last night and overheard my remarks. I..." His eyes were dulled by the first hint of uncertainty she'd seen in him. "I did not tell a soul about your Henry. I learned of him quite by accident. 'Twas desperation and wounded pride that made me use the information to force you to me." He sighed heavily. "My only excuse is that I was furious you returned my...my interest, yet would not spend time with me because I am no wealthy Englishman."

" 'Twas not that at all." Cat reflexively laid a hand on his arm. The tremor that shook him shuddered into her own body. The shiver of mingled delight and dread set her pulse racing with possibilities. "Knowing what you do of my...my background, you must see why I am cautious of men. Once before I allowed my heart to fool my brain into thinking a man could love me for myself, not my father's wealth."

"I assure you, I am interested in you *despite* your father," Gervase said cryptically. A muscle in his cheek twitched as he flexed his jaw, and the predatory light was back in his eyes, making them glow like banked embers.

Cat's breath caught as an answering flame kindled inside her, making the blood leap in her veins. "Very well. I will appear with you at the tourney processional, then we will see."

"Aye, then we will see." He stared deep into her eyes, luminous gray burning into wary purple. The rustle of the wind through the trees, the murmur of other lovers walking in the gardens faded. There was only the stirring presence of this tall, lean man whom she wanted beyond anything she'd known before.

Pray heaven she was not leaping from the pot into the fire.

The day of the tourney dawned gray and cool, but Cat didn't let that dampen her enthusiasm as she prodded a sleepy Etta from her pallet and sent Gamel to ready the horses. The castle was barely astir when she harried her escort over the drawbridge and on toward the field that would soon host the pageant.

Sir Philippe didn't share her excitement. "Only think what your mother will say when she hears of this," he wailed, pacing before one of the silken tents flying the Sommerville colors.

Cat rolled her eyes and struggled for calm. "I thought we had settled this last eve. Mama would have approved of my putting Sir Archie in his place. Do stop wringing your hands. You're getting your gauntlets in a snarl."

The knight's hands dropped to his sides. His eyes closed briefly in his own bid for patience. "But to ally yourself with a knight who is a stranger to us..."

"You trusted him enough to sell him Thor."

"Thor is a horse. You are milord's firstborn. His beloved daughter. His—"

"His greatest trial." Cat grinned. "Come, what harm can there possibly be in accompanying Sir Gervase as he and the other combatants enter the lists? He's hardly likely to try and ravish me before the hundreds of spectators."

Philippe gasped. "Has he tried to... to seduce you? Is that the reason he came to your defense? Because he thought...?"

"Thought I'd be an easy mark?" Cat finished for him. "Nay. I admit I, too, feared that at first, and kept Gamel or Garret near whilst he and I made plans for the processional. But Sir Gervase has not done or said anything improper." Indeed, he had made no improper suggestions. His gaze did not stray down her body as most men's did, never lingered overlong on her breasts or sought to divest her of her clothes.

Perversely, she found his restraint unflattering and annoying. She knew he still desired her, for hunger burned in his eyes when he thought she wasn't looking. Something held him back. Guilt for having accidentally ruined her reputation? Regret for the differences in their stations? Mayhap he sought to go slowly, to assure her of his respect before wooing her. Or win a fortune in tourney prizes, then court her more openly, more as an equal. 'Twas an oddly pleasing notion.

Philippe grunted. "Well, I suppose there's no harm in it. He could hardly carry you off before a throng of spectators. But..." His frown returned as he eyed her gown. "I doubt Lady Gaby would think your garb appropriate."

"'Tis one of Mama's actually, left behind when she departed in such haste. I thought the cut most modest." Cat touched the high neck and turned in a slow circle, watching the velvet ripple around her feet. Adorned only by a wide gold girdle at her hips, the gown barely hinted at the shape beneath.

"But 'tis black. A most unsuitable color."

Actually, it suited her rebellious mood exactly, but she doubted Philippe would appreciate the sentiment. "Sir

Gervase's surcoat is black and there wasn't time to make him a new coat.''

"We might have something we could loan—"

A blast of trumpets cut across Philippe's objections, followed immediately by the arrival of Gervase and his men.

Gervase inclined his head, but made no comment on her gown. Which would have been disappointing if she hadn't caught the appreciative gleam in his eyes. "It seems 'tis time, my lady.''

"Indeed it does.'' Stepping forward, she stroked Thor's nose. "You are looking very fine,'' she murmured, letting them all think 'twas the horse's trappings she admired, not the man who walked beside him. Commanding, she thought, though she'd applied the term to few men outside her family. The armor and mail beneath the black surcoat added considerably to his muscular frame. The silver eagle embroidered across his chest and repeated on the shield his squire held was a simple yet powerful device.

"Did I tell you we will enter with Etienne de Vigne's party, not the English?'' Gervase asked as Philippe lifted her into the saddle of her palfrey.

"Nay, but 'tis not a problem. I am half-French myself and feel none too affectionate toward the English at the moment.''

Gervase blinked. "You are?''

"Aye to both. My mother is French, and I would cheerfully skewer Archie if ladies were allowed to ride in the melee.'' Grinning, Cat took the silver chain Oscar had procured for her and handed one end to Gervase just as a second blast of the trumpets summoned the combatants to line up for the processional. "Is aught wrong?'' she asked Gervase.

"Nay. I had not realized you were half-French."

Cat wondered why that disturbed him, but there was no time to reflect on that, for they began to march into the field. There was a good deal of jostling and nervous laughter. 'Twas unusual for the women to lead the knights in on chains like war trophies, but the crowd roared its approval. She looked back at Gervase, who walked behind her, chain in hand. Their gazes locked.

Fire flared in his. *'Tis us against the rest of the court*, his eyes seemed to say.

Aye, Cat silently replied, smiling. *We are in this together*. Deeply touched by the intimate bit of communication, reminiscent of the sort she'd seen her parents share, Cat's spirits soared. They didn't falter until the spectacle was over and it came time to part from Gervase and take her place in the canopied galleries. As she mounted the steps to the seats reserved for the nobles, she passed by Clarice and her cronies.

"See, I told you she had no shame," Clarice hissed. "First a horse trainer, now a French knight so poor he had to barter for his horse."

Cat's cheeks flamed, but she kept her head high all the way to her chair. As she sat, she was conscious of the curious stares and ugly whispers rustling through the assembly.

"Someone should cut out that woman's tongue," Oscar said.

"Aye." Cat was stunned by how quick people were to believe the worst. She and Gervase had not been alone with each other, yet they were accounted lovers. She was relieved when the appearance of the herald drew attention from herself.

Potbellied and pompous, he unfurled his scroll and, accompanied by many trumpet flourishes, announced the pairings for the jousts. On the previous day, any knight who wished to compete had made the rounds of the various lodgings and touched his sword to the shield of one with whom he desired combat. Most matches were expected. Lord Henri Gaston, the leader of the French, was to fight the duke's champion and so on down through the ranks of the two countries who had fought for so many years.

Exhausted by the events of the past few days, Cat drowsed in her seat and tried not to fall asleep. A gasp from Oscar jerked her wide-awake. "What? Has one of our men drawn a bad opponent?"

"Archibald de Percy has challenged Gervase... winner to get the other's armor, sword and horse."

"Nay." Despite his soft looks, Archie was accounted a skilled jouster. One of the best who'd come to Bordeaux. "Have you seen Gervase practice? Does he stand a chance, do you think?"

"Philippe said Sir Gervase acquitted himself well," Oscar replied. "Considering he rides an unfamiliar mount."

The lump spread to her belly. This was her fault. If she hadn't given Archie such a cruel set-down, he never would have made such an outrageous proposition and Gervase would not now be jousting for his life on an unfamiliar mount.

"God be with you," she murmured.

Chapter Five

Gervase and Archie were the fifth pair to fight. By the time they approached the tilt barrier, Cat's nerves were as brittle as parchment. "Tell me what is happening, Oscar, for I do not think I can bear to watch." Eyes closed, she mouthed a fervent prayer for the horse she loved and the man she...she-

The impact of wooden lances shattering against lacquered steel hit her like a physical blow. "Oscar?"

"Gervase rocked him, but they both kept their seats. They're being handed another set of lances." The second run proved just as inconclusive, and Cat began to relax. Mayhap the contest would be judged a draw. Emboldened by hope, she opened her eyes just as the men once again took aim at each other.

There was a terrible beauty in watching Gervase manage the long lance as Thor pounded down the left side of the wooden barrier to meet Archie's oncoming charge. At the last moment, Archie shifted so the point of his lance would hit Thor's chest. His goal was to cut the horse from under Gervase.

"Nay," Cat gasped, shooting from her chair.

Gervase dropped his lance and jerked Thor hard to the right. Archie's lance missed the stallion's side, caught

Gervase's leg and flipped him from the saddle to sprawl on the ground.

"Foul," cried Oscar. The crowd surged to its feet, some people screaming for blood, others for justice.

"Merciful heaven," Cat whispered as Archie leapt from his horse, drew his sword and closed in for the kill.

"He's up," Oscar cried. "He's up and fighting. Jesu, but he wields that broadsword as though it weighed naught."

"Who?" Cat strained to see over those in front of her and beheld a miracle. Gervase was not only up, he fought like the very devil despite the fall he'd taken.

"Gervase's style puts me in mind of Lord Ruarke."

Aye, her father did fight with the same controlled fury and lightning reflexes. And her father never lost. Hope blossoming in her chest, Cat watched Gervase parry Archie's every thrust with strokes so crushing he soon had Archie backed up against the tilt barrier. Archie dropped the point of his sword and tore off his helmet, a clear sign he capitulated.

"Archie didn't fight honorably," Oscar growled. "Serve him right if Gervase ran him though."

Gervase did not. Keeping his sword on his opponent, he tugged off his helmet and inclined his sweaty head. "By rights, your armor and horse are now mine," he shouted. "I waive them in exchange for a public apology to Lady Catherine Sommerville for the vicious lie you started that besmirched her good name."

Cat's gasp was drowned out by the one that swept through the assembly. Archie had not started the rumor about Henry and herself. And 'twas not a lie. She'd admitted as much to Gervase. Why was he now seeking to restore her tarnished reputation?

Barely conscious of the glances cast in her direction, she stared at Gervase. He stood straight and tall, armor gleaming in the late-afternoon sun. For her honor he'd sacrificed the ransom he could have claimed for Archie's horse and armor... a fortune to a man of such modest means as Gervase St. Juste. Her throat tightened, and her eyes filled with tears.

"How romantic," whispered the woman to her left.

"How chivalrous," murmured another.

Archie turned, an ugly sneer twisting his features as he scanned the gallery. Hatred blazed in his eyes when he found Cat. "I apologize, my lady," he shouted, sounding not at all sincere.

Cat inclined her head. "Accepted."

"Well done, Sir Gervase," exclaimed the duke. "Minstrel," he said to the gaily clad lad at his side, "I charge you to compose a ballad to this knight's noble defense of his lady's honor."

"I am not his la—" Cat began, but her protest was cut off by the crowd's shouts of approval.

Gervase saluted them with his upraised sword, sheathed it, then turned and walked from the field to a burst of wild cheers.

Cat saw blood on his shoulder and cringed. "Oscar, I'm going to see how badly Sir Gervase is hurt."

"But Philippe is due to joust next."

"You stay and watch. I'm only going as far as the lists," she added over her shoulder as she left the galleries.

"Gamel and Garret are yonder, take them with ye."

Cat nodded, though she had no intention of taking any of the men from the joust. A sense of elation filled her as she worked her way through the crowd. Most eyes were on the next combatants. The few who noted her passing

smiled and offered congratulations. Margery waved gaily
from her seat higher in the stands, and even Lady Ela
unbent enough to incline her head.

How fickle they are, Cat thought—not for the first
time. 'Twas one of the things she disliked about life at
court. At the moment, the only thing she did like was
Gervase St. Juste. She realized that her feelings for this
mysterious man had just undergone another abrupt shift.
Why had he done this? Bah, she was no closer to understanding him than she'd been when they met.

Once clear of the throng around the tilt field, Cat
picked the St. Juste banner from the others fluttering in
the breeze and followed it to his camp. In contrast to the
half-dozen large silken tents belonging to her father,
Gervase had only a single canvas, one worn and patched
in places. He sat before it on a stool while his squire
worked to remove his armor. Just as she reached them,
the lanky youth lifted off the breastplate, revealing a
trickle of blood on the garments beneath.

"Oh, his lance slipped between the plates of your armor." Cat bent to examine the bloody rent in his padded
gambson.

"What do you here?" Gervase demanded.

"I saw you were wounded and came to see if—" Cat
turned her head and discovered his face was level with
hers "—if you needed...aught," she finished, her mouth
suddenly dry.

"'Tis just a scratch."

"Still it should be cleansed and bandaged."

"I've been tending my own hurts for years. I can—"

"This one you got in defense of me, and I will see it's
properly seen to." Cat straightened. "Armand, if you will
bring me water, clean cloth and...do you have a medicine chest?"

The boy's prominent Adam's apple bobbed as he swallowed. "We... I have a bit of salve we use for the horses."

Cat frowned. "Run over to the Sommerville tents. You should have no trouble finding them, for the banners fly higher than any of the others. Tell whoever is there that Lady Cat needs the medicine chest for Sir Gervase."

"Aye." The boy looked first to Gervase, who nodded grudging permission for the errand, then dashed off. Leaving them alone.

Unease shivered down Cat's spine. She hadn't been alone with a man since Henry convinced her to run away with him. Her eyes flickered to the surrounding tents, empty now. From the tourney field came the roar of the crowd. It sounded muted, distant. Very distant. "Let us get your gambson off so I may judge the extent of the damage," she said briskly.

Gervase ducked away from her hands. "Where are your guards?"

"I... I left them to watch Philippe ride in the joust."

"Did you now?" His steady gaze took on a speculative gleam. "'Tis not wise for a lady to wander about on her own."

"No harm would befall me here." Still Cat backed up a step, or tried to. He grabbed her arm. She looked down at the tanned hand, so large it could encircle her wrist twice. "Let me go."

"Nay. Not yet, at any rate."

Cat's body shook, her mind whirling with a dreadful sense of foreboding. "Wh-what? What do you intend?"

"Why, to take you on a bit of a ride." A sardonic smile lifted one corner of his mouth, but his eyes remained dark, cold. "You've been saying how much you miss riding."

"I've changed my mind. I do not wish to ride right now." This couldn't be happening. How could she have been taken in by another man? Cat tried to wrench free, but he held her fast.

Truly frightened, Cat opened her mouth to scream. He yanked her down onto his lap and cut the sound off with his wide palm. The other arm was around her middle, holding her immobile.

"You see," he whispered into her ear, "I'm kidnapping you. 'Twill be some time till we're missed, and even then, the good people of the court will doubtless think you've done it again, run off with an unsuitable lover. I'll leave them a note that will convince them of that."

Just after dark it began to rain. The chilly droplets slid over Cat's forehead and down her nose to drip steadily onto her bound hands. She ducked her chin into the neck of her tunic and wished she'd given in when Gervase had ordered her to change into male garb before they left. But no, she'd been too angry for that. Instead she'd hissed, spit and fought till he'd made good his threat to gag her and carry her off across his saddlebow like a prisoner of war.

What a fool she'd been to trust him. She wasn't certain which was worse, Henry who'd seduced her into running away with him, or Gervase who'd lulled her into a false sense of security. His hot glances, his pretense of passion held in check had been just that, a sham. Even his grand gesture, seeming to give up a rich prize to salve her honor, had been a trick. All the time he'd wanted one thing—to kidnap her. Doubtless he planned to bed her, then wed her and demand her dowry.

"Shall we stop and seek shelter?" Perrin whispered.

"Nay. We need to put more miles between us and Bordeaux," Gervase replied. He shifted to reach behind him, then settled a woolen blanket or cloak over Cat's head and shoulders.

She sat up straighter and shook it off.

"Don't be a fool," he growled. "You'll catch your death of cold in that thin gown."

Cat snarled at him through the linen gag, prompting him to curse and remove it. " 'Twould serve you right if I did and cheated you of your chance to rape me," she spat.

"Rape?" He snorted. "Nay, but I'd sooner bed with the devil than you, my fine English lady. 'Tis ransom I'd have, and that I can get whether you are sick or well."

"Ransom?" Cat turned her head, blinking against the rain that sluiced over her face.

He looked down on her, his expression hidden in the shadows cast by the visor of his helmet. "Aye, ransom. Your sire will pay handsomely to have you returned to him."

That he would. An icy fist clenched tight around her heart as she thought of her parents receiving a demand for coin in exchange for the life of their daughter. *Oh, Papa, Mama, what have I done to you... again?* "You bastard," she hissed, teeth chattering now with fury, not the cold. "You are a beast of the lowest form. Worm... maggot... vulture..."

"Cease your shouting or I will replace the gag."

"Do it, then, you viper, for I'll not shut up till I've denounced you to the heavens and roused the whole countryside."

Gervase cursed and tied the damp linen over her mouth again. Not out of fear they'd be heard, for the path his scouts had found sent them through a stretch of forest denuded of people and game by the cursed war. Nay, 'twas his own conscience she pricked with her accusations. Though she was everything he hated—vain, petty, shallow and English—he did not want to harm her. All he wanted was his due...enough coin to rebuild what Ruarke had despoiled when he'd attacked defenseless Alleuze.

Still Gervase kept an arm securely fastened around his captive's slim waist. He had a bruised cheek and bloody scratches on his arms from her initial attempts to escape him back at the tourney field. Despite her fragile appearance, the lady had claws as sharp as the cat for whom she was named. He'd not underestimate her ability to do damage, nor risk having her break her neck in a tumble from his horse. Fortunately the gelding he rode was patient and nerveless.

Farther back in the little cavalcade, Armand had Thor on a short lead. Strapped to the stallion's back was Gervase's family's sword...a relic too precious to be left behind, no matter that he hadn't exactly redeemed it, unless one counted Archie de Percy's public apology. With most of the Sommervilles at the tourney field, Gervase had sneaked behind the largest tent and cut his way in to retrieve his sword and leave the ransom note addressed to Lord Ruarke. In the pack were the Sommervilles' medicine chest and the boy's clothing Catherine had refused to wear. Mayhap when she got over her initial anger...

Gervase snorted. Though they'd been hours on the road and she was likely exhausted, Cat sat ramrod straight, her body as far away from his as was possible considering she sat across his thighs. Damn but she was a temperamental bit of baggage. By the faint light filtering in through the canopy of leaves, he saw her hair was black with rain, her face ashen by contrast. From his vantage point, he could see her breasts strain against the layers of velvet plastered to them, the nipples pebbled by the cold.

Heat shot through his loins, mocking him, infuriating him. "What's done is done, my lady," he growled, removing the gag again. "You are my prisoner and will stay so till your sire pays your ransom, but I do not wish to treat you ill. You harm only yourself by your stubborn refusal to take the shelter I offer. Could you not hate me just as well while wrapped up in my cloak?"

"I will take naught from you," she croaked.

"You will do as I say." Gervase bundled her into the cloak despite her awkward attempts to thwart him. "There now. Sit still and when we stop for the night, you will take off those wet things and put on the sturdy woolens I brought for you."

"Bloody hell I will," she replied in a muffled voice.

"Your prisoner giving you trouble?" murmured Perrin.

"Naught I cannot handle." Gervase sighed. It might have been easier to sail to England, besiege Ruarke Sommerville's castle and demand his due.

"Wake up." A hand jostled Cat's shoulder.

"In a moment, Etta," Cat mumbled sleepily. "I must have danced too hard last eve, for I swear I ache in every bo—"

"Get up, we've no time for lazing about," commanded a hard, familiar voice.

Cat opened her eyes, shocked to find a man crouched beside her bed, glaring at her. Not just any man, but the one who had haunted her nightmare. Gervase St. Juste.

"Up. We must break camp and be on our way," he grumbled.

"Camp?" Cat blinked, refocused on the men moving about the small, dim clearing, and the enormity of her situation came crashing in on her. It hadn't been a nightmare. She was Gervase's prisoner. "Sweet Mary!" She sat up, tumbling hair across her face. She dragged it back with an impatient hand and realized the blanket had pooled at her waist, revealing her linen shift to the gray dawn...and the eyes of her captor. Cursing, she clutched the blanket to her chest. "What happened to my clothes?"

"They were wet...I removed them when we stopped to—"

"How...how dare you?"

He sighed. "It was too dark to see anything, and frankly I was too tired to have cared in any case." He picked up a stack of brown cloth and tossed it onto her lap. "Now get dressed. We haven't much time."

Cat loosened her grip on the blanket long enough to flick the clothes away. "I prefer to wear my own things."

"Impossible. I'm afraid I had to cut them off."

"Cut them off." Cat felt violated.

He stood, and she saw he'd changed from his tourney finery to a gray tunic worn over a suit of heavy mail. The metal shirt still bore the stains of his battle with Archie. Had anyone tended his wound? Bah, he was her captor, and she the victim. His next words made that exceedingly clear. "They were unsuitable for this journey in any case. Dress, and we'll leave."

Cat clenched her teeth, wanting to leap up and fly at him but painfully aware her shift was thin as cobwebs and came barely to her knees. She lifted her chin instead. "I will not."

"You will." His eyes narrowed to flinty slits. "Either that or I will mount you before me clad only in what you wear."

"You wouldn't dare."

"Oh?" He rocked back on his heels, arms folded across his chest. The gesture not only met her challenge, it made him look even larger and more formidable. "I would dare anything... anything at all... to secure what is due me."

"Due you!" Cat scrambled to her feet, blanket and all, hugging the wool about her like a shield as she faced him. "'Tis ransom you speak of, not some holy quest or God-given right."

"In this case, they are one in the same."

His blunt assertion took her aback for an instant. Then she thought of Henry and his protestations of undying love. What he'd loved was her estates. What Gervase wanted was an excuse to justify kidnapping. Where money was concerned, men apparently had slippery consciences.

"Your reasons do not matter to me. I will not dress in these rags nor move from this—" Her brave words ended in a yelp as he grabbed her arm.

"Then you shall ride as you are. Perrin," he called over his shoulder. "Tell the men to mount up."

"But I haven't eaten or... or been give a moment of privacy." So she might relieve herself.

Gervase cocked his head, seeming to find her embarrassment amusing. "There's food and a bush yonder that you may use...after I have your word you will wear these clothes and not attempt to escape if I give you a few moments of privacy in which to don them and attend to your other... needs."

Cat bristled, unused to being laughed at or ordered about. "If you do not let me use this bush of yours, you may find your own clothes are in no fit state to wear."

He chuckled. "I've had worse poured on my head from the walls of keeps I was besieging." Then he sobered. "What is it to be? I have little time and less patience for your willful ways."

Willful she might be, but Cat was not stupid. Escape was her top priority, but she'd not succeed clad in her shift, barefoot with no idea in which direction lay Bordeaux. Better to mask her hatred, feign compliance and wait for a better chance. "For the moment, you hold the upper hand. I will wear the clothes."

"I'd also have your word you'll not try to escape if I give you a few moments of privacy."

"Why trust my vow? You hold us English in contempt."

"Look on it as a test, of sorts. If you pass, I may grant you leave to ride alone... without the gag."

Cat glared at him, aware he was toying with her. Two could play at that game. "Very well. I give you my solemn oath that I will not try to escape if I am permitted to dress and attend to myself in private. Do you wish me to kiss your sword to seal the pledge?" she asked with false sweetness.

Not my sword, Gervase thought, but her offer did provoke a stimulating image. He quashed it, a bit disappointed she'd given in, for he enjoyed matching wits with her... and mayhap other things, as well. "That won't be necessary," he said more harshly than was warranted. "Just see you are quick. I will wait here. If you are gone overlong or there is more thrashing about in the brush than I deem necessary, I will assume you have broken your pledge and come looking for you."

She nodded curtly, but her eyes flashed defiance. Holding the blanket carefully about her, she knelt to retrieve the pile of clothing, then turned and walked toward the brush with the regal bearing of a queen. Unfortunately, she'd given no thought to her rear guard...or lack thereof. Gervase was treated to an unrestricted view of her backside swaying provocatively beneath the thin, knee-length shift before she vanished.

"She gave in, I see," Perrin observed.

Gervase jumped guiltily. "Aye." Good thing, for he doubted he could ride another mile with her in his arms. He'd won this skirmish but was vividly aware a battle yet waged between them. The outcome was not in dispute, and the contest might have been amusing were they not on a desperate, hurried journey though dangerous territory with a vengeful host likely on their heels. "Still I'd not trust her as far as I could throw Thor. Speaking of which, I will ride the stallion and let her have the gelding, on a stout lead."

"Is that wise? What if she can't keep up?"

"Then I'll take her up with me, but I'd prefer to be unencumbered in case we are set upon by any of the outlaws so prevalent in the land these days."

Catherine Sommerville stomped out of the brush in Armand's best clothes, the blanket rolled under one arm. Knowing they must travel near several cities and stop to get supplies, Gervase had hoped to pass her off as one of his men. But the young squire had never filled the hose in quite so stunning a fashion, and of course there was no disguising her breasts. He supposed she'd pitch another fight if he asked her to bind them.

"Why are you standing about gaping?" his captive snapped. "The sooner we are away the sooner my father may ransom me."

The day went downhill from there. The rain that had tapered off when they'd made their brief stop near dawn fell again as a nasty mist. It seeped through the layers of wool to his weary muscles and aching bones, making Gervase too aware he'd gone three runs in the jousts, fought a fevered sword battle, then been in the saddle for nearly a full turn of the sun. As the sullen skies began to darken with yet another nightfall, he heartily wished he could stop and rest. But his neck prickled with the knowledge that Philippe might well be on their trail.

Though Gervase had left a note claiming the "lovers" had eloped to Bayonne, the ruse might not have fooled the Sommervilles into riding south whilst Gervase went east. As an added precaution, some of the vanguard was dragging branches behind to wipe out their tracks. Just in case they were pursued, Gervase rode in the rear of the cavalcade with the best of his fighters while Perrin led with their prisoner's mount securely tied to Sir Vallis's. If they were attacked, the knight was to immediately spur ahead and get the lady away.

Gervase straightened as Perrin rode down the column of men toward him. "What is it?"

"I wondered if you were going to call a halt?"

"Did she ask it?" Gervase immediately looked ahead to the small figure muffled in his cloak. Impossible as it seemed, her spine was as straight as when they'd started out.

"Nay." Perrin lifted his visor, looking older than his six and twenty years. "She has asked for naught, not food, nor water nor respite from the journey. But the horses are exhausted, and so are the men. We cannot risk riding through the mountains in the dark in any case."

Gervase lifted his eyes to the forbidding ridge of black rock that lay ahead of them. Well he remembered the narrow, tortuous trail through those peaks, with its sharp turns and treacherous drops. "You are right."

"Thank God." Perrin sighed then smiled. "You've been so unlike yourself today. So quick to anger, and showing us that temper Grandfather thought he had beaten out of you."

"Aye, the old man would be most disappointed at my display of de Lauren meanness if he were yet alive." He sighed, too, and the tension that had gripped him eased. If his wits had been addled, 'twas from guilt. He had finally struck the first blow at the man who had murdered his family, yet deep in his heart he despised his methods. That accounted for part of his sharpness; his lady prisoner was responsible for the rest. He'd learned the hard way to show naught of what he felt lest it be criticized by his grandparents. But Catherine got under his skin as no one and nothing ever had. He could admit none of this, not even to Perrin. Instead he said, "If I've pushed too hard, 'tis because I feel Sir Philippe's vengeful breath on the back of my neck."

Perrin nodded and cast a worried glance at the shadowy trail behind them. "Aye, my nape's been prickling, too, but we've men posted a goodly distance back. If there'd been any sign of pursuit, our lads would have reported in. Lyle has found a likely place to camp for a bit."

Gervase gave permission to stop, but waited till he'd spoken with the rear guard and posted a watch on the trail before he rode into the small camp Perrin had established. He was not surprised to find all in order, the horses watered and picketed with their feed, the men unrolling their oiled ground cloths and blankets beside the stream that cut through the wooded glen. His men were used to hard living, both on the battlefield and since they'd come back to Alleuze. What did surprise him was the aroma of roasting meat.

"What fool ordered this fire built?" Gervase demanded, striding toward flames that danced under a pine bough.

"I did." The lady he'd thought to find prostrate with exhaustion stepped in front of him, hands on hips, face shiny from a wash in the stream. A few tendrils of hair clung wetly to cheeks pale except for the flush anger had lent them. Only the circles under her eyes revealed the weariness they all felt.

"Ah, hoping to attract the attention of our pursuers?"

"In this mist?" She glanced meaningfully at the wisps of smoke forced to hug the ground by the heavy, damp air. "But if you've a mind to smother it and deny us a hot meal, suit yourself." She stalked to the base of the pine and ducked under the bit of canvas someone had rigged as an awning. Regal as a queen despite her page's garb, she settled herself on a nest of blankets and awaited his verdict.

Witch, Gervase thought. Infuriating, tempting witch. "Where did this come from?" he asked, mouth watering as he stared at the small pig Armand turned on the makeshift spit.

"The lady's horse kicked it up when we rode in," the boy replied. "She marked where it'd gone and sent Vallis and some of the others after it. Must we put the fire out, milord?"

"The wonder is she didn't run away whilst you were all galloping about the forest hunting wild boar," Gervase grumbled, but he hadn't the heart to deny his men a hot meal. God only knows when they'd get their next one.

"Nay. She's right about the smoke not rising in this weather."

Angry about that, among other things, he went down to wash up in the stream. Then he checked the perimeter of the camp, examined the horses for strain or lameness and set the guards for the night. All of these things Perrin and Vallis had already seen to, but it gave him something to do besides return to camp and match wits with his prisoner. Prisoner, ha!

Settling down on a rock at the edge of the water, Gervase glared at the camp fire through the trees. The promise of warmth and light drew him against his will, much like the woman who'd kindled both the blaze in the clearing and the one in his gut.

He looked up as Perrin approached. "I wasn't certain you'd want any, but I've brought your dinner." Perrin held out a piece of bread covered by a thick slab of meat.

"I'd be a fool to starve on principle." He bit through the crusty skin, relishing the rich juices that filled his mouth.

Perrin grinned, unslung a wineskin from his shoulder and hunkered down on a nearby rock. "The lady said much the same thing when I pointed out she was cooking a meal for her captors. She said she'd be a fool to starve herself to spite us."

"Likely she thinks to lull us into inattention, then escape." Gervase didn't pass up the food, however. They ate quickly, filling their empty bellies and passing the wineskin between them. When he'd licked the last of the juice from his fingers, Gervase washed his hands in the cool water and stretched. "Judas, but that was good."

"Aye. I'd never have thought of catching the little beast. 'Twas Lady Cat who spied it and sent the men to chase it down. By the time they returned, she'd selected two forked branches to brace the spit and a third to skewer the pig."

Gervase glanced through the leaves at the lady who sat before the dwindling fire. Soft light flickered over her pale oval face. "How comes a high-born lady to know of such things?"

"Why don't we go and ask her? At least we could thank her for the food," Perrin added when Gervase balked. "Or are you determined to sit here and brood?"

"Is that what you think I'm doing?" Gervase snapped, then he realized Perrin was right. "Damned. How is it that I can face a whole troop of English soldiers without a qualm, yet this one fragile lady ties my guts in knots?"

Perrin laughed. "I'd hardly call her fragile, not when she stood the ride as well as any of us and cooked our dinner."

"Aye, she's an unusual woman." He didn't want her to be, but she was. Nor did he want to think of himself as a coward. So he stood and walked through the trees to the fire. She was unaware of his approach, her attention on a story Vallis spun about a childhood boar hunt that had ended with the inexperienced hunters being chased up a tree by a determined sow.

Cat Sommerville's low, musical laughter filled the glade, blending with the tinkle of the stream. It occurred to Gervase as he watched the mirth spread over her face, making her skin and her eyes glow, that he hadn't seen her laugh as freely at court.

His men spotted him, of course—he'd have taken them to task if they hadn't—but there was little ceremony between them, for they'd been to hell and back together, so no one stood as he ducked under the dripping pines and entered their circle.

Cat's breath caught audibly. "I . . . I didn't see you." She looked discomforted as a child found filching sweetmeats.

Was she trying to seduce one of his men into helping her escape? Gervase's narrowed gaze swept the upturned male faces, searching for guilt. He saw weariness and something more touching . . . relief for a few moments of amusement snatched from the jaws of fear and desperation. He'd not deny them their simple pleasure, but he would watch her. He'd not forget she was deucedly clever. Inclining his head, he sat down across the fire from her. "I came to commend you on a fine meal and ask where a high-born lady learned to roast suckling pig over an open fire."

Her sigh of relief seemed exaggerated. "My . . . my parents traveled around a bit and took us with them. There being so few inns, we often camped out in the woods or meadows."

"Ah. I assume you waited in those huge silken tents while the maids slaved over opens fire to—"

"The lads turned the spits, 'tis true, but my mother oversaw the whole thing and taught us to do likewise." She chuckled. "My first attempt on my own was a roe deer my father had killed. I bade the boys put the meat on before the fire had burned down sufficiently. The haunch was charred on the outside and rare inside, but Papa ate it anyway and declared it was the bes—"

Gervase stood abruptly, unable to hear her speak in such loving tones of the man who'd pillaged his keep. "I advise you to seek your pallet. We must be up before dawn." He strode off into the night that was as black as his mood, confused by conflicting emotions where Catherine was concerned.

Bad enough he lusted after his enemy's daughter, but now he was coming to admire her bravery, respect her intelligence and even, God help him, like her. As he sought his bedroll on the camp's perimeter, Gervase steeled himself to resist her unusual lure.

It should have been easy... he'd spent a lifetime denying who and what he was. His wife had often castigated him for his coldness, his unfeeling nature, unaware of the needs that seethed beneath the shell he'd built up.

Catherine knew.

There was some force inside her that pierced the barriers he'd erected and touched the inner core of him. He must fight it, for to give in, to open himself to his enemy's daughter, was...

Unthinkable.

Chapter Six

They broke camp at dawn after a simple meal of bread and hard cheese. Cat was so bone weary she could scarcely wash her portion down with a bit of ale. Splashing cold water in her face cleared her head, but she couldn't stifle a moan of pure misery as Perrin boosted her up into the saddle. She drew small comfort from the groans of the seasoned fighters who seemed every bit as sore as she was.

All save Gervase. He appeared fresh and hale as he bounded about the clearing in the predawn gloom giving orders and checking with the scouts who'd ridden in from their back trail. The bitter news that no one seemed to be following them haunted Cat as the cavalcade set out through forest toward the black bulk of the mountains jutting into the sky. The storm had blown itself out during the night, but lingering clouds blocked the horizon and the mists clung stubbornly to the hollows as they left the woods and began their ascent up the rocky path.

Her frustration and desperation grew with every step the gelding took. Where was Philippe? Why hadn't he ridden out and rescued her ere now? She knew Gervase had left a note in the Sommerville tents when he'd gone to reclaim his sword. Doubtless he'd threatened to harm her if they were pursued, but Philippe should have ignored that and come anyway... her father would have.

Gervase now rode at the head of the column, but the man must have eyes in the back of his head. The moment she fell behind or edged toward one of the side trails cutting away from the main route they followed, he looked back and speared her with a hard, reproving glance.

The mountain pass wound sharply to the left and entered a narrow canyon, forcing them to ride single file. Glancing up the sheer granite walls, Cat saw a hawk wheel in the thin ribbon of sky. Free. Oh, to be free. Her heart soared with a longing so fierce it brought tears to her eyes. She blinked them back sternly, fearing if she allowed one to fall 'twould unleash a torrent to rival the rush of the river in the gorge below. Instead she stared down at the churning torrent, mesmerized by its headlong dash to the sea.

Her uncle Alex owned a fleet of sailing ships and loved the sea almost more than the land. He'd taught his own children as well as his nieces and nephews to swim... and to sail. If she could reach the water, she might be able to fashion a raft from tree branches and sail to Bordeaux. If she didn't make it that far, better to slip under the wild gray than to be imprisoned in Gervase's dank tower... or worse.

"I've water in my pouch if you thirst, my lady."

Cat glanced over at the squire who was her guard for today. Tempted as she was to snap at him, Armand wasn't responsible for her predicament. He was a comely lad of fifteen whose kindness reminded her of her cousin Richard. Armand had grown up near Alleuze, Gervase's estate, and apparently the place for which they were bound. Times were hard there, Armand had told her at supper. The previous year the keep had been attacked by the English and rendered nearly uninhabitable, the fields burned and the stock driven away, leaving the people destitute, close to starving. For some reason they blamed her father. When she'd asked why that was, Vallis had silenced him with a growl.

Cat had every intention of pursuing the subject when she could get the squire alone. "I am not thirsty at present."

"If you need aught, let me know."

"Just my freedom," she said.

"Would that I could." His troubled gaze went to Gervase's wide, armored silhouette at the head of the column. "But..."

"I know," she said gently. "'Tis the lot of prisoners to chafe at their confinement and seek to escape."

"Escape." His brown eyes widened in horror as they surveyed the treacherous drop from the trail to the floor of the canyon. "Oh, please, my lady, do not attempt it. You...you'd be killed."

"And you would be punished most severely for losing your lord's ransom prize," she teased.

Armand straightened. "Better he should beat me bloody than you should break your neck."

"Hmm. A sobering thought, that." Cat eyed the water again and weighed her chances. Not here, for the boy was right about the fall, but if the trail should dip closer to the bottom...

"We don't wish you to come to harm," Armand murmured. "'Tis just the money, you see, we need it something fierce."

"Greed. It always comes down to that, doesn't it?"

"Nay. We are not greedy. We want only what was stolen—"

"Armand," Vallis said, riding up on Cat's other side as the trail widened a bit. "Go forward and see if your lord requires aught. I'll watch her ladyship for a time."

"I'd not keep you from other, more important duties," Cat said as the squire reluctantly left.

"There's naught more important to my lord than guarding you." An unexpected smile softened the veteran's scarred face. He was weathered by time and battles, his voice deep, his manner gruff, but she was used to such men, had been winning her way around them all her life.

Last night's meal was a prime example. Her mother had oft remarked that the way to a man's heart was through his stomach, not his loins. Not that she wanted any man's heart, but because she'd been kind, many of the men now looked at her with less hostility. Unfortunately, the one man she needed most to lull into carelessness hadn't been fooled by her pretense of acquiescence.

Gervase St. Juste's hard, assessing gaze had followed every move she made last night and this morn. He'd placed her in the middle of the march with guards before and aft. Friendly though they were, Cat knew these men were staunchly loyal to their lord and wouldn't help her escape. Yet. But she'd not give up.

"'Tis a strange sort of kidnapping," she remarked, watching out of the corner of her eye as Vallis flinched. Good. "I must say you men don't seem like the sort of soulless brigands—"

"We're honorable men," the knight protested.

"Hmm." Cat glanced ahead to Gervase astride Thor. This morn the stallion had balked at being mounted, yet unused to his new owner. She'd hoped to see the knight dumped on his head. When he'd controlled the restive war-horse without resorting to whip or spurs, she'd felt betrayed anew. "Not only is your lord a kidnapper, he's a thief. He pledged his sword for the purchase of Thor, yet when he left he took both horse and sword."

"The sword's been in his family for generations. He could hardly leave it behind. And the horse..." Vallis shrugged.

"Is a fine beast and too good to pass up." Cat sighed. "I suppose Papa will have to ransom us both."

"I think my lord hopes to keep the horse and breed it with the few mares we have left at home."

"He thinks to raise war-horses?" As seemed to happen so often, Cat found her glance drawn ahead to her chief captor. What manner of man was he?

As though sensing her regard, he turned in the saddle. He'd raised the visor of his helm, but the distance was too great for her to read his expression. Still a shiver worked its way over her skin, and her lips tingled with the memory of their kiss. No other man had ever made her feel so... so restless and achy with longing. He desired her, too, she knew that. He'd not tried to kiss her again, but the wanting was there. It blazed in his eyes when he watched her. What would happen when they reached this Alleuze? Thus far he'd left her alone, doubtless because he was busy guarding his back, but once safe behind his own walls, he'd be free to force himself on her. Or would it be force?

Cat tore her gaze away and looked down at the surging river. Better the water than whatever might wait at Alleuze.

Gervase breathed a sigh of relief when they left the high trail and descended to the floor of the canyon. He had no great liking for heights, even less for small, dark spaces. It was the war, of course. Wasn't everything. He'd been captured while trying to wrest a French castle from its English occupants and held in the oubliette for a week before his forces broke in to rescue him. Seven days without food or water or even light, stuffed beneath the floor in a cell no bigger than a casket. Aye, it had been like being buried alive. It haunted him still.

Repressing a shiver, Gervase dragged his thoughts back to the present danger. With a soldier's eye, he scanned the narrow valley, probing each bush and rock for signs of ambush. There was no way a force from Bordeaux could have gotten here before them, but other dangers lurked in the land these days. Disaffected soldiers and lawless brigands who'd kill them for their mail and horses. What they might do to Catherine didn't bear thinking on.

Here the river formed a large pool, the stony banks fringed with reeds and young saplings. Birds swooped low over the water, snapping up bugs in the noonday sun. They'd passed this way a dozen times over the years. He knew the trail continued along the pond for a goodly distance before climbing back up into the mountains. He'd planned to water their mounts here briefly, then press on. 'Twould be foolish to linger, but mindful of Cat's strained face and drooping shoulders, he called a halt.

Gervase handed Thor over to Armand and walked over to where Cat sat surveying the tranquil scene from atop her horse. "Will you step down and rest a bit?" he asked, uncertain of her mood.

She surprised him by smiling ruefully. "I'd love to, but I fear my legs would fail me and I'd land in a heap at your feet."

"I know the feeling." Gervase reached up and lifted her from the saddle to the beach, his hands lingering on her waist as he gave her a moment to catch her balance. His own limbs felt none too steady, but he knew it wasn't fatigue. Her nearness made his pulse pound like an untried lad's. For a long moment he stared into her lovely eyes, a deeper purple even than the violets that grew in the shade beneath the trees. Tiny flames danced in them. Desire? Or anger? Before he could decide which, she pushed against his chest. Reluctantly he let her go.

"I—I am fine now." She sounded a trifle breathless, but her steps didn't falter as she picked her way among the rocks to sit on a large one at the pond's edge.

Gervase followed, rummaged in his tunic for a square of linen, dipped it into the water and offered it up, only to find his high-born lady splashing handfuls of water on her face and neck like any common traveler.

She drank deep from her cupped hands, then tilted her wet face toward the sun. "Ah. That felt so good." Her sigh of contentment cut through him like a blade. What would it be like to tip her back on the riverbank and wring cries of pleasure from those lips?

"Would you like ale? Bread?" he asked tightly.

"Nay." She opened one eye, speared him with it. "Why are you doing this?"

"I—I thought you might be hungry."

"Not that." She straightened, droplets scattering as she gestured to the men and horses taking their ease along the river. "This... this mad scheme to kidnap me."

Gervase stiffened, his pleasure in their surroundings shattered by the reminder of who she was. Not just some lady he'd taken for profit, but Ruarke Sommerville's daughter. "'Tis not some mad scheme. You are my prisoner, and will remain so till I have the ransom from your father."

"What will you do with me?" She was frightened, yet held his gaze steadily. More bravely than many men he'd faced.

"We go to Alleuze . . . what is left of my home. There I'll hold you till the ransom money comes."

"Do . . . do you swear not to harm me?" Her voice shook then.

Perversely, it pleased him, because she shook him. "I'd be a fool to harm so valuable a hostage."

"Will you force me to share your bed?"

"Force? 'Tis not my way. Come now, no need to look so glum. I'll not deny I desire you, but I hardly think you are immune to me, either, sweetling. I imagine we will amuse ourselves much as you and Henry did."

The remaining color leeched from her face. "How long do you expect I will be forced to stay with you?"

Gervase shrugged. "A few weeks . . . more mayhap depending on how long it takes your sire to raise the sum I will demand."

"Which is?"

Gervase named the amount Bernard had suggested, and felt a qualm when she paled, her hand fluttering up to her throat. "Do you not think he can raise that much?" he asked anxiously, not certain whether he was worried or pleased. If the ransom went unpaid, the lady would be his guest indefinitely.

"He . . . he can, I think, but 'twill ruin him."

"Good."

"Good!" She exploded off the rock with startling energy. "What kind of beast are you to ruin a man you've never met?"

Gervase stood slowly, anger burning deep in his soul, searing away the desire he felt for her. "True, we never met, but those of my family who did have cause to regret the meeting. 'Tis for them I do this. For them and the living who will die without help." Hatred churned like acid in his belly. He turned on his heel and stalked away before he spewed it out.

Vallis called him over to check Thor's cinch strap, and he eagerly immersed himself in the dozens of details that someone else could have overseen. There were water skins to fill, the order of march to set. He was speaking of that with Perrin when a cry went up from the river.

Catherine.

His heart in his mouth, he raced to the spot where Armand stood, Catherine's cloak clenched in one bony fist.

"She was here a moment ago, my lord," the boy exclaimed. "I swear I only turned away a moment to fetch the bread she—"

"Has anyone seen Lady Catherine?" Gervase shouted, turning in a circle to scan the cliffs that rose sharply on all sides, echoing back his frantic words. "Quick, check up the way we came," he commanded Vallis. "Lyle, take ten men and search the banks of the pond." The weeds and young trees offered little in the way of concealment...even to one as slim as she. He didn't see how she could have run away without someone having seen her, but five minutes of frantic searching yielded nothing.

"This is ridiculous." Gervase shielded his eyes with one hand and scanned the valley again. "There are only two paths out of here, and she has taken neither. She cannot have escaped . . . unless she has turned herself into a bird or a fish. The first is impossible, the second . . ." His words trailed off as he stared at the water. 'Twas calm near the shore, but deep and swift moving in the center where the river current ran strong.

"Surely she wouldn't have attempted it," Perrin said, but he looked toward the distant spot where the pond gave way to falls and rushing river. "She couldn't swim so far undetected."

"Nay. But she could have drowned herself right handily." Despite the heat of the sun, Gervase shivered, recalling their argument. Angered by his unwanted attraction to her, he'd hinted he'd make her his mistress. Had that taunt pushed her over the edge, literally? "Tell the men to look along the shore. She may have become trapped by a sunken branch."

Gervase swung onto Thor's back and walked the stallion through the shallows, searching, searching. As he probed the murky green depths, he was haunted by the knowledge that her death was on his conscience. God, how could he have agreed to this mad scheme? It seemed they'd lost her when a shout from the far bank gave him hope and drew him thither.

"I...I think I've found her," Armand stammered. "Look there, among the weeds." He pointed to a swath of reeds extending some ten feet into the water. "Does that not look like blond hair floating near th-the surface?"

It did. Gervase leapt from the stallion, unbuckled his sword, tossed it onto the ground and made for the water.

"Take off your armor," Perrin cried. "It'll drag you down."

"Drowning is no more than I deserve." Gervase waded in, his eyes focused on the pale swirl in the center of the reeds. It couldn't be her. It couldn't be. But it was. Recognition stopped him a foot away. The same cold water that lapped at his chin tugged the strands of blond hair to and fro just beneath the murky surface. Her face was in profile to him, a pallid blur amongst the thick stalks and verdant leaves of the rushes.

She was dead. Because of him, she was dead. He closed his eyes against the pain.

"Gervase?" Perrin called from the shore. "Do you need help?"

Aye. But he knew there'd be none this side of hell. "I . . . I have found her." Gervase crossed himself, swallowed the gorge that filled his throat and gingerly reached for her shoulders.

She exploded out of the water like a wild thing, arms and legs flailing. A booted foot caught him in the stomach. It drove the air from his lungs and sent him staggering back. Off balance, he foundered and fell. As the water closed over his head, he wondered if he'd drown, weighted down, like so many before him, by the heavy armor intended to protect him. Not yet, by damn, he thought. I have too much unfinished . . . too many dependent on me.

Gervase struggled to stand, feet slipping on the slick river bottom, hands clawing at the reeds in search of something, anything to give him leverage. His lungs burned, and black dots danced before his eyes. Fight. Fight.

Seconds later something grabbed his arms and dragged him up from the muck. Coughing and choking, Gervase broke the surface. About him all was noise and confusion. He heard Perrin shouting for help, felt his friend's capable hands steady him as he found his footing. "Catherine?" he gasped.

"Here." Her face bobbed a foot from his.

Disbelieving, he raked the hair from his eyes. "Y-you aren't dead," he managed to say as he gulped in welcome air.

"Neither are you . . . more's the pity." Hair and leaves plastered to her head, lips blue with cold, she nonetheless glared defiance and hatred.

"Come," Perrin interjected. "We can sort this out on dry—"

Gervase shook off his grip. "You were trying to kill me?"

"Nay. I was trying to escape and you got in the way." She was treading water, he realized.

"You can swim?"

"Obviously."

"And breathe under water?"

One wet brow quirked. "With the aid of a hollow reed."

"Clever," he conceded with grudging admiration. "Obviously you meant to wait till we'd left...what then?"

Her teeth chattered; she steadied them. "I'd build a raft from these saplings and float downstream to Bordeaux."

Incredible. "I can see I've underestimated you."

"Aye, sir, you have." She must be exhausted and cold, God knows he was frozen, and she'd been in the water far longer than he, but she was unbowed. There were no tears over her failed plan, only steely determination in her level stare and firm jaw.

"Gervase!" Perrin pleaded, tugging on his arm. "You'll both have the fever and clotted lungs do you stay here chatting."

"Not chatting, fencing," Gervase said thoughtfully. Learning about each other. Catherine Sommerville was small and beautiful, like Marie had been. But there the similarities ended. As he watched Vallis pull the sopping lady onto the bank, he felt another grudging surge of admiration for his clever, brave little captive. He must take care not to underestimate her again.

* * *

They made camp on the edge of the gorge. Gervase was angry because they hadn't been able to travel farther, but the men were wet, tired and hungry. Cat was thrilled. She hadn't escaped, but she had slowed them down. Mayhap with luck Philippe would catch up with them on the morrow.

Wrapped in a cloak, she sat cross-legged before the canvas shelter Armand had rigged for her and watched over the preparations for dinner. "Those fish should be turned again."

Vallis set aside the blade he was sharpening and went to do as she had bid with nary a complaint at being assigned to help with woman's work. They were used to fending for themselves, he'd said, to cooking, mending and tending their own wounds. Had they no women? she wondered. Specifically, had Gervase a woman? A wife? "The fish must be almost ready, I think, my lady, though you'd be the best judge."

Cat tucked the cloak more securely around her and went to check the dozens of fish baking on hot rocks in the camp fire. The men must know she was naked beneath the cloak, for her clothes dried on a nearby bush. Yet there was no leering or ribald comments. Truly these rough men were better mannered than the court fops whose eyes constantly dipped into a woman's bodice.

"Done," she pronounced. "Let the men eat their fill, then we will bake the rest of the catch to take with us."

Vallis nodded and handed her the first portion before calling the others to eat. She withdrew to her lean-to and ate with unladylike haste. The hot food chased the last of the chill from her body. Sighing contentedly, she set the wooden bowl aside and eased back among the pine boughs Armand had gathered.

Gervase materialized from the dark and sat on a boulder a few feet away. "I see you've recovered from your *ordeal.*"

"Aye," Cat said warily. "And you?"

"I am no stranger to wet and cold, but Armand will be up half the night oiling my armor so it won't rust."

"I'm sorry for that."

"For my rust or his lack of sleep? Never mind," he said harshly. "I already know the answer to that."

"What do you expect?" she asked in kind.

"I expected a weak, biddable woman. One who would cling to the bow of her saddle and do as she was told, not one who would leap into the lake and try to swim away."

"Then you have not met the women of *my* family." She tossed her damp braid over one shoulder. "Your wife must be a pallid creature indeed to give you so warped an opinion of women."

"My wife is dead." He whipped his head around, glancing away from the camp fire and into the dark night. His memories must have been equally black, for his jaw clenched and unclenched.

She had her answer, and his obvious pain should have brought pleasure. It didn't. "I ... I am sorry," she said softly. "My younger sister lost her husband not long ago, and I know—"

"You know naught." He turned on her, his eyes blazing now. "How did he die, this sister's husband?"

"He'd gone to Dover on business, took sick of the plague and died. They'd been married only six months."

"Would you like to know how my wife died?" Something ugly moved in his eyes. "She killed herself ... after the English finished with her, she threw herself from the tower."

"Oh, my God," Cat breathed; no other words would come.

"'Twas the devil's work, not God's. But the devil will soon pay his due. I'd speak of it no more." He looked away again, watching as Vallis took the last of the fish from the fire and set it to cool. "Why did you suggest extra fish be caught and cooked for the trail?"

"Vallis says there is little game to be had up ahead."

"Would you not like to see my men and me grub for roots?"

"And starve along with you? Nay, I am too practical."

"You are not like other women."

"Nay, I am not." Nor was he like other men. Cat bit her lip, studying her captor's profile in the flickering light. He was a hard man, but not a harsh or cruel one. "If you take me back, I promise my father would reward you."

"What incentive would he have to beggar himself if I return his daughter?" Gervase growled.

"I don't understand why you must ruin him? If it is money you want, would a fat purse not suffice?"

"I want more than money. I want justice."

"My father is a just man," she said slowly, searching his unrelenting features for some sign of what he wanted.

"Your father is a ruthless murderer."

"Nay! You are mistaken."

"And you are naive. He was proclaimed the hero of Poitiers for the men he killed, not the fine cut of his armor."

Cat blinked. "'Twas a battle. Men on both sides died. I know that doesn't make it right, but if you want to affix blame for what happened, better the kings who ordered the fighting."

"This is not about Poitiers. 'Tis about what Ruarke Sommerville did afterward," Gervase snapped.

"What? What did he do?"

"Your clothes are dry, my lady." Armand held out the garments, eyes darting uneasily from her to his lord.

"In a moment," she said. "I'd finish this discuss—"

" 'Tis finished. You have ten minutes to dress and prepare for the night ere I return." Gervase stood, staring down at her with an intensity that sent dread racing down her spine.

"What then?" she asked, but he'd whirled away and disappeared into the darkness.

"You'd best hurry, my lady," Armand whispered. "Sir Perrin said milord was ever so angry you tried to escape."

Cat dressed behind the blanket Armand held up as a curtain and sought a few moments' privacy behind a nearby bush. Gervase was waiting for her when she stepped back into the circle of light cast by the dwindling fire. Unconsciously she raised her chin to meet the challenge. "I'd bid you good sleep, sir knight, but you deserve to be haunted by nightmares." Dismissing him, she ducked into the safe haven of her piney bower.

No sooner had she lain down than someone crawled in after her. A big, muscular body crowded against hers in the scant space. Gervase. None other would dare.

"Get out." She sat up. He grabbed her wrist and dragged her down across his chest. "Nay." Nails clawing at his arm, she tried to twist away.

"Cease." In a swift, lithe movement he flipped her onto her back, arms pinned above her head in one hand, torso pressing her to the ground. One powerful thigh was thrown over her legs, stilling them. Trapped. She was well and truly trapped.

Panting with exertion, Cat stared up at the face a scant inch from hers. 'Twas too dark to see his expression, but she could feel their hearts beating in wild counterpoint to each other... and something more alarming. His manhood swelling against her thigh. "Nay," she cried, renewing her struggles.

"Be still." He let her take more of his weight, making her aware of the power he leashed. "Be still or you'll goad me into doing that which you fear."

Cat ceased fighting, but didn't relax, couldn't. "So... 'tis not just my father's ruin you want," she said.

"I'd be a fool and a liar if I denied you stir me. I've been long without a woman and you're uncommon fair. But your honor... such as it is... is safe with me. I'd sooner bed a pox-ridden whore as Ruarke Sommerville's get."

Cat went limp, relieved by the reprieve, shocked by his vehement hatred. "Then what do you in my bed?" she snapped.

"This." He shifted slightly. Something rough slid over her right wrist and tightened. Leather.

Outrage spilled through her. "You would bind me?"

"I've no wish for another swim tonight." He fastened her hands together securely yet not painfully. "I will leave your ankles free... for now. But if I find you out of bed before I call you in the morn, they'll be tied, as well."

"What of tomorrow? Will my hands be tied when we ride?"

"They will."

"Beast," she hissed, longing to go for his eyes.

"You brought this on yourself. Remember—if you are tempted to escape me again—that I have precious little left in life. What I do have, I mean to keep."

Chapter Seven

It was hours till dawn and the sky yet dark when Gervase gave the order to march. Conscious that if they'd discovered his trick and were following, the Sommervilles would not stop to frolic in mountain lakes or bake trout, he was anxious to make better time today. He rode at the head of the column, aware of the censorious glances of his men. Not usually given to softness, they had, however, taken exception to his treatment of Catherine.

"Was it necessary to bind her hands?" Perrin demanded from beside him, eyeing the trail. "There's nowhere she could go."

"So I thought yesterday. I'm lessoning her. And mayhap saving her impetuous little neck. If she tried to dash off, she might well tumble over a cliff and cheat me of my ransom money."

Perrin wasn't fooled by Gervase's harsh words. He'd seen the stark terror in his friend's face when they'd thought the girl drowned. He witnessed the profound relief that had replaced it when they'd found her alive. And he heard the fondness beneath the gruffness. He knew, too, how much of himself Gervase hid, even from himself. "She is not the haughty lady I thought her at court, nor the vicious witch we'd expected. I find it hard to believe she sprang from so vile a man as Ruarke Sommerville."

"Mayhap she favors her mother, as my mother did hers."

"Thank God she was naught like her sire...mad Odell."

Gervase nodded, recalling the tales his grandfather had told of old Odell whose father had died a raving lunatic and older brother had perished in a fire of his own making. "Grandfather said Uncle Bernard was mad, too, but I never saw any sign of it."

"Nor did I. Though I never warmed to him, I don't think Bernard is to blame for the sins of his kin. Any more than Lady Catherine is for her sire's."

"The lady is not being punished for her father's sins but for her own foolhardiness. Judas, who'd have thought a woman would go to such lengths to escape?"

"She has courage and determination." Perrin grinned. "And she's right handy to have on a march. Suckling pig two nights ago, trout last night. I wonder what she'll serve up this eve?"

"Your tongue, if you don't keep it between your teeth." Turning from Perrin's wide grin, Gervase fixed his gaze on the path ahead. He was not going to think about Catherine. She was his prisoner, naught more. But he found it impossible to forget how it had felt to lie with her in the dark, her soft body molded to the hard planes of his, her breath warm on his cheek. The memory brought with it the same damned quickening in his loins.

Dismayed, he shook off the forbidden desire and concentrated on the road. As they rounded an outcropping at the crest of the ridge, the peaks of the Monts du Forez stretched out before him like the humped back of a sleeping dragon. 'Twould take days to wind their way through the forested valleys and the narrow trails that crisscrossed the mountains. He'd chosen this route on purpose. 'Twas less traveled than the one around the mountains and less touched by war. There'd be more chance of finding game in the woods or buying supplies in the villages along the way.

Just then the sun broke over the peaks, setting fire to the clouds, while far below, the rocky summits glowed red in the reflected light. The awesome power of God's majesty lifted Gervase's spirits. Mayhap 'twas a portent that his own dark trials were about to end. He hoped so, for he was soul weary of death and destruction...and of the misery and hunger that followed them as day did night.

"Come," he said, motioning his column forward. "I recall there is a cluster of farms in yon valley. They may have a bit of barley or a few chickens they'd be willing to sell."

"Barley and chickens," Cat muttered when the word was passed down the line. "All men think of is their stomachs." But she knew that wasn't true. The memory of Gervase's body pressed so intimately to hers still burned. Nor was she fool enough to think 'twas hatred alone that fueled the fire between them. Of all the men on God's green earth, why did her traitorous body have to harken to his? Even knowing 'twas only lust didn't ease her mind. Tales of her parents' tumultuous courtship were proof that matters seldom ran smoothly between men and women. But to think that she could desire a man who would bind her like a prisoner.

Cat chuckled. She was a prisoner, but by no means resigned to that state. Her smiles and hot meals had already turned some of the St. Juste men from wardens into friends. Soon one of them might be moved to pity and help her escape. True, the treacherous track they rode offered little hope of that, but the valley into which they descended might. If not one of the soldiers, mayhap she'd persuade someone at these farms to aid her. Beneath her cloak, she worked at the thongs on her wrists, gritting her teeth as the leather chafed flesh used to velvet cuffs.

"We're near there," Vallis said. "The place Lord Gervase mentioned lies just yonder. You can see the huts through the trees." As they rode into the clearing, several large birds rose up from the ground behind the buildings and began circling.

"What are they?" Cat asked, alarmed.

"Vultures," Vallis spat, cursing. He fingered the scar that ran down his cheek into his graying beard. "It bodes ill."

Gervase's terse command to halt rang out, stopping everyone in their tracks. Cat saw him lean toward Perrin, then motion for two of the men-at-arms to follow him. The hooves of their horses kicked up clumps of earth from fresh-plowed fields as they fanned out and approached the buildings. Naught moved in the yards. No smoke rose from the chimneys, yet a pall hung over the place.

A sense of foreboding raised gooseflesh on Cat's arms as Gervase circled wide around the first hut and disappeared behind it. "What is it? What do you think's happened?"

"Naught good," Vallis muttered. "I think I'd best loose your wrists." He drew his dagger, sliced the thongs, then the lead rope attached to her horse. "If my lord gives the word to ride, don't hold back."

The waiting frayed Cat's nerves. It seemed an eternity had passed before Gervase cantered out from behind the hut. His sword was sheathed, his visor up. When he skidded to a halt beside Perrin, Cat saw his face was ashen, his eyes bleak and angry.

Brigands. The word flashed down the column, leaving fear in its wake. Men tightened the grips on their weapons and cast measuring glances at the encroaching forest.

"The attack took place yesterday, I'd guess," Gervase called out, quieting the murmurs. "Their trail leads off to the north. I've sent Lyle and Simon to make certain they're gone." He snapped out orders to search the area, then rode down to where she waited with Vallis. "Vallis, there is one who yet lives. Bring bandages, though I doubt there is much we can—"

"Let me come," Cat said. "My mother is an accomplished healer, and she taught me to tend the sick and the wounded."

Gervase's eyes met hers, black with some emotion she couldn't name. "I doubt you practiced on wounds such as these."

"I—I can stitch rent flesh." It turned her stomach, but her mother had impressed upon her the importance of putting the patient's welfare above her own squeamishness.

"Nay. 'Tis not a sight for your delicate eyes." With that, he wheeled away, and Vallis scrambled after him.

Delicate? Cat nudged the gelding after them, as much to prove Gervase wrong as to help the injured. In the confusion of securing their position, no one stopped her. When she rounded the corner of the hut and saw the bodies she wished someone had.

Dear God, there were so many... ten... a dozen... sprawled on the ground like broken dolls in dark pools that once had been red. The scavengers had already begun their work. Averting her eyes from the grisly sight, she urged Jock over to where Vallis and Gervase knelt on either side of a body lying across the threshold of the nearest hut. She dismounted, shocked to find her legs nearly too weak to hold her, and tottered over to them.

The victim was a man. The gaping hole in his chest, the gurgle in his lungs as he struggled for breath spelled his doom. And well the poor man knew it.

"Do... do not waste time on me," he whispered, his eyes filled with pain and urgency. "My wife... lies within. I... I tried to reach her, but... my strength failed. See... see to her."

Through the open doorway, Cat glimpsed a woman, lying on her back, her skirts thrown over her face. Blood flecked her pale thighs and lay beneath her in an ominous puddle.

Vallis started to rise, but it was Gervase who walked within. He slowly drew the skirt from the woman's face, shuddered and bowed his head. When he walked out, his expression was haunted, his gaze unfocused. He didn't seem to notice Cat as he hunkered down beside the fallen peasant. "She is fine. They... they tied her up, but otherwise, she is in no pain."

That at least was true. The woman was dead, had likely died in pain and fear, but Gervase had sought to ease the husband's passing with the lie. Cat's throat tightened. Tears filled her eyes, mercifully blurring the tragic scene.

"Thanks be to God," the man whispered. "Do not let her see me... like this," he pleaded. "Take her... take her with ye."

"Aye," Gervase said thickly. "Can you tell me who did this?"

"Two soldiers . . . rode in last eve . . . asked for food . . . water. They. . .they offered to pay. My brother and I saw no harm. When I went to fetch the goods, they felled him . . . signaled to others. Six . . . mayhap eight more. . .rushed out of the woods." His eyes closed. "The screams . . . the screams went on all night."

Cat's stomach rolled up into her throat as she thought of what these people had endured.

"Were they English?" Gervase asked harshly.

"Nay. French. . .from Arles. I. . .I heard them say they were on their way there . . . to join their master . . . Jean Cluny."

"I know that name, but 'tis odd he ranges so far north. And chooses so small a target. Merchants are his usual style."

"They were hungry. . . and bored."

"Bored!" Cat exclaimed, appalled. "How could they do such a thing for. . .for sport? You must go after them."

Gervase looked at her as though seeing her for the first time. "What do you here? Damn, you will learn to stay where I put you." Grabbing her arm, he hustled her back to her horse. "What if the brigands were lurking in the huts? What if . . . ?"

"You are hurting me," Cat said.

He stopped. "Merciful heavens, did I do that?"

Cat looked at her raw wrist, then at his horrified expression. "Nay, 'twas my own foolishness in thinking I could break the leather thongs. What is it?" she asked, unsettled by his ragged breathing and tightly clenched jaw.

"God, I am sick of death and violence." His eyes darted around the clearing where his men went about the gruesome task of gathering the bodies. "What if they come again? What if the peasant was mistaken and there are more than eight or ten of the fiends? What if I can't keep you safe?"

"Shh." Cat laid a hand on his arm, alarmed by the tremor that shook him. "I am not worried. I know you will guard me—" Her words ended in a squeak as he dragged her against the hard wall of his armored chest, both arms wrapped around her as though he feared someone would try to snatch her away.

"Catherine," he moaned into her hair. "Jesu, I could not bear it if aught happened to another woman in my care. I was a fool to bring you here. Damn my thirst for revenge. No matter what your sire did, 'twas wrong of me to take you."

The intensity of his remorse shattered Cat's anger, and she found herself soothing the man who'd kidnapped her two days ago. "All will be fine. You will keep me safe, I kno—"

"I couldn't protect Marie. She trusted me to protect her, and I left . . . left her to die."

"Marie? Was she your wife?"

Before Gervase could answer, Perrin joined them and asked anxiously, "Is aught wrong with Lady Catherine?"

"What?" Gervase blinked, then shook his head as though to clear it. He looked at Cat, blinked again and all but shoved her away. "I was comforting her," he said gruffly.

"Ah." Perrin nodded in apparent understanding, but Cat was completely baffled by Gervase's strange behavior. "'Tis a terrible sight. It reminds me of what we found when we returned to Alleuze last year."

Gervase's throat worked convulsively. He squeezed his eyes shut, and she could practically feel the battle he waged with what must have been terrible memories. His anguished expression tugged at her healing nature. She wanted to put her arms around him and hold him as she would a wounded child, she but sensed he'd reject any such gentleness. Finally he opened his eyes and looked at Perrin. "If you can do what is needful here, I will ride out and see if Lyle and Simon have found any sign of the brigands."

"Fine. Be careful," Perrin said.

"You, too. And watch out for Lady Catherine," Gervase added, though he didn't look at her before he stalked away.

Feeling oddly shaken, Cat wrapped her arms around her waist. "What happened here reminded him of what was done to his castle."

"Castle is too grand a name. Alleuze has only one tower, but there is a stout curtain wall around it and a score of dependency buildings inside. Or there were... before the attack."

"Tell me about it." *For Gervase would not.*

"We were away fighting at the time."

"But his wife was there?"

Perrin nodded and looked away just as Gervase disappeared into the forest. "Marie was there and we were not."

"Gervase said she... she killed herself."

The lines around Perrin's mouth deepened. "The leader of the brigards raped Marie and killed her daughter because the baby's crying annoyed him. Driven mad by the loss of Eva and her own ravishment, Marie jumped from the tower window."

Cat remained silent for a few moments, horrified. She then spoke. "Poor Gervase, to lose both his wife and his daughter in so cruel a manner," she whispered. "It explains much. I—I see now why he is hard and angry." She looked down at her clenched fists, then up at Perrin's compassionate face. "He hasn't cried for them, has he?" she asked with sudden insight.

"If so, he shed his tears in private, but I doubt he cried. Gervase is not much given to displays of emotion."

Cat's surge of horror became outrage. "What makes men do such things?" she cried.

"There is a wildness that comes over men after a battle . . . a need to conquer that can spill over into rape if their commanders don't maintain discipline. But what was done at Alleuze . . ." Perrin shook his head. " 'Twas much like what happened here. Senseless violence. The work of beasts masquerading as men."

"On that we are agreed. I thank you for telling me about Alleuze." Emboldened by Perrin's openness, she asked, "For some reason Gervase blames my father for that attack, doesn't he?" At Perrin's nod her frustration grew. "He is wrong! My father would never do such a thing."

"We have proof to the contrary. Our people had gotten word of their plight to Gervase's uncle Bernard. He was coming to help Alleuze and saw your sire riding away . . . recognized his banners."

"What?" Cat exclaimed. "But . . . but that's impossible."

"Bernard has no reason to lie about such a thing. Now if you will excuse me, I must see to burying the dead."

Numbly Cat watched him walk across the yard. So this was why Gervase not only wanted money, he wanted to ruin her father. Now she understood how deep his hatred must run.

She looked away from the bodies being arranged for burial and up at the clouds blotting out the sun. Just so had the lives of these poor people been snuffed. When Gervase had taken her captive, she'd called him an outlaw. Now she realized her fate could have been far worse had he truly been a ruthless brigand. He desired her and hated her father... reason enough for most men to have ravished her, yet Gervase had treated her honorably. Could she somehow convince him he was wrong about her father?

"My lady." Vallis hurried across the clearing, a bundle held awkwardly in his arms. "My lady, see what we've found." He folded down a corner of the blanket to reveal the face of an infant. The child bleated weakly, rooting against Vallis's mailed chest in a vain search for food. Vallis colored. "Here, my lady, you'll know better how to deal with this."

Cat pushed aside her own worries and took the babe. "I fear none of us is equipped to deal with this. What we need is a cow or a goat. I see pens for animals, but they stand empty. Have the men search the woods and see if one escaped the brigands."

"We cannot," Vallis protested. "Gervase left orders to have the dead buried by the time he and the others returned."

"We cannot let this infant starve."

"It isn't safe to linger here. Mayhap we will come across another farm and can barter for some milk."

"That would take too long. The babe already grows weaker. I will search for a goat myself."

* * *

Gervase caught up with Lyle and Simon two miles from the farms. "What have you found?" he asked his trackers.

"Ten horses, traveling at a modest pace, passed along this trail sometime late yesterday." Sim pointed to a broken branch and a pile of dung. "I'd say the bastards had no fear of pursuit, for they left a trail a blind man could follow."

"Doubtless they think themselves stronger than anyone hereabouts. I'd love to prove them wrong," Gervase muttered.

Lyle tugged at the mustache he wore in the vain attempt to make his baby face seem older. "Shall I go back for more men?"

"Nay." Gervase sighed regretfully. "Much as I ache to punish them, there are scores of people at Alleuze depending on our mission. Nor do we know whether these bastards plan to meet up with more of their kind. We could find ourselves facing a superior force." His hand tightened on the hilt of his sword, and he swore that if they should chance upon these men, he'd see they paid . . . as Ruarke Sommerville would soon pay. "Scout ahead for a few miles, while I go back for the rest of our party. We will rendezvous here in one hour."

Tempted as he was to dally until Perrin had buried those ghastly reminders of the massacre at Alleuze, Gervase rode swiftly back to the settlement. When he cleared the trees, he saw half-dug holes, abandoned shovels and eight unburied bodies.

"What the hell?" Had the brigands doubled back and attacked his men? Drawing his sword, he urged Thor forward.

Armand ran out of the last hut, the one doubtless belonging to the brother of the peasant they'd been unable to save. "My lord, welcome back. Did you find the outlaws?"

"Nay, I did not. What is going on here? Where is everyone? Why are these people not buried?"

"Lady Catherine sent them into the woods to find a goat."

"Whatever for?" Gervase exclaimed.

"For milk."

"She desires milk . . . now? By all that's holy!"

"'Tis not for her," Armand said quickly, "but for the babe, the small girl-child Vallis found rolled in a sleeping pallet in this hut. Lady Catherine says 'tis likely the mother did it to save her baby's life before she was . . . killed. Only now there is naught to feed the babe, so Lady Catherine says—"

"Enough," Gervase snapped. "I ordered these people buried with all haste so we might leave this accursed place."

"And so they shall be." Catherine walked out of the hut, a bundle tucked into the crook of her arm. "Vallis found evidence a few of the goats ran into the forest. As soon as the men have located them . . . pray God one is female . . . we shall bury the dead and leave. We have no other hope of feeding this poor mite, and I know you'd not want her to die." She opened the blanket, giving him a peek at the babe's tiny white face.

Eva must have looked just so . . . still . . . dead. Gervase's stomach lurched, his muscles clenched with the need to ride away from this place and the terrible reminders of the day he'd lost his own wife and daughter.

As though sensing his turmoil, Thor shied. Under cover of quieting the stallion, Gervase got his own emotions under control. But he still couldn't look at the child. "The goats are likely miles from here by now, if they've not been eaten by some predator. We will wait one hour, no longer. I'd be well clear of this place before dark," he growled.

"Could we not spend the night here?" she asked.

"Nay!" He could no more spend the night here than he'd been able to sleep in the master chamber at Alleuze where Eva had died. Unwilling to let her see how deeply he was affected by the stink of death and destruction that hung over the farm, he turned to Armand. "Find Perrin and inform him of these new orders."

Well aware that both his squire and his lady prisoner thought him harsh and unfeeling, Gervase strode across the clearing to the half-finished grave, stripped off his gauntlets and began to dig. The effort of lifting shovelfuls of thick clay while wearing full armor soon had him sweating and aching. He concentrated on the physical strain, closing his mind to the memories that threatened to suck him down into madness. He'd finished one grave and started another when Perrin approached.

"We found three of the goats," Perrin said. "I thought we might roast the two males and take the female with us."

"Turn the males loose."

"We could use the fresh meat."

"I'd have no more killing." Gervase kept his eyes averted from the compassion he knew he'd find in Perrin's and dug on.

"Fine. Give your shovel to another and come rest a moment," his cousin said gently.

Gervase shook his head and continued working. He heard Perrin sigh and braced for an argument, welcomed it for the chance to vent some of the impotent fury building inside him.

"I demand you come out of there and speak with me," cried an imperious voice. Catherine stood on the rim of the hole he'd dug, hands on hips, eyes mutinous.

"Demand all you like," he growled. "I give the orders here."

"Well, I am not staying to listen. And my horse goes with me." With an arrogant toss of her head, she started for Thor.

"Stop her," Gervase shouted, but his men had seemingly been turned to stone. Cursing them and her, he scrambled out of the fresh grave and went after her, his cramped muscles screaming in protest. He caught her as she grabbed the stallion's reins. "I think not," he snapped, tearing the leather from her grasp.

Catherine flinched but didn't back down. "Ah, I thought that would get your attention. Now I—"

"You dare much, lady. I am in no fit mood for any of your little games."

"I assure you, this is no game." She folded her arms and matched him glare for glare. "While I appreciate your sentiment against more deaths, we need the meat, and the goats will be spared the fear of being stalked by the beasts of the forest."

Gervase ground his teeth over an oath. "Fine, have them killed then. I care not what happens to the goats or any other damn thing." Spinning on his heel, he found his place at the graves had been taken by another. Perrin stood between him and the site, braced for confrontation. Gervase took one step toward it when Catherine's voice stopped him.

''I know you do this to ease your pain, but think what will happen to us if we run into those brigands and you are too exhausted to fight them.'' She laid a gentle hand on his arm.

He shook her off. ''You know naught about me and my pain.''

''I know this reminds you of what happened at Alleuze, but working yourself to the point of collapse will not bring them back and may endanger our lives.''

A shudder ran through Gervase as her words pierced the haze of rage and guilt that had enveloped him since entering the clearing. ''Damn but you're a cold one if you can ignore this.''

Tears filled her eyes. ''If you think me unaffected by their suffering, you are wrong. But wailing and gnashing our teeth ill serves the living...who should be our prime concern.''

Gervase sighed. ''You are right,'' he said grudgingly, surprised but grateful for her levelheadedness. Most women would have been more hindrance than help. Marie had fainted at the sight of blood, even someone else's, he recalled. Guilt clawed at his conscience. Bad enough he'd never loved her, but to think ill of her now she was dead. And that was his fault, too.

He shook his head to clear it, then looked down at Cat. Despite her calm practicality, her face was pinched with strain, her eyes rimmed by mauve shadows. ''I am sorry I shouted at you.'' The apology sounded rusty, but she smiled.

''Naught matters but getting away from here.'' She glanced at the forest. ''Do...do you think they are still nearby?''

"Nay, but do not worry, I won't let anything happen to you."

Her smile faded. "Because I am a valuable hostage?"

She was far more than that, but he dared not tell her how much he'd come to care for her. "I will keep you safe because I will not fail another woman." 'Twas more of himself than he'd shared with anyone, and she seemed to understand.

Instead of pressing for details, she nodded. "Let us eat and rest, then, for I am sore weary." Taking his hand in hers, she led him toward a small camp fire. He followed, unaware that he'd put himself in another's keeping for the first time in his life.

Chapter Eight

Cat woke to the sound of furious screaming. For a moment it blended with her nightmare about murdering fiends, then she realized 'twas the babe. "Hush, hush, little one." She fumbled about the darkened lean-to, picked up the child and rocked it. The babe arched its back and screamed even louder.

"What is wrong with it?" Gervase growled from without.

"Jolie, I have called her. And I don't know what's wrong."

"It's probably hungry."

Cat pushed aside the blanket over the entrance, blinking against the firelight. "I fed *Jolie* before retiring."

"Don't you know they require frequent feedings?"

"How would I?" Cat snapped. "I've never been a mother."

"I thought all women knew such things."

"Oh, aye, we're born with it the same way males are the ability to wield a sword." Grumbling about the stupidity of certain males, she thrust the child at him. "Here, hold her whilst I find the milk."

"I'll get it." Seconds later he returned with a cloth and a bowl of the milk Simon had earlier coaxed from the goat. "Here."

Awkwardly juggling the babe in one arm, Cat dunked the linen into the milk and presented it to the child, who latched on and drew down with surprising vigor. "She's stronger than she was," Cat murmured. "Only see how she drinks."

Gervase wasn't looking at the babe. His gaze was fastened on the thigh left bare where Cat's tunic had ridden up. The hunger in his face made her skin tingle and heat curl in her belly. She should order him away, or cover herself with the blanket. Cat did neither, returning her eyes to her task as she pondered this desire that afflicted them both. 'Twas madness to even consider coupling with him, and yet she burned with curiosity. What would it be like to give full rein to the needs boiling inside her? To lie beside him, let him touch her and touch him in return?

Cat looked up and found him watching her. Their gazes tangled, yearning violet with burning silver. She felt the tension build inside her, inside him, sucking the air from the tent till she could scarcely draw breath.

"You shouldn't stare at a man so," he whispered. "It drives all the good intentions from his head."

"I might say the same thing to you," she replied.

"Aye. I suppose you might." He reached out and cupped her jaw. His fingers were cool, yet a rush of heat suffused her cheek as his thumb gently stroked it. In the half-light, his eyes seemed to glow. "This is wrong."

"I—I know." She trembled. "But sometimes it feels right."

He nodded, the corners of his mouth tilting up in a sad half smile. "Why you?" he murmured, his words mirroring those thrumming through her own mind. "Why does it have to be you?"

"The lure of the forbidden?" she suggested, struggling to keep her tone light though her heart thundered in denial.

"Aye, you are that. A siren song so sweet it makes me want to forget who and what we are to each other."

Cat's throat tightened with unshed tears. "Gervase, I... I could forgive you for kidnapping me for the sake of your people." *Even though you are wrong about my father.*

"If only things were that simple." His hand slid around to the back of her neck, coaxing her to lean forward. "Would to God things were as simple as this." He lowered his head.

Cat's mouth went dry as she watched his lashes sweep down to cover the glittering intensity of his gaze. Her own eyes drifted shut on a moan as his mouth closed over hers. This wasn't the hungry taking she'd expected. Instead his lips moved over hers with a tenderness that made her feel cherished. Aye, warm, secure and, above all, cherished. His tongue slid along her lower lip, wetting it and drawing it between his teeth to be gently suckled. A shiver rippled through her body, warming her muscles and melting them like butter in the sun.

"Catherine." He cupped her head in both hands as his tongue swept inside, stroking over hers with shocking intimacy. She should have been frightened, but felt instead a strange quickening in the secret recesses of her body.

Moaning softly, she leaned closer, mimicking the seductive rhythms of his mouth with the shy thrusting of her own tongue. Dimly she heard someone whimper, thought it was herself until Gervase tore his mouth free and she realized the babe protested at being wedged between their bodies. "Poor thing," she crooned, jostling it till the mewling ceased and the now-sated infant went back to sleep. "I'll put Jolie down and—"

"Nay." Gervase's breathing was as ragged as Cat's, but his expression held none of the regret she felt. " 'Tis just as well. This foolishness can lead nowhere. Nor would I want it to." He jammed a hand through his hair. "Lusting after Ruarke Sommerville's daughter. I am truly cursed."

"Wait." Cat laid the babe out of harm's way in the corner of the lean-to. "You are wrong about my father. He is not the one your uncle saw riding from the keep."

"I do not wish to speak of it."

Damn him. Why must he be so closemouthed? "You must. At least tell me when this happened."

"Last summer." His jaw tightened. "And before you deny it again, I made inquiries when I first arrived in Bordeaux. Your precious papa was in France last summer... on campaign."

"That is so," Cat said slowly, then her chin came up again. "But my father would not do such a thing. I know he has killed, but only in war when 'twas either that or be killed himself."

All the gentleness leached from his face. "So, war justifies the slaughter of helpless women and children?"

"Of course not, and I am certain my father never did any such thing. He is a man of honor... even in war."

"Honor!" he spat. "I know he besieged Alleuze in my absence and when my people surrendered, rode within to rape and pillage."

"Nay," Cat gasped, horrified as much by his accusations as the vehemence with which he spoke.

"Aye. The blood of my wife and daughter are on his hands." He glared at her, disgust replacing the desire of moments ago. "By rights, I should rape you and send you back to him...broken as my Marie was when *he* was done with her. Do not gasp and shrink away. We both know you are no maiden. Or mayhap, given what passed between us moments ago, you think 'twould not be rape. I assure you, I feel ruthless enough to make it so."

Terrified by the fury darkening his face, Cat closed her eyes. When she opened them, he was gone. As she released the air pent up in her lungs, she realized the only thing that stood between her and rape was Gervase's sense of honor. How long could that bulwark withstand the pressure of his hatred?

Somehow she had to convince Gervase that, his uncle's claims to the contrary, her father was innocent. Would it make a difference if Gervase knew she was innocent, too, untouched by Henry Norville despite their elopement? Nay. What better way to repay her father's supposed crimes than by despoiling his daughter. Clearly escape was even more imperative.

"He didn't mean it, you know," Perrin said the next morn.

Startled from her own private hell, Cat looked over at the knight riding beside her. "Who?"

"Gervase. I overheard your argument last night." Perrin's gaze slid from hers, as had most every other man's this morn.

At the time she'd been too busy with the unfamiliar task of feeding and changing the babe to care. Now her cheeks burned. Doubtless they had listened and watched while she'd nearly surrendered her virtue to a man who hated her. "I am quite certain he meant every word he uttered."

"Nay. Gervase would never harm a woman. If Marie's whining and nagging didn't drive him to murder..." Perrin cleared his throat. "I should not have said that. 'Tis unkind to speak ill of the dead, and 'twasn't her fault she was weak and spoiled."

So Gervase's wife hadn't been perfect. Doubtless he'd loved her anyway. Cat's mother was not weak, but her habit of nagging and butting her nose into her husband's business had caused many a stormy argument between the two. Still Ruarke was devoted to his Gaby, loved her to distraction and respected her opinions... most of the time. Theirs was a marriage based on trust and respect. The sort of bond Cat had hoped for with Henry. Clearly her judgment in men was lacking. Had Gervase's gallant defense of her honor not convinced her to trust him, she wouldn't have gone alone to tend his wounds and ended up playing into his hands.

"Gervase will not harm you," Perrin repeated more forcefully. Which of them was he trying to convince? "You will be released, unharmed, when the ransom's paid."

Seeing a slight crack in her kidnappers' unity, Cat pressed. "I disagree. What better revenge than to take my father's money and return me either dead or ruined?" Mayhap even pregnant. Dear God, could she live with that stigma?

"Gervase is not capable of doing such a thing."

"Neither is my father, yet you all believe the worst of him. I pray you help me to escape before Gervase's obsession with vengeance results in more deaths. Mine."

Perrin shook his head. "I would not go against Gervase, nor would it be safe for you to try to make your way back alone."

"I am willing to take my chances," Cat said urgently.

"On what?" demanded a horribly familiar voice.

Cat gasped and looked up to find Gervase reining in on her other side. "On taking Jolie with us to Alleuze."

"Jolie?" Gervase scowled, then grunted. "Ah, the babe. We will leave it at the first hut we come to."

"Then she will surely die," Cat replied. "The peasants have too many mouths to feed. Why should they squander what they have on a babe who is naught to them? And a girl-child at that."

"I will give them coin to buy food."

"And stay behind to make certain they do not toss Jolie out and spend it on themselves?" Cat challenged.

"You have a poor opinion of our peasants."

"Not at all. These people have lived in a war-torn land for most of their lives. They are hungry, frightened and suspicious. While the people who farm my family's demesne lands are fairly treated, I have seen those who are not so fortunate in their overlord. People who are bullied, beaten and taxed to the brink of starvation. They would not react any differently than would the peasants here, I think. They would take your money and use it to keep themselves and their children alive. *Their* children."

Gervase sighed. "You are likely right. The goat and the babe slow us down, but I do not want any more harm to come it."

Lyle rode up, his round face lined with concern. "There are people on the trail ahead," the scout reported.

"Who? How many?" Gervase drew his sword.

"I don't know. We heard voices around a bend in the road, but dared not venture too close for fear of being seen. Vallis stayed on guard whilst I rode back to warn you."

Gervase nodded, gave orders for everyone to withdraw into the woods and wait while he went forward with Lyle.

"He should have taken you with him," Cat murmured to Perrin as she watched the two men disappear.

"Gervase knows what he's about," Perrin replied. "But I'll be certain to tell him you were concerned for his safety."

"Of course I am," Cat said stiffly. "If aught happens to him, how will I get home again?"

Perrin grinned. "And that is the only reason?"

"Aye." But it wasn't and they both knew it. Cat looked away from his knowing smile and stroked the babe's back. Vallis had rigged a blanket sling that held Jolie securely against Cat's chest, yet left her hands free to control her horse. A concession to the threat posed by the outlaws. Apprehension shivering over her skin, Cat glanced anxiously about the thick, dark woods. What if those murdering fiends lurked in the brush, watching, waiting to pounce on them? *Merciful Mary, keep us safe.*

"Someone comes," Perrin hissed.

Cat released a sigh of relief when Gervase rode into sight, his visor up, his sword sheathed. " 'Tis naught but a troop of players," he explained, reining in beside Perrin.

"Thank God for that," Perrin replied, and the rest of the men echoed the sentiment.

Gervase grunted. "The bad news is that they were attacked by the outlaws late last night." He held up a hand to still the flood of questions. "The bastards came at them whilst they slept around their fire. 'Twas done for sport or meanness, for 'tis well-known the jongleurs were as hard hit as the peasants by this continual war and unlike to have anything worth stealing."

"Were any hurt?" Cat sidled Jock closer.

Gervase glanced her way, face bleak, eyes shuttered as they'd been at the peasants' farm. "Their leader is dead. The others escaped into the night with minor bumps and scrapes." His jaw relaxed fractionally. "At least the women are unharmed."

Sensing his pain, Cat longed to reach out and hug him but knew he'd reject such gentleness...at least from her. "I will see what I can do to ease their hurts, and they can come with us."

"Absolutely not!" Gervase said so sharply Thor shied.

"But we cannot leave them on their own with no one to—"

"There are two other men to protect the women, and such folk are used to seeing to themselves," Gervase snapped.

"In England, 'tis a knight's duty to assist the weak and aid the downtrodden," Cat said with asperity.

Gervase ground his teeth over an oath; Perrin choked on what sounded like a chuckle. The other men shifted uneasily.

Cat pressed her advantage. "Pity the French are not so...charitable, but I insist we at least see to their wounds."

"You are in no position to give orders," Gervase grumbled. "Nor can we play nursemaid to every unfortunate we meet." But he surprised her by not only agreeing to let her tend the players, but by taking food from their lean supplies to feed them.

The four wretches huddled by the side of the road under Vallis's guard were pitiful indeed. Ila and Faye, mother and daughter respectively, clung together clad in torn shifts little better than rags. They bore scratches and bumps from their panicked escape and were utterly terrified, but had been spared the fate of the farmers' wives.

Once Cat had cleaned their wounds and they'd eaten a bit of roasted goat, they recovered enough to help with their menfolk. The fire-eater, Tearlach, a brawny man in his middle twenties, had nasty gashes on his arms from fighting with the outlaws. Bevis was in the worst shape, a gangly young acrobat whose leg had been broken apurpose by the leader of the brigands.

"He snapped poor Bevis's leg over his knee," Ila explained, "and would have done for the other one if Tearlach hadn't rushed out from behind a tree and distracted that fiend whilst Bevis crawled off into the brush."

"Someone should hunt the vermin down and dispose of them," Cat said as she finished setting Bevis's leg with branches and torn blanket strips. "I've done the best I can, but..."

Bevis nodded, his face ashen, his wheaten hair slicked with sweat. "'Twas too badly broke to mend straight. Still I thank ye for yer efforts, my lady. I'll just have to learn to dance on my hands. 'Twill be a novelty, at least."

Cat looked away, eyes filling with tears. Most players, except those who found posts with a great lord, lived hand-to-mouth. A crippled acrobat was like to starve.

Gervase left the rocks where his men sat eating and talking amongst themselves. "Can you tell me anything about the outlaws who did this?" he asked Tearlach.

"They were soldiers...ten men mounted and armored, with swords. What they hoped to gain by attacking poor folk like us..." He shook his dark, shaggy head.

"They wanted us." Faye sidled closer to Gervase and measured him with hot brown eyes. Her face was dirty, her hair tangled, but her flesh was firm and ripe beneath the skimpy gown Gervase's men had recovered along with the rest of the players' meager possessions. "Me especially. My thanks for saving me from them. I have little of value, but if there is something I can do for ye." She wet her lips and gazed up at him with open invitation.

Watching them, something twisted and splintered in Cat's chest. Jealousy? Nay, she'd not let it be. Annoyed with him and with herself, she averted her gaze, busied herself with repacking the remaining medicines in the chest.

"'Tis your friends you must thank for saving you, and Lady Catherine for the tending of your wounds," Gervase said in a flat voice that gave no hint of his mood. "Now we must be on our way."

"Surely ye won't abandon us," Faye exclaimed.

Cat jerked her head up, ready to protest his decision no matter her feelings about the nubile young dancer.

"Nay. I'd not be so...uncharitable." Gervase spoke to the players, but his wry gaze was focused on Cat's face. "We will escort you to the nearest village."

"They won't let us stay," Faye whined. "Because of the outlaws that infest the countryside, the villagers have become wary of letting strangers into their midst. They'll lock us up in some barn for the night and send us away come morn."

"Not if I give you coin to pay your way till your wounds heal," Gervase said, looking at Cat. A few brisk orders sent men scrambling. Bundles were shifted so the women could ride on the pack animals. Faye's hints she'd prefer to ride with Gervase were summarily dismissed. Bevis was slight enough to be mounted behind Armand, his splinted leg sticking out at an odd angle. Tearlach preferred to walk, which was fortunate because he was too heavy to ride double, and there were no extra horses.

"I'm used to it, and I'd keep my body fit." He stepped up beside Cat's horse. "In payment of yer kindness, I'd entertain ye with a story or two to ease the tedium of the journey."

"I would enjoy that." Cat smiled. Tearlach was handsome in a brawny sort of way, his speech polished as a court jongleur. She looked up, caught Gervase scowling at her, and her smile deepened. "I'd enjoy that very much."

Cat's pleasure wore thin after the first hour. How frivolous seemed the tales of courtly love when death might await them round the next bend. But she laughed at Tearlach's witticisms and tisked at his bawdy jokes. 'Twas almost a relief when Jolie stirred and whimpered for her next meal. Knowing they couldn't stop, Cat drew the skin of milk from behind her, found the feeding cloth and proceeded with the skill of a longtime mother.

"Is your child a boy or girl?" Tearlach asked.

"Girl . . . but she isn't mine." Her gaze on the little mouth sucking diligently, Cat told him what had befallen the farmers.

"They are a foul bunch. We were lucky to escape with our lives. They wanted to wait till light and search for us, but Maslin, their leader, said they had to reach Arles in four days." He frowned. "Mayhap yer lord husband should make camp and wait to make certain they have left the area before proceeding."

"Gervase is not my husband."

Tearlach's eyes widened. "I—I apologize, my lady, I naturally thought so...so polished a lady as yourself..."

"You mean I don't look like a common whore?" Cat chuckled. "Nor am I." She hesitated, wondering how much to tell him. Though she didn't know Tearlach well, he might try to help her escape if he knew her circumstances. Tempting as that was, she didn't want to see him harmed on her account. And if anything, Gervase had watched her more closely since the players had joined them.

Unease tingled down her spine, and she knew he had turned to watch her...again. Don't look, she warned herself, but the curiosity that had plagued her from birth drew her head up. Turned in his saddle, Gervase stared back from the head of the cavalcade. His eyes bored into hers, piercing in their intensity.

Shivering, she wrenched free of their spell. "Sir Gervase also rescued me from the outlaws." A lie was less dangerous.

"Did he now?" Tearlach's gaze was skeptical, but he launched into another story.

"Would you rather ride back there with them?" Perrin asked.

Gervase whipped his head around. "Nay. Why should I?"

"To spare the crook in your neck."

"Careful I don't put a crook in that smug smile of yours," Gervase growled. "No doubt she thinks to exchange her favors for that muscle-bound player's help in escaping from me."

"Lady Catherine doesn't seem the type...otherwise she'd have used her, er, charms to convince you to return her to Bordeaux."

"Charms! The only thing she's done is flay me with the sharp side of her tongue." Liar. Gervase's blood heated as he recalled the feel of her mouth yielding to the pressure of his, the slide of that tongue against his own. Sweet. Seductive. Potent.

Perrin chuckled. "Aye, she's a handful. Willful and proud, yet selfless and caring. She may be English, and a Sommerville, to boot, but I much admire her."

"I see the little witch has ensnared you, too."

"Nay, she has eyes for you, not me." He looked side-long at Gervase. "I know how you feel about remarrying, but she is worth two of Marie. This one wouldn't fold under pressure as your first wife did. She'd work beside you to realize your dreams. Forget this quest for revenge and wed her instead. Mayhap her father would dower her with enough coin to rebuild Alleuze."

"Perrin," Gervase warned. "Cease such talk."

"Aye, my lord." Eyes icy, Perrin looked away.

Gervase sighed. "Don't let us quarrel about her. I swear she is driving a wedge between me and my men. Day and night they sing her praises. 'Lady Catherine has the healing touch. Did you ever taste the like of her baked trout? What a gentle soul she is to care for that wee babe,'" he mocked, mimicking them.

"Aye, insisting we take the child was a stroke of genius. Only think how much easier 'twill be for her to escape with the puling serf's brat tied round her neck."

"You refuse to see any bad in her," Gervase snapped.

"Nor you any good. I suppose 'tis her fault that you cannot keep your eyes from her."

"Aye. Nay." Gervase snorted. "I do not deny I desire her. It makes no sense," he added angrily, unused to confiding such things. "She's the daughter of the man responsible for so many deaths, yet to my everlasting shame, I'd bed her in an instant." Nor was his interest solely a thing of the flesh. Perrin was right. There was much to admire about Catherine. He'd called her selfish, yet she was the first to offer help to another. By contrast, he saw the war had hardened him to others' suffering. He did not like that and sought to mend his ways.

"'Tis not surprising you desire her. She is beautiful, and we've lived like monks this past year. I cannot recall the last time you bedded a woman."

"Neither can I." Yet he'd not felt the lack till he'd met Catherine. Even Clarice's blatant overtures hadn't stirred him.

"Why not ease yourself with the young player, Faye?" Gervase's nose wrinkled. "Nay."

"I agree she's in sorry need of a bath, but one might be arranged, and she certainly seems eager enough."

"She's not to my taste," Gervase said flatly. "Now if we can leave off discussing my lack of bed partners, there is the matter of these brigands who are a half day ahead of us. If they should loiter, we might come upon them."

The tension between them faded as they fell to discussing the number and placement of outriders. Grateful as he was for that, Gervase's nerves remained tight as bowstrings as they rode steadily onward. Despite the fact that Vallis and Lyle were up ahead, he feared they might be ambushed. In places the forest pressed so close to the trail they were forced to ride single file, in others the low-hanging branches afforded an excellent perch from which men might swing down and disarm his.

As the day wore on, Gervase considered stopping and waiting a day to let the brigands get farther ahead of them. He even considered turning back. But with no hope of replenishing their dwindling supplies, he couldn't risk that. So they traveled on till the forest began to thin. Calling a halt, Gervase rode to the tree line and scowled at the trail ahead.

It lacked an hour till sunset, yet the narrow dirt ribbon stood out pale against the dark stone as it wound its way up the face of the next mountain.

"We'll be obvious as a fly on blancmange," Vallis muttered.

Shielding his eyes, Gervase ran them up the trail from bottom to top and back again. "So would anyone else. I don't see anything moving up there."

"We were delayed whilst my lady tended the wounded players. The whoreson brigands are likely on the other side. If I recall correctly, the town of Le Vigan lies in the next valley. God spare them." Vallis crossed himself.

"They've the town wall to hide behind . . . providing they are not tricked or forced into letting these monsters inside." Their safety was not his worry, but he had responsibilities enough. Thanks in part to Catherine. Damn but she attracted unfortunates the way a dog did burrs. A flash near the crest of the mountain caught his attention. "Wait . . . what is that?"

"I saw it, too. Light on something shiny."

Alarm sent Gervase's heart racing. He thought he saw shapes moving on the trail. Another flash confirmed his worst fears. "Sunlight on armor. Quick, get back under the trees lest they spot us." He stared at the mountain till his eyes ached, trying to decide whether the distant figures were going up or down. After a few moments the flashing ceased. Had the men gone over the top or found shade?

"What will we do?" Vallis asked.

Gervase expelled air, but the tightness in his chest remained. "We haven't much choice. The horses are too

tired to go on and there is no shelter the way we came."
He wheeled the weary stallion and headed back to where
the others waited. "We will make camp inside the woods.
There will be no fires, and no one will stray beyond our
patrols. For any reason."

Gervase expected no complaints from his men or the
players; they were used to deprivation. But each night
Catherine had gotten fires for cooking and hot water for
washing. He looked over to catch her reaction just as
Tearlach extended his arms and lifted her from the saddle. With the child between them, their bodies didn't
touch, still Gervase thought the man's hands lingered
overlong before releasing her waist. Her simple smile of
thanks set his teeth on edge. The way she subtly arched
her back reminded him of the long hours she'd spent on
the trail, the strain doubtless made worse by the weight
of the babe.

He had the oddest wish to knead the knots from her
tired muscles, not as a prelude to seduction but simply to
offer aid. He found himself standing in front of her with
no memory of having moved. "Water could be heated if
'twould ease you," he said awkwardly.

She smiled. "That sounds like heaven, but I'd not endanger us all for my comfort. I will be fine once I've
worked out the stiffness." Turning, she lifted the braid
she'd taken to wearing. "If you could untie the sling, I'd
greatly appreciate it."

His noble urges of a moment ago fled. Now he wanted
to nibble the pale flesh she'd exposed. Would it taste as
sweet as her lips? Would she moan and lean back against
him?

"Gervase? Is aught wrong?" She glanced over her
shoulder.

Everything. "Nay." He loosened the knot, trying his damnedest not to touch her. His fingers brushed her nape and came away burning. The delicate shiver that shook her said she was as affected by the accident as he. "Catherine..."

She turned, holding the squirming infant before her like a shield. "I know." Her eyes were deep-set pools of longing. "I wish...I wish we had met years ago."

Gervase nodded. "I...I wish that, too. But 'tis too late. Even if I could offer you the kind of life you deserve, neither I nor my people could forget what your father did."

"You are wrong. My father didn't attack your home. Your uncle is either blind or a liar. If you could meet my father, you would know he could not do such a thing." She walked away, but her words lingered in Gervase's mind.

He'd not met the man, but he was coming to know and respect his daughter. Catherine spoke often of the things her father had taught her—like breaking a horse without whip or spurs. Would such a man be capable of rape and murder? But then, why would Uncle Bernard lie about seeing him at Alleuze?

Chapter Nine

Clouds obscured the moon, rendering the night as dark as Gervase's thoughts. Were the outlaws out there somewhere in the forest, waiting to attack the sleeping camp? With the wind moaning through the trees, making the bushes writhe and twist, 'twas impossible to tell if anything was on the move.

Afraid fatigue might cause his men to drowse at their posts, he'd agreed to take the second watch—from midnight till dawn—himself. Jumbled as his emotions were, there was no chance Gervase would sleep tonight.

"My father is innocent," Catherine had said, her gaze level, open, honest, willing him to believe.

Bah! She'd say anything to protect her precious sire. And he was only tempted to believe her because he lusted after her.

The snapping of a twig behind him brought Gervase around swiftly, sword drawn, body tensed in a fighter's crouch.

"'Tis just me, milord," purred a soft voice. Faye slipped from the shadows.

"You should be abed," Gervase mumbled.

She sidled closer, a blanket wrapped around her shoulders. "I came to thank ye for rescuing us. I've brought a bit of wine.'' As she stuck out the wineskin, the blanket parted, revealing a slim, naked thigh. "Are ye... interested, m'lord?"

Gervase's pulse raced, his blood heated and pooled in his loins. Perrin was right, it had been overlong since he'd bedded a woman. 'Twas abstinence that fed his unnatural desire for Catherine, and here was his chance to quench that thirst. "Aye, I find my mouth is suddenly dry." He reached for the wine, uncorked it and took a sip.

Faye stepped nearer, one slim hand on his chest, her legs brushing against his. Her eyes glittered provocatively.

Gervase's body quickened, but his mind remained curiously detached. Her musky woman's smell clogged his nostrils, making him long for Catherine's light, clean scent. Her hair was dark and tangled. He thought instead about unplaiting Catherine's thick braid and plunging his fingers into golden silk.

Cursing under his breath, Gervase shoved the cork into the wineskin and handed it back. "My thanks. Return to camp now."

Faye pressed herself against him. "But ye've a need I'd ease, milord. I'm accounted quite talented in that regard."

"I'm certain you are." His manhood urged him to find out. "But I am on watch." 'Twas a better excuse than the truth. He put his hands on Faye's shoulders to turn her away and caught sight of someone standing in the shadows. "Catherine?"

She stiffened as though he'd struck her, her face stark with misery. The tears shimmering in her eyes lanced through him like a hot blade. Despite all that had happened to her, she'd never cried till now. Her pain became his own.

"Catherine." Shoving Faye aside, he started toward her.

"Look out! Behind you!" Catherine screamed.

Instinct sent Gervase diving for the earth. He tucked, rolled and came up with his sword in one hand, body tensed to repel an attack.

"Hold! Mercy!" A fat man holding a cross before him staggered from the brush, fell to his knees and began to pray.

Gervase straightened slowly, weapon poised, wary eyes scanning the gloom for some sign this was a trick. "Catherine. Behind me," he commanded, wanting her close. "Who are you? What are you doing here?" he demanded of the blubbering man.

"I'm Father Ambroise." The man held the cross higher, his many chins quivering. "P-please...they took everything I had."

"Who?" Gervase relaxed fractionally as the priest began to blurt out a tale of ambush and thievery.

"Gervase!" Perrin charged onto the scene, sword aloft, three more men panting in his wake. All four checked their headlong dash when they spied the priest. "Who's this?" Perrin asked.

"A priest who had the misfortune to run into the brigands." Gervase sheathed his weapon and ordered the three men-at-arms to search the woods for any sign the priest had been followed.

"They're long gone." Father Ambroise heaved himself to his feet and shook his long black gown. Smeared with dirt and rent in places, it seemed to support his story, as did the scratches on his face and hands. "Disrespectful bastards. I told them I was a man of the cloth, but they buffeted me about, made sport of me. I—I feared they might even kill me."

"You'd not be the first. They've left death and pain in their wake," Gervase said grimly. "How did you manage to escape?"

"They found the skins of wine I was taking to Brother Bartholome. Whilst they were guzzling it down...with no appreciation for the fine vintage, I might add...I sneaked into the bushes and hid. My ass ran off the moment those fiends relieved her of the wineskins... faithless jade. I've been searching for her ever since." He peered anxiously at Gervase. "You haven't seen her wandering about, have you? She's a poor beast, but beneath my saddle are hidden the holy relics—"

"How come you to be carrying something so sacred and valuable without an armed escort?" asked Gervase.

"Well..." Father Ambroise's eyes, tiny as raisins in his pudding face, darted about evasively.

Gervase's suspicions returned. "Father..."

"Shame on you, interrogating poor Father Ambroise in such a fashion," Catherine exclaimed, stepping around Gervase and approaching the priest. "And after all he's been through."

The priest—if he was one—seized her hand like a lifeline, kissing it with what seemed undue fervor. "My lady, a thousand pardons for not acknowledging you sooner."

She smiled. " 'Tis we who should apologize for keeping you standing about when you are obviously hurt and exhausted. Come, I have medicines, food and drink at camp." She turned to leave.

Gervase caught hold of her arm to stay her. "Lady Catherine, I want to tell you..." *To explain about Faye,* he intended to say, but her cold look froze the words in his throat.

"'Tis not necessary. I assure you, I understand perfectly." Wrenching free, she marched away, her head high, the fat priest wheezing along behind her.

The knot in Gervase's chest wound tighter. He, who never explained, wanted to run after her, force her to listen. And then what? She was his prisoner, his ransom prize. There could be nothing between them. Mayhap 'twas better to end things this way.

Perrin's chuckle jerked Gervase from his gloomy thoughts. "I think the good father is a pardoner. You know, one of those priests who goes about to fairs and such selling absolution from broken vows and missed fasts."

"Aye, mayhap you are right." Gervase scowled. Despite the church's efforts to curtail such activity, many less devout clerics found it a way to make themselves rich. "Seems there are many types of thieves about on the roads these days."

"And we've had the misfortune to run into most of them. I suppose we'd best see if we can locate his ass, for Lady Catherine will doubtless insist on bringing him along and we're running short of mounts...unless you'd like to ask the lady to ride with you. Thor is strong enough to carry so slight a weight as hers in addition to your—"

"Absolutely not!" Gervase roared. "And we're leaving these leeches she's saddled us with at the next village we come to."

"Even the babe?"

"Aye. Especially the babe." Watching Catherine's eager if clumsy efforts to tend the infant tore at him, a constant reminder that Marie had been an indifferent mother to their child. If she hadn't been, would Eva have survived? Nay, he didn't want to blame anyone but Ruarke Sommerville.

The next day was the longest and most miserable Cat could ever remember. The weather had turned hot and humid; Jolie was fussy, and Cat's heart ached unbearably.

Gervase was a lecher, a worm, she told herself over and over. No better than Henry, for all his protests of honor. When she hadn't been quick enough to yield to him, he'd sought easier prey. Bah, Faye was welcome to him.

"I think the mite's cutting teeth," Ila said when they paused to rest in a wide place halfway up the mountain.

"Well, I wish they'd hurry and come in," Cat snapped, nerves worn thin by a night spent tossing, turning and yearning for what wasn't to be.

Jolie howled, face red and mottled, fists waving in the air.

"I'm sorry, sweetling. Oh, I wish there was something that would ease her discomfort."

"Here, let me take her a spell." Ila settled the bundle over her shoulder. "A bit of marjoram on the gums might help."

"We'll not find any herbs growing here." Cat glanced about their desolate surroundings. The sheer face of the cliff abutted the trail on the right and fell sharply away on the left. A few scraggly bushes clinging precariously to the stony soil and the scavengers that wheeled high overhead were the only signs of life. They'd been lucky to find water, she thought, watching the men lead the horses one by one to the trickle spilling from a cleft in the rocks.

Armand walked up carrying wooden cups and a leather skin. "Milord said we'd have to make do with water. The wine and ale must be rationed, having been depleted by the extra people.''

Angry as she was with him, Cat nonetheless gave Gervase high marks for generosity. A lesser man might have left those extra people by the side of the road. After all, they weren't Gervase's responsibility, and he was anxious to reach home. She took a cup and drank deep of the cool water. Ila did the same, then splashed a bit on Jolie's red face.

''I hate water,'' Faye announced. She rose from the rock where she'd been sitting. ''I'm going to ask Sir Gervase to make an exception for me. And he will, too.'' She flung a sly, smug glance in Cat's direction, then flounced off.

Don't look. Don't care, Cat warned herself, but her eyes followed the little hussy up the path to the spot where Gervase stood by himself. He'd removed his helmet, baring his sweaty head to the merciless sun. How tired and unhappy he looked. How she wished she could help him, Cat thought in the second before Faye reached him and his expression altered. Unable to bear seeing the tenderness she knew would replace his bleakness, she looked away.

''If I didn't know better, I'd think ye were in love with the curt young lord,'' Ila said thoughtfully.

''Nay.'' It came out more sharply than she'd intended. Cat sighed, idly pleating her dusty tunic. Mayhap if she'd been wearing gowns... ''He hates me.''

''Ye've not seen him follow ye about with his eyes.''

''Lust,'' Cat countered. ''He desires me... or he did before Faye joined us.''

Ila shifted Jolie to her other shoulder. The babe had quieted, which made Cat feel even more like a failure. ''Faye thinks she sees a way to do better than Tearlach.''

"Faye and Tearlach?" Cat looked over to where the sword swallower helped with the horses, his bare back and muscular arms glistening with water. "He is a hard worker."

"But not as handsome as Lord Gervase."

Cat sighed. Few men were. Unconsciously she looked for Gervase, alarm knotting her belly when she realized he and Faye had vanished. Had they sought out one of the small caves that dotted the mountainside?

"He sent her packing," Ila said, chuckling. "She's gone off to have a talk with Tearlach. About time, too. Yer knight took his horse up ahead to scout the trail, no doubt."

"He's not my knight."

Ila cocked her head, the lines around her sharp black eyes crinkling. "What is he to ye, then? Tearlach says his lordship rescued you from the outlaws, but I think there is more."

Cat opened her mouth to answer honestly, then reconsidered. It served no purpose to admit she'd not only been kidnapped, she'd been stupid enough to become enamored of her captor. The players had no horses and no weapons, except Tearlach's collapsing sword. "I'm grateful to Sir Gervase for saving me when my escort and I were attacked. 'Tis all."

"Is it?" Ila said, gray brows rising. "No wonder he watches ye so close, then. Must expect a fine reward for saving ye and returning ye to yer family."

Cat choked on a mouthful of water.

"Easy, dear lady." Father Ambroise bustled up and thumped her on the back. "I hope this rough living is not causing so fragile a lady as yourself to sicken."

"I am fine." And glad of the interruption. "But I'm not at all fragile," Cat added, smiling. Though she didn't approve of the cleric's calling, which made him little better than a merchant hawking his wares, he was a jolly rascal.

"All ladies are of a delicate disposition," the priest said stoutly, obviously hoping to pry open her purse with a bit of flattery. "A litter should be rigged for you. I'll speak to Sir Gervase myself about it."

"About what?" demanded that very knight, staring down at them like the wrath of God from atop his black stallion.

Father Ambroise stepped back. "Th-the Lady Catherine is far too delicate a woman to be riding about astride a—"

"Delicate?" Gervase threw back his head and laughed. "She may look like a lily, but I assure you her silken petals hide a core of tempered steel. Come, we must ride on if we're to reach the safety of Le Vigan's walls by tonight."

Tearlach and Faye were the last to join the procession, emerging from behind a boulder as the line of march passed by. His face was set and angry, hers tearstained. Watching them, Cat's own fury mounted. Men! Insensitive brutes the lot of them, who did their thinking with something other than their minds.

The trail widened and Cat edged Jock forward till she came abreast of Gervase. "Sir, a word if I might."

Gervase raised one dark brow, then gestured for Vallis to hang back. "I'd like to apologize for—"

"'Tis to Tearlach you should apologize. And to Faye, too," Cat snapped. "Turning the poor girl's head with your looks and position, causing her to cast aside a man she might wed when all you offer her is a few nights' fun tussling about in the bushes."

"So, you enjoy tussling in the bushes." He smiled, a soft, knowing smile that made her insides twist with need . . . and regret.

"I do not know . . . that is, of course not."

"What, did your young man . . . what was his name, ah, Henry . . . did Henry never oblige you by—"

"You bastard. How dare you fling that in my face." Intent on escape, Cat jerked back on her mount's reins, but Gervase caught the bridle and stayed her.

"Hold! This is a dangerous place to lose control of that temper of yours," he warned, casting an eye toward the sheer drop to the distant valley floor. When he looked at her again, the tension in his face eased. "I shouldn't have goaded you. The only defense I can offer is that my nerves are stretched tighter than lute strings. This trip was treacherous enough when we began. Now there's the added threat of outlaws lurking somewhere up ahead and six more defenseless souls to protect."

Cat nodded stiffly. "And I shouldn't have flown at you, 'tis just . . ." She averted her eyes, wishing she didn't recall the way her blood heated when he kissed her. How awful to crave with every fiber in her being that which she could never have. "I'm frightened. For all of us. I don't think I've ever been truly afraid before. 'Tis sobering to realize you were right. I have been cosseted, spoiled and sheltered my whole life."

"I was wrong about you. As wrong as I have ever been about anything," Gervase said, his voice suddenly deep and raspy. "You are braver than most men I know, loyal and compassionate. As these good people you've saved will attest."

Cat forced herself to laugh before he made her cry. "You make me sound like a faithful hound."

"And witty, too, which my hound is not." He grinned, then sobered. "This has been difficult . . . far more difficult than I'd imagined when I undertook this scheme. I wish . . ." He sighed. "It doesn't matter. The course is set. I've no choice but to go on."

"But you do," Cat said earnestly. "You only kidnapped me because you thought you had a grudge against my father, but you are mistaken in that. You have only to return me to him, I will explain, and all will be as it was before."

His expression hardened. "I doubt any of us will come through this journey unchanged. We are approaching the summit. I want you back in the middle of the line where 'tis safer."

"I will, if you'll promise to leave Faye alone. Ila tells me Tearlach is interested in wedding the girl."

"Really? She did not seem like a betrothed woman when she sought me out last night," he said, frowning.

"She sought you?" When he nodded, the pain in her chest eased. "I am sorry I misjudged you."

Gervase blinked. "You believe me, just like that?"

"Aye." Cat paused, seeing a way to drive home a point. "You are not the sort to lie about such things. Nor have you any reason to do so since we are naught to each other. If you desired her, you would have—" She stopped. "Why did you wince?"

We are naught to each other. 'Twas the truth, yet he wished it weren't so. "I am just surprised you would trust me, after . . ."

"After you kidnapped me." She pursed her lips. "'Twas wrong, but I forgive you. 'Twas done in the mistaken belief you were righting a wrong done to you. We have only known each other a short time, but I realize you are a good man. I hope you think the same of

me . . . and mayhap wonder how such a person as myself
could have sprung from an evil man. I am hoping you
will soon believe me when I say you are mistaken about
my father.''

Gervase wanted to believe her. But having lived with
the army, he knew men could be different in battle than
they were at home. There was something about war that
brought out the beast in some. Most damning of all, his
uncle had no reason to falsely accuse Lord Ruarke of
murder. Still now was not the time to quarrel over what
neither of them could change. Instead, he changed the
subject, a ploy that ever served him well. ''You doubtless play a hell of a chess game, my lady.''

Surprisingly she accepted his response with only a
slight frown. ''Mayhap I'll give you a game when we
reach Alleuze.''

He rewarded her with a smile. ''Aye. Get back to the
middle of the line, now.'' He paused. ''I—I did not tus-
sle about in the bushes with Faye last night. And I think
you know why.''

Cat nodded, shocked by how quickly his words made
her heart leap. ''You will be careful, won't you?''

''Recent events to the contrary, I am always careful.''
He lowered his visor and moved away, leaving her to
watch, her chest feeling oddly tense and hollow. If only. . .

From the back side of the mountain, Gervase stared
out over the broad, grassy plain, noting every tumble of
rocks and clump of trees that might hide a band of reiv-
ers. There were far too many for his comfort, especially
along the river that cut through the valley. The track to
Le Vigan, some four miles to the north, lay close to the
river . . . too close. He had no desire to find himself
trapped with his back to the water, not clad in so much

steel and with the memory of his near drowning so fresh. He said as much to Perrin.

"Aye, but how else are we to go?"

"I know of a lesser-used trail along the foothills," Father Ambroise interjected.

Gervase whirled. "I told you to wait with the others."

"Aye." The priest's fleshy lips pursed. "I'm the last man to put myself at risk, but I'd reach Le Vigan without running into those devils again, and I like not the look of yon road."

"Nor do I." Gervase glanced skyward. The sun had just poked above the peaks, bathing the valley in soft light and lengthening the shadows beneath the trees. "How do you know this trail?"

"As I told dear Lady Catherine, I come here each year to attend the fair at Le Vigan . . . the folks expect me, are eager for the chance to remit their sins—"

"Get on with it," Gervase growled, despising the overfed cleric and his greedy calling.

"Aye, well, in the hills a mile north of here dwells a friend of mine, Brother Bartholome."

"Another pardoner?"

"Nay." The priest gave a self-deprecating shrug. "He's a much better priest than I. He's a hermit . . . most dedicated. However he does have a fondness for Gascon wine."

"The wine you say the brigands stole from you."

"You don't believe me?"

"Let us just say I find it odd you escaped the outlaws unharmed, and we found your mule with your packs intact."

"Except for the wine. They beat me and took it," he cried. "I assure you I am not in league with those villains. Here . . ." He rummaged in the pack behind his saddle and produced a feather. "I swear it on this feather from the archangel Gabriel's own wing."

Gervase looked at the bedraggled white plume and laughed. "Where on earth did you get that?"

"From the bishop's legate in Avignon. 'Twas blessed by the pope," the priest assured him most earnestly.

Then he's a bigger crook than you are. But time was wasting, and Gervase much preferred the trail along the mountain to the one in the center of the valley, exposed to any who might be watching. "Very well. Show us this track, but I will slit your fat gullet if we fall into a trap."

With the women in the middle, Gervase in the lead of a ten-man group and Perrin commanding a like number in the vanguard, they set out along the hillside trail. Gervase hoped they'd be less visible moving through the deep shadows beneath the trees, but faces were grim, nerves stretched taut by apprehension. *Damn,* he wished he'd never begun this foolhardy scheme. If he hadn't wanted revenge, his men would be safely at Alleuze trying to scratch a living from the rocky soil and Catherine would be at court, mayhap betrothed to Sir Archie.

Well, that he didn't regret. The thought of her wed to another was . . . intolerable. Still his conscience prickled. What would happen to her after she was ransomed and returned to her world? Thanks to him, no decent man would take her to wife. The only other option open to a woman was the convent, but he couldn't see his high-spirited, hot-passioned Catherine as a nun. In seeking to ruin her sire, he'd ruined her, as well.

"Milord!" Lyle hurtled down the trail and drew rein so sharply his mount danced. "There are men up ahead."

A spate of questions drew the unwelcome news that five men waited in the trees a quarter mile on. The outlaws? If so 'twas only half of them. The other five were out there somewhere, waiting to ambush the rear of the column or leap out on the vulnerable middle. Turning in the saddle, Gervase whispered, "Swords out. The woods have eyes." Barely heeding the ripple of voices as the orders passed from man to man, he reviewed his options. Few, and none of them good.

His men were superior in number and fighting ability, but strung out as they were, 'twould be easy for the brigands to hide in the thick forest and pick them off one by one. Retreat wasn't an option. Nor was remaining here.

Armand rode up the line. "Perrin sent me to ask what your orders are, milord."

"We go forward." Gervase swallowed against the sudden tightness in his throat. "Close ranks. Watch your backs and the man behind, sing out if you see anything. We will keep to this pace for a quarter mile...till we reach the spot where they wait. On my signal, we will charge past their position. Once the women and the players are safely by, we will wheel, stand and prepare to repulse the brigands' attack."

Armand's eyes widened. "You think they'll do that, even though there are fewer of them?"

"I would if I saw my prize bolt from the trap." Gervase smiled faintly. "And, too, they will likely think we flee in panic and think to pick us off one by one. When we turn on them—

"The element of surprise will shift to us."

"Good lad." Judas but he looked so young. "I will want you and Lyle to go with Lady Catherine and the others."

"But...but my place is with you. Who will act your squire?"

He'd not need one. This skirmish would be swift, merciless and dirty, not a chivalrous encounter between knights who fought by a code of honor. And he wanted the lad out of it, but he couldn't dent Armand's pride. "Vallis will stand behind me. We cannot leave the lady and the others unprotected. I will fight the better knowing you and Lyle look to their safety."

Armand grudgingly accepted the task and went off to spread the word. When he'd gone, Gervase motioned Lyle to him and repeated the orders, adding, "When I give the word, I want you and Armand to sweep by with Catherine and the players. Ride like hell. Don't stop for anything till you reach Le Vigan's gates."

The veteran soldier frowned. "But ye'll need every sword."

"One more won't make a difference. And protecting the noncombatants would divert our attention from the fighting."

"Aye," Lyle muttered, and returned to his post.

Gervase spared a quick glance at Catherine's stricken face. *I am sorry, for so many things.* But there was no time for guilt or recriminations. Turning, he jammed his visor down and gave the order to move out, conscious that never had he ridden into battle with so much to lose. If aught happened to her, he'd never forgive himself.

Somewhere out there the brigands watched and waited.

Catherine shivered, eyes darting nervously about as they plodded through the woods. After the hot climb up the face of the mountain, the cool, damp shade had been most welcome. Word of the ambush changed everything. Now the shadows cast by the thick canopy of leaves gave the forest a sinister quality. At any moment she expected bloodthirsty savages to leap out and devour them. Frightened as she was, she balked at Gervase's plan.

"You must let us ride on alone, Lyle," she said again. "He will need you and Armand to fight beside him."

Lyle sighed noisily. "I've got my orders, milady. Gervase would fight with only half a mind did he not know ye were safe."

"I forgot what a valuable prize I am," she snapped.

"If ye're thinking that's the only reason he's doing this, then ye're not half as clever as I thought," he growled back. "Now make ready...we're nearly there."

"I am not going to ride off and leave—"

"*A moi!* For Alleuze and God!" Gervase roared. The cry was taken up by his men, mingling with the thud of hooves as the horses were spurred down the woodland trail.

Catherine was swept along like a leaf caught up in one of the rushing mountain streams. The landscape passed in a blur of green and brown. Out of the corner of her eye, she glimpsed a figure in the brush. A bearded man, mouth agape, sword raised. Before he could strike, they were by him. Then they were flashing past the front of the column, leaving Gervase and the others behind. She tried to stop, but Lyle had the gelding on a lead rope and was racing to outstrip the wind.

Branches tore at Catherine's clothes, leaves slapped at her face, forcing her to bury it in Jock's coarse mane and cling for her very life. They rode till she thought the horses must surely drop from exhaustion for she could scarcely keep in the saddle her muscles ached so.

Finally Lyle slowed them to a walk, then, mercifully, called a halt. For a few moments they stood still, drooping in their tracks. "We've only come a mile, but the horses'll not stand the pace," he muttered.

"Nor will we." Struggling for breath, Cat braced both hands on the pommel and looked round the tiny glade where they'd paused. What she wouldn't give to plunge her sweaty body into a cool stream, but there was no water in sight. Uphill lay a tumble of boulders, some two stories tall. The downward slope was covered with thick brush and berry bushes. "How did you and Jolie fare?" she asked Ila, who had insisted on taking the babe.

Ila's hair flew around her in a gray tangle, and she gulped air like a beached fish but managed a smile. "Winded but alive." She peeled back the edges of the blanket sling and peered at the babe's sweaty red face. "What say ye, little one?"

Black eyes sparkling, Jolie crowed and beat her tiny fists on the pillowy breasts that had cushioned her ride. Obviously she was none the worse for wear. Bevis was another matter. He slumped against the neck of his mount, face gray, eyes closed. Had it not been for Faye, who rode pillion behind him, the injured acrobat would likely have fallen off during their wild dash.

"He fainted at the first jolt to his leg," Faye murmured.

Cat nodded. "'Tis just as well, poor man." Tempted as she was to try and revive him, mayhap 'twould not be a kindness. "Can you hold him the rest of the way, do you think?"

"Aye. He doesn't weigh much more than I do, and he'd stand no chance mounted alone," Faye said in a surprising show of selflessness. Mayhap there was hope for her after all.

"Where's the priest?" Armand asked.

Lyle swore. "Milord didn't trust that priest . . . feared he might be in league with the brigands. Guess this proves—"

"Hark! What is that?" Lyle cocked his head and stared back the way they'd come. The trail was hidden by a bend, but the sounds of someone crashing toward them were clearly audible. "Quick, everyone into the rocks." Grabbing hold of the gelding's reins, he dragged Cat off the trail and around one of the boulders while Armand did the same with Faye and Ila.

No sooner were they hidden, than Lyle said, "Armand, stay here with milady whilst I draw them off." He was gone before anyone could protest.

Over the terrified thudding of her heart, Cat heard Lyle dash off, followed closely...too closely, by the rushing hooves of other horses. How many? One? Two? More? *Dear God, keep them safe.* Biting her lip to still its trembling, she waited.

An eternity seemed to pass, yet no one came from either direction. It shouldn't have taken Gervase this long to dispatch the outlaws. Surely Lyle must have been overtaken by now. If the pursuers had turned out to be Gervase and his men, they would all have come back by now. That they hadn't, boded ill.

"Do you suppose they're dead?" Armand whispered.

Ila moaned and Faye sobbed. Cat saw the girl was near to collapsing and taking the unconscious Bevis with her. Her pathetic whimperings fed Cat's own sense of hopelessness.

"Fear is a more formidable weapon than any devised by man," her father had often said. "Yield to it, and you are lost."

What would her father do? What would Gervase do? Not stay here, clearly, and wait for the enemy to find them. Nor could they use the trail. Their best chance seemed to lie in going up. Higher ground might afford a view of the valley and some hint as to what had happened. Or mayhap a cave in which to hide.

"Come, we must leave here," Cat whispered. Before they went, she bade Armand change places with Faye, who seemed barely capable of holding herself together much less seeing to Bevis.

Taking the lead herself, Cat urged her terrified charges around one boulder, then another. There was a rough path of sorts, no doubt used by the forest creatures. As they climbed, the trees thinned and the slope grew steeper. But looking back over her shoulder, she could not see past the thick trees to the trail and whatever had ha—

"What are ye doing here?" inquired a rusty voice.

Cat jerked to a halt and gaped at the man who watched them from a flat-topped rock. Brigand, was her first thought, but if so, he didn't look the part. Thin to the point of gauntness, he wore a russet robe, so frayed and patched no pilgrim would even own it. His bald pate was compensated for by a gray beard that reached his waist. He rather resembled the wood sprites who peopled the tales told to children. "Who are you?" she asked.

"I might ask ye the same," he said, pale eyes wary in a thin, wrinkled face as weathered as the rocks.

Behind her, Cat heard Faye whimpering softly, and even Ila had taken to praying. Armand had ridden forward, but he was only a boy and encumbered with Bevis's unconscious weight. 'Twas up to her. "I am Catherine Sommerville, and these are my companions. We were beset by brigands. Y-you aren't one of them, are you?"

"Me? Nay, I'm Brother Bartholome."

Cat relaxed fractionally. "The friend of Father Ambroise." Clearly hermiting wasn't as profitable as pardoning.

"How come ye to know Father Ambroise?" he asked more warily.

"He is, or was, traveling with us, but we became separated whilst escaping and know not what happened to the priest or to any of our... our guard." Her thoughts swerved to Gervase, then away, the pain of wondering if he was all right nearly unbearable. "Could you offer us shelter?"

"I'm a hermit. I've no fit place for visitors." He cocked his head. "Besides, ye've not told me who ye are. What's a girl doing riding about dressed as a lad and leading—"

"I will explain all, I swear, only we are exhausted and this man is wounded. Could you not at least take us to a place where we might rest? And give us a bit of water? I have a few coins—"

"Nay, I have forsworn wealth and worldly things." Brother Bartholome stroked his beard, his sharp eyes flicking over them. "Nor am I supposed to seek the society of others, but I did not exactly seek ye out. I suppose 'twould not hurt to let ye rest in my cave till ye've recovered yer strength."

"Thank you, Brother. We'll not impose on your generosity." But where would they go? If Gervase and the others were dead, how would they get to Le Vigan and back to Bordeaux? If Gervase was dead, did she care if she lived?

'Twas then Cat realized she'd crossed over from caring about Gervase to loving him.

God help her.

Chapter Ten

Cat stood in the entrance to the cave, watching the misty valley far below. Fog rose like smoke from the river that snaked its way through the trees. Dawn's golden fingers crept in, banishing the darkness from the land if not from her spirit. She and the jongleurs had found warmth and safety in the hermit's cave, but of the others, there had been no sign.

Oh, Gervase. Where are you? She bent her head against the pain of losing him. A few lingering raindrops dripped from the overhang and splashed into the puddles at her feet. Last night they had mingled with tears that even now were close to the surface. At the sound of footsteps, she turned to find the good Brother Bartholome at her elbow with a cup of warm wine.

"'Tis locally grown, but quite fine."

"It could be vinegar and I'd not notice." Cat tried to smile, knew by his frown she had failed. "Thank you for your kindness." She drank deep, surprised to feel the heat of the wine ignite in her veins, steadying her limbs. "What is in this?"

"Herbs."

"What kind? Do they grow nearby?"

No reply. Typical. The priest was as sparing with his words as he'd been generous with his possessions, sharing his limited food stores and limitless healing skills with them. Still silent, he rubbed a gnarled hand over his face, then glared down the rocky slope at the trees ranged far below them like fat, black mushrooms. "No carrion birds. A good sign."

Cat shivered, recalling the vultures at the farms. "Does that mean no one is dead?" It seemed impossible.

In the harsh wash of daylight, Brother Bartholome looked more frail than he had last night by firelight, his skin stretched parchment thin over prominent bones. But she'd watched him work tirelessly to reset Bevis's leg, tend their other smaller hurts and milk his own goat for Jolie.

"Mayhap buried."

"What? Oh, the..." Cat stumbled and couldn't go on. "I...I think I would know if he was...gone."

"He who rescued you."

"Rescued?" Belatedly she recalled her story. "Aye. Sir Gervase, the knight who rescued me from the outlaws."

"Hmm." His pale eyes regarded her shrewdly. Too shrewdly. "I sense you are confused, daughter."

Cat sighed. "Aye." She leaned back against the solid wall of the cave, scarcely feeling the chill for the ice inside her. Suddenly the burden of her plight seemed too great to bear alone. "He kidnapped me...for ransom, but... Oh, Brother Bartholome, how do I explain what I do not understand myself?"

"You love him."

"Aye." Cat straightened, fists clenched at her sides. "But I should not. He stole me from my family to get money from my father, and he brought me to...to this."

"Do you insult my abode?" He smiled wryly.

The unexpected humor startled a chuckle from Cat. "Your cave is the nicest I've ever visited, and I do thank you for your hospitality, and the care of my friends. Nay, 'tis just . . ."

"Hmm." He glanced down the mountain.

"He can never love me. He blames my sire for the deaths of his wife and child and the destruction of his home."

"Is your father a murderer?"

"He . . . he has killed in battle, this I know, but women and children . . ." Cat shook her head. "He is not that kind of man."

"And what kind of man is this knight who kidnaps women?"

"I am not certain." Cat lifted her face to the freshening breeze, but it failed to scour away the pain and confusion. "He is strong and brave, loyal to his people and, though this scheme of his might not make you think so, he is honorable."

"And handsome? I recall women value that in a man."

"Some women, but an error in judgment taught me to value men's deeds over their looks."

"And that is what confuses you, is it not? You do not trust your feelings for a man who would stoop to kidnap and ransom."

"He's desperate and deeply scarred by this cruel war. His people are cold and hungry because their fields were burned and their homes destroyed. What he seeks is justice . . . and the coin to provide for his dependents. How can I fault such noble goals?"

"You plead his case most eloquently."

"Aye, I do. Yet all the while I decry his methods."

"You are a most unusual woman." His chuckle sounded rusty. "I thought as much last night when I realized that the man I'd seen bravely leading his flock up through the rocks was a lady."

"My parents taught me to do what was needful." Cat looked down toward the valley, scanning the broken ribbon of brown that marked the trail they'd taken yesterday. "I have to go and see for myself what has happened."

The hermit stroked his beard. " 'Twould be better if I went."

"I couldn't send you into danger for a matter that is not your concern," she said gently.

"And I could tell you that all men are my concern." He cocked his head. "For all I know, your sire may indeed have butchered the people of Alleuze. Men, even good ones, can sometimes run to madness during a battle. But I do find that as the branches are pruned, so grows the tree. You, my lady, were tended by a wise and gentle gardener."

"If by that you mean my parents too often spared the rod, I fear you are correct. I'm far too willful for my own good."

"You've a stout yet kind heart. I know of few priests who tend their flocks as assiduously as you have these poor people you've taken under your wing. Now if you will wait here with them, I will go down and look for your knight."

Cat laid a hand on his arm. "But Brother, I should—"

"Nay. I can come and go more quickly and silently. I've lived here for twenty years and know every trail for miles about. Why, I could walk all the way to Le Vigan on the backs of these mountains and no one would see— wait, someone comes."

Cat started and looked around, but all she saw were rocks and trees, all she heard was the wind rustling through them. "Bro—"

"Hush. Into the cave. Warn the others to be quiet and don't come out till I call."

Cat hurried down the dark, twisting corridor that led into the heart of the mountain. 'Twas familiar ground for she'd paced it many times last night, forced inside by the rain, yet not wanting to disturb the others with her sleepless thrashings.

She slowed her steps on the threshold of the cave and peered inside. The single chamber was as large as the great hall back home in Wilton. At one end a candle burned on an altar hewed from solid rock. The other was lined with rough wooden shelves for storing the hermit's herbs and potions. A small fire burned within a circle of stones in the center of the cave, the smoke drifting upward to vent through a hole in the vaulted ceiling. By that meager light she made out the shapes of her friends still sleeping off the effects of their hazardous journey.

Satisfied they'd be quiet, she spun on her heel and rushed back to the surface. Careful to stay well back in the shadows, she stared at Brother Bartholome silhouetted against the dawn sky. His fingers toyed with the wooden rosary at his waist, and she unconsciously prayed with him. Then she heard the rattle of hooves on stone. Only one horse, she thought, but didn't relax. It could be an outlaw scout.

"Hello the cave," shouted a cheery voice.

"Father Ambroise. How good to see you." The hermit left the mouth of the cave and went out to greet his friend.

Cat started after him, then recalled Gervase's concern that the priest was working with the brigands. Sick with apprehension, she listened to the priests exchange news.

"Bartholome, I have had such a journey. Twice I've been beset by ruthless cutthroats," the priest exclaimed. "I'm a mass of cuts and bruises, and they stole your wine."

"I can live without the wine. Thank God for your safe deliverance from those devils."

"God had help from the sword of one Sir Gervase and his men." Creaking leather and loud groans marked the priest's dismount. His mule brayed in relief. "The fighting was fierce and bloody. I've never been so terrified in all my life."

Cat squirmed. What of Gervase and the others?

"And where are these men now?" the hermit asked.

"They search for the lady who was with us." Father Ambroise coughed. "If you've a bit of wine to ease my parched throat, I'll tell you the whole of it."

Cat could wait no longer. Bursting from the cave, she skittered down the trail in a hail of fine stones. "What of Gervase?" she demanded, grabbing the priest by the front of his fine robes and giving him a shake.

"Lady Catherine!" Father Ambroise made a hasty sign of the cross. "Thank God, you are alive."

"I know about me. What of the others? What of Gervase?"

"Alas." The twinkle fled Father Ambroise's eyes.

Cat's heart shriveled. "He . . . he is dead?"

"Nay. Well, I'm not certain. You see, he went to Le Vigan and they thought he was an outlaw, so they locked him up and—"

"Who are they? Why did Gervase go to Le Vigan?" Cat shouted.

"Easy, my child." Brother Bartholome patted her shoulder and gently pried her fingers from Father Ambroise's robe. "Clearly this tale is a tangled one. It's beginning to rain again. Come within where we can unravel the details in comfort."

Cat agreed, but there was naught comfortable in the story the priest told. Gervase and his men had been successful in overpowering the outlaws, killing or capturing all ten while suffering only minor wounds themselves. The victory soured when they found Lyle dead, herself and the others missing.

"Sir Gervase mourned the loss of his man, but was glad his squire had succeeded in getting you and the jongleurs safely away," Father Ambroise added. "We gathered up the dead, the wounded and the outlaws' booty and marched toward Le Vigan. Sir Gervase was like a hound on a scent, examining every tree we passed for some sign of you, my lady." He paused for a sip of wine, then continued. "By the time we reached the city I could tell his nerves were stretched thin by the battle and the uncertainty over your circumstances."

"I should have gone on to Le Vigan."

The priest shook his head. "Nay, 'tis a blessing you did not, for it seems the town was in league with the brigands."

"What?" exclaimed Brother Bartholome. "That's impossible. The mayor, George Berger, is an old friend. An honorable man."

"Aye, that he was, but he is mayor there no longer. When we arrived the gates were locked for the night and the watchman bade us come back in the morn. Sir Gervase refused, demanding to know the whereabouts of his people, three women, three men and a babe. The guard fetched the mayor. 'Twas not Berger, but a man named

Emile Sauveur who mounted the walls and shouted down that they had admitted no such a group. The knight called him a liar and threatened to besiege Le Vigan if they didn't show you at once."

"That doesn't sound like Sir Gervase."

"He was frantic to get you back. The mayor accused us of being the brigands who terrorized the area. Sir Gervase told him we'd killed the outlaws and had their bodies brought close to the wall. The mayor and his guard came out from the postern gate, a rough-looking lot, I thought. Sir Gervase bent and uncovered the face of the outlaw leader. Sauveur cursed, drew a cudgel from beneath his cloak and bashed the knight over the head."

"Merciful God!" Cat took a deep breath, fighting panic.

"Nay. He wore his helmet and was thus only dazed, but before we could go to his aid, the mayor had a dagger pressed to Sir Gervase's throat. He forced us to stand by whilst his guards dragged the good knight within the city."

"Sweet Mary," Cat whispered. "Why would they do that?"

"As I said, they were in league with the outlaws. It seems their leader was Vachel Sauveur, the mayor's brother." Father Ambroise looked away, and Cat knew there was more.

She clenched her fists so tightly her nails dug into her palms. "Will they allow us to ransom him?"

"Nay. Sir Perrin already offered everything we have—horses, armor, the outlaws' plunder and my sacred relics. Emile wants an eye for an eye. On the morrow, he plans to open the yearly fair with a drawing and quartering."

Gervase. Cat closed her eyes on a wave of pain so strong she swayed where she sat. A gnarled hand came up to steady her.

"We will pray for him," Brother Bartholome said. "And then we will find a way to get you safely back to Bordeaux."

Cat forced her eyes open, vision blurring with tears as she glanced around the circle of concerned faces. Armand, Ila with baby Jolie in her lap, Faye, Bevis propped up on his elbows. She'd known these people only a few days, yet the terrible things they'd survived together made it seem like a lifetime. "I would greatly appreciate your help in seeing my friends to safety, but I must find a way to free Sir Gervase."

Wouldn't you know they'd lock him in a cellar, Gervase thought as the door banged shut, trapping him in the dark. The clang of a bar dropping across the door shattered the last of his nerve. It was the oubliette all over again. Shivering, he lay on the dirt floor where they'd tossed him, dazed as much by the turn of events as from the blow Emile had dealt him.

He must have slept, because when he awoke his flesh was nearly as cold as the ground. His body ached from the battle he'd fought with the outlaws and from the cuffs meted out by the guards as they dragged him through town. Apparently Vachel Sauveur had been a popular man.

Damn, how had Le Vigan come to this? he wondered, postponing the moment when he'd have to deal with his surroundings. Last year when he'd passed through here, it had been a quiet little mountain town. Remembering the bleak faces of the few townsfolk he'd glimpsed as he'd been hustled from the gate, he decided Emile was not their *elected* mayor. Doubtless he and Vachel had taken over the town and used it as a base from which to loot the countryside. How many were they? Would Perrin be able to get into Le Vigan before tomorrow's festivities?

And where the hell was Catherine?

Concern for her forced Gervase to open his eyes. The yawning blackness forced them shut again. Damn. Damn, he hated the dark. Sweat broke out on his back, sliding down his spine beneath the woolen tunic. Panic lapped at the edges of his mind, sucking at it as the tide did the sand. *Idiot. You'll be no use to anyone if you do not get past this unreasoning fear.*

Clenching his teeth, Gervase rolled over, forced his eye open and looked around. As his eyes grew accustomed to the gloom, he realized the darkness wasn't total. A bit of light came in through a small opening high on the wall. This wasn't an oubliette, but a storage room. He crawled around it, using his hands and nose to assess the contents. Kegs of wine, sacks of grain, spices, dried meats, wooden chests and even bolts of cloth. Likely the ill-gotten gains of Vachel's raids.

They'd given him naught to eat or drink, so he helped himself to wine and meat, then dragged a keg over, stood on it and peered out a window scarcely larger than his face. It gave him a ground-level view of the town square, where preparations were under way for tomorrow's fair. From the position of the sun, he guessed it was nearly noon. Already some of the merchants had set up their stalls. A pie man hawked his wares to the crowd gathered to watch the building of a gallows.

Gervase's blood ran cold when he realized Emile intended to have him dragged up those steps hanged, drawn and quartered come morn. Not without a fight. Not without knowing for certain that Catherine was safe.

He jumped down and searched for anything he might use as a weapon. They'd stripped him of his mail, armor and boots, leaving him clad in a woolen tunic and hose. Accustomed to the weight of his armor and sword, he felt vulnerable as a naked babe. From the bottom of one of the chests, he unearthed an ordinary eating knife and set to work trying to loosen the door hinges. He'd been working for some time when a shout from the market square drew him back to the window.

A troupe of traveling players entertained a growing crowd of townspeople and Sauveur's soldiers. A woman with pale braids and swirling crimson skirts danced to the sprightly chords of a flute, while a brawny, bare-chested man strode about swallowing and disgorging a sword.

He knew that man. 'Twas Tearlach.

Bloody hell! Was he in with the brigands, too?

Nay, Tearlach had fought beside him in battle yesterday, felling outlaws right and left with a borrowed weapon. Damn, why had Tearlach brought his troupe here? Didn't he realize Le Vigan was a den of thieves? He must, for he'd been there when Gervase had been taken. So what...?

Catherine!

Gervase groaned out loud, frantically searching the crowded square for the dancer with the blond braids. Catherine. It must be her, for Faye had dark hair. Damn her impetuous hide. Glad as he was to know she was alive, he'd throttle her for this. The players had moved off, taking their audience with them, but Gervase spotted another familiar face.

Father Ambroise stood in the doorway of the fine stone house across the way, talking with Emile Sauveur himself. Seen in daylight, Sauveur resembled a great dirty bear, his hair tangled and matted, his girth stretching the seams of a velvet surcoat that likely belonged to some dead noble. Whatever was the priest about? Gervase wondered, watching Sauveur's coarse features slide from belligerent to wary to resigned as the priest spoke. Finally Sauveur shrugged and nodded curtly.

Flashing that slippery smile of his, the priest made the sign of the cross over Sauveur's forehead, then bustled off. Dieu, was there no limit to what filth Ambroise would bless for profit? Gervase wondered, vaguely noting the thin, tattered priest who hurried after the pardoner. No doubt a pupil. Judas, what had France and the church come to?

Gervase stayed at the window till dusk fell and people drifted off to their homes, alternately buoyed by hope that his friends were nearby and strangled by fear that they'd been caught by Sauveur. Call it the desperate hope of a condemned man, but he knew Tearlach and Ambroise were here to free him. What terrified him was the certainty that Catherine was right in the middle of this scheme. Even if Perrin and his men had somehow gotten inside the town, too, how could they overpower Sauveur's soldiers? Last night the man had boasted of having a hundred mercenaries.

Damn. Better they had left him to his fate than that Cat and the others should perish trying to rescue him. Sick with dread, Gervase climbed down from his perch. His legs were stiff and cramped from remaining in one place for so long. He paced between the kegs and sacks, scarcely noticing the darkness for his own troubled thoughts. When the cramping eased, he went to work on the door hinges. Made of iron, they were impervious to his blade, but he hacked away at the wood holding them in place, working by feel till his hands were torn and slippery with blood.

A flare of excited voices pulled him back to the window. Torches had been lit in the square. The soldiers had rolled out kegs of wine and sat drinking under the stars. They'd finished the gallows and set up two chairs in front of it. So Emile might view the hanging in comfort, Gervase mused, then he saw something that raised his gorge. They'd propped Vachel's dead body up in the other chair.

"''Tis only fitting my brother should watch while his murder is punished,'' Emile shouted, stepping back to study the scene. The torchlight caught in his eyes, making them glitter with unholy fire. "Fetch Vachel a cup and let us drink to the morrow and the knight's death.'' Emile was either drunk, mad, or both.

Gervase's stomach knotted. He started back toward the hinges, his flagging muscles spurred by what he knew lay in store if he didn't get out. The grating of the bar being lifted stopped him mid-stride. Had Emile sent for him? Did he intend to torture him first? Palming the eating knife, Gervase ran to flatten himself against the wall behind the door, braced for a fight.

It creaked open, flooding the room with light from the smoking torch in the guard's hand. "Still don't know why Emile's letting him have a priest,'' the man grumbled.

"All men, even one such as this knight, are deserving of God's blessing,'' intoned Father Ambroise. He stuck his head into the store room and exclaimed, "Why, he's gone.''

"What?'' Shoving the priest aside, the guard blundered in. Just as Gervase tensed to ambush him, the guard grunted and pitched forward, landing facedown on the dirt floor.

"Gervase?" hissed a familiar voice.

"Perrin?" Gervase looked around the door, scarcely able to believe 'twas his cousin who stood on the threshold wearing an odd assortment of rags with a sword in one hand and another in his belt. "By all that's holy... how did you get in here?"

"By God's grace and Lady Cat's clever ruse," Father Ambroise replied, grinning broadly. "Some of the townsmen recalled me from last year and so the guards admitted me for the fairing."

"I'm supposed to be a tumbler," Perrin said, his fair skin flushed with embarrassment.

"And Catherine?" Gervase asked, voice low and raw.

Both men looked at their boots. Perrin sighed. "Well, Tearlach said, and I was forced to agree, that a troupe of players without a dancing girl would be most suspect. Especially since Emile knew we were likely still in the area. 'Twas hard enough to disguise the rest of our men as farmers and merchants come for the festival. That we did with the clothes, goods and wagons Vachel has stolen. But Faye was so terrified, I thought she'd give the whole thing away. So..."

"So naturally Catherine put her head into the lion's mouth." For him. The tightness in Gervase's throat spread to his chest.

Perrin laid a hand on his shoulder. "She's been guarded every moment, I swear. And she has been invaluable in organizing the townspeople. They were skeptical of us, but the presence of a woman eased their fears that we might be another band of brigands wanting to seize the town. They are armed as best we could and ready to rise up against the outlaws on our signal."

"Where is she now?"

"In hiding at the home of Master Michel, the wine merchant. 'Twas he who supplied the wine the soldiers have been drinking so liberally. With any luck, many will be too drunk to fight."

Gervase nodded. "She should not have endangered herself for me," he said stiffly, fear knotting in his gut. "Damn. Why would she put herself at risk to save me?"

"Because she loves you," Father Ambroise said cheerfully.

"I don't want her love," Gervase snarled. But he did. The need to love and be loved by her was a physical ache deep in his soul. If only, he thought, then stopped himself. It couldn't be.

"We've no time to discuss this now," Perrin said. Handing Gervase one of the swords, he herded him out the door and into the musty corridor. "I know you'll feel as naked as I do without armor, but got up as we were, there was no way to bring it with us. Besides, Emile's men have set aside their mail . . . excepting for those atop the city walls. Come." He led the way up the stairs of the old building and paused to look out the door.

"Our men?" Gervase whispered as they moved into the street. 'Twas deserted with nary a torch to dispel the gloom.

"In place at strategic points around the town. Each has a group of townsmen under his command. Vallis will bar the doors of the barracks and contain the mercenaries within. I thought you and I would each take one of the two gates, where the fighting is bound to be the fiercest. The citizens who are not armed will lock their doors and hurl things down on the mercenaries as they pass through the alleyways . . . chamber pots, hot oil, whatever they have on hand that might hurt or hinder."

Gervase nodded. "We've had that done to us often enough to know it can be effective." He looked around with a commander's eye, noting things only dimly glimpsed when the guards had hustled him from the gate to his prison.

The town had been built into the side of the mountain, its streets narrow and winding. With space so precious, the houses abutted one another. Their roofs stood out black against the sky, like the teeth of some giant beast. Their walls rose from the cobbled streets to form a series of linked canyons. 'Twould not be pleasant to be the quarry, chased through them with no avenue of escape, Gervase thought.

Cautious as a trio of hunted hares, they crept to the next corner. A dark figure dashed from the shadows to meet them.

"Thank God, I've found ye," Tearlach whispered. "'Tis the lady. Emile's found out she's at the wine merchant's and he's got the house surrounded."

"Sweet Mary save her," Father Ambroise murmured, but he prayed alone, for the others had raced off into the night.

"Sweet Mary save me," Cat whispered. Her prayer was drowned out by the rhythmic thud of the battering ram against the front door of the wine merchant's house. Though she was in the topmost chamber on the third floor, the vibrations shook her.

She never should have come here. Better to have taken her chances on the streets. At least she could have run instead of being caught like a hare in a snare. If only she'd gone with Dame Sofie, the merchant's wife, and her maids to take medicines and bandages to the makeshift infirmary in the church. But with Emile already combing the town for the mysterious dancing girl he fancied, Tearlach had deemed it too dangerous.

Her stomach rolling with fear, Cat considered going downstairs and out a rear window. A peek from the third story showed a half-dozen soldiers in the back courtyard readying a second ram to assault that door. What to do? Where to go?

In her mind's eye, she saw Emile's ugly face. The thought of his brutish mouth and filthy hands touching her made her flesh shrink inside her garish costume. There had to be a way out. There had to be. Hands shaking, she snatched the linen sheet off the bed and began tearing it into strips. Even after they broke down the outer door, 'twould take time to search the house and come to this room. Likely the men at the back would be drawn in to help, leaving the yard deserted. She'd fashion a rope from the sheeting, climb down it and sneak...

A noise from the window brought her around just as a man slid in over the sill. Gasping, Cat grabbed up her only weapon, an iron candlestick, and ducked down behind the bed. Stealthy footsteps marked his progress across the room. He cursed softly when he saw the trunks she'd piled against the door.

"Catherine?" he whispered.

"Gervase? Oh, Gervase." She leapt to her feet and launched herself at him.

"Oh, Catherine." The word became a groan as he caught her and held her close. He was answered by her soft moan as their lips met, meshed. He tasted of wine and desperation. All too soon he wrenched his mouth free. "Are you unhurt?"

"Aye." She wrapped her arms around him, clinging as fiercely as he did to her. "I am so glad to see you." Then the thudding at the front door pierced her joy. "You shouldn't be here."

"Neither should you." He set her away, his eyes glittering in the dimness as they raked her from head to toe. "We have to get you out of those clothes."

"I've longed to hear you say those words," she teased. "But do you think this is the right time?"

His grin was a brief flash of white in his tanned face. "I should have known better than to worry you'd be too weak with fear to escape with me."

"Escape? How?"

"I'll show you... only you cannot go where we must in that skirt and tunic. Are there no other clothes about? Hose, mayhap?" Three of the maids slept in the room, and a quick search of their meager belongings yielded nothing he deemed suitable. He was interested in the rope she'd fashioned from the sheet. 'Twill make a good decoy," he said, tying one end to a storage chest.

The crack of splintering wood and a lusty cheer sent them both to the window just as the soldiers rushed into the house.

"Damn." He tossed the free end of the sheeting out the window, then turned to her. "Take off the skirt and let us flee."

"Nay, Faye's tunic barely covers my rump." Catching the back hem of the skirt, Cat passed it between her legs and tucked it into her belt, fashioning pants of a sort. "Though I don't understand why you are so concerned about my clothes."

Moments later, she understood all too well, unfortunately. They were not going down into the backyard, but up, onto the roof. Gervase had a short rope tied to the chimney. He climbed it first, then pulled Cat up after him.

Mouth dry with fear, she looked down at the ground a heart-wrenching distance below. "I don't like this at all."

"You'd like Emile even less . . . trust me on that. And trust me to see you safely away from here." He held out his hand.

"I do." She took his hand, her fears lessening as his warm, callused palm closed over her icy flesh.

The confidence reflected in his level gaze and cocky grin made her smile back. "That's my brave lady. We are going across the rooftops to the church. Not that I think Emile would honor its sanctity, but in a few minutes he's going to be too busy fighting for his life to worry about you."

Crashing and swearing from the room below warned them that her former hiding place had been breached. As Emile's shaggy head appeared in the window, Gervase tugged Cat back behind the chimney and shielded her with his body.

"Bloody hell, she's climbed out the window," Emile roared, obviously having fallen for Gervase's ruse with the sheeting. "Don't stand there gawking . . . find her."

Cat released the breath she'd been holding and slumped against the chimney. Her respite was short-lived.

"Emile's men will be running about like headless chickens. Come." Gervase tugged her to her feet. "I must get you to the church and then take the eastern gate."

Cat swayed, dizzied by the height. "I don't know if I can."

He caught her, steadied her. "You can," he declared, and proceeded to prove it. Cat knew without his strength and agility she'd not have made it. The slate roofs were steep and slippery as glass beneath her feet, but Gervase guided her every step. Together they negotiated one roof, then two. Soon they were flying over them.

The voices of Emile's men drifted up from the valleys between the buildings, rough and determined in their hunt. Despite that reminder of what was at stake, Cat had never felt as free and alive as she did at this moment with the wind in her hair, her hand held securely in Gervase's. He would keep her safe. Until this moment she had not realized she'd been unconsciously searching for a man who could do that. Protect her.

Now she'd found him. Exhilaration sent her pulse racing in time with their feet as they crossed the roofs. They moved in unison, she and this hard, lean man who had once been her enemy. How odd the quirks of fate, she thought. If not for his misguided quest for vengeance, they might never have met. But they had, and the fire that burned between them was unquenchable.

He felt it, too, she realized when he finally called a halt atop a tall building on the market square. "I knew you could do it," he said, panting with exertion, eyes bright with triumph at the close call they'd escaped. Together.

"I'd not have done so without you." She leaned her shoulder into the solid wall of his chest, heart soaring when his arm came up and folded her close.

"And I'd not have been free if you hadn't conceived that harebrained scheme. A dancer," he grumbled, fingering the thin silk skirt, damp and filthy from their harried run. "If you ever put yourself in danger again, I'll wring your little neck."

"I love you," Cat blurted out, then wished she could suck the words back inside.

His smile fled, his handsome features congealed into a mask as rigid as the mountain peaks rimming the town. "You must not," he growled, peeling her hands from his arm.

"I—I cannot help what I feel," she whispered, searching his eyes, black and grim now, for some sign he cared. It was there, the briefest flicker in their shadowed depths. "Gervase..."

The tolling of the church bells cut through her plea.

"Our attack begins. Armand awaits in an upper room of this building. I will lower you down, and he'll see you to the church. The priests are there and the women. You'll be safe."

"What of you? Will you be careful?"

"Aye." He sounded distracted, anxious to be off. She wanted to tell him again that she loved him, but feared the unwanted burden might make him more reckless, not more cautious.

Chapter Eleven

Cat awoke with a start, dazed and disoriented. Judging by the light streaming in though the open window, 'twas afternoon. Of what day? And where was she? Her eyes flitted from the blue bed hangings to the equally unfamiliar room beyond. A tapestry brightened one white-washed wall, the few pieces of furniture were finely made. Ah, 'twas Dame Sofie and Master Michel's own bedchamber, she realized, memory returning. When the fighting had finally ended, Dame Sofie had insisted Cat come home with her and literally forced her out of her clothes and into bed.

It was over. That happy thought chased out the fatigue of the flight across the rooftops and long hours tending the wounded. Thanks to a combination of too much drink and the element of surprise, the outlaws had been routed, with minimal loss of life. The citizens of Le Vigan could put their lives back in some semblance of order.

What of Gervase? Where was he? She'd last seen him near midnight when he'd brought the injured Armand to the church to have his arm bandaged and reported that the battle had been won. Gervase had shrugged off her pleas to rest and gone to supervise the punishment of the vanquished. Had he gotten any sleep?

Anxious to find out, Cat sat up. Her muscles screamed in protest over last night's activities and drove her back into the nest of covers just as the door opened.

Dame Sofie's round face peered in. "Good. The lady's awake." She advanced with a horde of servants trailing after her. Not servants. Cat recognized the wives and daughters of the town's leading citizens. She'd thought them maids because they carried platters of food, buckets of steaming water and piles of clothing. They'd worked side by side with her last night, yet now they looked on her with deference and awe.

"Did ye sleep well?" the cloth merchant's wife asked shyly.

"Aye," Cat replied, puzzled by their behavior. "Is aught wrong? Was Gervase ill? Hurt?"

"His lordship is fine. All is well." Dame Sofie stood expectantly by the bed. "Will ye eat first? Or bathe?"

"It does not matter, but I can see to my own needs."

"Nay. We'd not hear of it." She looked horrified and the other women echoed her sentiments. "There's a feast to be held this eve in honor of the victory over Emile and his savages."

"'Tis our desire to see ye gowned and coiffed as becomes an honored guest," said the shy young woman.

"If not for ye, we'd still be *his* prisoners," added another.

Cat started to protest, feeling woefully inadequate to the role of heroine, but their hopeful expressions stopped her. "Very well." She gingerly sat and tossed aside the covers. "But Lord Gervase is the true hero. If not for him..." She shuddered, thinking of what would have happened had Emile captured her.

The tension of the moment was shattered as they all rushed forward to help. 'Twas like being swept into the center of a storm, albeit a gentle, well-meaning one. She was stripped and bathed, the scratches she'd gotten from the tile roofs rubbed with salve and bound with soft cloths. They plied her with seeded cakes and sweet wine. 'Twas a bit overwhelming, being the focus of so much goodwill. Apparently sensing Cat's unease, Dame Sofie finally sent the others away.

"What of my friends?" Cat asked, wrapped in a borrowed bed robe and seated on a stool before the fire.

"The priests are seeing what can be done to set the church to rights," Dame Sofie replied. Her pudgy fingers gently worked the snarls from Cat's wet hair. "The Sauveurs used it to stable the horses they stole. The jongleurs are in the solar below. The babe has a score of nursemaids hanging on her every breath."

"Sir Gervase and his men?"

"Silas, the goldsmith, won the right to put them up. So many wanted the privilege of tending our saviors, we drew lots to choose the lucky household. After the banqueting, you'll be lodged in the mayor's house for the rest of your stay."

"Nay. Not the house Emile used as his headquarters."

"Rest easy, my lady. The maids have spent the day clearing out the stink of his presence. Even the mattresses and bed linens have been burned and new ones put in their place."

"But surely you and Master Michel will move in there."

"We hope to, still the elections are not till next week. 'Tis possible the people will choose another over my Michel." But not likely, said the woman's proud smile.

All the while she talked, she dressed Cat in a linen shift and hose as fine as spiderwebs. Over that went a close-fitting tunic of gold silk and a sapphire blue surcoat, the armholes cut deep to show off the girdle belted low on her hips. The woman knelt and twitched the skirts into place. "Is . . . is it all right?"

"Finer than any I saw at court in Bordeaux."

"Bordeaux?" Dame Sofie's eyes rounded. "Ye . . . ye're English."

"You need not say it like that. We are at peace."

"If not for this cursed war, there'd be no leaderless soldiers cast adrift to terrorize the countryside." She sighed. "But that is hardly yer fault, and I must say ye are kind and gentle for all ye're English. How come ye to speak as we do?"

"I am half-French." Cat realized that since being with Gervase, she had switched to the dialect he spoke. "My mother came from Arles. She taught me the tongue of the Languedoc."

Dame Sofie gasped as though this were a greater sin than being English. "Is that where ye were bound when Sir Gervase saved ye from the brigands? If so, ye'd best have a care. There's a man in Arles—nay, more a monster Jean Cluny must be. Emile and Vachel sent tribute to him four times each year for the right to 'conduct business' hereabouts. As a lord might those vassals who owed him homage, except his rents were extracted in blood."

"Monstrous, indeed." Cat's first thought was that she must tell Gervase. Her next was to wonder if this Jean Cluny could also have been responsible for the attack on Alleuze. Suppose his men sported colors similar to her father's? Gervase's uncle might have seen them and . . .

The pealing of the church bells brought Dame Sofie to her feet. "Come. 'Twouldn't do for the guest of honor to be late."

Cat's steps lagged as they drew near the market square. "What of the gallows?" Surely they'd not eat with the bodies of the outlaws swinging over their heads.

"Gone. Sir Gervase ordered the gallows torn down the minute the last of the outlaws were hanged."

"He hanged them all?" Cat was aghast.

"Of course." Dame Sofie's soft features hardened. "'Twas no more than they deserved. Sir Gervase was for letting some of the younger ones go, but Michel knew we couldn't afford to. Thieving and killing is all they know. Once the knight and his men were gone, the brigands would fall on us like wolves on sheep."

Cat nodded in grudging agreement. What a terrible toll the war had taken on France. Back home, the fighting seemed distant. Families groused over the heavy rents levied to finance it and cried for the loss of a loved one, but their lives went on much as ever. Their fields and homes weren't being burned, they weren't being terrorized, even in peacetime. 'Twas tragic. Her compassionate heart cried out to help them.

A cheer went up as they rounded the corner of the mayor's house and entered the square. Men and women came running to touch Cat's hands, some even kneeling to kiss the hem of her skirts. Embarrassed yet moved to tears, she blindly followed Dame Sofie to the head table set at one end of the square.

Gervase and his men were already there, but she had eyes only for the tall knight. He rose from the throne-like chair, took her hand and bowed over it gravely. The cheers rose to a deafening din. As he raised his head, she saw his eyes were also suspiciously moist, but he managed a wry grin. "Ah, I see you are as discomforted as we by all this fuss."

"Aye, but do not let them hear you say so. 'Twill hurt their feelings." She found Dame Sofie seated at the nearest table, beaming as widely as a proud parent. "They are so grateful and do not know how to express it."

"I understand... believe me." His gaze turned intent. "But if you ever put yourself at risk again to help me..."

Cat lifted her chin. "I'd do it again in a heartbeat."

"Children... quit your squabbling," Perrin put in from Cat's other side. "You're alarming our hosts."

Pasting on a smile, Cat allowed Gervase to seat her beside him, then folded her hands in her lap and looked out over the crowd. The cobbled yard, bounded on all four sides by the tall stone buildings, was packed with people dressed in their feast-day best. Some sat at the trestle tables that had been set up, others were cross-legged in the grass rimming the yard. Rays of late-afternoon sun slanted in from the narrow streets. She watched the light catch on a bit of gold embroidery here, a stray jewel there. Obviously the townsfolk had wasted no time in reclaiming their property from Emile Sauveur's chests.

Master Michel stood, holding up his hands for silence. When he had everyone's attention, he launched into a lengthy, dramatic recounting of their year under Emile's thumb and their deliverance from that purgatory. He was a portly man of middle years, with a big belly and a gift for oratory. The tale was punctuated by weeping, growling and finally a collective cheer that rocked the shops on their foundations.

All throughout the long story, Cat was conscious of Gervase beside her. He looked unbearably handsome in a borrowed surcoat of blue velvet that turned his eyes to smoke and strained to contain his broad shoulders. They sat so close his long leg pressed against the side of hers, warming her through their clothes. When they both reached for the wine cup they shared, their fingers brushed, chasing fire across her skin.

Hearing his quick gasp, she knew he'd felt it, too, and looked up at him. His gaze did not waver from Master Michel, but a muscle twitched in his cheek as he flexed his jaw. Stubborn man, she thought. His determination to ignore what lay between them strengthened her own to have him. While Master Michel droned on, Cat planned and plotted. By the time he'd finished...finally...she had hatched and rejected a dozen schemes.

"I hope we won't be expected to speak," Perrin murmured as the crowd applauded their leader's fine words. "Naught we could say or do would live up to *that*."

They weren't. A toast was proposed and drunk, followed swiftly by another and another, till Cat thought she'd pass out in the trencher she and Gervase would share. As though she'd spoken the need aloud, a trumpet blast announced the arrival of food. Six men approached the head table, staggering under the weight of a platter the size of a door. In the middle of it a whole boar lounged on a bed of boiled onions.

"Impressive," Cat murmured. "Who found time to hunt?"

"'Twas none of our men, but the boar obviously has a bit of fight left in him," Gervase whispered, grinning.

Indeed, the men were having difficulty with the beast. It was heavy, and the wooden plank greasy. While the men fought to keep hold of the slippery board, their burden shifted alarmingly from side to side. Wine gravy dripped from the edge of the platter. The last man stepped in it, lost his footing and danced to stay upright.

His corner of the platter dipped, the boar slid toward the low side. The front man swore and tried to level the board, but he overcompensated and the boar nearly went off the front. The apple popped from its mouth and bounced in the grass.

"Set it down! Set it down!" cried the cook, a tiny little man who ran around them like a nervous hen.

Cat smothered a giggle, looked over and saw that Gervase was having trouble controlling his mouth, too. "Don't laugh."

"I'm trying not to," he muttered, biting his lip. Their eyes met and locked in a moment of shared mirth, of perfect understanding that reminded Cat of last night's frantic race for freedom. Now, as then, his gaze was unshuttered, giving her a glimpse of the happy man he could be, if not for the ghosts that haunted him. Why could he not see how well suited they were? Why could he not let her share his burdens and lighten them?

"Gervase..."

"Shh." He placed a callused finger over her lips. "I know there is much you would say, but not now. Not here."

Nervous as a bride on her wedding night, Cat paced the bedchamber in the mayor's house. 'Twas late, very late. The fire she'd lit in expectation of sitting before it with Gervase had burned down to embers in the hearth. Long shadows crept out from the corners of the room to meet at the foot of the bed, dispelled only slightly by the single candle on the bedside table.

What was keeping him?

Frustrated and worried, she kicked aside the trailing hem of her borrowed bed robe and stalked to the window. The feasting had seemed interminable; she'd left the moment the fruits and nuts were served, certain Gervase would follow directly. He hadn't.

Like most of the houses in the town, the mayor's was several stories high. There was a reception hall on the ground floor, a dining hall and a smaller solar for private meetings above them. The master chamber occupied the third story and commanded a view of the courtyard, deserted now except for a few men who'd passed out at the tables and been left to sleep off the wine. Gervase was not among them. She'd been pleased to see he cut his wine with half as much water, thinking he wanted to be alert when he came to her. Alert and...capable.

Now it seemed he wasn't coming at all. Cat sighed. He had said he'd talk with her. Could he have forgotten? Should she swallow her pride and go to him?

Someone knocked at the door, and she flew to answer it. Perrin, not Gervase, stood in the gloomy corridor.

"Is it Gervase? Is he hurt?" Cat said quickly.

Perrin shifted uneasily. "Nay. He is unharmed. He, er, sent me with a message." His gaze flicked to her face, then slid away. "On the morrow, I am to take you back to Bordeaux."

"Bordeaux? But...but what of the ransom?"

"He no longer wants it."

Cat flinched, the rejection as stinging and personal as a hard slap. "How will he restore his lands?"

"I don't know." He sighed. "I would like to leave at first light, if you think you can be ready."

It sank in then. "You? You are to take me, not him?"

"Aye. He will go on to Alleuze."

'Twas the final straw. "We'll see about that."

Cat stormed out of the room. Fists balled in her skirts, she hiked them up and raced the short distance to the

gloomy stairwell lit only by a single torch. Negotiating the
steeply winding steps in near darkness forced her to slow
her pace. By the time she'd reached the next floor, her
temper had cooled enough to let reason assert itself.

Gervase was not a man to be prodded by angry words.
They were far more likely to make him retreat inside
himself. What was needed here was cleverness, she
thought, pausing outside the door of the master bedchamber. Beyond the barrier of metal-banded oak planks
was the man she loved. The man who cared for her, at
least, whether he would admit it or not. She knew the
bond between them had been strengthened by the danger they'd survived the night before. Coming so close to
losing someone did that. But he'd not act on his feelings. Because his damnable honor would not let him
move past the fact that he had kidnapped her.

If only she could force him to realize it mattered not to
her how they had begun, 'twas the ending that mattered.
They were destined to end their days together. She'd felt
it from the first, when he was an unknown man staring
in at her from the darkened garden. Somehow she must
convince him of that. Which meant she could not let him
send her back to Bordeaux.

She could always kidnap him and force him to wed her.
The notion made her giggle. Imagine throwing Gervase
over her saddlebow and riding off with him. Impossible.
He outweighed her by several stone, and he was three
times as strong. Still . . .

Cat eyed the door speculatively. There was one weapon
at her disposal. Something he'd not fight or ignore—desire.

* * *

"What are we goin' ta do?" the soldier whispered.

His comrade squinted at Le Vigan through his good eye, the one that wasn't swollen shut from the blow he'd taken when the gate fell. "Leave, I guess. We're a half mile off, but I know those men patrollin' the walls are townspeople, not ours. 'Tis obvious they've done for Emile and the rest."

"Aye." The first man shifted to lean against the rocks in which they'd taken refuge when they'd run as far from Le Vigan as their legs would get them. "Do ye think anyone else got away?"

"Nay. We'd not have escaped if we hadn't been mannin' the gate." Conscious that they'd run off and left their companions, they avoided looking each other in the eye.

"What do ye suppose got into the townspeople? A twelvemonth we've been here and they've always behaved like cowed sheep."

"Dunno, but something set them off, that's sure. Who'd have thought they'd have the guts to attack a hundred armed men." He frowned. "Wonder where the rest of our troop was?"

"Drunk, most like. When I came on duty, the wine merchant was offerin' free wine on account of the fair. I...I nearly stayed behind to drink, but then I recalled how Emile had put out the eyes of the last man who shirked guard duty."

"Aye. He were a fierce leader. We'll not find another as quick and clever at findin' an easy mark."

"There's his brother...Maslin."

"Aye. That's it. We'll go to Arles and tell Maslin what happened here. He'll take us in...and mayhap come back to wreak vengeance on this pissant town."

Chapter Twelve

Gervase shifted in his sleep, embracing his lover as the first shimmering tendrils of the dream engulfed him, accepting the illusion of what he dared not take in reality. Catherine.

"Catherine," he whispered.

"I'm here." Sliding her arms around his neck, she opened eagerly for the questing edge of his tongue. She tasted of sweet wine and even sweeter desire. The groan that rumbled through him as he took control of the kiss was answered by a moan of surrender. Tightening his embrace, he explored her with a thoroughness he'd only imagined. Nay 'twas better than he'd ever imagined. He felt her breasts swell beneath the garment she wore, groaned again when she rubbed them against his chest, seeking surcease from the ache he knew was building there.

He dragged his mouth from hers, stringing kisses along the column of her neck and across her collarbone. Her nipples peaked, hard and sensitive as he parted the robe and stared at her in the firelight. "Beautiful..." He brushed his knuckles over the upper swell of one breast, then cradled it in his palm, making her moan softly.

"Small and perfect and more beautiful than I dreamed," he whispered, lowering his head. "I should not, but..."

She gasped in surprise as his mouth settled over the taut peak. The gasp became a cry of pleasure as he drew down with devastating gentleness. "Gervase! Oh, Gervase!" She tunneled her fingers into his hair to hold him close, urging him on with whimpers of pure delight. Her head fell back in abandon, the breath ragged in her throat as he transferred his attentions to the other breast and suckled hungrily.

The feel of Catherine straining against him stoked the heat in Gervase's veins to a fever pitch. Never had he wanted anyone as fiercely as he did the slender woman coming apart in his arms. Desire surged through him in waves, a primitive need to conquer that warred with the urge to savor the joining he'd craved since their first meeting. Balanced on that knife point, he dragged his mouth from her breast and kissed her again. His tongue plundered in blatant imitation of the more intimate act to come. He drew her against him, hands planing down her spine to cup her buttocks and draw her up into the juncture of his thighs.

Her wriggling had dislodged the folds of her robe. His naked manhood pressed against the satiny smoothness of her belly. Her hips rocked in time to the same pulse that throbbed deep inside him, seeking, pleading without words.

"Catherine," he gasped, dragging his mouth from hers. As he tensed to mount her, his eyes opened again. 'Twas exactly as he'd dreamed a dozen times. She lay beside him, her hair spread across the pillows like a banner of sunlight, her eyes dark with passion. Her skin was flushed, her breasts rising and falling in time to her quickened breathing, the nipples swollen and wet from his kisses. So beautiful. So real.

Too real.

He blinked, struggling to separate illusion from reality. The dream had never been this vivid or gone this far. "Catherine?"

"Aye. Please, Gervase, I'm so empty without you."

"You're real." Swearing, he drew back, or tried to, but her grip on his neck was firm, and he was still dazed.

"I am as real as what we feel for each other," she said calmly, but her eyes glinted with unshed tears.

"You shouldn't be here." He tugged the robe closed.

Her chin angled up. "I am not leaving."

Nor did he want her to go. He wanted to drag her beneath him, wrap those long legs of hers around him and plunge deep into her waiting heat. She must have read his desire. Her eyes turned to smoke; her lashes fluttered self-consciously. Though he knew she was no virgin, she managed to look like a maid flushing over her first flirtation.

"Why do you send me away?"

Gervase sighed. He hadn't realized this would be so hard. "I am trying to repay you for saving my life."

"Ah." The blushing maid vanished and the little warrior returned, scowling fiercely. "So you have decided . . . without a by-your-leave . . . to reward me by sending me back to Bordeaux."

"It is better this way," he said stiffly, missing her already. Who would he fence with, laugh with when she was gone?

"Not for me. I will wither and die without you."

"You will find another to wed." The idea of his Catherine married to someone else turned his voice harsh and raw.

"Could you do that, send me off to wed another?" Nay! "Aye."

She reached up and cupped her hand to the stubbled line of his jaw, her eyes deep and luminous. "You are lying, my love."

Gervase sighed. Turning his head, he kissed her palm. "It cannot be, Catherine. You must go back."

She shook her head, sending sparks of candlelight shimmering through her hair, making it crackle with vitality. Aye, she was more vividly alive than anyone he had ever met. Like a ray of sunshine burning away the darkness in which he'd lived these past few years. "How can you deny what is between us?" she asked in a small voice, as a single tear ran down her cheek.

Unable to resist, he lay down beside her and drew her head into his shoulder. "Because I care for you, care what happens to you." He gently stroked her hair. The springy tendrils curled around his fingers, smelling of rosemary and Catherine. Her sigh as she relaxed into his embrace twisted something deep inside him. "'Twas bad enough when I thought the outlaws had captured you. Worse when you put yourself in danger to save me."

"I was not afraid." She raised her head, eyes shining with such purity of purpose that his heart clenched.

"I was... for you. I knew then that if anything happened to you, I'd never forgive myself. So I am sending you back."

"But why? The brigands are vanquished. 'Tis only another two days to Alleuze and safety."

"You will not be safe there," Gervase said, low and tight.

"Why? Oh, Vallis said the walls were not in good repair, but surely if 'tis safe for your people, I will—"

"'Tis not a matter of walls, and you know it." Out of desperation, he let the fierceness of his desire blaze forth. "If I took you with me, I'd not be able to keep my hands from you."

Her smile was dazzling, smug and wholly feminine. "I counted on that when I crept into your bed. I want your hands on me."

"Catherine. You deserve naught less than marriage, a home and a family. I can offer you none of these things."

"Because your estates are in ruin."

"Aye. Bad enough my people and I must scrabble for our living. I'd not subject you to that."

Cat knew then that he loved her... even if he hadn't admitted it. "But my dowry portion is huge. With it we could—"

"Nay." He looked aghast. "After what I did, 'twould be dishonorable to wed you and take your dowry."

"Many an heiress has become a kidnapped bride. I assure you there would be no force involved. I'd gladly wed—"

"Do you not realize how wrong that would be? I couldn't."

But he wanted to. Cat splayed one hand on his chest, loving the solid feel of his muscles beneath her palm. His skin was deeply bronzed under a whirl of crisp black hair. What would it be like to touch him all over? She wanted to find out, but she wanted more. She wanted to wed him and work by his side for the rest of her life. "Do you hate me because of what you think my father did? Is that why you won't marry me?"

"Nay." His pained expression mirrored her own anguish. "I can't hate you, not when your every deed proclaims your kindness, your bravery, your compassion. If you were a lesser woman, I might punish you and your father by wedding you for your dowry."

Prideful dolt. 'Twould serve him right if she took *him* prisoner and refused to release him till he'd wed her. *Wicked girl,* her conscience chided. But he had kidnapped her first. And he did love her... she was certain he did. What harm would there be in giving them both what they wanted? Each other.

Cat peered up at him through her lashes, found him staring into the fire, his eyes stark and bleak as their lives would be without each other. Despair gave her the courage to press on. "I do not care for fine clothes, was bored and repelled by life at court and heartily wished myself home training horses. I am not going back. Not ever. If you send me with Perrin, I will escape and make my way to Alleuze."

"You wouldn't!"

"I would. And if you send me from your bed, I will only return...again and again till I have worn down your resistance and you finally agree to wed me." She cocked her head, grinning cheekily. "Do you know I considered tying you to the bed and holding you prisoner? 'Twas a sound plan, only I feared you'd awaken before I had you bound. But I still may try it."

"Catherine." Exasperated, he glared at her.

"That may work on lesser creatures, my lord, but my father can out shout and out glare you any day. I was weaned on such displays and am not the least intimidated." She marked it a victory that he did not flinch at the reference to her father.

"What am I to do with you?"

Cat smiled, but not too broadly. Her mother had taught her not to gloat. Men hated to have their noses rubbed in a woman's victory. "Follow your heart," she said softly.

"I should not," he said, but instead of moving away, he tunneled his hands into her hair. Letting it slide through his fingers, he spread the golden tendrils across the pillow. "Like ripe silk," he murmured. "I've dreamed of doing this, of wrapping myself in your hair and losing myself in your body. Ah, the nights I lay awake, hot and throbbing with the need for you."

Cat felt the throbbing echo low in her belly. She was vividly aware of the herbal scent rising from the linen sheets to mingle with Gervase's clean male scent, of the sudden warmth infusing her body, of the breathless rush of air in her lungs and the aching need for his touch. She framed his face with her hands. The rasp of his whiskers tickled her palms and tingled down her arms. "And I for you," she whispered, shy, uncertain and unbearably excited. "I do not want to wait any longer."

"Nor do I." He kissed her, hands fisting in her hair, dragging her head back to give him greater purchase, his mouth hot, hard and hungry.

With a soft groan that was part surrender, part triumph, Cat opened to him, her tongue dueling with his. This was what she'd wanted, waited for all her life. She followed where he led, learning what pleased her, pleased him. Then she took what he'd taught her and blazed new trails, taking and giving even as he did. By the time he raised his head, she was clinging to him, senses reeling, swamped by the rising passion she saw reflected in his smoky eyes.

"Catherine! You near make me lose control just kissing you." He threw aside the covers. Candlelight rippled over his lean, muscular body, giving her a heart-stopping glimpse of his rampant erection in the second before he pulled her close.

"Sweet Mary!" Cat gasped, and tried to move away.

"Easy, love." He caught her waist with one hand, stroked her hair from her face with the other. "I didn't mean for you to think I'd take you like a starving animal...though I admit you do make me hungry as one," he added, grinning wolfishly. "Nay, we've waited too long for this to see it end in a quick tumble."

"G-Gervase, there is something I need to tell you about Henry," she said, staring up into eyes black with desire.

"Nay, there'll be no talk of your other lovers in our bed." His kiss held a hard echo of his anger, but when she whimpered in wordless complaint, his mouth instantly gentled. His tongue slid over her lips in silent apology before slipping between them to tease and seduce.

She was lost. Well and truly lost. Her fears drowned in a wave of pure sensation. It wasn't necessary to tell him this was her first time; he'd be gentle and caring with her. Shivering, Cat twined her arms around his neck and kissed him back, letting go of doubt and uncertainty, welcoming the heady rush of desire building inside her.

Feeling her go pliant in his embrace, Gervase was swept by euphoria and fierce male triumph. He set out to win her, to pleasure her so thoroughly he'd wipe every other man from her mind and brand her as his own. Before he sought his own release, he'd make certain she was satisfied.

Cat shivered as his hand slid up her ribs. The callused palm left a trail of fire in its wake, had her arching off the bed as it settled over her breast. He molded and shaped it, plucking the sensitive nipple into a hard peak. Her blood heated and raced, sending fire streaking to pool in her lower belly.

His mouth left hers and stitched tiny biting kisses from her jaw to the swell of her breast, opening the robe as he went. "So beautiful," he murmured against her heated flesh. "Proud and bold as you are." He saluted the nipple with a flick of his tongue, smiling when she groaned. "You like that?"

"Y-you know I do," she managed to say, her nerves so finely drawn with anticipation she was shaking. "Please..."

"Aye, I do want to please you...in every way I know." His mouth closed over the aching peak, drawing down more greedily than he had earlier.

'Twas what she wanted, needed, and she told him so, his name falling like a litany from her lips as she clasped his head to her breast. She cried out in disappointment when he left off suckling her, but 'twas only long enough to transfer his affections to the other engorged nipple. As he settled in to pleasure it, his hands moved over her body, kneading and stroking her from ribs to hips and back again.

Molten heat washed through her in waves, arrowing down to the hidden cleft at the juncture of her thighs. There the throbbing built, the coil tightening till the ache was nigh unbearable. She shifted her legs, seeking to ease the emptiness.

The feel of Catherine twisting in his embrace, the soft, pleading sounds his touch drew from her, ripped at Gervase's control. He wanted to part her thighs and plunge into her, yet held himself back. Not yet. He had to bring her to fulfillment first, because when he entered her he knew he'd not last long.

"Don't stop," she ordered when he left her breast. Her flushed face and smoky eyes were nearly his undoing. Nearly.

"I'm not." He nipped at her tummy, kissed his way down her lower belly to the nest of golden curls at the top of her thighs.

"Gervase?" The wary confusion in her voice told him this, at least, was new to her, and he was glad.

Grinning, he looked at her slender body sprawled in the circle of pale light. "Trust me, you'll like this better than all that has gone before." With that, he gently spread her legs, his fingers sliding through the soft hair to the slick, wet folds and the secrets they guarded.

Cat tensed, not certain what to expect. The hot rasp of his breath where she'd least expected it made her gasp. The tip of his tongue burned like flame on her sensitive flesh, drove her mindless with ecstasy. It was too much. It was not nearly enough. She arched against his mouth, offering herself shamelessly, letting the flames carry her higher. Higher. Until the world exploded all around her.

Gervase heard her sob his name, felt her shudder then go limp in his arms. Aroused to the point of pain, he took in her flushed face, her passion-hazed purple eyes and knew he'd made a start. For her sake and his own, he began again, touching and tasting, wooing and seducing until she was as hungry for him as he was for her. When he felt her body begin to convulse a second time, he knew he could wait no longer. Parting her thighs, he rose over her and plunged into her narrow velvet sheath.

Cat gasped as pain cut through the haze of passion. He trapped her, from above and from within, his superior weight driving the air from her lungs, the rigid length of his arousal stretching her to the limits.

"My God, you're a virgin," he gasped.

"I was," she replied through clenched teeth.

"Why... why didn't you tell me?"

"I... I tried to, but you wouldn't speak of Henry."

She'd had no other lovers. Gervase struggled to hold himself still, for the notion touched him deeply. "I . . . I could withdraw."

"Really?" she sounded curious but not insistent.

"I could try, but I've wanted you very badly for what seems like my whole lifetime."

'Twas a balm to her sundered body, but she'd never felt so vulnerable, so intimately exposed to another person.

"There won't be any more pain," Gervase assured her, shaking with the effort to hold back, to give her time. He kissed her throat, the tender place behind her ear. "You liked what came before," he reminded her.

"Aye." She eased her nails from his shoulders.

"You'll like what comes next even better," he promised.

"Really?" Cat turned her head and found his on the pillow beside her, face drawn in agony, eyes glittering with suppressed needs. He was suffering on her account as she had on his. Only it wasn't really his fault. Such was the lot of women, but the earlier love play had been . . . wonderful, exhilarating. She wanted to recapture that feeling. "It doesn't hurt so much now."

Her reward was a dazzling smile. "I'm glad." He kissed the tip of her nose, and then her mouth, his lips and tongue tender as they coaxed a response from her.

She gave it willingly, welcoming the familiar syrupy heat that spilled through her as he began to move, gently setting her afire from the inside out. Gone was the sense of being invaded, replaced by a completeness that brought tears to her eyes. "I am truly yours now," she whispered.

"Aye." Watching the wonder steal over her face, Gervase felt his chest tighten. Or was it his heart expanding? Truly he'd never experienced such a sense of belonging, of having found the other half of himself. "Come morn, we will wed. For now, let me show you how much you mean to me," he rasped. Cradling her body in his hands, he lifted her for the deep, sure strokes that rekindled the fire between them.

Her arms wrapped around his neck, Cat clung to him with every fiber of her being, matching the pace he set, then quickening it as the flames inside her burned hotter and hotter. Each thrust of their bodies seemed to carry them higher, till suddenly the molten core inside her seemed to shatter on a wave of ecstasy so perfect she cried out, "Gervase. Oh, Gervase."

"Catherine!" Gervase groaned, and buried himself in the heart of the convulsions that shuddered through her. Consumed by the fire, he poured himself into her, body and soul. The stunning release left him spent and gasping for breath, still he gathered himself to move and spare her his weight.

"Nay. Don't leave me." She clung weakly to him.

"Never, but neither do I want to crush you." Groaning, he rolled to his side, carrying her with him. Her head pillowed on his shoulder, her eyes were dazed yet filled with joy. "I—I need you so, Catherine," he murmured, moved by the overwhelming sense of rightness he felt with her, yet unable to voice his feelings.

"Oh, Gervase. As close as you guard your thoughts, I never thought you'd admit you cared." She pressed her face into his chest and shuddered, her tears scalding his flesh.

"I do care. More than I can say, for words don't come easily to me. Please don't cry. It tears me apart." Gervase held her and stroked her hair as her sobs muted to sniffs. His heart ached for her, for them. It was done, the bond between them sealed forever. He wasn't sorry, how could he be? And yet when he thought of all they still must face... her father's wrath, his people's poverty... he felt like crying himself and screaming at the Fates.

"Your actions speak for you," she murmured at length, banishing his troubled thoughts. "You were so gentle with me, so tender and patient."

"Nay, I was not," he exclaimed, belatedly remembering she'd been an innocent. "Curse me for a fool. Are you all right?"

"All right? Oh..." She flushed and nodded. "And you? I fear I've marred your back with my nails."

"My back has borne worse. I wish I'd known you were a maid."

"What difference would it have made?"

"I'd have gone more slowly, taken more time to make certain you were ready for me."

Cat chuckled. "I assure you I was most ready, and I did try to tell you about Henry."

"I did not want to discuss your first lover."

"He was never that... as you now know." Her expression sobered. "We worked together training the horses and I fancied myself in love with him. Worse, I thought he loved me. 'Twas my dowry he desired, not me. I did not learn that till I'd already made the mistake of running off with Henry. Papa caught up with us before I was either wedded or bedded, but it cost me much."

Her reputation and her trust in men. Gervase recalled what a prickly thing she'd been when they'd first met. "Thankfully your father found you in time and made certain Henry could dupe no—"

"Papa did naught to Henry except send him away with a sound whipping. Henry died fittingly, however, killed by a jealous husband as he climbed out the wife's chamber window.''

Gervase chuckled. "Aye, 'twas his just reward for having ruined your reputation." And he felt a primitive pride in having been her first lover. How different she was from Marie, who had lain beneath him like a stone, murmuring prayers whilst she performed her duty. But there was no place for Marie in his marriage bed. "Are you certain you are all right? I know there was pain, but did you find some joy?''

"Joy?" Secure in his arms, basking in the reflected glory of their lovemaking, she teased, "'Tis a pallid word to describe what you made me feel. And well you know it," she added. "For your face is flushed with triumph and your chest swelled—"

"My chest? Your lessons are severely lacking if you think 'tis my chest that's swelling," he mocked, drawing her close so the heavy length of his arousal prodded her hip.

"Gervase. Is it possible . . . so soon?''

"I'd not have said so, but it seems you inspire miracles on several levels, my lady." He nuzzled her throat. "Only think, if we are this good together the first time, what 'twill be like when we've practiced a bit." Lowering his head, he kissed her with all the longing pent up inside him.

Cat welcomed the sliding edge of his tongue, tasting passion and possessiveness yet not startled by either. She wound her arms around his neck and arched against him, glorying in the groan that shook him as he took her wordless invitation to deepen the kiss. They were both breathless by the time he lifted his head. "Oh, Gervase. I love you so," she murmured.

"I—I know." 'Twas a start, she thought. At least he accepted her love. His gaze was soft, tender. "Much as I'd welcome the chance to show you I care, you are new to this and doubtless sore. I'd not have you suffer on the morrow when we ride out."

How gentle he was. How considerate. Despite the fact that he thought her father his enemy, he had treated her with naught save honor. And now love. Cat gazed up at him, seeing the shadows that still haunted his eyes. What a hard life he'd had, she thought, filled suddenly with the need to make it up to him. She could not restore his estate, nor the lives of those he'd lost, but she would cherish him with every breath in her body. "I fear I will suffer more if you ignore me," she said softly, running her hands down between them and touching him.

Gervase groaned, eyes squeezing shut. "I've spawned a monster," he whispered. But he didn't push her away. Body taut as a strung bow, he shuddered beneath her questing fingers. 'Twas novel and exciting to have a woman take the lead. He supposed he'd best get used to it...in bed and out, for his Catherine was not one to meekly follow orders. "Enough," he cried at length, control stretched to the breaking point. "You'll unman me."

"Never." Cat relished her ability to make him shiver and groan as he did her. The word ended on a squeak as he tumbled her onto her back and entered her in one sleek thrust. She groaned his name, filled to overflowing, body and soul.

Eyes luminous, glittering with passion and much more, he slowly stoked the fire she had kindled. It flared and burned and twisted between them, then consumed them. Cat's last thought as she tumbled back to earth wrapped securely in his arms was that she hoped tomorrow never came. She wanted to stay here in Le Vigan, locked up with Gervase forever.

Would that they could stay here forever, Gervase thought as he felt Catherine relax against him, their limbs still entwined. Her breath, soft and warm on his chest, stirred the hair over his heart in the same way she ruffled his senses, awakening them the way spring rain did the parched earth. 'Twas as though he'd been dead and only now was coming to life. For Catherine.

I need you, Catherine. I...I love you. The words lifted his weary soul, but he dared not utter them. The feeling was too new. Too strong. He'd loved his parents and lost them both. Because he was tainted, by his de Lauren blood, his grandfather had said. What if it was true? What if he lost Catherine?

His arm tightened around her. How slight and fragile she felt, he thought, alarmed suddenly. Much as he longed for home, he dreaded their arrival at Alleuze. There were many who'd lost family and property to the Sommervilles' raid. Many who would hate her for her name alone. Somehow he must keep her safe.

Chapter Thirteen

Gervase and Cat were married the next day, at noon in the market square with all the town watching and Father Ambroise officiating. Knowing he dared not linger for the three weeks required to have the banns read, Gervase had approached the priest and offered what coin he had to have them waived.

"I am no longer in the business of selling the church's dispensations." The priest had looked both affronted and much different with his plain robe and ringless hands. "However I will conduct the ceremony today because I know you must return home to succor your people. But most especially since Lady Catherine—to whom I owe a great debt for making me see the error of my ways—did confess to me this morn that you two had lain together."

Minx, Gervase thought and smothered a smile. He'd wondered why his not-overly-pious lady had insisted on rushing off to confession at first light. Now he knew. 'Twould seem she was most determined to have him.

Still, as he waited before the door of the church, along with the entire population of Le Vigan, Gervase regretted that Catherine had been cheated, not only of her beloved family's support on this special day, but of the fancy new clothes and elaborate fuss all girls dreamed about.

If she felt the lack, it wasn't evident in Cat's face as the women led her forward through the crowd. Nor was she exactly dressed in rags. Someone had lent her a tunic of cream silk edged in gold and over it a surcoat of purple samite shot with gold thread that gave off sparks in the noonday sun. An amethyst-studded belt girded her hips. Bound only by a thin gold circlet and veil at the crown, her pale hair flowed down her back and lapped seductively at her hips with every step she took toward him. Her cheeks were flushed a becoming pink; her eyes locked on his, glowing with love and pride.

Gervase's chest tightened, so filled with emotion he felt his heart might burst through his ribs. Though their beginning had been a rocky one, and many a stone yet littered their path, he could not imagine loving anyone as he did her.

As they turned to face Father Ambroise, Cat glanced sidelong at Gervase and whispered, "I've caught you at last, my lord."

Gervase choked on a spurt of laughter. "Aye, and I expect life with you will not be dull."

She grinned. "Nor would either of us want that."

He resisted the urge to hug her and kiss her breathless . . . at least till Father Ambroise had droned his way through what seemed like the longest wedding ceremony ever. The moment they were pronounced man and wife, Gervase swept her into his arms and took her mouth in a hungry kiss. But instead of conquering, he found himself surrendering to the potent sweetness of her love.

"We must leave tomorrow," he said when she let him up for air. "But today is ours. And tonight I will give you a wedding night to remember always."

"Last night was our wedding night, my love," she whispered. "But I've no doubt tonight...and every other that follows...will be very special." Smiling into each other's eyes, they turned to face the cheering crowd.

They did not leave the next day or the one after that. 'Twas four days later when Gervase finally pronounced the horses rested and the men healed enough from their wounds to continue. He had kept himself busy by day seeing to repairs to the town's walls and training Le Vigan's garrison. By night, he and Cat explored the passion they roused in each other. The bond between them grew with each hour they spent together...in bed and out.

Their special closeness had given her the courage to ask, "Could we not send word to let my parents know I am no longer your prisoner but your wife?"

He'd trembled violently. "Nay, hearing you'd wed your kidnapper would enrage them. They'd come after us and take you—"

"They would not," she'd assured him. Secretly she hoped her father would come and clear up the terrible misconception that he'd attacked Alleuze, but to voice that hope would only upset Gervase. "Please let me write them," she begged instead. "It...it tears at me to know they are worried sick thinking me the captive of some ruthless brigand enduring God knows what horrors when, in truth, I am well and happier than I've ever been."

"Ah, Catherine." He'd sighed and hugged her tighter then grudgingly agreed she could write to her parents once they'd reached Alleuze. "'Tis too dangerous to send a single man back to Bordeaux now. Once we are safely home, I must send word to my uncle of the change in plans and our wedding. The same messenger can carry your letter to the nearby port and thence by ship to Bordeaux, which will be quicker in any case.''

"Thank you. Thank you.'' She'd kissed him soundly, thinking how lucky she was to have found a man who loved her enough to not only overlook her father's supposed perfidy but allow her to write to the man he hated above all others.

Cat looked upon their time in the little mountain town as the happiest of her life, and knew Gervase shared her reluctance to leave. But there was no escaping his duty to his people. They left at first light with an extra pack animal to carry the foodstuffs pressed on them by the grateful people of Le Vigan. Master Michel and the town fathers had wanted to give them more... everything the Sauveurs had pilfered from the town and from those they attacked on the roads. Gervase had refused.

"I but did what anyone would have, seeing the predicament you were in.'' Gervase swung onto Thor's back, his armor winking dully in the gray light of dawn. "Give the coin and goods back to those from whom Emile and Vachel stole.'' He set his heels to the stallion and led his party out through the town gates.

Riding well back in the group, Cat hunched her shoulders under her borrowed cloak and tried to ignore the weight of the leather pack Dame Sofie had persuaded her to take.

"My Michel and the others feel quite strongly that Sir Gervase and yerself should have something for risking yer necks to save ours,'' the woman had explained the day before. "Brother Bartholome told us conditions was bad in Alleuze... so we decided that we'd place this in yer keeping for them. We were right happy to have back that which the brigands took from us, but no more. What's in this pack is not rightly ours. 'Tis coin and jewelry taken from travelers and from other towns. There's no way of knowing to whom it belongs and many of the poor souls are dead.'' She'd looked at Jolie sleeping by the hearth. "Keep some by to pay the wee one's way, for the sake of her dead parents.''

Cat had been unable to dispute the fact that though she and Gervase would provide for Jolie, the babe deserved some recompense for being orphaned. And then there were the players. Bevis would never tumble again, and had decided to remain in Le Vigan to act as town minstrel, but he needed coin for an instrument and suitable garb. Ila, Faye and Tearlach were afraid to chance staying on the road and had chosen to try their luck at Alleuze. Brother Bartholome was staying to tend the flock at Le Vigan while Father Ambroise traveled on at least as far as Alleuze. All of them were owed something for their pain and suffering at the hands of the Sauveurs, but Gervase's example had shamed them into saying they didn't want anything, either.

Cat had decided that wasn't right. Integrity was all well and good, but it wouldn't put food on the table or clothe them come winter. So she'd taken the tainted gold and jewelry into her keeping . . . without Gervase's knowledge. It hurt her to sneak about, but she excused her actions by thinking that the man was long on honor and short on practicality where money was concerned . . . otherwise he'd not have turned his back on her ransom.

With that to ease her conscience, Cat rode behind Gervase through the winding forested trails. Used to the rolling countryside of southern England, she was constantly awed by the landscape, the rugged mountains punctuated by deep ravines. The contrast of stark limestone cliffs and lush, hidden valleys. The draining heat of the day that swiftly gave way to night so cold she huddled against Gervase for warmth. Not that he complained, but camped in such close quarters and forced to sleep in their clothes in case of attack, sleep was all they did.

These byways were lightly traveled, which didn't surprise Cat at all. What she did wonder about was why an army had bothered to pass this way and harass Alleuze. Particularly when she saw the keep, perched halfway up the side of a cliff, its pale walls seemingly one with the limestone.

"'Twas taken by treachery," Vallis explained. His head was bandaged from the wound he'd suffered in the fighting at Le Vigan. Armand had been injured, too, and his arm was still in a sling. "The bastards claimed they were merchants with wares to sell...flour, sugar, salt. Things the people of Alleuze had not tasted for months."

That her father never would have done. If he'd been told to take Alleuze, 'twould have been by siege, not trickery, but Cat would waste no more breath protesting her sire's innocence to those with closed minds. Somehow, someway she'd prove them wrong. But that was a task for next week or next month. Today she had to get through meeting her husband's people.

The thud of the drawbridge settling to earth jolted her from her reverie. Nerves ajangle, she rode through the massive barbican and under the iron teeth of the portcullis. A track so narrow they were forced to ride single file led straight up, abutted on one side by the cliff face and the other by a solid wall topped by a walkway. These impressive defenses should have been bristling with archers. Instead one withered old man looked down on them, smiled and raised a bent pike in welcome.

Thus far things did not look too bad, Cat thought. The image of well-being began to fade when they entered the lower bailey. The charred remains of two large buildings, likely the stables and barracks for the garrison, clung to the east wall. Work had begun to clear away the wreckage, for several carts full of blackened stone and twisted timbers stood about. But not much progress had been made. She wondered where the workmen were.

That question and many others were answered as they filed through the second gate house and into the inner bailey. Cat had a brief impression of a stout tower silhouetted against the bright blue sky and of more destruction . . . burned timbers, broken stone and shattered furniture . . . before the shouting began.

"Gervase! Gervase!" People tumbled from the crumbling doorways of the keep and the ruined dependency buildings. A veritable wave of pinched faces and gaunt bodies. Bald old men, skinny women and gangly children, all dressed in clothes so mean and filthy no serf at Wilton would have worn them to clean out the garderobes. They surged around Gervase and his men, shouting their names, touching their boots and crying.

"Ye were so long gone we feared ye'd up and got yerself killed," exclaimed one man. He was of middle years, but his left leg was missing below the knee and he limped along on a crutch.

Gervase had removed his helmet and now handed it to one of the boys. "I'd not be so inconsiderate as to leave you to shoulder all this alone, Leon." He smiled ruefully. "Though we've had quite a time getting here."

A woman stepped up beside Leon, her hand brushing his arm in a gesture that bespoke familiarity. "Ye are well come, milord."

"Dore, has your husband been misbehaving?" Gervase teased.

Leon's expression darkened. "I've little choice in the matter, as ye can see," he snapped. His venomous words snuffed out the smiles. People shifted uneasily and looked away.

"If ye'll come within, there's a bit of ale I've been saving against yer return," Dore said, hand clutching Leon's sleeve.

He shook her off. "Where is she? Where's the heiress what's going to set things to rights?" he demanded.

Alarm skittered down Cat's back. She saw it reflected in the quick glance Gervase shot her over the crowd. The others saw it, too, turning on Cat like a pack of wild animals. Their lips drew back from yellowed teeth, their eyes narrowed.

"Murdering English bitch," someone screamed. The crowd surged forward. A filthy hand reached for Jock's bridle.

Vallis was quicker. Muttering an oath, he placed himself between Cat and the angry mob. "Hold! Leave her be!" he cried.

Cat reached for the eating knife at her waist and began to pray. 'Twasn't the Almighty who came to her rescue, but Gervase. Shouting her name, he charged forward and swept her onto his lap. "Stay back!" he ordered, one arm wrapped around Cat. He'd pulled no weapon, nor did he need one, the fire in his eyes enough to hold the throng at bay. "Lady Catherine is in no way responsible for her father's deeds."

"After what Sommerville did to us, how can ye protect his daughter?" Leon shouted.

"Because she is my wife," Gervase told them, Thor dancing sidelong in response to his rider's tension. "Aye, wife," he replied to his people's strangled shouts of disbelief.

If anything, the mood of the crowd turned uglier. Cat had once seen a mob in London tear a thief limb from limb. "Gervase," she murmured. "I'm afraid. Please take me away from here."

" 'Twill be fine," he assured her, his voice hard with conviction. Then he shouted, "The man...or woman...who lays a hand on her will be banished from Alleuze."

Welcome to purgatory, Cat thought.

"What will you do?" Perrin asked anxiously.

Gervase placed his elbows on a crude table and stared out over the dimly lit hall. 'Twas quiet now except for the slurp and crunch of eighty souls gulping down the first decent meal they'd had in months. "They'll come around."

Perrin snorted. "Nay, but the only thing that diverted them from taking their hatred out on poor Lady Catherine was your offer of the food and drink we'd brought from Le Vigan."

"They are good people. They'd not harm her," Gervase said, wishing the words didn't sound so hollow.

"Once they were good people. Now they are little better than animals, hounded by fear and hunger and memories of murdering brigands who attacked them by night. Will your threats make them forget 'twas her father who entered Alleuze by guile, then burned and raped and tortured for the sport of it?"

Gervase sighed and glanced about the once-fine hall, a place of light and laughter, now a blackened husk. The walls were scorched by the fire upon which the brigands had forced the cook to roast the castle cattle. When the food ran out and they tired of the torture, they'd consigned the furniture to the flames, laughing and dancing about, from all reports, while the timbers two stories overhead smoked in the terrible heat. Then they'd departed, taking with them everything of value...including the golden candlesticks Gervase's great-grandsire had brought home with him from the Crusades.

"What was done to Alleuze went beyond waging war," Gervase murmured half to himself. "'Twas wanton destruction of the most cruel and malicious sort. I...I have difficulty believing the man who sired and raised Catherine could do such things."

"Aye." Still... Perrin thought again about the contrast between the terrible deeds ascribed to Odell de Lauren and the goodness of Abella de Lauren, Gervase's mother.

"When they come to know her, the people of Alleuze will value her as we do."

"If they don't stone her first," Perrin muttered.

Gervase shifted and stared at him, alarm plain in his weary face. "You don't seriously think anyone would...not after I threatened them with banishment." In such perilous times, 'twas the worst punishment he could devise, akin to a death sentence.

"I think the hatred of those who were here runs deeper than those of us who were not. And we cannot be with her every moment. Thankfully she agreed to eat in your chamber, but what of tomorrow? Surely you can't expect to keep her under lock and key. Knowing Lady Catherine, she'd chafe at such confinement."

"Or rebel." Gervase sighed and rubbed a hand across his eyes. Jesu, he was bone tired. He'd known there would be a few rough moments when he brought Catherine here, but he'd underestimated his people's thirst for vengeance. "I will assure her safety...with my body if needs be."

"Oh?" Perrin's glance turned sharp. "And what of the band that has twice attacked our small herd of cattle? Will you go after them or let them take the meat from under our noses?"

"Nay. We need the food to last the winter." Because the land near Alleuze was so steep and rocky, the pasturelands lay on the plateau several miles away. "I'll take twenty of the men with me and leave you in charge here."

Perrin complained, but Gervase stood firm. Despite his faith in his people, he'd not leave Catherine unguarded.

'Twas not easy living in a mountain keep with eighty or so people who hated you. After two days in her new home, Cat decided hell came closer to describing it than purgatory.

She sat on the camp stool she'd carried into the small enclosed garden behind the tower. Jolie slept in a basket at her feet, while Ila drowsed on a blanket nearby. Tearlach and Faye were helping Father Ambroise clean the chapel, for no one at Alleuze would lift a finger to help. Her friends were as much outcasts as Cat herself, tainted by their association with a Sommerville. All her life Cat had been proud of her name and her lineage. She still was. 'Twas why it hurt so to see it hurled at her head like a curse whenever she left her room. Which was not often, for Gervase had ordered...nay, asked...her to keep to herself till he returned from dealing with the cattle thieves.

Brigands, thieves, murderers, this land abounded with them. The dregs of humanity left by the receding tide of war to roam about and prey on those weaker than they. She'd come to France in hopes of finding a place where she'd fit in. Now that dream seemed further away than ever.

Disgusted, Cat stood to pace, kicking at the weeds that choked the stone path. The master chamber overlooked the garden, and their first morn here she'd awakened in the lumpy, musty pallet to find Gervase staring out the window.

"The sun is out at least," she'd murmured, slipping her arm around him to offer comfort. She'd hoped this tragic place with its scarred walls and layers of dirt would look better by day.

"Aye." He kissed her hair. "I used to follow my grandmother around while she tended her roses. She covered them in leaves to shield them from the icy winters and watered them when the hot summer sun was drying. I am glad she can't see what's come of them." A tremor shook him. "My parents died when I was two and ten. I missed them all my life. Now I am glad they died. I sometimes wish *I* had not made it back from the war."

"Oh, Gervase." Unable to bear his anguish, she wrapped her arms around him and hugged him tight. "I am so sorry."

"Hush." He'd clung to her then, as needy as he'd been when he'd wakened her in the heart of the night and loved her with a passion that had bordered on desperation. "I've not wished that since I met you," he softly assured her. "You are my light, the only joy I've known after what seems a lifetime in hell. But this is no place for you. Even if you were...accepted...conditions here are too rough. There is so much to be done, but no men to do the work save myself and my soldiers, and now we must go off again to rid us of some new threat. I...I should send you back."

"Nay. Do not, for I won't go," she had insisted. "My place is with you. Together we will make a home here." But now, with Gervase and the others gone, Cat's spirits flagged. Bad enough his people hated her, but they seemed to have little interest in cleaning up their home. From her window, she'd seen them moping about, half-heartedly poking at the burned timbers and tumbled stone without making much progress toward bettering their situation. Small wonder they were mired in past tragedies, living as they did surrounded by reminders of them. If 'twas up to her, she'd have the refuse toted away, the walls scrubbed and whitewashed. But 'twasn't up to her, and unless she could change their poor opinion, it might never be.

A weed caught on the hem of one of the gowns Dame Sofie had given her. As Cat bent to free the fabric, something pricked her. "Ouch!" Scowling, she sucked at the bit of blood on her finger and searched for the culprit. The glossy leaves and sharp thorns of a rosebush peered out from the brush.

A rosebush?

Kneeling in the scrub, Cat gently freed the plant. 'Twas small and scraggly, with nary a bud on it, but 'twas a rose. Gervase's grandmother's rose.

Cat rocked back on her heels, the tears that rode too near the surface these days filling her eyes. Somehow it had managed to survive the hooves of the brigands' horses, when they'd used the garden for a tiltyard, and the months of neglect that had followed. But it was weak and stunted from lack of food, light and proper care. Like the people of Alleuze.

The thought struck her fast and deep. Hard on its heels came another notion. She'd wronged these poor folk, thinking them lazy or uncaring because they did so little to help themselves. Without food, how could they have the strength to work? Without guidance, how could they know what to tackle first? Without hope, how could they have the heart to even begin?

Cat jumped up, her mind awhirl with plans. Thanks to Dame Sofie, they had money for food, and more, enough for an army of workmen to restore Alleuze. As her mother had done Wilton.

Smiling, Cat recalled her father's tale of coming home from waging war on the Sommervilles' enemies, the Harcourts, to discover that his wife of only a few months had sold the plunder in the storerooms and used it to rebuild Wilton. How he used to laugh, his eyes glowing with love and pride for his beloved wife. Cat wanted to see that same expression in Gervase's face when he came back from thwarting the cattle thieves.

"Ila! Ila, watch baby Jolie for me," Cat exclaimed.

The old woman sat up, alarmed. "Are we attacked?"

"Nay. We are saved." Cat bent to kiss her wrinkled cheek and stroke Jolie's downy head for luck. "I must go out... with Tearlach and Father Ambroise... and mayhap Vallis if he is up to the journey." Aye, Gervase would be most wroth if she went hying about the countryside alone.

"Where do ye go?" Ila demanded, looking dubious.

"To... oh, what was the name of that town we bypassed on our way here? We saw the walls in the distance. Brissac or something like that. It cannot be more than a few hours away."

"Aye. There is a Brissac not far away. 'Tis a good-size town, larger than Le Vigan. My parents and I went there to sing and dance at the yearly fairs. But whatever do ye want there?"

"Food and workers. Dozens of workers."

* * *

"Should we not make camp? It feels like rain, and 'twill be dark in a few hours."

Gervase shifted in the saddle and glared at the storm clouds racing across the sky. "Nay, Henri, I'll risk a wetting to sleep within Alleuze's walls tonight."

"He means in that woman's arms," Leon muttered.

"I make no secret of the fact that I enjoy my *wife*," Gervase snapped. "But that is not the only reason I'd reach home tonight." He glanced at the men drooping in their saddles. Several had crude bandages peering through the rents in their mail. By dint of hard riding and Henri's keen tracking, they'd surprised the thieves. The fighting had been brief, but fierce and bloody. While they'd regained most of the stolen cattle and scattered the brigands, the leader and twenty of his men had escaped. From a prisoner, Gervase had learned a chilling fact.

That leader was Maslin Sauveur, brother to Vachel and Emile. Maslin had learned, from two survivors of the battle, what had happened at Le Vigan and was determined to avenge his kin. "He took the cattle hoping to draw ye from yer tower, but didn't know ye'd move so fast," the outlaw had whined. "But ye'll get yers. Maslin Sauveur rides for Jean Cluny of Arles. Cluny'll not be pleased to hear his men have been murdered. He'll send men to kill ye and burn Alleuze to the ground."

The knowledge that he had only a short time in which to prepare for a siege had sent Gervase rushing back to Alleuze. Goaded by his desperation, they arrived well before dark. A profound sense of relief surged through Gervase as he cantered into the courtyard and swung down from Thor. His gaze instinctively went to the narrow second-story window, but no familiar face appeared there.

Perrin rushed down the steps of the keep, his face and arms grimy from a day obviously spent working in the rubble. "We didn't expect you back so soon."

"Where is Catherine?" Gervase asked immediately.

"She's in her room, as far as I know." Perrin turned slowly, looking first to the empty tower window, then to the clusters of castle folk. "But I've been occupied trying to clear the filth from the hall. Dore, have you seen the lady?"

The housekeeper sniffed and studied her worn boots. "I'm not her nursemaid."

She knew something. Gervase took her scrawny arm and gave her a little shake. "What have you done with Catherine?"

"N-naught," Dore stammered. "Sh-she rode out."

"Out! Out where?" Gervase roared so loudly the stone keep shook and his people cringed.

"Easy, Gervase." Perrin laid a hand on his shoulder. "You're frightening them so they can't answer."

"Dore," Gervase said through his teeth, "where is my wife?"

Ila pushed her way through the crowd, Jolie in her arms, Faye trailing in her wake. "She's gone on an errand to Brissac."

"Brissac?" Gervase echoed. All he could think was that she'd found life at Alleuze too harsh and had left him. He tried to tell himself 'twas for the best . . . for her, but his heart ached.

"Aye, to Brissac . . . to fetch food and workmen," Ila added. She prattled on about outlaw plunder and roses trying to grow among the weeds, but Gervase was past heeding her.

"Bloody hell, how could you let her go?" he demanded.

"I...I didn't know." Perrin looked to the guards. "By whose order was the gate opened?"

The guard shrugged. "What care we where she goes?"

Gervase pulled off his helmet and threw it, heedless of the dents in the precious metal as it bounced on the stones. "You should care, by God. How could you let her hie off like that? What if she falls in a ravine? What if she is attacked by...?" Holy Mother. Maslin was out there somewhere. He whirled, reaching blindly for Thor's reins, ready to ride out again.

"Wait." Perrin grabbed his arm. "You are near dead on your feet, and the others, as well. Let me go and look for her."

"Nay. I must go and with every man I can muster," Gervase said grimly. He stared at those around him, filled with a bleak, silent rage, at them for having allowed Catherine to leave, at the perilous times that made even an errand of mercy a death march. "I know you'd as soon see her dead, but I will go after my wife and could use the support."

'Twas a measure of the love they bore him that every man capable of riding and carrying a weapon ran to arm...even those who had just ridden in.

Early-morning light filtered through the canopy of trees, dappling the party riding through the forest. Another mile and they'd break into the open and begin the climb into the mountains, Cat thought, well pleased with what she'd accomplished in only a day. Behind her rumbled carts filled food, building supplies and the common laborers who would do the menial tasks assigned by the craftsmen she'd engaged, with the priest's help.

Forward of the baggage wains rode the master stonemason and the carpenter, both deep in discussion with

Father Ambroise, who'd quickly proved his worth as a wage negotiator. There had even been enough coin to hire the ten men-at-arms Vallis had insisted on as a precaution against trouble on the return trip.

"How much longer do you think?" she asked the knight.

"I pray we'll reach Alleuze by nightfall." Vallis's grizzled mustache twitched as he glanced about.

"Oh, good. I want to be home and the work well under way before Gervase returns."

"Aye. If milord sees ye've come safely back, he may only beat me instead of skinning me as I well deserve for letting ye talk me into this mad scheme," Vallis grumbled.

"You only agreed to bring me because I threatened to follow after you on my own."

"Humph. And ye'd have done it, too. Though why ye couldn't leave the task to Father Ambroise and me, I don't know."

"Because you have no knowledge of building and even though Father Ambroise swears he's finished with being a pardoner and wants naught more than to serve as priest at Alleuze, I didn't want to test him unduly by handing him so much coin."

Vallis grunted. "I agree that the latter argument has merit. No sense tempting a man." He cleared his throat. "I was surprised by yer knowledge of building."

"It seemed my mother was always making improvements to Wilton, so there were constantly masons and carpenters underfoot. 'Twas impossible to live there and not pick up at least a rudimentary understanding of such things."

"Yer lady mother saw to the repairs?"

"Papa was busy raising war-horses and seeing to our defenses. Mama must keep busy, for she has a restless spirit and a rampant curiosity which I fear she passed to me."

"Aye. Ye've a tendency to leap before ye look."

"Come, now, don't fret. We're almost out of the wood—"

"Beware!" someone screamed, and the peaceful forest suddenly teemed with armed men.

She had a swift impression of mailed men with harsh faces before Vallis pushed past her, putting himself between her and danger. The din was terrible, rough shouts blending with the shrieks of terrified horses and wounded men. She pulled the eating knife from her waist and prepared to defend herself. And none too soon, for a filthy hand reached out of the crowd and snatched at her wrist.

Cat screamed and lashed out. Blood spurted, the hand vanished, to be replaced by another. This one was gauntleted, and her blade skittered harmlessly off the leather and steel. He reached for her, she evaded him, looking up past an armored chest to a face she'd thought never to see again.

'Twas Emile Sauveur. The ghost of Emile Sauveur.

Shock held Cat immobile for a moment. The ghost took advantage of that and grabbed her arm. The strength of his grip convinced her here was no apparition come back from the grave. Screaming and kicking, she began to struggle in earnest. Her boot connected with his thigh and he grunted, his hold on her easing.

Cat jerked free, set her heels in the gelding's ribs and urged him away, but the fighting was thick around her and she could hear the outlaw scrambling after her.

A shout rang out about the chaos. "St. Juste! St. Juste!"

Gervase, here?

Whipping her head around, Cat saw her husband, his sword rising and falling in the gloom as he slashed his way toward her.

"Gervase!" Even as she spoke, her horse shuddered and stumbled. It would have taken her down with him had Gervase not reached her. His arm snaked around her waist, yanking her from her saddle. "Oh, Gervase, I—"

"Quick, swing on behind me," he commanded.

With an agility born of fear, Cat did as he bade, wrapping both arms around his waist. Through the metal links of his mail, she felt his muscles shift and bunch as he battled the brigand. She was a liability to Gervase, she realized, and would have slipped off Thor's haunches but worried any movement would distract him. So she clung there, praying with all her heart.

Used to the muted violence of the tourney, Cat was stunned by the carnage raging all around her, amazed by the terrible grace of Gervase's strokes, the stamina with which he beat back the thrusts of his beefy opponent. Her throat tightened and tears welled as she realized he battled with all his heart and soul for the very lives of those under his protection.

A grunt of pain vibrated through Gervase's big body, jerking her from her reverie. She felt him shudder and tightened her grip in an instinctive attempt to add her puny strength to his. He swore, then marshaled himself to counter a swift downward blow. Steel screamed down steel as their blades met and caught for an instant before Gervase sent his enemy's sword spinning off into the woods. With a growl of triumph, he swung again.

The man who bore Emile Sauveur's face yelped and ducked. Obviously realizing he was overmatched, the coward wrenched his horse to one side and spurred away from the fighting. Seeing him run, his men disengaged and fled in all directions, crashing through the woods like terrified rabbits.

"Hold," Gervase cried when his men made to pursue. "If we give chase they could turn and entrap us." The men of Alleuze sagged in their saddles, the forest silent except for their ragged breathing and the moans of the wounded.

Cat pressed her forehead to Gervase's sweaty back. "Thank God, you came when you did," she murmured.

He raised his visor and glared at her over his shoulder. "God's mercy won't spare you the beating you deserve for leaving Alleuze and putting yourself in mortal danger," he growled.

"Aye." Cat licked her dry lips. "'Tis my fault, but—"

"With you there is always a but. I care not what harebrained scheme you were about, you were told to stay put." His diatribe was ruined when he swayed, his eyes rolling back.

"Gervase?" Cat grabbed hold to steady him. "What is it?"

Cat spied the blood dripping from his hand to stain the fallen leaves. "Perrin! Vallis! To me, quickly!" she cried.

Perrin arrived in time to keep Gervase from pitching out of the saddle, then lowered him to the forest floor. Cat knelt and pressed trembling fingers to the rent in the shoulder seam of his tunic. "Get his mail off and let me bind this before he bleeds to death."

Ten men scrambled to obey, but as she watched his life force bubble out, Cat feared her skills wouldn't be enough to save him.

Chapter Fourteen

"My lady. My lady, the fever has broken."

"Wh-what?" Lady Cat jerked upright in the chair where she'd slept these past few nights.

Poor thing, so stiff and tired, Dore thought. "The fever's broken," she repeated gently.

"Really?" Lady Cat whipped around to stare at Gervase. He lay in the center of the big bed she had purchased in Brissac, his face white as the pillow beneath his head, his hair slicked back with sweat, his lips dry and cracked. Three days of battling fever and raging delirium had gouged dark hollows around his eyes. The rasp of his breathing was scarcely audible above the whine of the wind at the shutters, but the mere fact that his chest yet rose and fell was nearly a miracle.

"I...I didn't think ye could save him." Dore sank to her knees and kissed Lady Cat's hand.

"'Twas God's will, not mine," Lady Cat murmured, head falling back against the chair, tears running down her cheeks.

Tears of joy and relief, Dore thought. "Aye, 'twas surely that, but He had a right good helper in ye, my lady. When they carried my lord in, 'twas plain he'd lost so much blood I expected him to die that night, but not ye."

She smiled faintly, recalling how the lady, blood spattered and white with fright, had nonetheless browbeaten the stunned castle folk into tending their fallen lord.

Barking out orders like an army commander, Lady Cat had bade them carry Gervase upstairs, strip him of his garments and lay him on a blanket before the fire. She had his wounds stitched closed by the time the bed was ready to receive him. Nor had she left his side since, sleeping in the chair or in a pallet on the floor, eating and drinking whatever was pressed on her. 'Twas her hands that changed his bandages, wiped his fevered body and spooned watered wine between his parched lips, her hands that had mixed the herbs to fight infection and restore the blood.

Such strength of will was surprising in one so delicately built, Dore thought, looking at the small hand she held in her work-worn ones. Such dedication to a man she clearly loved went against everything Dore had thought of Ruarke Sommerville's daughter. For days now, she'd been looking for ways to make amends. "I've a tub set up in the solar if ye'd care to bathe."

Lady Cat started. Her eyes, haunted by shadows nearly as purple as they were, widened. "'Tis most thoughtful of you, Dore, but I'd stay till he wakes so I know he is all right."

Her gaze rested on his face, caressing it. Her lip trembled. "I . . . I feared I had lost him."

Dore squeezed her hand. "We would have had ye not wrestled the devil for him."

"Wrestled the devil." Lady Cat smiled. "We must remember to tell Gervase so when he wakes . . . he'll like that."

"Aye. He will... but I fear he'll be most angry when he sees how tired ye are, my lady. If only ye'd come away, wash and rest a bit, I'd sit with him."

Lady Cat cocked her head. "I appreciate your concern for me, but I must admit it surprises me."

"And me, as well." Dore held her gaze. "I hated ye when ye first came. We all did for yer sire's cruelty against us. But... but I see now Gervase was right when he said we shouldn't hold yer father's sins against ye. 'Tis clear from all ye've done... not just in saving his life, but in trying to restore Alleuze... that ye're an angel, not a monster."

"Oh, my heavens." Cat straightened. "I forgot all about the mason and the workmen." She glanced at Gervase, then at the door, torn by conflicting duties. "Here I paid for their time and—"

"Fret not, my lady," Dore said soothingly. "Perrin took them in hand, and my Leon, as well. The rubble's been carted away, the hall scrubbed and whitewashed. I'm surprised ye didn't hear the carpenter and his helpers hammering away in the lower bailey." She went and opened one of the narrow shutters that covered the arrow slit, flooding the room with gray light. "Come see."

Cat sighed, so tired she could scarcely move. Nay, 'twas relief that had robbed her limbs of their strength. He was alive. Alive and like to stay that way. 'Twas time for her to rejoin the living, as well. Groaning, she got up and hobbled to the window.

Though the sun was not yet over the mountain, the courtyard teemed with activity. All traces of Alleuze's trial by pillage and fire had been removed. Where once there'd been debris piled against the bailey wall, now marched a row of new buildings. Smoke rose from the chimney of one she marked as the kitchen. The smith stood at his forge in the doorway of another, pounding a piece of hot metal. In the open air, men clad in naught but knee-length braies toiled to shape tables and benches from a dwindling pile of lumber. Over the top of the wall, she noted a new course of stone had been added to reinforce the outer defenses.

"Oh, 'tis wondrous. More than I'd dreamed they'd accomplish," Cat breathed. "They've worked miracles."

"At yer behest, my lady," Dore replied. "We've food in our bellies, a roof over our heads and hope in our hearts, thanks—"

A groan sent both women back to the bed. Gervase's eyes were open and clear for the first time in days.

"Catherine," he murmured, smiling up at her.

"Oh Gervase. You know me."

"Aye. Why should I not?" He tried to rise, groaned and fell back. "Jesu, what ails me, I'm weak as a babe?"

"You don't remember the brigands?" Cat asked anxiously, fussing with the large bandage on his shoulder to make certain he hadn't reopened the wound again.

"Which ones?" His frown deepened. "Now I recall . . . you went to Brissac and were attacked."

"And you saved me." Cat took the cup of watered wine Dore had poured and pressed it to his lips.

Gervase drank, scowling at her over the rim. When he'd finished, he let go the storm that had built inside him. "Catherine, if you aren't the most exasperating—"

"I know." She sat down and burst into tears.

"Now see what ye've done," Dore snapped.

"Me?" Gervase watched in amazement as his housekeeper bent to cosset the woman she'd openly scorned.

"Poor lamb, worn herself to the bone tending ye and what thanks does she get? The moment ye're out of danger ye rail at her. Ingrate," she added, spearing him with a condemning glance.

Gervase blinked, off kilter and struggling for balance.

"Nay, nay. 'Tis all my fault," Catherine said between sobs and sniffs. *His Catherine crying?* "If I hadn't gone off like that, he...he wouldn't have been so gravely wounded."

"Damn right," Gervase murmured, but Dore cut him off.

"'Tis true, but there's no point fretting over the past," said the woman who'd been haunted by the past this twelvemonth. "Ye've done yer best to make up for that one tiny mistake."

"Tiny mistake!" Gervase exclaimed.

Dore glared at him. "Aye, and 'twas done for a good cause. When ye see what miracles she's wrought here."

"The only miracle I see is that she is still alive." But Catherine's uncharacteristic silence troubled him.

"I meant the improvements to Alleuze," Dore said.

Gervase stared at Catherine's bowed head, waiting for her to speak. When she didn't, he grew more uneasy and looked around, noting the same scarred walls and the same lack of furnishings. No, the bed was new. "No wonder I dreamed I'd gone to heaven and slept on a cloud." He shifted gingerly on the wool-stuffed mattress. "Whence came this bed?"

"From Brissac," Dore said.

"Brissac! You went alone to Brissac, endangered yourself and, indeed, all of us, for a bed?" Gervase shouted. He tried to sit, but a wave of dizziness sucked him down.

"Gervase!" Catherine leapt from the chair, her hands on his chest, pressing gently, tears streaming over her cheeks. "Please do not move, for your wounds aren't yet healed. When they are, I promise you can beat me to your heart's content."

" 'Twould serve you right if I did," he grumbled, but exhaustion drained the rage from him.

"She didn't go for a bed alone," Dore said.

"Dore, please do not argue with him," Catherine pleaded.

"I cannot let him think ill of ye, my lady."

"Let him think what he likes so long as he is still."

Gervase looked from one concerned face to the other, conscious suddenly of Catherine's pallor, of her lank hair and the dark circles beneath her eyes. "What has happened? Are we besieged? Have the brigands returned?"

"Nay. All is well," Catherine said quickly. "At least I think it is. I've been so busy with you, I—"

"How long? How long have I been ill?"

'Twas Dore who answered, "Three hellish days and nights when ye lay racked with fever and we didn't know if ye'd live or die. That ye did is thanks to yer lady wife."

Gervase scanned Catherine's face, seeing the love and devotion in every weary line. "Have we no servants that my wife must kill herself tending me?"

"I wanted to. I needed to," she cried.

Guilt. Gervase understood it well. His quest for revenge had landed her here, in harm's way. "It seems I owe you my life. In which case, I'll only beat you a bit," he teased, but instead of rising to the bait, her tears began to fall anew. "Catherine! Please, I cannot stand to see you weep so. Is aught wrong?" He reached for her, groaning as pain lanced through his shoulder.

"Nay, do not move or you will tear out the stitches." She flung herself across his waist, hands braced on his upper arms. "I swear naught is wrong," she insisted, lashes spiky with tears.

She lied. Gervase opened his mouth to say so, caught Dore's warning glance and hesitated. Tired as he was, Catherine looked exhausted. Whatever was wrong would wait till they were rested. "I will lie still," he said, "if you will sleep."

"First you must eat." Catherine leapt up and ran to the hearth where a pot sat just off the coals. "I've some broth."

"I hate broth," Gervase grumbled. "Besides, I'm not hungry."

"Now the real work begins," Dore said grimly, shaking her head. "He is the worst of patients. When ye say eat, he'll refuse. When ye say sleep, he won't be tired."

"Nay. He will eat," Catherine said, hurrying back with bowl and spoon. "Won't you, Gervase?"

When he saw how her hands trembled and her lips, too, Gervase gave in. "Of course I will." Ignoring Dore's wry chuckle, he swallowed a bit of the thin, tasteless liquid. Between spoonfuls, he managed to slip in a few questions. He was pleased to learn that none of the men had been seriously hurt—besides himself—relieved there'd been no sign of the brigands. There was still the threat of this Jean Cluny, but mayhap the beating his men had taken would convince them to leave Alleuze alone.

When the bowl was empty, Cat set it aside and fussed with the dressing on his shoulder. Even her gentle probings made the damn thing ache abominably. 'Twas not the pain that made him suck in his breath and groan, but the certainty that his tyrannical little wife would withhold bad news out of concern for his health. "Will you send Perrin to me?" he asked.

"Not till you are stronger," she said, straightening.

"Catherine." He caught hold of her hand. "I do not blame you for these injuries of mine."

"Thank you," Cat murmured. Unable to bear the tenderness in his gaze, she turned away to rummage in her chest of medicines. She did not deserve his forgiveness. She had been wrong to go to Brissac, headstrong, impetuous, willful and wrong.

As soon as Gervase was safely asleep, she'd seek out Father Ambroise, confess her sins and ask for a penance to atone for nearly having cost Gervase his life. Something involving a great sacrifice...aye, that was it. She'd wear sackcloth and eat dry bread crusts the rest of her life. And she'd mend her ways. She'd be cautious, meek and biddable. Even if it killed her.

Gervase recovered with his customary speed and was out of bed in five days, anxious to see what progress had been made in setting Alleuze to rights. The details reaching the sickroom had been sketchy, for his little tyrant had kept visitors to a minimum and forbidden all talk of serious matters.

With Catherine beside him, he entered the hall to break his fast, eager for some physical activity to relieve his pent-up energy. Just inside the doorway, he stopped short. The whitewashed walls and fresh rushes underfoot were expected, the new trestle tables and benches were not.

"Did you buy these in Brissac?" he asked.

"Nay," Catherine murmured. "They were made here."

"By whom? 'Twould take time to cut and cure so much wood."

"Come, take your seat at the high table," she urged.

Gervase's eyes widened as he caught sight of the dais at the far end of the hall and the cloth-draped table upon it. "Where...?" he began, then other things registered.

The tallow candles in the piked wheels hanging from the beams overhead. The whole garments his people wore in place of their torn ones. The brown bread and broken meats on the platters the servants carried in. "Where did all this come from?" he demanded.

"Can we not speak of it after you eat?" Catherine asked.

"I would hear your explanation now."

"But you should not be standing so long."

"Then do not keep me waiting," he said softly.

Haltingly Catherine said, "I bought these things with the coin Dame Sofie pressed upon me when we left Le Vigan."

"You took part of the Sauveurs' plunder after I expressly refused to?" he asked, aghast she'd gone against his wishes.

"Aye." Catherine looked down at her toes, her head covered by a coarse brown scarf that was nearly as ugly as the shapeless russet robe she wore. "I most humbly beg your pardon."

Humbly? Gervase doubted Catherine had ever been humble in her life. He waited for the "but" she usually tacked on to any explanation she made. 'Twas not forthcoming. Indeed, she'd been in a strange mood ever since he'd regained consciousness in their new bed. A bed she'd thus far refused to share on the grounds she might roll in the night and reopen his shoulder.

As if such a thing were possible. He'd seen the stitches himself, so numerous and so stout he could have wielded a sword without straining them. Still she insisted on sleeping apart from him, as remote and distant as the waning moon. She tended his wounds and brought him his meals. She oversaw the running of the castle and the progress of the repairs. If he called for her, she came at once. If he offered advice on the restoration, she saw it carried out without question or complaint. If he spoke to her, she replied. If he teased, she smiled, but all the while her expression remained set and distant.

The spark that had lit Catherine from within had been extinguished, and he knew not how to rekindle it.

"Why did you defy my orders?" he asked again.

"I didn't, exactly, but..." She clapped a hand over her mouth to keep back the rest of her words, then mumbled, "I am sorry, my lord. It won't happen again."

"What is amiss?" Perrin asked, coming up behind them.

"Did you know where she got the coin for this?"

Perrin's gaze flickered to Catherine's bowed head, then back to Gervase. "Aye. And I did not say so because we feared to make you angry whilst you were yet healing."

"Well, you were right, I am angry," Gervase snarled. Conscious that his temper was fraying and not wanting to argue with Catherine in front of Perrin, he took hold of her. "We will go where we can be private and you will explain how you came to defy me in this."

"Gervase, be reasonable...." Perrin began, but Catherine forestalled him by pronouncing herself willing to go with Gervase and assuring his cousin she'd be safe.

The exchange, with its hints of closeness between the two, increased Gervase's frustration. Glaring at Perrin, he tugged Catherine out of the hall and slammed shut the door to the hall, sealing them in the dark entryway. Once the walls had been hung with the primitive weapons carried by his ancestors. He was glad the brigands had taken them, otherwise he might have been tempted to hack at the thick oaken door to alleviate his rage.

"Well?" he growled, propping his good shoulder against one wall to bolster his flagging strength.

"I am sorry I went against your wishes. I won't do it—"

"Nay, you will not," he grumbled, frightened by her attitude but uncertain how to snap her out of it.

"If that is all, milord, I'd attend chapel," she said dully.

"Cease calling me 'milord' like I was some chance acquaintance," he shouted.

"Gervase, then," she said dutifully, head still down.

"And must you wear that shapeless sack?"

She ran a hand over the coarse wool and he could only think how it must chafe her soft skin. "I vowed I would, but if you forbid it, I will, of course, comply."

"I don't want your compliance, dammit, I want..."

When he didn't continue, she peered up at him through her lashes, eyes flat. "You have only to tell me, and I will obey," she said. A phrase he was growing to hate.

"I want my Catherine back!"

She blinked. "I am here, my lo—Gervase."

"Bloody hell!" He turned away and jammed a hand through his hair, wincing as fire radiated from his half-knit muscles.

"Please have a care for your wound," she urged, her hand gentle on his arm. That touch, the first born of something other than healing, sent flames of a different sort licking through his body to settle in his groin.

Mayhap she held herself aloof from him for fear he was not yet healed. Healing be damned. He pulled her into his embrace, cut off her squeak of surprise with a hard kiss, his tongue stealing past her parted lips to taste and subdue.

"Nay, Gervase." Panting, she wedged her arms between them and pushed. "I...I am late for chapel. Father Ambroise is waiting to hear my confession." Free of him, she fled.

Gervase let her go because he'd hold no unwilling woman. The ache in his chest was only partly due to his recent wound. What had happened to make her act so? She wasn't afraid of his anger or of being punished for having taken the money. Nay, she seemed...indifferent. 'Twas an enemy he knew not how to fight.

Determined to seek answers, Gervase opened the door and strode into the noisy hall. The voices fell silent so swiftly he thought they'd all been stricken mute at once. Scores of eyes watched him wind his way through the trestle tables to the dais, some of them curious, others condemning.

Perrin scowled at him. "What have you done with Catherine?"

"Naught." Gervase sank gratefully into a new high-backed chair intended for the lord of the castle. Obviously it had been bought with the disputed coin, but he was too worried to care.

"Wine, my lord?" Armand inquired a trifle coolly.

Gervase sighed and nodded. "I swear I have not harmed my disobedient wife. She's gone to confession."

"She spends much time with Father Ambroise. Though I do not understand what she can have to confess," Armand said stoutly.

Gervase drained the cup and slammed it down. "I do. 'Twas a sin to defy her husband and take the Sauveurs' plunder."

"I...I suppose." Armand's beardless face scrunched. "But how can it be a sin to use the money if so much good came of it?"

"We would have survived without new tables," Gervase said.

"True." Perrin took the chair to his right and leaned forward. "But what of the kitchen? Would the cook have been able to make our meals in a lean-to when the icy winter winds blew? And what would Oliver have put into the pot? A few stray hares and a bit of wild onion. Without the wine, grain and dried meat the lady bought, we'd have starved. And what of the outer defenses? Would they have held without the extra course of stone? Nay, I think not. But most of all, our people wouldn't have lived to see winter if the food hadn't given them strength and their improved surroundings the will to go on."

Gervase gazed around the hall. Eating had resumed and, with it, conversation. Though there were far fewer folk at Alleuze than there had been when he first went off to war, they were heartier and happier than he'd seen them in six long years. "Very well, I grant you the coin was put to good use, but—"

"You didn't want to profit from ill-gotten gains," Perrin said. "Lady Catherine reasoned you would feel that way."

"Did she?" Gervase growled. "It seems she is well versed in what is on my mind, whilst I have no idea what maggot is in hers." He sipped from the cup the squire had refilled, but the wine didn't wash the bitterness from his mouth. "I do not suppose either of you can tell me what ails her."

"I didn't know the lady was ill," Armand exclaimed.

Perrin sighed. "She works too hard."

"I don't think it's fatigue, but I am not well versed in the ways of women," Gervase muttered. Marie had often called him insensitive for not correctly interpreting her sighs and crotchets. "Still something is wrong.

Catherine hasn't once nagged at me or crossed me since I recovered.''

"Most men would count that a blessing," Perrin teased.

"Mayhap she realizes this was a mistake and wants to leave," Gervase whispered, appalled by the thought.

"Nay," Perrin exclaimed. "She loves you and the people of Alleuze. She's happy and busy here." He jerked his chin toward the nearest trestle table where six boys gobbled bread and talked excitedly. "Two days ago one of them spotted a pig in the woods below the keep. When word reached Lady Catherine, she bade Vallis ride out and see if it was one that had escaped when the brigands took Alleuze. Indeed several pigs had fled and bred in the forest, for there is now a whole herd of them living wild. Thus far the boys have rounded up eight of the beasts and penned them in the lower bailey awaiting slaughter. We'll have fresh meat, soap and such. But more important, there are a pair of sows and a boar to ensure stock for next year."

Gervase nodded slowly. Food wasn't the only thing Catherine had given Alleuze. She'd given them hope and a reason to look to the future. The castle folk had finished breaking their night's fast and prepared to shoulder the day's tasks. In the past they'd done so with lagging steps and grim faces. Now they smiled and joked with one another, their laughter as bright as the sunshine spilling into the clean, cheery hall. All this was his little wife's doing, he thought, deeply touched.

"'Tis Lady Catherine," someone shouted above the din. Instantly the hall fell silent and all eyes, including Gervase's, went to the doorway where she stood. Shadows hid her expression, but her posture seemed uncertain, hesitant.

"If they slight her..." Gervase stood, ready to defend her.

"Nay, they will not." Perrin tugged him back down.

"Bring food for our lady," Dore commanded. A dozen people scrambled to obey. People who had spit and hissed at Catherine on her first day here jostled for the honor of bringing her bread, filling her cup. The rest hustled toward the door to offer escort. Swept up by a tide of goodwill, she was brought to the table and seated at Gervase's right.

Gervase half expected her to be intimidated by such boistcrousness, but she laughed and joked, answering questions about the day's work with the ease of long practice. "Obviously much has happened whilst I was healing," he said to her when the throng had left her to her bread and wine.

"They've worked so hard. Only wait till you see," Catherine replied, her eyes shining with a hint of her former vivacity. She was even more beautiful than when they'd first met, though seeing her in such mean garments grated on him.

"'Tis thanks to your efforts that things have been set to rights," he said gently. "And while I still do not like the manner in which it was financed, could you not have found coin to buy yourself a gown?"

Her smile faded and she lowered her head. "This gown is more fitting to my...station."

"Station? Does being my wife mean you must dress as a serf?"

Anger flickered in her gaze but was quickly stifled. "I meant no offense, my lord," she murmured. "Since my garb offends you, I will leave."

"Wait!" Gervase made a grab for her, but she evaded him, hurrying from the hall as though the hounds of hell pursued. He would have liked to follow, but his limbs felt weak suddenly, and his heart so heavy. "What ails her?" he cried softly.

"I know not." Perrin frowned. "I thought she wore those mean garments because many of the tasks that needed doing were dirty and she insisted on working alongside the women, but..." He stroked his chin. "She does spend time with Father Ambroise."

"Of course." Gervase's eyes narrowed to angry slits. "'Tis that pesky, money-grabbing priest. He has somehow found a way to lay his hands on a portion of the Sauveurs' treasure and turn Catherine against me. I must see him at once."

That proved easy, for just then the priest strolled into the hall. That he looked much altered, his garments plain, his gut slimmer, in no way muted Gervase's anger.

"Father Ambroise...get you here to me," Gervase roared.

The priest blinked but hurried forward. "'Tis good to see you up and about, Lord Gervase," he said, taking uninvited the chair Catherine had vacated. "I have prayed long and—"

"I bet you have." Gervase grabbed the front of his robe and hauled him up so their noses nearly touched. "Prayed for my swift demise, no doubt, so you might have free rein here. But we will speak of that anon. Now tell me what have you done to Catherine?"

"To Lady Catherine? Why, naught, save hear her confession, I assure you." His eyes bugged and sweat dotted his forehead.

"Ah, now we come to the meat of it. How much did you charge her for the absolution of these trumped-up sins?"

"Naught." He looked affronted. "I told you I was through with that sorry business. I've written to the bishop asking if I might serve as priest here...with your support, of course."

Gervase sighed, his anger fading. From Dore he'd heard the priest had cleaned the chapel with his own hands, said mass and heard confessions...all without asking for a sou. "I will consider it. Only tell me what penance you've levied on my wife."

"I—I cannot disregard the sanctity of the confessional. Even if you are trying to choke it out of me, my lord."

"Sorry." Gervase eased his grip. "Can you say if the wearing of sackcloth was your idea?"

Father Ambroise slid back into the chair, rubbing his neck. "Nay. She insisted 'twas fitting penance for her sins."

"Sins? Good lord, man, I kidnapped her and she's the one atoning?" Gervase scowled darkly. "And the other things? The meekness?" The refusal to share his bed?

"I should think you'd be pleased the lady was more biddable."

"Nay. Much as she sometimes angered me, I want my Catherine back...sharp tongue, willfulness and all. The question is, how do I win her over when she's closed up like a clam?"

"I might say 'tis no more than you deserved," Perrin muttered. "You've done that to me...and others...for years."

"I have? Aye, I have." Gervase sagged back into the chair, his jaw clenched so tightly his teeth hurt. My God, he'd not realized till now how damaging such behavior could be. What if he couldn't find a way to draw Catherine out and her guilt over his wounding festered till it poisoned her as his grandparents' hatred for the de Laurens had poisoned him? He could not let that happen. She was too good, too precious to be lost as he had been till she came into his life.

"How can I reach her?" he whispered.

"By giving of yourself," Perrin said just as softly. "By talking to her of the things that trouble you."

Chapter Fifteen

As Cat entered the hall that night, an odd mix of dread and anticipation knotted in her belly. Though it was very difficult to hold herself aloof from Gervase, she looked forward to seeing him, to sitting beside him and talking of simple things the way her parents had. Of the day's events and the morrow's plans.

She passed slowly between the rows of trestle tables, pleased by the bustle of activity, noting what had been done and what yet needed doing. Under Dore's watchful eye, the maids set thick slices of bread at each place to serve as plates for the roast pig that turned on the spit in the new kitchen. Pitchers of wine waited on a serving table to be passed along with a steaming potage of beans and onions. New rushes crunched underfoot as Cat approached the dais, but somewhere she must find herbs to strew in them, rosemary and thyme to keep them fresh-smelling.

Which brought to mind the garden, plucked clean of choking weeds and ready to receive the seeds she'd harvested from the few plants that hadn't been killed off. There was basil, marjoram, borage and several others, plants native to this clime. Dore had named them for her and promised to tell her what they were used for. But there were vital herbs missing, things needed for flavoring the food and, more importantly, for medicines. Cat thought longingly of the extensive gardens at Wilton. She'd ask her mother for cuttings to bring to Alleuze. If she ever saw her mother or Wilton again.

A wave of homesickness struck Cat, and she sank into the small chair beside Gervase's high-backed one. The vague pain that had lurked in the back of her mind all week intensified. All she had worked so hard to accomplish now seemed . . . tainted, hollow. Though he had allowed her to send the letter to her parents as promised, Gervase had insisted she not reveal her whereabouts lest they come and try to take her back.

"My lady, shall we serve the meal?" Dore asked, jerking Cat from her dark thoughts.

"We will wait for Lord Gervase."

"He's not coming down."

"What?" Cat noted with alarm that no manchet trencher had been set at Gervase's place. "Is he ill? Why wasn't I told?"

"He said we weren't to trouble ye, my lady."

"Not trouble me?" Cat exploded out of her chair and ran from the hall. Lifting her skirts, she took the narrow, winding stairs two at a time. Breathless and frightened, she burst into their chamber and stopped short. The room was dark save for the faint light from the fire in the hearth. Gervase sat cross-legged before it on a folded blanket, his eyes shut, another blanket draped across his shoulders.

"Gervase?" she whispered. When he didn't reply, Cat crept forward, her eyes locked on his shadow-draped profile. "Gervase, what are you doing?" she asked, kneeling beside him.

"Praying."

"But you can't sit here in the cold and dark."

"I should have sackcloth and ashes, but there wasn't any cloth to spare and Father Ambroise said 'twould be a pity to scatter ashes about when you've only just finished cleaning."

"Why sackcloth and ashes?"

"I'm atoning for my sins."

"What sins?" Cat felt his forehead, worried his faint voice and odd notions heralded a return of the fever. He felt cool.

"I kidnapped you against your will and did seek to hold you for ransom," he muttered.

"Aye, well, that's true enough, but I forgive you and—"

"I cannot forgive myself."

Cat understood—couldn't forgive herself for having caused his wounding. "Will you not at least eat something?"

"Nay. I am fasting."

"Fasting?" she shrieked, her vows to speak mildly forgotten. "You need food and plenty of it, recovering as you are from a wound that nearly killed you. I forbid it, do you hear?"

Gervase smiled and tweaked her nose. "Ah, Catherine. I hear, and am right glad to see my little tyrant returned."

She rocked back on her heels. "Why are you really doing this, Gervase?" she demanded sharply.

"I am trying...in my own clumsy way...to make you see how damaging guilt can be. Yours over my wounding, mine over kidnapping you. But mostly the guilt my grandsire foisted on me."

"Jacques St. Juste?" Cat settled down beside him, startled by his openness. "The man who raised you after your parents died?"

"Aye." He took her hand. "'Tis the first I've spoken of this to anyone save Perrin, and he doesn't know the whole of it because I couldn't bare my shame even to him."

"Oh, Gervase. 'Tis said a burden shared is lighter than one borne alone. Let me help you." She linked her fingers with his, as though sensing his need for her strength.

"Old Jacques blamed Mama and me for my father's death, even though 'twas the English who slew him."

"How unfair," Cat cried. "Why would they do that?"

"They didn't like my mother, had, in fact, opposed their only son's marriage to Abella because her sire, Odell de Lauren, was reportedly an evil man. To appease them, Mama pretended to be an orphan without kin, but after Papa was killed, she feared Alleuze would be overrun by the English and sent in secret for her brother, Bernard. He came with an army, ran the enemy off and restored the keep to us. I was only two and ten at the time and terribly impressed with the dashing uncle I had not known I had."

"How strange you did not know him."

"'Tis a twisted tale." Gervase's courage and his voice faltered. Cat's gentle squeeze on his hand restored him somewhat. She deserved to know the truth. "My maternal grandmother, Solange, died soon after my mother's birth. The mysterious circumstances surrounding her death revived rumors of insanity in Odell de Lauren's family. Solange's parents went to Crenley and demanded their grandchildren. Odell let them take my mother, but refused to give up Bernard, who was six and his heir."

"So they were raised separately. What a sad, sad story."

He looked for signs of repugnance in her, but found only compassion. "I grew up knowing none of this, but my own parents were most strict with me, whipping me even for childish pranks. After Papa died, Jacques, his father, told me it was because they sought to tame my tainted de Lauren blood. Mama died soon after my father... of a broken heart and old Jacques's meanness, I think. My life changed then."

"Not for the better, I take it."

Gervase shrugged, and Cat feared he'd retreat again and tell her no more, but he went on. "Jacques claimed that my mother had brought with her the curse of the de Laurens. That her bad blood, and mine, were responsible for Papa's death. The only way to purge me of the evil was to bleed me."

"Gervase!" Cat grabbed his arm to steady herself.

He put a hand on her shoulder and squeezed. "'Tis all right. The leeches came only once, for my grandmother... normally a timid soul... threatened to kill herself if I was bled again. Jacques gave in, but he found other ways to mold me into a 'better person.' All displays of temperament and emotion were strictly forbidden. To laugh, to cry, to shout was to release the unnatural passions he was certain I harbored within me."

"I see," Cat whispered, horrified. It explained so much. Why he had been cold, remote and harsh. To think his own grandfather had purposely made him that way. She thought of her own childhood, supported by loving parents, two sisters and doting grandparents. Then she thought about the abuses Gervase must have suffered. Tears filled her eyes and she blinked them back, needing to see his face. "How...how could you stand it?"

"I thought I deserved it. Jacques's treatment of me filled me with such fury, such an impotent urge to hit him back, that I was certain I must be as evil as he said I was."

Cat's chest ached with unshed tears. She wanted to throw herself into his arms and sob for the injustices that had been heaped on him, but a river of tears would not wash away his pain. "If you were evil, you would have kidnapped me, raped me and killed me for what you thought my father did." She smiled through her tears. "If anything, there is too much honor in you."

"I did not think so when I realized the woman I had kidnapped was kind and compassionate, not vain and cruel." He hesitated, looking deep into her eyes. "Mayhap now that you know about my family you will change your mind about this marriage."

"Never." Cat wrapped her arms around his neck and hugged him tight. "I love you, Gervase. For now and for always."

"And I you," he said softly.

"Gervase?" Her lower lip trembled. "Do you mean it?"

He paused, thinking of the de Lauren curse and the old fear that it had been responsible for his parents' deaths. If he lost Cat, he wouldn't survive. He wasn't going to lose her...not ever. "I love you, Catherine St. Juste, with all my heart."

"Oh, Gervase." Tears spilled down her cheeks, but he knew they were happy ones. "I never thought you'd say those words."

"Come, I'll prove to you I mean them." He toppled her onto his lap, smothering her gasp in a kiss. By the time he raised his head, they were panting as though they'd run up a hill.

Cat looked up into her husband's smoldering eyes, her fingers brushing over the bandage on his shoulder. "We should not. Your wound isn't sufficiently healed."

"For days you have made excuses to avoid our bed. Have you changed your mind about this marriage?" he asked slowly.

"Gervase! How can you think such a thing? I want to be with you now more than ever," she cried. "I didn't want to hurt you."

"What I have in mind will not harm me, and I have missed you most sorely, my love."

"And I you." Sighing, she melted in his arms. Her fingers twined in his chest hairs. "Gervase, are you nude all over?"

"Nearly." He nuzzled her throat. "I've left my braies on so you can have the pleasure of undressing me as I intend to you." He plucked at the neck of her robe. "Jesu, but this is coarse stuff. I'll warrant it has chafed your skin raw."

Cat smiled ruefully. "Aye, it has."

"Then you must let me tend you. Is there some of that salve you rubbed into the scuffs left by my armor?"

"Aye." The knowledge that some of her bruises were in very private spots made her shiver deliciously. "In my medicine chest, there by the bed."

Gervase nodded and made to stand with her in his arms, but pain lanced through his barely healed muscles. "Damn, I . . ."

"'Tis no matter." Scrambling off his lap, Cat stood and offered him her hand. "We will walk together."

Indeed, it did somehow seem fitting to cross the room, fingers linked as their lives were, as their bodies soon would be. Still, when they stopped beside the bed, Gervase jested, "Here I'd hoped to impress you with my strength." Grinning, he sat and pulled her into the V of his thighs.

"Oh, I am impressed, my lord." Cat gazed pointedly at the large bulge in his linen drawers. "Most impressed."

"Are you now? Well, that's a start." He slowly pulled the scarf from her head and attacked the braids coiled over each ear. Sliding his fingers through the silken curls, he gently massaged her scalp, smiling as she sighed and let her head fall back. "'Tis a pity to keep such bounty covered."

"'Twas a penance," she murmured.

"I know. 'Twas not necessary. I didn't blame you."

"Ha!" She straightened, eyes flashing. "You were furious with me. If you hadn't been nearly dead, you'd have beaten me."

"Never. Though I don't remember ever being as frightened as when I saw you besieged by the outlaws." Taking flint from the bedside table, he lit the night candle. "It seemed to take a hundred years to reach you." He fumbled briefly with the laces of her robe, then whisked it off over her head.

Gasping, Cat made to cover herself with her hands.

"None of that." He gently forced her arms down to her sides. "Think of me as your physician, called to treat these sores." His smile faded when he saw the red welts marring her skin. "Damn. Only tell me which salve to use." He tugged the medicine chest from beneath the table and opened it.

Cat reached for the crock of yarrow and goose grease, but he took it from her and bade her lie down on the bed.

Even as she complied, she said, "This isn't necessary. I can do it my—"

"Hush. 'Tis little enough after all the hours you spent tending my wounds. Not to mention all you've done for my people."

"Our people," Cat said, stretching out on her belly.

"I like the sound of that." He tisked over a particularly large spot on her shoulder. "Let me know if I hurt you, love, my hands are not used to such tender work."

Cat relaxed, his touch incredibly light and gentle. When he asked if she was all right, she nodded. "Aye. It . . . it just seems strange to have someone doing this for me."

"I know. You are used to being in control."

"Me?" She raised her head and glared over her shoulder. "You make me sound like some kind of despot."

"Tyrant," he corrected. "A most beautiful tyrant."

Her father called her mother that sometimes, but she would not mar the moment by bringing up her family.

He resumed stroking her skin. "Even with the improvements you've made, our life here won't be easy. For your sake, 'twould be better if I had not wed you, but..." He sighed. "But I am a selfish bastard and could not give you up."

"You are not selfish. Time and again you warned me we would have a rough road ahead of us, but I cannot live without you, either." She sat and framed his face with her hands, bringing it down for a kiss that held both passion and promise.

"Love me," Gervase murmured when she lifted her mouth.

"I do. Oh, Gervase, I do with all my heart."

"Lie with me, then . . . and do not fret over my wounds." The candlelight reflected the depth of his feelings, a love that mirrored her own. In time, mayhap that love could bridge his hatred of her father. For the moment, it was enough that he'd lowered his barriers at last and no secrets lay between them.

"Aye," she whispered, arching up against him.

"Catherine. It's been so long." He buried his face in her neck and gently lowered her onto the bed, aligning her soft body with the hard planes of his. "I need you so very, very much."

"And I you." She offered her mouth eagerly, shifting to cradle the strength of him between her thighs.

Gervase groaned and dragged her closer, struggling for control as their mouths mated. She was so small, so fragile that she deserved exquisite care, but she was driving him crazy. It wasn't just the feel of her catching fire in his embrace, but the knowledge that she was giving herself to him on every level nearly sent him shuddering over the edge. As he rose up to roll her under him, white-hot pain shot through his shoulder.

"Bloody hell!" Gervase rasped.

Cat sprang back from him. "What is it?"

"Naught. I but moved too quickly." Eyes shut, he willed the agony away as he had so many greater hurts in the past. When he opened his eyes, her troubled face hovered over his.

"We will sleep," she said, and moved away.

"Later." He halted her retreat by throwing a muscular leg over her slender ones. "If you struggle, you might well injure me." His eyes glinted with triumph. "Only trust me to know what is best...for both of us." His hand glided up her ribs to capture her breast. Gaze locked on hers, his fingers gently plucked at the nipple, making it swell and sending fire through her veins.

"You do not play fair." With a sigh of surrender, Cat lay back and gave herself over to his care. When his mouth replaced his fingers, drawing down on her with satisfying greed, she arched into his embrace. Shock waves rippled to the aching core of her. Against her thigh she felt the proof of his desire throbbing to the same beat that drove her. She reached down between them, pushed aside the encumbering linen and filled her hands with his hot flesh. Like velvet-covered steel.

The breath hissed out between Gervase's teeth as her small hands caressed him. "Easy, or we'll be done ere we've begun."

"Good, for I can wait no longer. Come, fill me... complete me," ordered his little tyrant, trying to tug him atop her.

"I will, but not like that." He rolled onto his back, bringing her with him. One minute she lay sprawled on his chest, the next she was sitting up, straddling his waist. Her gasp of shock, the blush that suffused her skin as she hastily drew her hair about her, made him laugh. It felt good. In all his years of marriage to Marie, never once had he laughed in bed. "You would hide your charms from me, lady wife?" he teased, parting her mane and ogling her breasts.

She went crimson, yet she didn't cringe. "I feel exposed."

"You are, but only to me. You know I'd not harm you nor do anything that would shame you." As he spoke, he palmed her breasts, kneading them gently, watching with a connoisseur's eye the way hers turned to purple smoke. "See, this is not so bad. I can touch your sensitive breasts." He grazed the hardened peaks with his fingertips, smiling at her sharply indrawn breath. "Yet you have the upper, er, hand, and are in complete control."

"I am?" Cat's senses were spinning so she'd tangled her hands in his crisp chest hairs to keep her balance.

"Aye. For instance, if you want me to kiss your breasts, you have only to do this...." Sliding his hands around to her back, he urged her forward till her nipple touched his mouth. "Cat?"

"Aye." The word became a hushed moan as he drew the sensitized flesh into his mouth and suckled, setting her afire again. Inside her the pressure built, and her hips answered, rocking against him in an instinctive search for surcease. His hands rushed over her, kneading her back, cupping her buttocks, then slipping between her thighs to explore the secret folds. Tighter and tighter the coil grew until she feared she'd explode.

"Take me, Cat," Gervase growled. Shuddering with the effort to restrain himself, he helped her lift. "Ah." His groan nearly drowned by hers, he sheathed himself in her burning heat.

For an instant, Cat sat still, stunned by the sheer size of him. He filled her, stretched her, yet there was no pain, only a sense of completeness. She stared down at him in the candlelight, his handsome features starkly defined by the power of his need. The corded muscles in his jaw and neck stood out in testimony to the battle he fought for control. She didn't want control, she wanted to give in to the wildness he'd kindled in her.

Moving her hips experimentally, Cat rose up on his shaft, then lowered herself. The burning heat intensified, clawing at her loins, forcing her to move again.

"Aye, take us there, my lady, my love." He put his hands on her hips to steady her till she'd found the rhythm. They came together hotly, fiercely, bodies straining to give and take till neither knew who led or who followed. Yet this went beyond a physical joining.

They were forging a link between their very souls. Shuddering with the force of her emotions, she sought to tell him what he meant to her. One look at his eyes, passion hazed yet shining with love, told her no words were necessary. The coil inside her flared then splintered.

"Aye, love. Now," Gervase whispered. With quick, sure strokes, she carried them higher. Her cry of release came seconds before he growled her name and buried himself deep in the heart of the contractions, utterly consumed by the feel of her body tightening around his, by the love he poured into her.

It was going to be all right, Cat thought dimly moments later as she floated back down to earth, locked tight in his sweaty embrace. They had each other, naught else could harm them.

Seeking a bit of privacy from the chaos of ongoing repairs and preparations for the coming winter, Gervase headed for the small garden at the back of the tower. He'd been tempted to ride out, for he did his best thinking on horseback, but his little tyrant had caught wind of the plan.

"Nay, what if you are attacked by Maslin?" she'd cried.

Though he was reasonably certain Cluny's outlaws would not be back, he hadn't wanted to worry her or take from their work the twenty men she'd thought necessary to guard him. 'Twas what came of allowing a woman to stick her nose into men's affairs.

Allowing? Gervase snorted as he opened the garden gate. There was no *allowing* with Cat. He knew they'd quarrel over her willfulness all their lives, but he wouldn't try to tether her... unless she put herself in danger.

"Well, what do you think?"

Gervase turned, startled to find Cat had followed him. Bright sunlight glinted on the braid she'd pinned in a coronet atop her head. The deep blue of the gown the maids had fashioned for her intensified the color of her eyes. "You look beautiful."

"Not me, silly," she replied, beaming with pleasure nonetheless. "The garden."

He looked where she pointed, surprised to see the sea of weeds had been transformed into neat if sparsely planted beds divided by gravel walks. "'Tis just as it was in my mother's day," he murmured. "When did you find the time?"

"'Twas not all my doing. Ila knows a great deal about plants and Faye was eager to learn. They did most of the work."

"At your behest." He drew her into his embrace, back to front. His chin resting on the top of her head, he studied the tranquil scene, senses lulled by the scent of warm earth mingling with the sweetness of the woman in his arms. "Thank you."

"I enjoyed it. At home I often supervised the planting of the herbs." The words were lightly said, yet they caused his gut to clench. Would she ever think of Alleuze as home? Unaware of the pain she'd caused, Catherine went on, speaking of the herbs they lacked and her plans to obtain them. "Would you reconsider and let me tell my mother where I am and ask if she could send some packets of seeds and mayhap plant roots, as well?"

Gervase tightened his grip on her. "If they know where you are, your father will come and take you from me," he reiterated.

"Not if they know I'm wed and happy." She shifted to look up at him. "By the by, where did your note say to send the ransom?"

"The message I left in your father's tents said only that we had eloped to Bayonne in the south of France. The plan was for my uncle to send the ransom demand and pick up the money in the small port of Sete. 'Tis only a day's journey from his home outside Arles." He nuzzled the top of her head. "But of course that note was never sent." The day they'd arrived in Alleuze, he'd kept his promise and sent word to Bernard of their marriage and his decision not to ransom Cat. The same messenger had also carried a letter bound for the English court at Bordeaux. With any luck, her parents had already received it and knew she was safe and happily married.

Still her heart was heavy. Cat lifted his hand and kissed the scarred knuckles. "I wish I could see them again. I...I know you hate my father, but would you punish my poor mother, too?"

"I had not thought of that." Restless now, Gervase took Cat's hand and led her to the back of the garden. There, enclosed by a short wall, were the gravestones of the St. Justes, from his great-grandparents to his parents, and finally the stone that marked Eva's final resting place. "I know what it is to fear for your child and be unable to help her. When I learned of the attack, my first thought was for her... little did I know she was already dead and buried."

"You must have loved them very much."

"I loved Eva...she was so small and fragile. Like a bud that will never have a chance to flower." He bowed his head against the painful memories. "But Marie... nay. Better she had gone to the convent, as she'd wished, but her older sister, to whom I'd been betrothed from childhood, died and Marie's father insisted she fulfill the contract."

"But I feel your sorrow every time her name is mentioned."

"Guilt." Gervase exhaled, but the tightness in his chest remained. "She begged me not to go off to war and leave her here, but to allow her to return to her parents' home. Out of spite for the coldness she showed our daughter, I made her stay. I truly thought Alleuze so far removed from the fighting that there would be no danger." He raked a frustrated hand through his hair. "Jesu, I'd not have risked any of their lives had I—"

"You are not to blame." Cat threw her arms around him and hugged him with all her strength. "You could not have known. We must not dwell on our past mistakes, but look to the future. Our future." Cat tugged his head down and kissed him with all the love pent up inside her. Gradually she felt the tension ease from his big body, knew the exact moment when he forgave himself, for his mouth gentled and his hands moved over her as though she were made of spun glass.

"How did one so young become so wise?" he murmured.

She was not wise, merely desperate to see him as happy as he had made her. "I am like my mother in that," she said pointedly.

Gervase drew in a deep, cleansing breath and released it slowly. With it went the last of his despair. Thanks to Catherine. "You must write and tell her you are well...or as well as can be a noble lady consigned to scrabble a living from—"

"Hush." Cat silenced him with a swift kiss. "I am content. We are young, strong and clever. We will prosper."

"Aye, with you beside me, I know we will."

A horn sounded, the high, wavering note shattering the still autumn air.

"Someone comes," Gervase cried, turning toward the gate.

"Brigands?" Cat asked, hurrying to keep pace.

"Nay. Two longs blasts on the horn would signal that. But I can't think who would venture so far into the wilds."

Her father? Cat quickened her steps, but the colors of the party riding in through the gates were unfamiliar to her.

"'Tis Uncle Bernard...de Lauren," Gervase muttered.

"Are you on good terms with him?"

"Aye. Though Jacques detested him, Bernard was ever kind to me." Gervase scowled. "But he is not a frequent visitor. I hope he hasn't come to argue about the ransom."

Cat hoped not, too. She had mixed feelings about meeting the man who had accused her father of murder. She was grateful, on the one hand, for she'd not have met Gervase otherwise, yet wary of he who had hatched the plot to kidnap her.

Chapter Sixteen

Cat disliked her uncle by marriage on sight.

Bernard de Lauren was handsome, in a soft sort of way, tall and elegant with gray eyes a trifle paler than Gervase's and a touch of white in his brown hair. His fine clothes were the only jarring note, a red velvet surcoat embroidered with gold thread and precious stones, and the rings that winked from every one of his fingers as he bent to kiss her hand.

If he was so wealthy, why had he not done more to ease the plight of his nephew's people? she thought a trifle angrily. Her papa would not have stood by if one of his brothers or their children needed aught.

"I can see why you wed her," Bernard said silkily. "She is indeed very beautiful . . . such unusual eyes."

He reminded her of the fawning men at court. Cat's smile wavered slightly. Still he was Gervase's only remaining kin, and he did seem quite harmless. "If you will come within, my lord," she said sweetly. "You can take your ease and a cup of wine." She gestured for Bernard to precede them, then mounted the stairs on Gervase's arm. As they entered the hall, Bernard began exclaiming over the improvements made since his last visit.

"When was that?" Cat asked.

"Why, the day I drove off the English bastards who'd attacked Alleuze." Bernard's chunky chest puffed out beneath its layers of gold chains.

"You engaged them?"

"Nay. Base cowards that they were, they took to their heels the moment my outriders were spotted."

"Ah. Then how did you know 'twas my father who led them?" Cat asked more sharply than she'd intended.

"Catherine!" Gervase exclaimed.

" 'Tis all right," Bernard said, still smiling. "Her loyalty to her sire, however misguided, does her credit. I saw their banners, but knew not to whom they belonged till I went to Bordeaux to participate in the tourney. I recognized the red lion and made inquiries. Ruarke Sommerville is famous, or should I say infamous, throughout France."

Midguided, my foot. "Yet you did not stay to confront my father?" she asked, trying to curb her temper.

"Nay. I knew Gervase would want that privilege, but unfortunately Lord Ruarke was due to leave before Gervase could get to Bordeaux and challenge him."

"You wished to challenge my father?" Cat was appalled.

"Of course," Gervase growled. " 'Twould be the honorable thing to do, but he left ere the tourney began, and was thus once more beyond my reach...unless I wished to sail to England."

"Your message said you have decided not to pursue your feud against the Sommervilles." Bernard frowned his disapproval.

"If you have come to talk me into demanding a ransom for my wife, you have wasted a trip," Gervase said stiffly.

"Nay. I have come to offer my congratulations and meet the extraordinary woman who has bewitched you."

"I have not bewitched him," Cat protested.

"Well, you are lovely enough to," Bernard said, apparently unaware of her annoyance. "And this marriage certainly seems to agree with you, Gervase, I've never seen you looking better."

"Thank you, Uncle, and I appreciate you coming. 'Tis a long way, through hostile lands."

"Only two days' march." Bernard accepted a cup of wine from Dore and drank deep. "I must say," he added, scanning the hall again, "I had not thought you had the wherewithal to accomplish all this."

"Nor would I if it hadn't been for something that happened on our way back from Bordeaux." Over more wine and the food that followed, Gervase told his uncle all that had befallen them.

Genial as the conversation was, there was an air of suppressed tension about Bernard that made Cat's nape prickle. Yet when she looked over to see if Gervase felt it, too, he seemed perfectly at ease, chuckling as he told his uncle how he had found himself saddled with a babe, a troupe of traveling players and two priests.

"The brigands attacked us just outside Le Vigan," Gervase said, his smile dimming. "We killed them, including Vachel Sauveur, their leader. But I was in turn captured by his brother, Emile, who had taken over the town. I was due to be hanged the next morning, only Catherine devised a scheme to save me."

"She did?" Bernard's eyes flickered over her. "How enterprising of her. And you killed Emile, as well?"

"Nay, the townspeople executed him and his cutthroats," Gervase replied. "You speak as though you knew him."

"The name was known to me," Bernard said, turning the cup in his hands and studying it.

Gervase leaned forward. "We have reason to believe they were working for a man called Jean Cluny who hails from Arles. Have you heard of him?"

"Aye," Bernard said. "Who has not. What did you hear?"

"That he is a lord of brigands, who extracts fees from such bands in exchange for the right to pillage in a certain area."

"Outrageous," Bernard said. "What can be done about this?"

"About Cluny?" Gervase shrugged. "Little. But a band of his outlaws has been operating in the area. They lifted some of our livestock and made so bold as to attack Catherine on the road from Brissac. She says the leader resembled Emile, which makes me think it may be Maslin Sauveur. Though I managed to drive him off and there's been no sign of him since, I fear he may return to avenge his dead brothers. I won't rest easy till he has been eliminated. Could you lend me some men to help with that?"

"Of course," Bernard said at once. "Only tell me how many you will need and they are yours."

The door to the hall crashed open and a large man strode in, mail glinting beneath his surcoat, his hand on his sword hilt.

"What the devil?" Gervase growled, and stood, his hand falling to his own weapon.

"Be at ease," his uncle said. "'Tis my captain, no doubt come to say the rest of my troop has...settled in."

Cat stared at the man advancing through the gloom, his sword sheathed, his helmet still covering his face. Menacing. He might be Bernard's captain, but there was an air of menace about this hulking warrior. As he approached them, he lifted the visor of his helmet, and she saw his face.

Recognition came at once. " 'Tis him . . . the man who attacked us on the Brissac road." Cat leapt up and started for Gervase.

The brigand was quicker. Snagging her around the waist, he dragged her back against him. The cold edge of his dagger pressed against her throat. "Easy now, don't move."

"Cat!" Gervase lunged, sword sliding from its sheath.

"Hold!" Bernard cried. "Maslin is right handy with that blade. You wouldn't want him to cut such fair skin."

"Maslin?" Gervase stopped, eyes wide with horror. "Uncle? What is the meaning of this? Are you involved with this . . . this—"

"Involved?" Maslin laughed nastily. "Aye, his lordship's involved up to his fine white neck."

"That will do," Bernard snapped. "Is all secured?"

"Aye, easy as taking honey from a whore. The fighting men are locked in the barracks, the castle folk in the stables. Scared as rabbits, they be, offered nary a bit of resistance. Some of them fainted dead away at the sight of our swords and had to be dragged away by their fellows." He spat in disgust.

"If you've harmed any of them," Gervase snarled.

"You will do naught." Bernard shook his head sadly. "If only you'd stuck with our original plan none of this would be necessary, but nay, you had to wed the bitch."

Cat moaned softly, and Gervase's eyes flickered to her. The sight of her in Maslin's grasp, so small and vulnerable, made his blood boil. He wanted to charge across the hall and tear her from the hulking brute, but the knife at her throat stopped him. "If 'tis money you want, release my wife, and I will find—"

Bernard chuckled. "Your wife? Nay, she is not, nor never can be, your wife. You are cousins... first cousins. Her mother is my sister...and was half sister to your mother."

"Impossible. My mother's sister died years ago."

"So I thought, too," Bernard said.

"You lie," Cat whispered. "My mother has no family. They were all killed when a band of renegade French soldiers attacked them on their way to Chinon. She would have died, too, had my father not heard the fighting and rescued her."

"A very pretty story... and no doubt true as far as it goes. Our father was killed, and I fled, thinking Gabrielle dead."

"You left her to the mercy of the soldiers?"

"I was badly outnumbered. Had I known she yet lived, I'd have gone back and tried to save her."

Liar, Gervase thought, seeing his uncle in a new light. 'Twas like turning over a pretty stone and finding a slug beneath it. Dear God, his grandfather had been right. That issue paled beside another one...Catherine was not his wife, but his cousin.

Gervase stared at her across the toppled chairs. Her face was white, pinched with the agony they shared, her beautiful purple eyes magnified by pools of unshed tears. Her silent suffering tore him apart. "She is my wife," he said in a hard voice, willing the words to give her heart. "I will appeal to the pope for a dispensation."

"'Tis neither here nor there," Bernard said briskly. "For the lady goes with me to Crenley."

"Why?" Gervase rasped. "None of this makes any sense. What do you hope to gain by taking her to your castle?"

"A fortune. Enough coin to see me set for life. You see, I sent the ransom note to Ruarke Sommerville the moment I knew you had taken the wench. Her mother should be bringing the sum to Arles any day now."

"M-my mother? Why would she bring it and not my father?"

"Because then I'll have two hostages against his good behavior. Think you Ruarke would attack Crenley to get his money back whilst I hold his wife and daughter?" He looked at Gervase. "I had planned to share my bounty with you. After all, you did not look down your nose at me the way your father's people did. Why, after your father was killed by the English, I offered to take over Alleuze and the rearing of you, but they refused."

"Obviously I did not see you as clearly as they did."

Bernard shrugged. "They did not like my father and thought me like him. They were wrong, I'm far more clever than Odell. He was a brute and a tyrant, but his hasty temper did him in. I am never hasty. Every move I make is carefully considered. Come," he called to the men hovering in the doorway. "Take my nephew to his chamber and make certain he stays there."

"Ye promised him to me," Maslin growled.

"You were right, Gervase, Maslin does bear you a grudge for killing his brothers, and I fear he's most insistent about being allowed to punish you," Bernard said as casually as though they'd been discussing the weather.

Gervase's eyes widened. "Jesu, are you Jean Cluny?"

"Aye." Bernard's eyes glowed with pride. "I had not thought you clever enough to figure that out."

"Your men raped and killed scores of innocent people."

"Such is the aftermath of war," Bernard said offhandedly. Mad. He must be mad, Gervase thought. "If we did not do it, someone else would, but the English have already plucked the richest plums from our country. All that is left to us is the dregs. You curl your lip at me, nephew, but your aunt wed one who pillaged France. Your fair cousin—" he jerked his chin at Cat "—was fed and clothed on French plunder."

"My father never pillaged innocents," Cat shouted. "And I wager he never attacked Alleuze, either. I bet you did."

Bernard glared at her. "We stray from the matter at hand, and I would be gone from this dank castle of yours before dark." He turned to his henchman. "I cannot let you kill my nephew, Maslin, for he is the only one of my blood left, but I can give you something he values near as much as you did your brothers. His so-called wife. When I have Gabrielle as surety against Ruarke's good behavior, I will give Catherine to you."

Gervase knew he must act and quickly, or he'd get no chance. Dragging the knife from its scabbard, he leapt at Bernard. Something crashed into the back of his skull. The last thing he heard before the world went dark was Cat screaming his name.

Crenley Keep looked more like a fairy-tale castle than the home of a mad robber baron, its whitewashed walls glistening against the verdant backdrop of the surrounding forests, Cat thought, as the party clattered across the drawbridge and into the lower bailey.

Of the journey there, she recalled very little. Sunk in misery, her hands bound before her, she had stared at the

space between her horse's ears. Her mind's eye replayed
the dreadful scene in the hall over and over again. One
horrible revelation piling atop another. Bernard's perfidy, his association with the brigands, even the threat to
her parents and herself, all paled beside the one thought
that haunted her.

She was not Gervase's wife.

She could never be his wife because they were cousins.

Numb with fatigue and anxiety, she nonetheless roused
herself as Bernard called a halt before the tower. Here,
too, all looked neat and orderly. But the boy who ran up
to take the horses was thin and poorly clothed, his face
pinched with fear. The same fear was reflected in the
servants who crept out to offer food and drink to their
returning lord.

Bernard cuffed them from his path. "Bring the wench.
I'd see her safely locked away before I take my ease."

A hard-eyed soldier dragged Cat from the saddle and
hustled her up the stairs in his lordship's wake. In the
gloomy entryway, two blond girls of perhaps twelve years
huddled together. His daughters, Cat thought, scandal-
ized by the skimpy clothing that clung like paint to their
lean flanks and barely budded breasts.

"Ah, there are my pretties," Bernard exclaimed. He
pinched one on the rump and stuck his hand down the
other one's bodice. When she whimpered and tried to shy
away, he slapped her. "Here now, Leala, have you forgotten how to behave?"

"N-Nay," the girl stammered. "I thought...I thought
since ye'd brought her, ye wouldn't be needing us any
longer."

"I'd not bed my own sister's child." His eyes narrowed. "Get you to my chamber...both of you. As soon

as I've seen my niece properly settled, you can show me how much you've missed me.''

"Aye, milord," they said in unison. Hand in hand, tears steaming down their cheeks, they fled.

Dumbstuck, Cat watched them go. It seemed impossible that Gervase could be related to this... this monster. And Bernard said his father had been even worse. Small wonder her poor mother had claimed to be an orphan. Who would want to associate themselves with such a heinous family? And what of herself? Cat shuddered as she stared down at the veins in her hands, appalled to think their tainted blood flowed in her.

"Bring her," Bernard growled. He preceded them up the nearest stairway, through the solar, down a long, dim corridor and up a second set of steps. They passed several chambers, and she caught glimpses of beautiful hangings and costly furnishings. There was an order and a cleanliness about the place that surprised her. Beautiful Crenley might be, but the core of it was as rotten as Bernard's soul.

The chamber to which he led her was luxurious, the faint evening light streaming in through a pair of narrow arrow slits augmented by a dozen candles. A Persian carpet covered the floors; woven tapestries lent color to the walls. There was a fire in the hearth, food and drink arranged on the table before it. Two women stood beside the canopied bed at the far end of the room, obviously waiting to serve her.

Thinking of Gervase as she'd last seen him, sprawled senseless and helpless in a heap at Maslin's feet, her spirit rebelled. "I'd prefer the dungeon," she declared.

"I wouldn't hear of it," Bernard replied genially.

"Likely Maslin has beaten my husband to a bloody pulp and thrown him in some corner to die. I could not rest easy here knowing my lot is so much better than his."

"He is not your husband."

Cat lifted her chin. "He is, no matter what the church says. Gervase is the husband of my heart. I . . . I will not eat or drink or sleep till you call off that brute you left—"

"Tisk-tisk. Such a fuss you raise. I see you inherited your mother's stubbornness along with her unusual eyes." He chuckled. "You will have no more success in defying me than she had in defying our sire. He was going to sell her, you know, to a wealthy lord. 'Tis why we were on our way to Chinon. I was to have the coin." His smile became a snarl of rage in one of those alarming mood swings that seemed to strike him. "She cheated me of my due, but I'll have my revenge on her . . . and that rich English bastard who carried her off. Cursed English."

He really was mad. Cat trembled, partly from fear, partly from the urge to bolt. But he stood between her and the door.

"As to your threatened fast . . ." He glanced idly about the room, then back at her. "If you do not eat and drink everything set before you, I will torture these two and you will watch."

Cat gasped. "Y-you would not."

"I assure you I'd derive great pleasure from it." An unholy light blazed in his eyes, making them glow like hellfire.

"Very well." Cat dropped her own eyes, unable to bear the sight of his naked madness. "But—"

"But nothing," Bernard snarled. "I will give the orders and you will follow them . . . they will all follow them. Including your mother, when she comes. Ah, 'twill be

great fun making that proud beauty dance to my tune."
Rubbing his hands together, he turned and walked out
the door. Over his shoulder, he called, "You two come
with me. Tonight we will leave the lady to tend herself."

The maids scurried after him like frightened mice. Nor
did Cat blame them. Bernard's unstable mind was more
terrifying even than Vachel's and Emile's evil. With a
creature like Bernard, one would not know from one
moment to the next what terrible thing he might do. Had
he not left Gervase, his own flesh and blood, in the
keeping of Maslin?

The clank of the bar being dropped into place across
the door rang hollowly in the silent chamber. She was
truly Bernard's prisoner. Weak-kneed suddenly, Cat
stumbled over to the bed and sank down. Far from ap-
preciating the fluffy, wool-stuffed mattress or the scent
of roses that wafted from the crisp sheets, she despised
her comfortable surroundings. Escape was clearly her
first priority, but fear and exhaustion had turned her
brain to mush. First she must rest, then she'd formulate
a plan.

Despite her perilous situation, she fell asleep within
minutes. Her last thought before drifting off was of
Gervase.

"Heavenly Father, please let Maslin be so afrighted of
Bernard's wrath that he will not harm my husband."

Gervase regained consciousness by slow degrees,
fighting the moment when he must leave the safety of
oblivion and face the pain of reality. There wasn't a
muscle or bone in his body that didn't scream with the
agony of what had been done to him, still he didn't move
or cry out.

If they knew he was awake, they'd start in on him again.

Or rather Maslin would. Maslin had tried for countless hours to break him, but not kill him. "Milord said I'd pay if ye died," Maslin had growled that first day. "And he'd do it, too. Crazed, that one is...crazed for certain. But my brothers and I made a right good living working for Bernard." At the mention of his brothers, Maslin's lip had curled, revealing sharp yellow teeth. "I mean to see ye pay for killing them. There's ways of making a man wish he was dead without leaving a mark on his body. And I know them all."

Over the next two, or was it three days, Maslin had proved himself a man of his word, as adept at mental as he was physical persecution. He'd locked Gervase in his own chamber and slept in the great curtained bed while the lord of Alleuze lay blanketless on the floor, chained to the bedpost. Maslin took all his meals in the room, as well, devouring quantities of food under the nose of his starving prisoner.

The constant pain, the gnawing in his belly was naught to the fear that Maslin would make good his threats to torture the people of Alleuze. That and the clawing need to escape this place and rescue Cat prodded Gervase from his haze of pain. Silently he assessed his situation. He lay facedown on the wooden floor, shirtless, but he still had what was left of his braies on. Which hopefully meant his manhood was intact, as well. Dimly he recalled Maslin threatening to divest him of it just before he passed out the last time. Through his lids, he saw a glimmer of light. At least they hadn't left him in the dark.

"Ah, ye're awake." Maslin's voice skittered down Gervase's spine and clenched in his belly like an icy fist. "Drink?" his tormentor offered silkily.

Gervase shook his head, just the barest fraction, but the ache vibrated through his skull. Salt water was what Maslin offered, brine that burned the cuts inside his mouth and magnified the thirst a thousand times over.

"Right. We'll get on with it then." Maslin unlocked the chain at Gervase's ankle and picked up the cloth-wrapped cudgel, striking it against his palm. A warning. A promise.

Gervase tensed, the muscles in his back screaming in anticipation of the first blow. God, he hurt so he didn't know if he could bear any more.

"Maslin!" a voice called, hoarse with fear. "Come quick! There's an army at the gate."

"Has the drink addled yer wits?" Maslin growled. "No one would bring an army here."

"Come see fer yerself," the man shouted, and ran off.

Maslin swung toward Gervase, indecision contorting his already twisted features. "I hate to leave when ye've only just woke up, but I'll be back." He slammed the door behind him.

Gervase crawled to the wall, pulled himself up on the clothes chest and peered down into the courtyard. Thirty or so armed men streamed toward the lower bailey and the gate house. Before them, they drove the men of Alleuze—Perrin, Leon, Simon and even Tearlach. Obviously Maslin had pressed them into service to face this threat. Over the pounding in his head, he heard trumpets and screams.

Mayhap he could escape in the confusion. Teeth set against the pain, Gervase tried the door. It was unlocked and the corridor deserted. By the time he'd negotiated the stairs, he was sweating and so dizzy he could barely stand, but he pressed on into the hall. It was likewise empty, the food on the tables and the overturned benches evidence of the brigands' hasty departure.

The smell of roasted meat made his mouth water and his belly growl. Tempted as he was to sit and gorge himself, he knew he dared not linger. Still if he didn't eat and drink he'd not have the strength to make the courtyard, much less the stables. He grabbed the nearest cup, drained it and followed the wine with a hunk of bread. Anxious to leave, he snagged a bit of meat.

The door to the hall flew open, crashing into the wall with enough force to rock the timbers two stories overhead. In the doorway stood a huge knight in full armor, his sword up, shield at the ready. His head swung back and forth like a bear in search of prey. When he spotted Gervase, he roared, "You there...are you Gervase St. Juste?"

Gervase dropped the meat. "I am," he croaked.

"Bastard! Whoreson!" The knight stormed into the hall, his furious footfalls making the whole room shudder. Or was it just that he was so weak? Gervase thought, bracing a hand on the table. The knight stopped just shy of it. "Defend yourself," he bellowed, raising his sword and shield.

Gervase laughed grimly. "I'd oblige you, sir, but I have neither a sword, at present, nor the strength to lift it." He swayed, caught himself and asked, "Who the devil are you?"

"Ruarke Sommerville."

The roaring in Gervase's ears intensified. "Ah. You've come back to finish us off."

"Back! Back? I've never been to this accursed place before, but I will most assuredly finish you off when I've got my daughter. Where is she?"

"She is not here. My uncle took her. Torture me if you will, but first go after her." Gervase's stomach clenched, then heaved. Don't let me disgrace myself, he thought. The ground shifted beneath his feet as though a hole had opened.

"Damn and blast, what ails you?" Ruarke shouted, but the voice was fainter.

Nay, he was the one fainting. Gervase felt himself start to fall, tried to catch hold of the table, but his fingers slipped off and the floor rushed up to meet him.

"Bloody hell!" someone shouted. Hard hands gripped his shoulders and rolled him over.

Gervase groaned, the pain forcing his eyes open. A helmeted face hovered over him. "I think I'm going to be sick," he said. Appalled but helpless, he proceeded to do just that, dimly aware of the hands that supported him, while he emptied his stomach, then laid him back down on the floor.

"What ails you? Is it the plague?"

"Nay. Too long without food... ate too quickly." Gervase waged war with his belly and won. Swallowing hard, he looked up and saw Ruarke Sommerville sans helmet.

His rugged features proclaimed him a man to be reckoned with. There was strength in the firm jaw, a certain ruthlessness in the slant of his mouth and determination in his scathing midnight eyes. He would be an implacable enemy. "Where is my daughter?" As he asked the question, an unspeakable pain flickered in his dark eyes. "Tell me where she is." He grabbed Gervase by the shoulders and shook him.

White-hot agony tore through Gervase's body. He groaned and arched against it, feebly trying to twist away.

Ruarke released him instantly. "What is it?"

"Torture," Gervase gasped between his teeth. Black dots danced before his eyes, threatening to suck him into oblivion. He couldn't go, not till he'd told Ruarke where to find Cat, but speech was beyond him.

"Milord?" Gamel's face appeared behind Ruarke. "We've searched the keep and found no sign of Lady Cat. Should we begin questioning the prisoners, or has Sir Gervase talked?"

"Nay. He is hurt somehow, but I do not see where." Ruarke's hands were strangely gentle as they skimmed Gervase's body feeling for breaks. "He has a shoulder wound, but it is mostly healed. Fetch water... blankets... see if there is a leech or herb woman among the prisoners. I want answers from—"

"Ruarke!" A woman rushed in and knelt at his side. "Where is she? Where is Cat?"

"By all that's holy," the big man shouted. "I bade you wait in the forest till 'twas safe."

"I could not." Her voice was hoarse, her face shiny with tears, as she turned toward him. "Sweet Mary... Who is this? What has happened to him?"

"This is Gervase St. Juste," Ruarke growled.

The woman's eyes widened, great purple pools in her pale face. Gervase knew then where Cat had gotten her eyes, and her spirit. "You fiend. What have you done with my daughter?" She went for his throat.

Ruarke grabbed her wrists and held her back. "Easy, love, I'm as eager to punish him as you, but it seems someone has already done so, for he is sore hurt."

"Good," snapped his wife. "I know you have no stomach for torture, but I will do whatever it takes to make him tell us—"

"Shh," Ruarke murmured. "There is something odd going on here and there'll be no talk of torture till I know what. Nor will this man answer any questions in his present state.''

She glared at Gervase, then nodded. ''I will fetch my medicines.'' In a whirl of woolen shirts she left.

Ruarke stared at Gervase. Gone were all traces of the tenderness that had softened his features while he spoke with his wife. ''My wife will tend your hurts, then you will tell us where our daughter is. If you have harmed her...I will see you hanged.''

''I've not...hurt her,'' Gervase said. At least not intentionally, but a lengthy explanation was beyond him. ''Please...waste no time on me. My uncle has taken Cat. You must go—''

''If this is some trick to make me leave...''

''Nay, I swear. I...I will go with you.'' Gervase tried to rise, but pain sucked him back down.

Lady Gabrielle reappeared. ''Can you tell me where you hurt?''

''Everywhere. Maslin...very thorough in his torture.''

Ruarke grunted. ''I assumed he was your captain, for he tried to hold the gate against me. Who is he? Why did he torture you?''

''Uncle Bernard's tool.'' Gervase drank Lady Gabrielle's foul-tasting liquid and grimaced. ''He hurt me because I killed his brothers. Please, I beg you to go after Cat.''

''Where did this uncle of yours take Cat?'' Ruarke asked.

''To Crenley. Bernard took her to Crenley.''

Lady Gabrielle gasped, and the crock of salve slipped from her fingers into the rushes. ''Bernard de Lauren?''

The sweat on Gervase's body turned to ice. Nay. It can't be true. But even as he nodded, he knew it was.

"*Mon Dieu,* I thought he was dead," the lady said.

"And he you," Gervase whispered. "I—it seems we are related. I—I'm the son of your sister, Abella." And your daughter's husband. Only they weren't really wed. *Oh, Cat, I love you still,* he thought as the herbal haze sucked him into blessed oblivion.

Chapter Seventeen

She had never felt more frightened or more frustrated in her whole life, Cat thought as she paced the confines of her luxurious prison. 'Twas not for herself that she feared. She was safe enough, if bored witless after five days of confinement. Her nerves were stretched taut with the worry that any moment her mother would arrive with the ransom money and wind up in mad Bernard's clutches.

Equally terrifying was the thought that her father might come to rescue her. 'Twould be a futile effort. From her window she could see the walls and gate house, bristling with armed men. On the tiltyard in the lower bailey, a veritable army trained each day. Not that he expected a frontal attack or siege, Bernard had laughingly assured her. ''If anyone comes, I will merely use you to force their surrender.''

He would, too. The man was so crazed 'twas difficult to see how he could be related to her mother or to Gervase.

Gervase.

Her days were racked with anxiety for him, her nights by dreams of their brief marriage. They were vivid, sensual dreams from which she awoke fevered with desire, only to discover 'twas not Gervase's strong arms that held her but the tangled sheets. Then she'd recall Bernard's stunning revelation, bury her face in the pillow and cry bitter tears. She supposed she should feel unclean. 'Twas a sin to wed a cousin. What she felt was despair at the cruel trick fate had played, causing her to fall in love with a relative. Yet deep in her heart of hearts, she did not believe Gervase was blood kin to her.

The sound of the bar being lifted from the door scattered her thoughts. She was surprised to see evening shadows creeping across the courtyard three stories below. It must be one of the twins with her dinner, for no one else came near her.

Tonight it was Leala who carried the tray. As she bent to place it on the table by the fire, the sleeves of her gown rode up, displaying the fresh bruises that marred her thin arms.

"What happened?" Cat cried, hurrying to her side.

The girl shrugged. "He hurt Liana last night and I objected." No need to ask who he was. Young as they were, these poor things had been forced to share Bernard's bed in the six months since his men had overrun their village and killed their parents. "My lady...I am frightened for her. She is not as strong as I am, and lately...lately she has spoken of taking her life."

"Oh, Leala." Cat opened her arms and the girl flew into them, great sobs shaking her slender body. "I have got to find a way to save you," she muttered.

"Ye?" Leala raised her head, wisps of flaxen hair clinging to her wet face. "Why, ye are more a prisoner here than we...though at least ye're spared his bed."

"Only because we are blood kin." Though the last time he had come to gloat over her, Cat had detected an unsavory gleam in his eyes as he appraised her figure. Sweet

Mary, if he touched her she'd...she'd kill him. One more worry to add to the burden she bore. "There must be a way out of here."

"I fear not." Leala sighed. "The first night here we tried to run, but they caught us and dragged us back to *him*." She shuddered at the memory. "There are too many guards and they are too vigilant. And...and even if there was a way, Liana is too weak and frightened now, I fear she'd not keep up."

"If I had a weapon, we might be able to overpower the guard when you brought my food."

Leala's brown eyes bugged out. "Overpower the guard? Us?"

"'Tis worth a try. Do you think you could steal a sword from the barracks? Nay, 'twould be too heavy, too hard to conceal. A knife, then, could you steal one?"

"F-from the kitchen, mayhap, but even if ye got free of this room, what then? How would we get out of Crenley?"

"There must be a postern gate." Hearing that it was heavily guarded dimmed Cat's hopes. Nor, it seemed, were there any secret tunnels or bolt holes such as some castles had so that those inside might escape in time of siege. "At the very least, I must get out of this room," Cat said at length. "If I must dig a hole and pull the dirt in afterward to hide myself, that I will do. At all costs, I must not be here when my family arrives. If I am, Bernard will use me as a lever to capture them."

"Mayhap no one will come," Leala said softly. "We thought our grandfather would come and bargain for our release, but he likely knows what we have become and is ashamed—"

"Do not say such a thing," Cat exclaimed, hugging the girl closer. "None of what has befallen you is your fault.

If your family didn't come for you, they either didn't know where to look or assumed you dead." She shifted Leala so their eyes met. "When we are free of here, we will look for him."

Leala's gaze dropped. "Nay, I could not face him."

"Then you need not," Cat said soothingly, knowing how close to the edge the poor thing walked. "You can stay with me."

"Truly?" For the first time, hope lightened her wane features. "Do ye really think we can escape him?"

"Aye. My mother and my two aunts by marriage escaped from Edmund Harcourt by...wait, that is it." Cat released Leala and began to pace. "They put hazelwort in the ale and made the soldiers so sick they were helpless when my father and two uncles attacked the castle." She swung back to the puzzled girl. "Do you know if there is enough hazelwort in the garden?"

"Is hazelwort an herb?" At Cat's nod, Leala sighed. "I don't know it. My father was a wool merchant, my mother a seamstress. If we took sick, the herb woman came and did what was needful."

Cat tisked. "I could tell you what to look for."

"Ye should go," Leala whispered. "Put on my clothes, sneak past the guards and never come back."

"I couldn't leave you here," Cat said, aghast. Yet part of her wanted to snatch Leala's suggestion and flee.

"We are naught, Liana and I. Less than that now that the lord has ruined us, but ye are a fine lady."

"We are all going to leave here," Cat said firmly. "You are going to pretend that you have forgotten something in the kitchen, go down and get me a knife. Then return. Whilst you are gone, I will use some of the parchment his fine lordship gave me and draw a likeness of such herbs as we might use."

* * *

The walls of Crenley Keep were painted bloodred by the last rays of the setting sun. An ill omen, to be sure.

" 'Twill not be easily taken," Gervase said, studying the castle from the concealment of the forest a half league away.

Ruarke grunted. "Aye, the place is shut up tight as a clam, the wall walks thick with guards."

"Maslin said Bernard had some two hundred mercenaries." Ruarke had brought a hundred men with him, not that it mattered, since they could not attack or commence a siege with Cat inside. "We should try to get some men in, secure Catherine and then open the postern gate for your forces," Gervase said.

"Aye." Ruarke tugged off his helmet and ran a hand over his face. "Doubtless you are planning to volunteer, but your uncle or his servants would be certain to recognize you."

"But I visited here once. I could—"

"Find yourself in chains again. Would you waste Gaby's efforts to patch you together?" He glanced sidelong at Gervase. "My daughter would be most wroth did you get yourself carved into small pieces, and I must say the idea sits ill with me, as well."

Gervase grinned. "On that we are agreed." It had taken two days to bring Ruarke's army from Alleuze to Crenley. Thor's every step had jarred Gervase's barely healed muscles, but he'd refused to be left behind. "We must find a way to get her out of there."

"I'll challenge Bernard to meet me in single combat, winner take all," Ruarke growled.

"Bernard has no honor." But Ruarke did. He was big, brash and likely ruthless in battle, but he was honorable. Though he'd had just reason to kill Gervase out of hand, he'd held him whilst he was sick and believed his wild tale of kidnapping and betrayal. "Had I realized what Bernard was, I'd not have credited his lies and this wouldn't have happened."

"Gaby says he was always clever at duping people. Like deadly nightshade, with its lovely blossoms and poison berries. Besides, 'tis hard to see evil in your kin," Ruarke added.

Especially when you fear to find evil in yourself. "Had I not been so desperate for someone to blame and punish for hurting my people, I'd not have fallen in with his scheme so quickly."

"I know the feeling," Ruarke grumbled. "When Philippe sent word Cat had been taken, I dropped everything and sailed for France, driven by the need to wring your neck for daring to take my Cat." He sighed. "I'd have had you, too, but it took time to search Bayonne, then return to Bordeaux, discover where Alleuze was and hire men to guide me there."

"Thank God, you left before Bernard's ransom demands reached you, else Lady Gabrielle would have fallen into his trap."

"Nay. I'd never have let Gaby go alone to meet Bernard, or anyone else. I know, I know," he added, grinning ruefully, "you think it odd she came with me, but better to bring her, surrounded by all of my men, than to have her trailing after me alone. Which she most surely would have done."

"Hmm. A trait her daughter has inherited."

"Too true." Ruarke cocked his head. "They are a trial at times, my little tyrants. Yet I think you love our Cat as greatly as her mother and I do."

"Aye." With all his heart. Gervase dropped his gaze, fighting the unaccustomed sting of tears behind his lids.

Small good it would do either of them. Better they had never met, never known the joy they brought each other. The hopelessness of their forbidden love rose up to choke him. Truly he was cursed.

"Something will work out," Ruarke said gruffly. "Wait, is that wagons I see on yon road?"

Gervase followed the knight's gaze. A line of wagons stopped at Crenley's gate. Long moments passed, during which time they doubtless craved admittance. The drawbridge remained firmly up till a contingent of soldiers had ridden out from the sally port, examined each wagon and finally allowed them to enter. As the drawbridge creaked up behind them, Ruarke cursed. "I'd thought we might get inside posing as merchants."

"Mayhap a priest could get in," Gervase said. "Father Ambroise would help." He was at Alleuze, where a contingent of Ruarke's men manned the walls. Not that they'd likely be needed. Before they'd left, Ruarke had wrung from Maslin a confession. 'Twas he who'd attacked Alleuze and raped Marie.

"I needed money to pay my taxes to yer uncle and knew ye were away," the brigand had mumbled. They'd hanged him and his men in the lower bailey. It didn't bring back the dead, but Gervase had felt a certain satisfaction in seeing justice done.

Ruarke shifted in the saddle. "There's no guarantee Bernard would let the priest in or treat him well if he did. And, too, he might remember him from Alleuze. Come, we can do naught here." He wheeled his war-horse and started back toward their camp.

Grudgingly Gervase followed, but as he looked over his shoulder at the castle, he worried about Cat. "He would not starve her or mistreat her, do you think?"

"Nay, of course not," Ruarke said heartily. Too heartily.

Sunk in misery and frustration, Gervase rode back to camp, turned Thor over to a groom and took a seat by the fire.

"You must eat," urged a gentle voice.

Gervase stared at the bowl of potage in his hands, having no memory of how it got there, then up at Lady Gabrielle's anxious face. "I know, but..."

"Bernard is not stupid. He won't harm Cat... at least till he has the money." She sat down on a stool and handed him a hunk of bread. "You'll be no help to her if you faint from hunger."

Nag, Gervase thought, stifled by a wave of longing for his own little tyrant. "You are right."

"Of course I am." Lady Gabrielle turned and began badgering her husband to eat his portion. "I have been thinking on what you said about Crenley's impregnability, Ruarke. Being a coward at heart, Bernard has ensured that no one can enter by the usual routes, but there are other ways."

Gervase's spoon halted halfway to his mouth. "What ways?"

"Well, there are the shafts that lead from the garderobes down into the middens, which are accessible from outside the walls." She smiled at Gervase's grimace. "Quite right. No one worries about an enemy sneaking in that way because the shafts are too narrow to accommodate a man, and disgusting, besides. But at Crenley there is, or was, another shaft down which we pitched the kitchen garbage in winter. It piled up outside the curtain wall, and was hauled away come spring. The stench was horrific."

Ruarke set his bowl aside. "How wide was the shaft? On which side of the castle, facing the road or the woods? Where does it come up inside?"

"Wide enough for the carcass of a deer. Facing the woods and at the end of the garden farthest from the keep, so the smell would not bother those inside." Eyes bright with hope, she knelt before her husband. "'Twould take too long for our army to crawl within, and there is nowhere for them to hide, but I—"

"Nay!" Ruarke roared, rousing the men who slept in their blankets. They drew their swords, but seeing their leader by the fire, lay back down again. "You are not going inside."

"I am going," Gervase said with quiet conviction. Ruarke wanted to go himself, but conceded that Gervase's shoulders were a bit narrower, his build leaner and he did know his way around Crenley. What he didn't know of the upper chambers where Bernard might hold Cat, Lady Gabrielle supplied from her memory.

"When?" Ruarke asked when that was settled.

"Tonight. Every day that passes without word of your arrival will make him more suspicious . . . more unstable. And, too, I do not trust Catherine to sit idly by waiting. 'Twould be just like that brave little idiot to conceive some harebrained scheme to free herself before her mother comes and is trapped."

Ruarke and his wife exchanged looks. "You know her so well," the lady said softly. "And you obviously love her, no matter how things started between you. I wish..." Her voice trailed off, but he knew 'twas the ill-fated marriage she thought on.

"I, too, wish things were different, but a man cannot will away the blood that flows in his veins. If he could, I assure you I would not want even a drop of de Lauren blood in mine. And not just because it means Catherine is lost to me."

Lady Gabrielle laid a hand on his arm, her beautiful eyes, so like Cat's, dark with sorrow. "I understand. So great was my horror that some of my family's evil was within me, I never spoke of it . . . even to my own daughters. Every day I prayed that they would not turn into the monsters my father and brother were."

"And it seems they have not," Gervase said. "So it must have been for my mother. She and my father were most strict with me. Once I took a stick to a dog that had bitten me, and was severely punished for my 'cruelty.' At the time, I thought them brutal, now I see they hoped to whip the meanness out of me." Of Jacques's abuses he said nothing. 'Twas too private a horror to share with anyone save Catherine, who'd understood him so well.

"I would say they succeeded." The lady smiled sadly. "I was prepared to hate you. Now I'd appeal to the pope himself for a dispensation so you and Cat might remain married. After all, your mother and I were only half sisters. I never knew Abella, but Bernard mentioned a sister born to his mother several years before Odell wed my mother. I gather Solange died in childbed, and her parents took Abella to live with them. I recall wishing someone would come for me, but my poor mother had died birthing me, and her family were Scots from far-off Edinburgh."

Gervase nodded. "Like you, my mother never spoke of her sire's family. I did not know I had an uncle till my father was killed and Mama sent for Bernard. I wonder why he aided us?"

"Because he is a crafty bastard and no doubt thought you might one day prove useful to him," Ruarke said.

"And I did." Gervase hung his head. "I appreciate your offer to help Catherine and me. But we are cousins, and I do not think His Holiness would grant a dispensation. Jacques claimed the de Laurens and all who wed them were cursed. It seems he was right."

"Ruarke and I have done right well." Gaby patted his arm.

"Aye, so you have." Unable to bear her pity, Gervase stood. "I will rest a few hours, then ride to Crenley."

"And we will be right behind you, my boy." Ruarke clapped him on the shoulder, then muttered an apology when Gervase winced. "Are you certain you are up to this?"

"I must be. When I have Catherine, I will send her out through the garbage chute and open the postern gate."

"We will be waiting."

Why did Bernard have to choose tonight to request she join him for dinner? Cat wondered as she hurried after the steward.

Request? Nay, her presence had been commanded, and it was so far past the dinner hour that she'd been abed when the summons came. "Tell him I am not hungry," she'd muttered.

"Please, my lady." The poor steward had wrung his hands. "If ye do not come, he will kill me."

"Nonsense." But Raymond's haunted look had given her pause. Even if Bernard did not hurt the steward, he might well come and drag Cat from her bed. Ugh. Cat had shivered and bade Raymond wait outside, thrown on one of the gowns Leala had brought her and accompanied him. Her mind, however, was on Leala. Was she even now searching the gardens for the herbs that might aid them? Or had Bernard's dinner plans ruined Cat's?

The hall was ablaze with lights from a hundred flambeaux. Blinking against the sudden brightness, Cat saw the trestle tables were lined with hard-faced fighting men. Mercenaries or brigands, who watched her progress through the hall with the avidity of wolves spying a tasty lamb.

"Courage, my lady," the old steward whispered, his leathery face pinched with concern. "They'd not dare touch you."

"Th-thank you. But why would you care?"

"Your lady mother was kind to me...indeed to all of us...when she lived here. God rue the day you were brought here, for Lord Bernard is as mad as his father ever was."

"Would you help me get a message to my mother, warning her to stay away?"

"I couldn't. Naught comes in or out of Crenley that *he* doesn't know about."

Over the heads of the diners, Cat saw Bernard awaited her at the dais, dressed in royal purple and seated in an ornate throne of a chair. Despite the distance separating them, his gaze was no less intent than his men's. Surely he'd not touch his own niece. By the time she reached the dais, she was rigid with dread.

"Ah. So nice you could join me." Bernard's face was flushed, his speech slurred. Good, with any luck, he'd be facedown on the table in no time. But Cat underestimated Bernard's capacity for drink...and food. He consumed everything set before him. Capons in sauce, baked fish, lark pie and slices of roasted beef so rare blood dripped onto the linen tablecloth, turning her stomach.

Cat took a bit of the chicken, but her throat was so dry she had to wash it down with wine. 'Twas strong, and she looked about for water to dilute it, but there was none on the table. Sipping sparingly, she watched with mounting disgust the debauchery of the men in the hall. Some were so gone with drink they'd fallen beneath the tables, whilst others danced atop them. A few had grabbed the serving maids and dragged them into the corners. Obviously they didn't fear attack. Fools. If they only knew...

Her father would not let her mother come alone to Arles with the ransom. She must get a message out to him and douse the wine with a purgative to render the mercenaries helpless. When Crenley was secured, she and her father would go to Alleuze and free Gervase. Heartened by the plan and eager to see if Leala had found the necessary herbs, Cat stood.

"What?" Bernard demanded, eyes red-rimmed and glazed.

"I have eaten sufficient." Chin high to cover her fear, she turned to go, but Bernard caught her wrist.

"Aye. Let us quit this place. I have wine and sweetmeats in my chamber. What say we partake of them...in private? Though you're a bit old for my taste, I've a yen to tumble you."

Shock held her immobile; the bit of food churned in her belly. "How can you suggest such a thing? Y-you are my uncle." Gross as that notion was, 'twas the only way she could think to save herself.

"Am I?" His eyes darkened with something she couldn't read, then a sly smile spread across his face. "Mayhap I am too steeped in sin to care for one more." His fingers tightened, bruising her arm. "Come." When she resisted, he cursed, tossed her over his shoulder and carried her from the hall. Her screams were drowned out by the drunken shouts and lewd suggestions of his men.

* * *

The trip through the garbage chute was pure hell.
'Twas a tight fit, even though Gervase had stripped to his
hose. The stones were slippery with filth, the stench horrific through the cloth Lady Gabrielle had tied over his
nose and mouth. Worst of all, 'twas dark as a tomb. The
blackness closed around him, stifling him as his shaky
fingers searched for purchase on the slick rocks. His half-
knit muscles screamed in protest as he dragged himself up
the incline toward the faint bit of gray that marked the
end of the tunnel, but naught short of death would stop
him from saving Catherine. He might not be able to claim
her as his wife, but he'd never stop loving her.

So Gervase persevered, ignoring the scrape of rock on
his naked back, grateful for the lean build he'd inherited
from his father and the lifetime of hard living that had
tempered it. After what seemed hours in purgatory, he
reached the steel grate that covered the shaft. It swung up
and away just as Lady Gabrielle had promised. The creak
seemed to echo off the garden walls, and he hung in the
chute for an eternity, expecting at any moment to be
plucked from hiding and killed.

When no one came, he levered himself out of the hole
and flopped onto his back behind a large bush. Easing
the gag from his face, he gratefully gulped the fresh night
air. Conscious of the need for haste, he peered out to get
his bearings, spied a fountain in the near corner and
slunk over to it. Hastily he washed the worst of the filth
from his body, then drank.

There was no moon, which helped to hide him as he
crept through the garden, keeping the wall to his left side,
the long knife in his right hand. He had spotted the gate
and was making for it when a figure suddenly stood up.

Cursing silently, Gervase went flat on his belly. The
sweet scent of thyme filled his nostrils. Through the

herbal fronds, he watched the woman…'twas either that or a priest in a robe…stoop to pluck something. She held it up, muttered softly, then threw the plant away and took another. What an odd time to be culling herbs, he thought.

He prayed she'd soon fill her basket and leave, but she dallied, wandering about, picking and muttering. Hell! He had no time to waste. The next time she turned her back toward him, Gervase sprang up, darted forward and snagged her from behind. Beneath the light robe, her body felt so thin. "Do not fear. I won't hurt you," he whispered.

If anything, her trembling increased. Above the grimy, wet band of his hand, her eyes were wide with shock.

Now what was he to do with her? If he let her go, she'd likely scream the place down. He'd have to gag her, but mayhap he could get information first. "Are you a maid here? Do you know if there is a lady imprisoned by Lord Bernard?"

Her eyes bugged out. She made an inarticulate choking noise and nodded vigorously. Out of other options, Gervase lifted his hand a fraction. "I—I am Leala. Wh-who are ye?" she whispered.

"Gervase St. Juste."

"My lady's husband. Thank God, ye have come. Thank God. Thank God." She slumped against him.

"Don't faint," he urged, tugging her upright. "Can you tell me where the lady is kept?"

"Aye." Her cowl had slipped back, revealing pale hair and a beautiful, childish face. "But…but why do ye stink like a midden and…?" Her glance flicked to his bare shoulder and then beyond. "If ye are Sir Gervase, where is yer armor and yer army?"

"I was forced to climb up the rubbish chute, and as to my army, or rather Lord Ruarke's...it awaits beyond the postern gate and my armor with it. Do you know where my wife...Lady Catherine is kept? Is she unhurt?"

"That filth would not bed her, she is his lady niece."

Gervase blinked, astonished by the girl's vehemence in referring to her lord as filth and her assumption that if Bernard hurt Cat, 'twould be by bedding her. Because he had bedded Leala? Nay, she was but a child. "Would you like to help the lady?"

"I am helping her. 'Twas she who sent me into the gardens to gather herbs that we might dose the garrison...oh." Her eyes filled. "If only I'd been quicker. Ye are come and the soldiers have not been inca...incapa..."

"Incapacitated." Gervase grinned. No need to ask who had devised this bold, impetuous scheme. "Never mind that. We will have the element of surprise on our side. But I must make haste." He was torn two ways, wanting to go to Cat, take her in his arms and make certain she was all right, but ridden hard by the need to open the gate for the Sommervilles. "Leala, could you get a message to Lady Catherine? Tell her rescue is at hand. Bid her be dressed and ready but remain in her room till I come for her."

"Aye, my lord. Gladly. There are guards patrolling the grounds. Let me go to the garden gate and see if the way is clear." She did, beckoning him forward after a moment and pointing out the location of the postern gate. "It...it may not be anything, but when I passed by the hall on my way here, I saw many of the soldiers there drinking and making merry."

Gervase chuckled. " 'Tis excellent information. You are as clever as you are brave."

"I am neither, my lord. 'Tis for the lady's sake . . . she has been good and kind to me, even knowing what *he* made me."

She hurried off into the night before Gervase could question her further. But he knew. He knew what Bernard had done and the notion sickened him. Goaded by the overpowering thirst to punish Bernard for all his abuses, Gervase worked his way along the base of the tower, keeping to the shadows, out of the harsh pools of light cast by the torches. Twice he encountered guards on patrol. Much as he disliked killing from ambush, he couldn't afford to have them sound the alarm. He waited till the men passed him, then slipped out and disposed of them, hiding one body in the stables, the other under a wagon.

Wearing the garb stripped from one of the soldiers, Gervase approached the guard at the postern gate. "I've come to relieve ye so ye might join the merrymakin' in the hall," he growled.

"Ye're early." The man turned toward the long, narrow windows, from which spilled light and raucous laughter. That moment of inattention cost him his life. In another moment Gervase had the keys from his waist and opened the door.

"Thought you'd run into trouble," Ruarke said, ducking in through the low portal and stepping over the guard. "But I see you handled it right well. What of Cat?"

As he shucked off the too-tight tunic and donned his mail shirt, Gervase related all the girl had told him. By the time he'd buckled on his sword, the Sommervilles had filed in in goodly numbers and were fanning out along the wall. One party, under Ruarke, headed for the main gate to let down the drawbridge for those who waited

without. Gervase took the rest of the men and set out for
the hall. The torchlit courtyard was deserted except for a
few souls, so gone with drink they leaned against the
stones for support or sat on the ground moaning.

"We will wait here for the rest of the men in case some
of those inside are in better condition to resist," Gervase
said. "But I do not think this will take long."

A dark-clad figure hurtled around the corner of the
building. One of the Sommervilles caught the intruder,
but a soft, feminine cry of shock stayed his hand.

"Cat?" Gervase asked, hurrying over, but it was
Leala, not Cat who looked up at him.

"Sh...she's gone, milord," the girl sobbed.
"The...the guard at her door said *he* had sent the steward to bring her to the hall. But I looked in...she...they
are not there, my lord, and I fear..." What she feared was
clear.

Chapter Eighteen

Gervase's nerves wound tighter and tighter as he followed Leala to a side entrance and up the narrow, winding staircase to the second floor. He had to be in time. He had to!

"Bernard's is the first door on the right," Leala whispered.

Gervase nodded his thanks, then bade her find her sister and hide somewhere safe. When she'd gone, he stepped from the stairwell. Sword at the ready, his eyes swept the dimly lit corridor. Empty. And silent. Was that good news? Or ill? Palms wet, mouth dry with dread, he slipped down the hall.

He'd gone only a few steps when Bernard's door opened. A body catapulted out and into his, driving him back two steps. Instinctively he tensed to repel an attack, but the softness of the flesh pressed to his, the familiar scent wafting from it delayed the response.

"Catherine!" he cried, his voice raw with relief.

She clung to his arm, gasping for breath. "Oh, Gervase—"

"Get back here, you bitch!" Bernard exploded onto the scene, his face contorted with fury, bloody scratches on his neck. He spotted Gervase and checked his stride.

"Well, well . . . if it isn't my nephew come to rescue his bride." His glittering eyes raked Gervase from bare feet to wet hair. "I see you managed to escape from Maslin, but you look a bit worse for wear."

"Strong enough to take Catherine from here and see you pay for all you've done." Gervase tucked her shivering, unprotesting body behind him and brought his sword up.

"I've an army below. One shout and you'll be surrounded by my guards," Bernard retorted.

"They are a bit busy just now. I did not come alo—"

"Jesu!" Bernard exclaimed, his shocked gaze fixed on something behind Gervase. "G-Gabrielle?"

Turning slightly, Gervase saw that Lady Gabrielle had indeed defied her husband's orders to remain in the woods. Silhouetted against the black maw of the stairwell, she stared at her brother. "You are as evil as I remembered," she murmured.

"And you are as beautiful, damn you."

"Go back down, my lady," Gervase pleaded. "Take Catherine away from here and hide till this is over."

"Nay!" Bernard shouted, his voice echoing off the stone walls. "I've waited too long for this." He lunged at Gervase.

The shriek of steel drowned out Gervase's curse as his blade met Bernard's. The blow numbed Gervase's arm to the shoulder. Still he knew he could defeat the man . . . once the women were clear. "Run! Both of you." Gervase shoved Catherine toward her mother and parried Bernard's next thrust. "Lock yourselves in the nearest room till Lord Ruarke or I come for you."

"Sommerville is here?" Bernard demanded, stepping away from Gervase but holding his blade between them. The long scratches stood out vividly against his ashen face, and there was blood on his surcoat. Mute testimony to the battle Cat had waged.

"Aye...here, inside the keep and subduing your men," Gervase snarled. "But I claim the honor of killing you, for all you have done to me and mine. And, by God, if I find you've harmed my wife, you'll be a long time in dying."

"She will never be that. Never. She is your cousin, daughter of my lovely sister." He transferred his gaze to Gabrielle again. A sly, feral gleam blossomed there. "I'm so glad you've come home. 'Twill be like old times. But first I've this pesky nephew of mine to deal with." He leapt forward. Aiming blow after blow at Gervase's unprotected head, he beat him back.

Conscious of the women behind him and of what he stood to lose if he gave ground, Gervase rallied his flagging body in a stunning flurry of thrusts. Despite all he'd suffered at Maslin's hands, he was the better fighter. The knowledge dawned in Bernard's eyes, and his sword strokes grew more frenzied.

At last Gervase saw the opening he'd been looking for. Sparks flew from the blades as he slipped under his uncle's guard. Instead of countering the move or even yielding, Bernard let go the sword. Spinning away, he darted into the chamber and slammed the door.

"Bloody hell!" Gervase dashed forward, but 'twas too late, for he heard the bar clatter into place on the other side. "Damn, he'll not escape me!" He pivoted, intent on finding men and a battering ram. The sight of Catherine, slumped in her mother's arms, stopped him short.

"Catherine." Frightened, he knelt beside her. She stirred when he brushed the tangled hair from her forehead, her eyes opened, dark with fear. "Oh, love. Did he...harm you?"

"Nay." She left her mother's arms for his. "I fought him off. Still..." Her lower lip, bruised in one corner, trembled. "If you hadn't come when you did..."

"Shh." Shaking himself, he gathered her close, awkwardly patting her back as he murmured nonsense. Words of love and devotion he knew he had no right to utter, yet he'd come so close to losing her he could not stop himself.

"Gervase?" Lady Gaby touched his shoulder. "I will see to Cat whilst you find a way to get Bernard out—"

Her words were cut off by the purposeful thudding of heavy feet up the stairwell. The first person to round the corner was Ruarke Sommerville, his visor and sword both up. When he saw his wife, he stopped short. "Gaby, by all that's holy, I will—Cat? Is that you?" He left off shouting at his wife and knelt to embrace their daughter. "Oh, Cat, are you truly all right?" His love shone through the unknightly tears coursing down his leathered cheeks as he hugged her tight.

Gervase stood slowly. Much as it hurt to relinquish Cat, it had to be. At least she was in the capable hands of her loving parents. Turning away from the touching tableau, he motioned to Gamel and Garret, who'd followed Ruarke up the stairs. "Find something we might use as a ram to batter down yon door. 'Tis made of oak and banded with metal, so it must be stout."

"Who is within that chamber?" Ruarke demanded, letting go of his daughter and standing.

Dazed but over the worst of the shock, Cat watched her father and Gervase, astounded by the respect and, aye, liking, with which they discussed the matter of prying Bernard from his hiding place. When had this miracle happened? The joy of seeing them in harmony faded as she realized it no longer mattered. Gervase was not her husband, and Ruarke Sommerville was no longer his father by marriage. The pain bit so deep she winced.

"What is it?" her mother asked.

"Naught." Cat burrowed further into her mother's embrace, but the arms that had once been her haven against all ills had not the power to heal this, the most grievous of wounds.

"Bernard did not . . . touch you, did he?"

"He tried to." The horrible memory turned her voice raw. "I . . . I know he is evil, but to bed with your own niece . . ."

"Shh." Gaby kissed her brow. "Your father and Gervase will see he pays for that and all else he has done. Let us go to the solar below. There are two girls there who cling together and weep your name. Mayhap seeing you will calm them."

"Leala and Liana." Cat straightened. "Bernard used them ill, poor things. Aye, let us go and see to them."

Gervase swung away from the preparations to assault the door with an oaken bench. "You are hurt yourself, Catherine."

Ruarke shot him a quelling glance, then helped his wife and daughter to stand. Cat was steady on her feet, but he sent his squire with her. "Cat needs something to take her mind from all that has happened," he explained when the trio were gone. "Both from Bernard and from, well, the fact she cannot have you."

Gervase nodded and turned back toward the door, but not before Ruarke had seen the anguish in his expression. It touched him deeply. Normally he would have been in the thick of things, but he held back, letting Gervase position the men and set the cadence as they began to demolish the door. The boy needed something to occupy his mind, too, and he certainly knew what he was about. "You've obviously done this a time or two," he remarked, coming to stand beside Gervase.

"I've taken a keep or two...French keeps that had fallen into enemy hands."

Ruarke frowned. "Are you sorry to see peace declared?"

"Nay. I had my fill of fighting after my first battle, but a man may not simply walk away. I did my duty...'twas why I was not at home when the brigands struck." His eyes darkened as they focused on that loss, passed but not forgotten. "I will be glad to return to Alleuze and..." He stopped, his expression even more pain filled, and Ruarke knew he thought of Cat and of the marriage that was now nullified.

Such dark thoughts were diverted by a loud crack and the splintering of wood as the panels parted. His men started through the breach with himself and Gervase hard on their heels. Quick as they were, they found the chamber empty. "Where has that bastard gone?" Ruarke shouted.

"Here!" Gervase called, drawing them to the small alcove in the outer corner of the room. A privy had been built into the wall with a narrow window above it. Wedged crosswise of the window was a sword, tied to it, a rope made of bed sheets.

Motioning his men back, Ruarke joined Gervase at the window. 'Twas a straight drop from the window, four or five stories to the hilltop behind the castle. Far below them, a dark figure hung suspended against the moonlit wall. "Bernard!" Ruarke roared. "Quick, send men out around the castle to intercept him."

Bernard paused and looked up, his expression hidden by gloom and distance. "Ah, you got in more quickly than I'd expected, but you'll never catch me. You've taken Crenley, but you won't keep it. I've enough gold with me to buy an army and take it back.''

"You won't win!" Gervase cried.

Bernard's laughter echoed off the stone. "I already have. You'll never have Crenley or Catherine. I've seen to that." He began to move again.

"I'm going after him." Gervase sheathed his sword, grabbed hold of the sheeting and swung over the sill. But the knots were not strong enough to bear both their weights. Fabric ripped and went lax in his hands. He snagged hold of the sill, his curse ending in a grunt of pain as his arms were nearly pulled from the sockets. His fingers began to slip on the slick stone.

Far below, Bernard screamed, the ugly sound abruptly cut off by an ominous thud. Gervase knew he'd be next, but Ruarke leaned out and grabbed his upper arms. "Help me pull him up!" he called to those who waited behind him.

Eager hands brought Gervase quickly to safety. Shaky with relief, he leaned against the window frame and stared down at the body sprawled in the dirt at the base of the curtain wall. There was little chance Bernard could have survived the fall, but Ruarke sent men to check. He and Gervase were in the courtyard assessing their losses and making certain all was secure when Bernard's body was brought in, slung over the back of a palfrey.

"Well, that is that," Ruarke muttered, looking at Bernard's broken neck. "Foul as he was, he deserved to die more slowly, still I did not relish killing my wife's half brother."

Gervase nodded. "You are far more decent than he, for he'd have killed you in a heartbeat. It seems the evil in the de Laurens did not pass to the females, for my mother was kind and gentle, and the Lady Gabrielle also."

"My Gaby has ever hated being a de Lauren. And I must say she in no way looked like him." Ruarke stroked his chin thoughtfully as he studied Bernard's sightless gray eyes. "Did your mother much resemble him?"

"I have her gray eyes and black hair." His jaw tightened. "After the way I kidnapped Catherine, I understand why you would think me like Bernard, but I assure you—"

"Nay. I did not mean that," Ruarke said hastily. "Whilst I do not like what you did, I understand why you were driven to it. I would welcome you as a son by marriage." He sighed. "But we have already chewed that bone. What I meant to say was that when Gaby reluctantly admitted to me she was a de Lauren, I teasingly said she might be a gypsy girl substituted for Odell's at birth."

"A pleasant notion."

"Aye. And likely just that."

Gervase nodded and looked around, appraising the grim aftermath of battle. Though Ruarke had forbidden his men to loot Crenley, the keep had not escaped unscathed. An overturned candle had started a fire in the kitchen. It had been extinguished before it spread further, but 'twould take work to make the kitchen usable again. Broken furniture littered the hall and spilled out into the courtyard. Doors had been smashed, windows broken and the rush-strewn floors fouled by blood. There were dead mercenaries in need of burying, and terrified servants in need of calming before any work could be gotten out of them.

"I will stay to help with all this, if you need me, then I must leave for Alleuze," Gervase announced.

"Leave? But..."

"'Tis for the best," Gervase said quietly, though his heart was breaking. "No good can come of lingering."

"Gervase cannot be gone, Thor is still here," Cat said. Hands on hips, she confronted her father in the stable yard.

"He refused to take the stallion...said he hadn't the coin to pay, and—"

"But where has he gone? And why?" Cat demanded.

Ruarke sighed and scrubbed a weary hand over his face. The brilliance of the morning sun seemed pallid compared to the fire in his daughter's eye. Jesu, he was too tired for this. Two days had passed since the liberation of Crenley, and they'd all worked like serfs to set things right. Still he knew there was no avoiding her. "He left for Alleuze this morn, and—"

"Without telling me?" Her chin wobbled, and the light left her eyes. "Or saying goodbye?"

"He thought it for the best," Ruarke said gruffly, wishing Gaby were here, for he was no good at scenes like this. "He but sought to save you from a...a painful parting."

"Oh, he did, did he?" She folded her arms across her chest, one foot tapping on the cobblestones she'd helped scrub clean of blood and soot.

Recognizing the gesture, Ruarke tensed.

"Well, I am not going to be parted from my husband," she said.

"But...but he is not—"

"I do not care that we cannot be legally wed." Her chin came up, and Ruarke's heart sank.

He cast a desperate glance two stories up to the window of the master chamber. With the worst of the cleanup done, Gaby had retreated there to go through her father's and brother's things. "Your mother—"

"Mama will just have to understand that I must follow my heart in this. And so will you. Please, Papa." She laid a hand on his arm and looked up at him as she'd used to when she was a babe seeking to wheedle a sweetmeat. "I cannot live without him."

"But . . . but to live in sin."

"Royal princes wed their cousins," she reminded him. Then her eyes filled with tears. "I am sorry for the shame I'll bring on our name. Hopefully it won't ruin Philippa's chance to find another husband or Elizabeth's betrothal to Robert Ardley."

"I do not give a fig for what others think. And your sisters will be fine. All I want is for you to be happy."

"I will be. Besides, it does not feel like a sin. I cannot think of him as kin. He is my husband, and I will have no other."

"Aye, but—"

"Please say you won't try to stop me," she pleaded. "I'd rather go with your blessing than sneak off in the night."

Ruarke sighed, knowing well enough when he was beaten. She'd been wrapping him around her little finger from the time she was born. "Better to have you go with my blessing *and* a strong escort, I suppose," he grumbled.

"I love you, Papa." She stood on tiptoe, kissed his cheek, then darted off. "There is so much to do, and I'd leave within the hour."

"Dearling, what are you doing?" Ruarke asked.

Gaby looked up from the trunk she'd been ransacking. "Still going through Bernard's possessions. I've started an inventory of the plunder he amassed. We should try to find the owners.''

"Aye, but I doubt few of them are alive.''

"Likely you are right,'' she said unhappily. "We will sell what we can, then and use the coin to help the living.''

Ruarke grunted. "We'd best find a strong castellan to oversee the property. Even then I do not like trying to manage an estate from so far away.''

"Too bad Gervase would not agree to stay.''

"He's so stubborn…and honor-bound…he'll not take one crust he feels is not his.'' Ruarke grinned suddenly. "But that was before Cat went after him. If she were to ask…''

"For shame, setting your daughter on the poor man.''

Ruarke chuckled. "He'd best get used to it.'' He knelt beside her and peered into the trunk. "What is in this?''

"Bernard's personal possessions. Cat said he brought her up here to show them to her.'' She shuddered. "Among other things.''

"Oh, love.'' Ruarke hugged her close. " 'Tis all right, Bernard did not succeed, and Cat is on her way to Gervase.''

"I know.'' She put her head into his broad shoulder, soaking up his strength. "But I am troubled by that.''

"You are? But you gave them your blessing.''

"Cat is right to follow her heart. She'd not survive in a loveless marriage any more than I would. That does not keep me from wishing things were different.''

"Aye.'' Seeking to divert her, Ruarke nudged the small chest she'd been examining when he came in. "What is this?''

Gaby moved from his embrace and picked up the coffer. "Bernard told Cat this belonged to my mother.'' She reverently touched the rosewood cover. "Mama died when I was born, and I never had anything of hers nor knew much about her save that she was a Carmichael from Scotland traveling from Bordeaux to Arles. Odell bragged that he attacked the party in which she was traveling, killed off her kin and forced her to marry him."

Bastard. Vile bastard, Ruarke thought, but to voice his opinion would only hurt Gaby. "What is inside the chest?"

"'Tis locked. There doesn't seem to be a key for it, and I'd not ruin the finish by forcing it open."

"Let me see." He took the chest, pulled the eating knife from his waist and gingerly inserted the tip in the lock.

"The strange thing is, this coffer was in the pouch of things Bernard took down the wall with him."

"Greedy bastard did not want you to have it."

"Likely." She watched Ruarke work, but her mind was on the brief meeting with her brother. "Bernard was up to something."

"That's like saying grass is green."

"I don't mean the thieving. This was something... personal. Though it had been years since I'd seen him, I well recall the look Bernard got when he sought to hurt me. That same sly expression was in his face two days ago. He—"

"There!" Ruarke handed her the chest. "You open it."

Gaby slowly lifted the lid. It smelled musty, as though it hadn't been opened in a long, long time. "There's a small case of some sort." It was also made of rosewood and inlaid with silver vines. With her thumbnail, she flicked up one of the leaves and the halves fell open. "Oh, look." She held it out for him to see... two miniature portraits facing each other. A young man and young woman. "Do you think it could be my mother?"

He nodded, taking in the delicate oval face, the black hair peeping from the edges of the wimple. "You look like her. But who is the man? He also has black hair, and..." He leaned closer, tilting the portrait to better catch the sunlight. "Do you think his eyes are purple or blue?"

"Purple. His eyes are purple and hers are...brown, I think." She raised her head, her expression so hopeful it hurt. "It could mean naught. He could be my mother's brother. Or mayhap this is not my mother, but my grandmother and grandfather."

"Nay." Ruarke closed the case and pointed to the date inscribed on it. "If this is the date when they were painted, your grandparents would have been old, not young. What else is in here?" He frowned when he saw the coffer was empty, but his finger caught on the leather lining. "Wait, one corner is loose." He pried it down and removed a square of parchment. 'Twas so old it crinkled as he unfolded it.

"What is this?"

"It seems to be a legal document of some sort. Mayhap Odell's will or something giving Bernard title to Crenley. See what you can make of it." He handed her the paper and went to pour two cups of wine from the pitcher on the side table.

Gaby stood and walked to the window where the light was better. "Sweet Mary!" she exclaimed. "This is no deed or will, 'tis marriage lines...between one Elspeth Carmichael and Duncan Carmichael, her distant kinsman. They...they were wed in Bordeaux on the tenth of April, 1337." She looked at Ruarke, tears sliding down her cheeks. "Elspeth Carmichael was my mother's name. These portraits must be of her and . . . and Duncan."

"Agreed, but why are you crying?"

"You do not understand the significance," she said, jumping up and down. "Odell often boasted that he'd wed my mother a few days after he'd captured her and killed off the rest of the people with whom she'd been traveling through the Languedoc. I was born on the tenth of January in 1338."

Ruarke did some quick counting and whistled. "Nine months to the day after Elspeth's marriage to Duncan. And you have Duncan's purple eyes." He grinned. "You were likely conceived on their wedding night. You aren't a de Lauren."

"Nay, I am not." Gaby threw her arms about his neck, laughing and sobbing.

"I am so happy for you, love." Ruarke swung her around and around till they were both dizzy. With joy. "No wonder Bernard took the casket with him. He didn't want anyone else to know—"

"Wait!" Gaby exclaimed. "Quick, put me down."

"What is it?"

"Cat. Cat and Gervase," she explained, wiping the tears from her face with the back of her hand. "We must go after them to tell the good news."

Cat had not felt so wretched since the day Gervase had kidnapped her from the tourney. True, she and her escort had managed to catch up with him, but the stubborn fool had refused to allow her to "throw herself away" on him. She'd begged, pleaded, cried and finally threatened to follow him. He'd responded by plucking her from her horse, settling her across his lap and starting back for Crenley.

Fuming, she glanced skyward. The sun that had shone so brightly when she left Crenley at noon was now covered by a thick bank of storm clouds. How fitting, she thought. Swept by a strong sense of déjà vu, she burrowed her face into the neck of her cloak. All it lacked was a downpour. As if in answer to her summons, a cold raindrop landed on her nose.

Gervase swore. Tightening his hold on her waist, he unpinned his own cape and draped it over her.

"You need this," she insisted, trying to fling the cape off.

He stilled her gently but firmly and tucked the woolen garment securely around her. "I'll not have you catching congestion of the lungs."

"'Twill not matter, for I'll die of a broken heart," she murmured, the ache in her chest growing by the minute.

"I know, love." He nuzzled the top of her head, his fingers kneading her waist in silent sympathy.

"Then why must you take me back?"

"Because 'tis the right thing to do. Bad enough you would be forced to scrabble for your existence at Alleuze, but to live with me in sin." He sighed. "Only think of our children."

Children. Cat's hand slipped down to brush her stomach while her mind whirled. Her monthly flow was a week overdue...nay 'twas nearly two weeks. Given all she'd been through, that might mean naught. But 'twas also possible she already carried their child. Her fingers splayed protectively over the still-flat planes of her belly. She should feel fear at the prospect of bearing a child out of wedlock, but the possibility only strengthened her resolve.

"You can take me back this time, Gervase, but I will not stay. The moment you leave for Alleuze, I will follow."

Gervase cursed and grabbed her shoulder, turning her slightly so their gazes met. "Dammit. The outlaws have been wiped out, but there are still dangers."

"Then you had best take me with you."

"Nay." His jaw firmed to meet the challenge in her eyes. "Such tricks may work on your father, but not on me."

" 'Tis no trick. I love you and you love me. We belong together," she said desperately, fighting for all she was worth.

"Catherine." He squeezed his eyes shut and she measured the war he waged between love and honor. When he opened them, his eyes were dark and bleak. "We cannot—"

"Riders coming toward us at a fast clip," reported Gamel, one of the thirty men Ruarke had sent with his daughter.

Gervase looked up, spotted the plume of dust on the road and swore through his teeth. "There's no chance we can outrun them. Make for those trees over there. We will hide till they've gone by." Spurring his gelding to a trot, he led the way. Once inside the tree line, he dismounted and lifted Cat down. "Gamel, you and Garret take her back into the woods."

She clutched his arm. "I would stay with you, Gervase."

"Hush. For once, do as you are told." He kissed her quickly, then herded her toward her bodyguards.

Cat glared at her husband, but saw that protesting would only distract him. How had she come to fall in love with a man she could not control? she thought. Or mayhap that was one reason she loved him, because he was a challenge.

"Come, milady." Gamel led her to his horse.

"'Tis Lord Ruarke!" Oscar called out.

Gervase shoved his sword back into the sheath and looked at Cat. "Likely he's regained his senses and come to take you back."

"He would not," Cat replied, but as Gervase took her up before him and rode out of the woods, she worried about what could have sent her father after them.

"I thought to find you halfway to Alleuze," Ruarke commented as he drew rein before them, having ridden ahead of the rest of his troop.

"So we would be if Gervase had not decided to return me to Crenley," Cat snapped, nerves tight with apprehension.

"I cannot let her stay without benefit of marriage," Gervase said stiffly, his features set as chiseled stone. Against her back, she felt his heartbeat falter and knew that despite his fine principles, it was killing him to let her go.

"Indeed?" Her father grinned, eyes twinkling as they darted from her face to Gervase's. "Well, as it happens, your noble sacrifice won't be necessary, my boy."

"Ruarke! Shame on you for teasing them," his wife said, riding up with the rest of the men. "What my dolt of a husband is trying to say is that I am not your aunt, Gervase." She smiled, though her eyes were wet. "I am not a de Lauren at all."

"What?" Gervase exclaimed.

"Oh, Mama." It took Cat's stunned brain only a moment to move from her mother's joy to her own. "Gervase!" she squealed, turning in his arms so swiftly she nearly unhorsed them both. "We aren't cousins." She grabbed his neck and kissed him soundly. 'Twas a most unsatisfactory embrace—his mail was hard and the visor of his helmet banged into her nose. None of it mattered, for his lips were warm, hungry and possessive.

When he lifted them to catch his breath, a slow, seductive smile spread across Gervase's rugged features. His eyes lit with a fire that made her blood race. "You are my wife."

"So I've told you all along." Cat smiled through her tears.

"Cheeky wench," he said, but fondly.

Then he looked over at her beaming parents. "How...how did you find this out?"

"Return with us and we'll show you," her mother said.

"We can discuss Cat's dowry," her father added.

"Nay. I swore I'd not take one coin," Gervase growled.

Ruarke frowned. "But to give my daughter without a dowry..."

"It doesn't matter," Cat said quickly. Crenley was a rich estate, or would be with better, kinder management. She had no fear they'd starve. "We will do as Gervase wishes." This time.

Epilogue

Crenley Keep
September, 1376

Outwardly there were few changes to mark the passage of a year. Crenley Keep still looked beautiful, glistening and pristine against the backdrop of multicolored autumn leaves. Its walls were manned by armed soldiers, for even though the hostilities between England and France had not resumed, peace was yet a relative term and outlaws still a threat.

Inside those whitewashed walls, Crenley was much different, Gervase thought, turning away from the window and pulling on the first tunic that came to hand. Through the open casement drifted the sounds of laughter and good-natured jesting as the castle folk got ready for the harvest feast. The yield had been plentiful, the storage bins beneath the tower were bulging with grain, dried fruits, nuts and salted meats. More than enough to see them through the winter and send some to Perrin at Alleuze. There was much to celebrate. Much to be thankful for.

The door to the chamber opened and Cat bustled in, a crying babe in her arms, two toddlers clinging to her skirts. "Gervase, can you hold Ruarke? I've so much to do and he won't settle."

Taking in her flushed face and harried expression, Gervase hustled across the room and accepted the warm, squirming bundle that was their three-month-old son. "Where are all the maids?" he growled, jiggling the baby on his shoulder till he quieted. "Bad enough you work yourself to a frazzle, must you—"

"Everyone is busy...there are a thousand things to do." She handed hunks of bread to the older ones and herded them over to sit by the fire. Though the day promised to be warm and fair, the mornings were chilly, a forewarning of cold weather to come. "With Liana gone to the convent, Leala and the others are shorthanded in the children's building," Cat explained.

He looked at the pair of orphans happily gumming their food and smiled. There were now so many waifs about the place that he had trouble recalling their names, ages and the circumstances that had rendered them kinless. But all were welcome.

Originally he'd been skeptical of her plan to take in those children left homeless by the war, especially since she'd been busy setting Crenley to rights and carrying their own babe. Cat had stood firm. "My Scottish cousins, Ross Carmichael and his wife, Megan, have been taking in orphans for years. I visited them once and thought 'twas a wonderful thing to do."

He had to agree, 'twas a wonderful thing, and it gave him great pleasure to see the starvelings who arrived at their door transformed into strong children with a brighter future. A few of the older boys were already being trained as pages, and marriage portions would be provided for the girls when they were ready.

"Oh, why are you wearing that old tunic?" Cat demanded, breaking into his pleasant reverie.

Gervase shifted the now-sleeping babe and looked at the brown tunic he wore. "'Tis fine enough. There'll be mock jousting after the feast, and I'll have to change into my mail."

"'Tis not fine enough." Scowling, she bent and rummaged through the trunk at the foot of their bed. The one she'd insisted be brought from Alleuze to replace Bernard's. "Here." She thrust a pile of clothes at him, took back the baby and laid him gently on the coverlet. Her hand lingered, stroking the blond fuzz on his head. "He's so beautiful. Like a sleeping angel."

"Hmm. And more like the devil when he's awake." Little Ruarke had inherited more than just his mother's coloring... he had her temper, too. And, he hoped, her good Sommerville blood, though he no longer thought of himself as cursed. People made their own way in life. "I wish your family could see him."

"Aye, well, 'tis a far ways to England," Cat said briskly. Too briskly.

Eyes narrowing, Gervase watched as his wife bustled about the room, straightening a pillow here, moving her tapestry frame an inch, then putting it back. Though normally bursting with energy, she seemed...anxious. "Is aught wrong, love?" he asked, catching her by the window and drawing her into his arms.

"Nay." She turned and laid her head on his chest, her arms wrapped around his waist. "I'm just nervous."

"You? Never."

"Aye." She looked up at him, frowning. "I love you."

"And I you." Gervase held her close, amazed to feel his loins tighten. A year wed, and it seemed they couldn't get enough of loving each other. This morning had been no exception. He'd wakened to the pleasurable touch of his wife's hands exploring his body. "How long before we must go downstairs?" he asked, rocking his hips against hers.

She moaned softly and stretched up on her toes, lips parting as she melted into his embrace. All too soon she broke the kiss. "Now, I fear," she murmured, looking as disappointed as he.

"I'll make up for it tonight . . . all night."

"I hope so," she said cryptically.

"What does that mean?" he asked.

Spinning away, she went to the trunk that held their clothes. "Only that you might be too tired," she teased.

"Never," he taunted, earning a hot, smoldering look. The easy give-and-take between them was the same as always, but he couldn't shake the feeling she was up to something. Though working to restore Crenley had taught them to compromise, there were still times when she took a notion and refused to budge.

"Hurry and get dressed," she urged. Drawing off the plain tunic she'd worn to oversee the preparations for the feast, she pulled on one he'd never seen before. A crimson surcoat embroidered with silver thread that matched the one she'd handed him. Hers hugged the slender figure she'd regained soon after giving birth. Little Ruarke had been born in the summer, nine months to the day after their wedding in Le Vigan.

Gervase had broken out in a cold sweat when he'd learned he was going to be a father. What if Bernard had destroyed Elspeth and Duncan's marriage lines and they had never found out the truth? Their son would have been born a bastard, tainted by his parents' blood ties. That fear had paled beside the anguish of possibly losing her in childbirth. Even knowing that her mother had borne three healthy daughters hadn't helped. But Catherine had survived the ordeal much better than Gervase had. And now look at her.

"Is that a new surcoat?" he asked, stepping behind her and tugging her braid from the neck of the garment.

"Aye." Her nervousness was marked by the number of times she pinned and repinned the braid atop her head.

"Catherine ... we promised to keep naught from each other. I would know what is bothering you," he said at last.

She stared at him, her eyes wide and troubled. "I am only nervous ... about today. Oh ..." She looked to the window. "Was that a horn? Can they have arrived already?"

"Who? Perrin and the folk from Alleuze came yesterday. I wasn't aware we were expecting anyone else."

"We are ... only I thought I'd have more time." She twitched her skirts, plucked at the embroidered hem of his surcoat and scowled. "'Twill have to do." Lifting the babe from the bed, she bade him bring Rolf and Etienne.

Curious and uneasy, Gervase picked up the orphans and followed her down the stairs. The hall was deserted, but the courtyard teemed with people ... those of Crenley and Alleuze. Their chatter gave way to cheers when their lord and lady appeared. Over the heads of the throng, Gervase saw the inner gates open and an armed troop ride in.

Who? he wondered, alarmed till he recognized the red-and-black banners fluttering in the crisp autumn air. Sommervilles.

"Catherine, 'tis a messenger come from your family," Gervase said, smiling. His smile became a frown when he realized it was not a messenger, but Ruarke and Gabrielle. "Curious we had no word of their coming. I hope naught is wrong."

"I...I think all is well," Cat said, nearly strangling on her nervousness. What if he hated her for going behind his back?

"Catherine! You knew of this and didn't tell me."

"Aye," she admitted in a small voice, clutching her son to her breast like a shield. "But..." Before the explanation could leave her lips, her father's men cleared the gates. Behind them came the horses. Four large gray stallions and twenty mares, each led by a mounted groom, for the animals were too valuable to be driven like palfreys.

Gervase handed the two small boys to a maid and started down the steps to the courtyard. Cat hurried after him, wanting to explain, yet afraid to risk an argument in public. She'd intended to tell him tonight, not expecting her parents till tomorrow.

"Gervase!" her father shouted, reining in at the foot of the stairs. "Greetings. You look surprised to see us."

"Aye. I am wondering why you need so many warhorses," he said slowly. "Are our countries at war again?"

"Nay." Ruarke glanced at his daughter. "Never say you didn't tell him?" When she didn't, couldn't, answer, he grunted. "The horses are yours, my boy," he bellowed.

"Mine?" Gervase glanced between his beaming father-by-marriage and his apprehensive Catherine. "Why?"

"Cat's dowry." Ruarke swung down from the saddle and lifted his wife from hers. "I couldn't let her come to you empty-handed, and you said no coin," Ruarke went on, seemingly oblivious to Gervase's dark scowl. "So..."

"So you and your daughter thought of a way around me," Gervase growled. As usual.

"I told you we should ask him," Lady Gaby said, but her dancing eyes said she'd been neck deep in the scheme.

"They'll make a fine start to your herd," Perrin said, slipping from the crowd to examine the nearest mare.

Gervase looked at the animals, sleek and proud, their beautiful coats gleaming in the sun, and felt his anger fade. "I should not accept them."

"But...?" Cat asked, cocking her head. "I think I hear a 'but' at the end of that. Please... Papa wants so much for you to have them, and I—"

"You are too used to getting your own way." Gervase kissed the tip of her nose. "But it does seem a pity to ship them all the way back to England, and I do deserve something for taking such a willful bit of baggage as yourself off his hands."

"Well, now that's settled, where is this grandson of mine?" Ruarke demanded, trudging up the steps.

"Here." Cat laid the baby in her father's arms.

"He has my hair," her sire exclaimed. The sight of his huge finger stroking the tiny head brought tears to her eyes. "And look at that fist," he added as the babe awakened and waved his hands about. "He'll soon be strong enough to wield a sword."

Cat's throat tightened. Though he'd never once complained at having three daughters and no sons, she'd often wondered if her warrior father didn't wish for a boy to follow him. As though sensing how unsteady she felt, Gervase put his arm around her.

"By the time he's old enough to ride, he'll have his pick of mounts," Gervase said. "I thank you for the horses, though they weren't necessary... Catherine is prize enough."

Her heart too full for words, Cat nestled back in her husband's embrace. Later, when they were alone, she'd tell him how much his simple, honest love meant to an heiress who'd been pursued for her money and kidnapped for revenge. As it turned out, there was no need to tell him.

In the sweet aftermath of their loving, while their hearts still raced together, he whispered in her ear, "I love you, Catherine. You complete me in ways I never thought possible."

She raised her eyes to his, basking in the glow of love returned equally and openly. "Aye, my love, we are two halves of one whole." No matter how they had begun, they belonged together... always.

* * * * *

presents
award-winning author

DALLAS SCHULZE

with her new Western

SHORT STRAW BRIDE

A heartwarming tale
you won't want to miss!

Coming this November

Coming soon from

Harlequin® Historical

Most Unsuitable…
from award-winning author

Margaret Moore

A delightfully wicked new series set
in Victorian England that opens with

THE WASTREL

the magical story of a disowned heiress
and a devil-may-care bachelor

THE WASTREL ISBN 28944-8 will be
available in November, wherever
Harlequin Historicals are sold.

And keep an eye out for the next in the series
THE DARK DUKE
in the Spring of 1997

HARLEQUIN ®

Scandals

A passionate story of romance, where bold, daring characters set out to defy their world of propriety and strict social codes.

"Scandals—a story that will make your heart race and your pulse pound. Spectacular!"
—Suzanne Forster

"Devon is daring, dangerous and altogether delicious."
—Amanda Quick

Don't miss this wonderful full-length novel from Regency favorite Georgina Devon.

Available in December, wherever Harlequin books are sold.

1997
Reader's Engagement Book
A calendar of important dates
and anniversaries for readers to use!

Informative and entertaining—with notable
dates and trivia highlighted throughout the year.

Handy, convenient, pocketbook size to help you
keep track of your own personal important dates.

Added bonus—contains $5.00 worth of coupons
for upcoming Harlequin and Silhouette books.
This calendar more than pays for itself!

 Available beginning in November at
your favorite retail outlet.

HARLEQUIN ®   Silhouette®

Merry Christmas, Baby!

A romantic collection filled with the magic
of Christmas and the joy of children.

SUSAN WIGGS, Karen Young and
Bobby Hutchinson bring you Christmas wishes,
weddings and romance, in a charming
trio of stories that will warm up your
holiday season.

MERRY CHRISTMAS, BABY! also contains
Harlequin's special gift to you—a set of
FREE GIFT TAGS included in every book.

Brighten up your holiday season with
MERRY CHRISTMAS, BABY!

Available in November at
your favorite retail store.

REBECCA

43 LIGHT STREET

YORK

FACE TO FACE

*Bestselling author Rebecca York returns to "43 Light Street"
for an original story of past secrets, deadly deceptions—and
the most intimate betrayal.*

She woke in a hospital—with amnesia…and with child.
According to her rescuer, whose striking face is the last
image she remembers, she's Justine Hollingsworth. But
nothing about her life seems to fit, except for the baby
inside her and Mike Lancer's arms around her. Consumed
by forbidden passion and racked by nameless fear, she
must discover if she is Justine…or the victim of some mind
game. Her life—and her unborn child's—depends on it….

Don't miss *Face To Face*—Available in October, wherever
Harlequin books are sold.

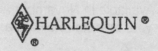

HARLEQUIN ®

®

43FTF

You are cordially invited to a

HOMETOWN REUNION

September 1996—August 1997

Bad boys, cowboys, babies. Feuding families,
arson, mistaken identity, a mom on the run...
Where can you find romance and adventure?
Tyler, Wisconsin, that's where!

So join us in this not-so-sleepy little town and
experience the love, the laughter and the
tears of those who call it home.

WELCOME TO A
HOMETOWN REUNION

The Murphys and the Stirlings have been
feuding for fifty years—ever since Magdalena
left Clarence at the altar, or vice versa.
Two generations later, Sandy Murphy and
Drew Stirling are unwilling partners in an
advertising campaign, and sparks fly. Everyone
in Tyler is wondering if history will repeat itself.

***Love and War* by Peg Sutherland,**
Available in November 1996
at your favorite retail store.

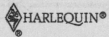

HARLEQUIN®

Harlequin® Historical

If you're a serious fan of historical romance,
then you're in luck!

Harlequin Historicals brings you
stories by bestselling authors, rising new stars
and talented first-timers.

Ruth Langan & Theresa Michaels
Mary McBride & Cheryl St. John
Margaret Moore & Merline Lovelace
Julie Tetel & Nina Beaumont
Susan Amarillas & Ana Seymour
Deborah Simmons & Linda Castle
Cassandra Austin & Emily French
Miranda Jarrett & Suzanne Barclay
DeLoras Scott & Laurie Grant...

You'll never run out of favorites.

Harlequin Historicals...they're too good to miss!

HH-GEN